big

NATE

SAY GOOD-BYE
TO DORK CITY

More

adventures from

LINCOLN PEIRCE

Big Nate From the Top

Big Nate Out Loud

Big Nate and Friends

Big Nate Makes the Grade

Big Nate All Work and No Play

Big Nate: Game On!

Big Nate: I Can't Take It!

Big Nate: Great Minds Think Alike

Big Nate: The Crowd Goes Wild!

Big Nate's Greatest Hits

big NATE
SAY GOOD-BYE TO DORK CITY

by LINCOLN PEIRCE

Andrews McMeel
Publishing®

Kansas City • Sydney • London

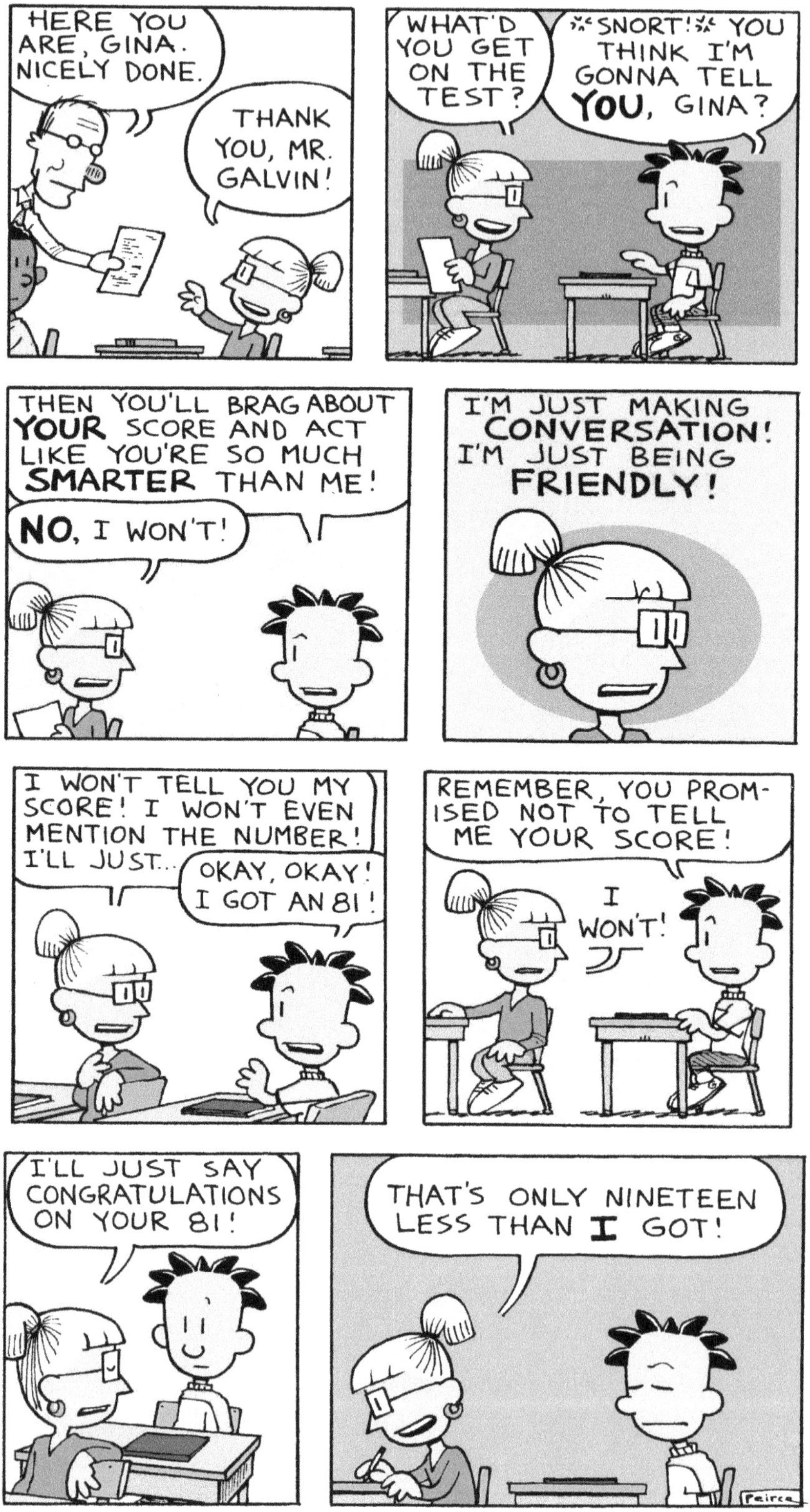
HERE YOU ARE, GINA. NICELY DONE.
THANK YOU, MR. GALVIN!
WHAT'D YOU GET ON THE TEST?
SNORT! YOU THINK I'M GONNA TELL YOU, GINA?
THEN YOU'LL BRAG ABOUT YOUR SCORE AND ACT LIKE YOU'RE SO MUCH SMARTER THAN ME!
NO, I WON'T!
I'M JUST MAKING CONVERSATION! I'M JUST BEING FRIENDLY!
I WON'T TELL YOU MY SCORE! I WON'T EVEN MENTION THE NUMBER! I'LL JUST...
OKAY, OKAY! I GOT AN 81!
REMEMBER, YOU PROMISED NOT TO TELL ME YOUR SCORE!
I WON'T!
I'LL JUST SAY CONGRATULATIONS ON YOUR 81!
THAT'S ONLY NINETEEN LESS THAN I GOT!
Peirce

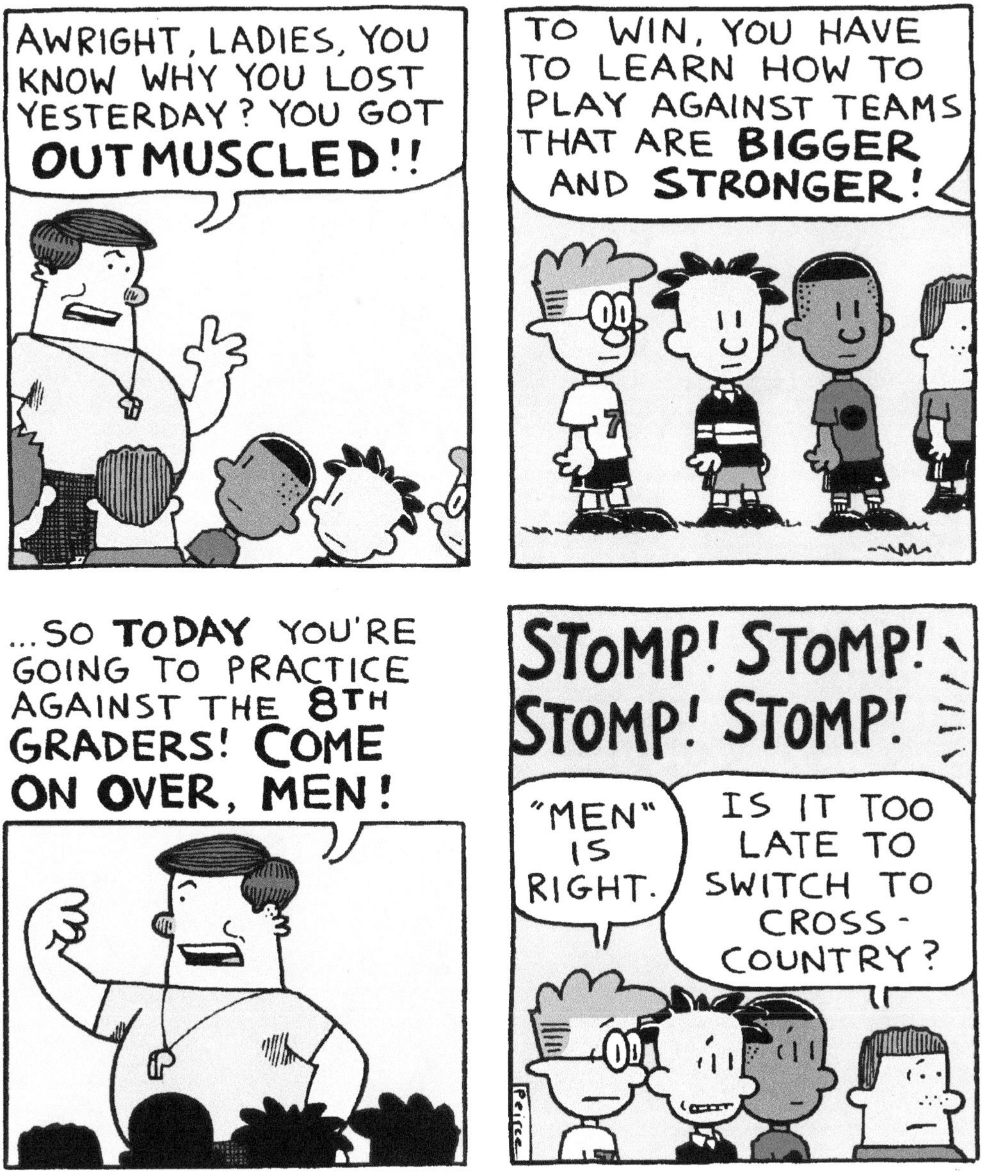
AWRIGHT, LADIES, YOU KNOW WHY YOU LOST YESTERDAY? YOU GOT **OUTMUSCLED**!!
TO WIN, YOU HAVE TO LEARN HOW TO PLAY AGAINST TEAMS THAT ARE **BIGGER** AND **STRONGER**!
...SO **TODAY** YOU'RE GOING TO PRACTICE AGAINST THE **8TH GRADERS**! **COME ON OVER, MEN**!
STOMP! STOMP! STOMP! STOMP!
"MEN" IS RIGHT.
IS IT TOO LATE TO SWITCH TO CROSS-COUNTRY?

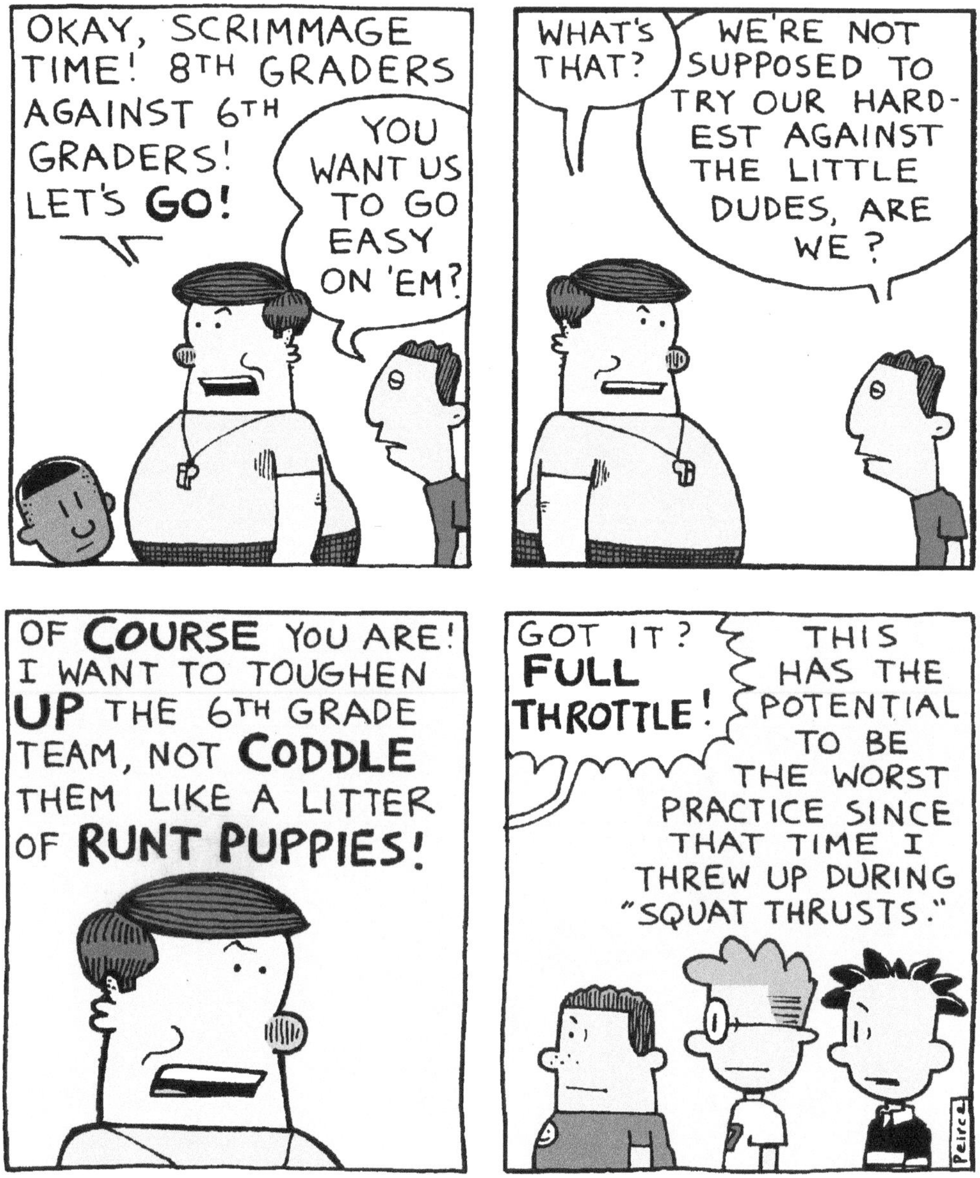
OKAY, SCRIMMAGE TIME! 8TH GRADERS AGAINST 6TH GRADERS! LET'S **GO**!
YOU WANT US TO GO EASY ON 'EM?
WHAT'S THAT?
WE'RE NOT SUPPOSED TO TRY OUR HARD-EST AGAINST THE LITTLE DUDES, ARE WE?
OF **COURSE** YOU ARE! I WANT TO TOUGHEN **UP** THE 6TH GRADE TEAM, NOT **CODDLE** THEM LIKE A LITTER OF **RUNT PUPPIES**!
GOT IT? **FULL THROTTLE**!
THIS HAS THE POTENTIAL TO BE THE WORST PRACTICE SINCE THAT TIME I THREW UP DURING "SQUAT THRUSTS."
Peirce

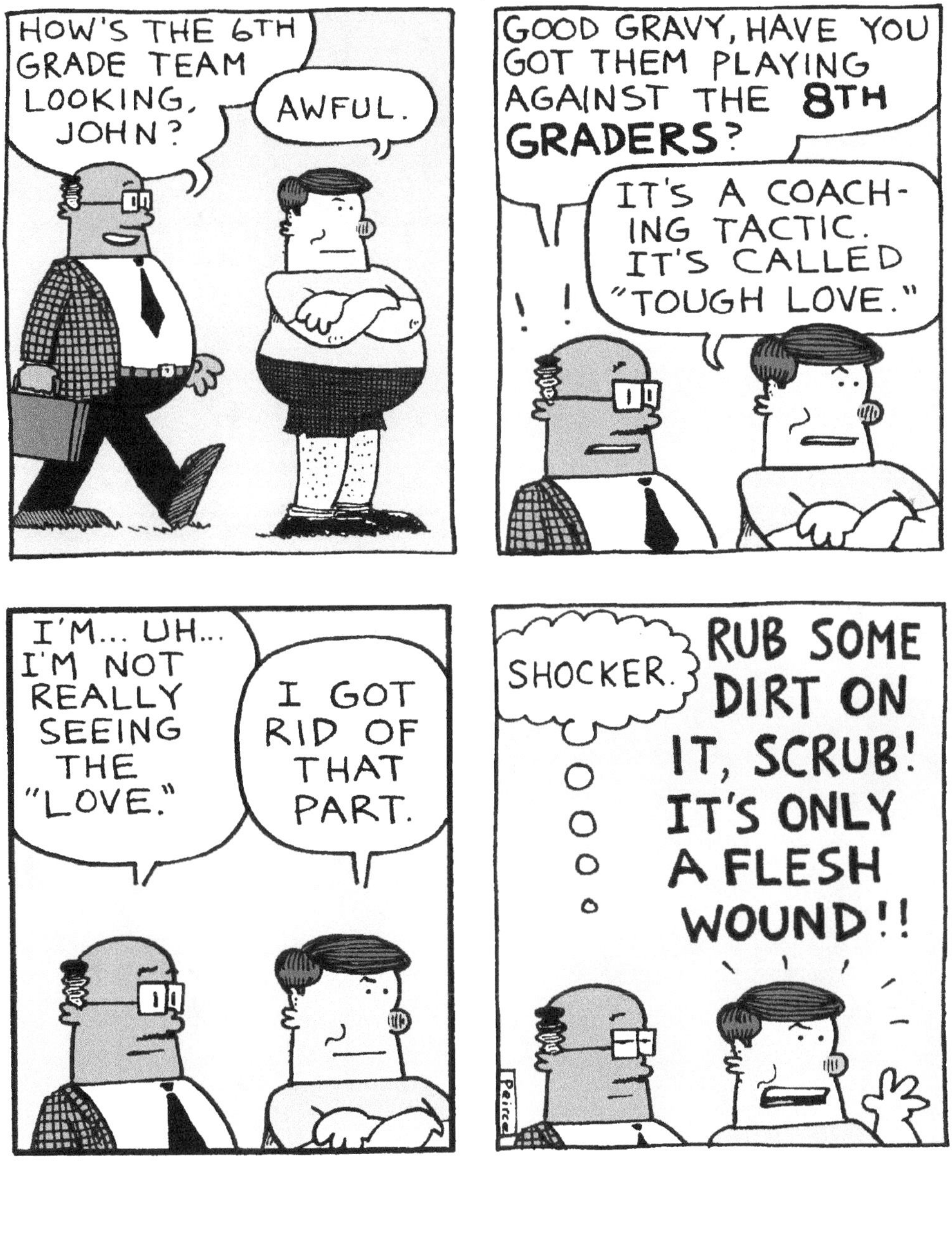
HOW'S THE 6TH GRADE TEAM LOOKING, JOHN?
AWFUL.
GOOD GRAVY, HAVE YOU GOT THEM PLAYING AGAINST THE 8TH GRADERS?
IT'S A COACHING TACTIC. IT'S CALLED "TOUGH LOVE."
! !
I'M... UH... I'M NOT REALLY SEEING THE "LOVE."
I GOT RID OF THAT PART.
SHOCKER.
RUB SOME DIRT ON IT, SCRUB! IT'S ONLY A FLESH WOUND!!
Peirce

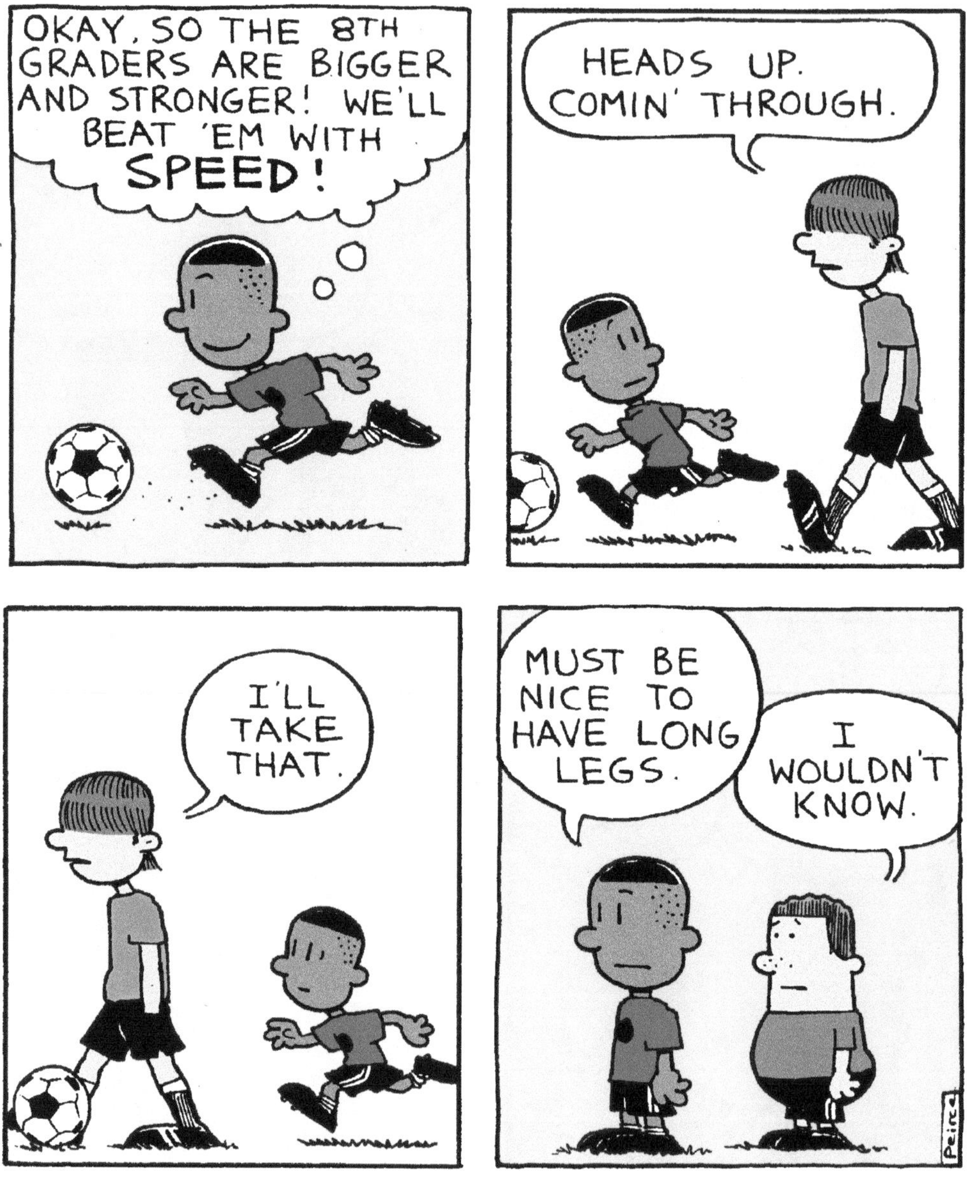
OKAY, SO THE 8TH GRADERS ARE BIGGER AND STRONGER! WE'LL BEAT 'EM WITH **SPEED**!
HEADS UP. COMIN' THROUGH.
I'LL TAKE THAT.
MUST BE NICE TO HAVE LONG LEGS.
I WOULDN'T KNOW.
Peirce

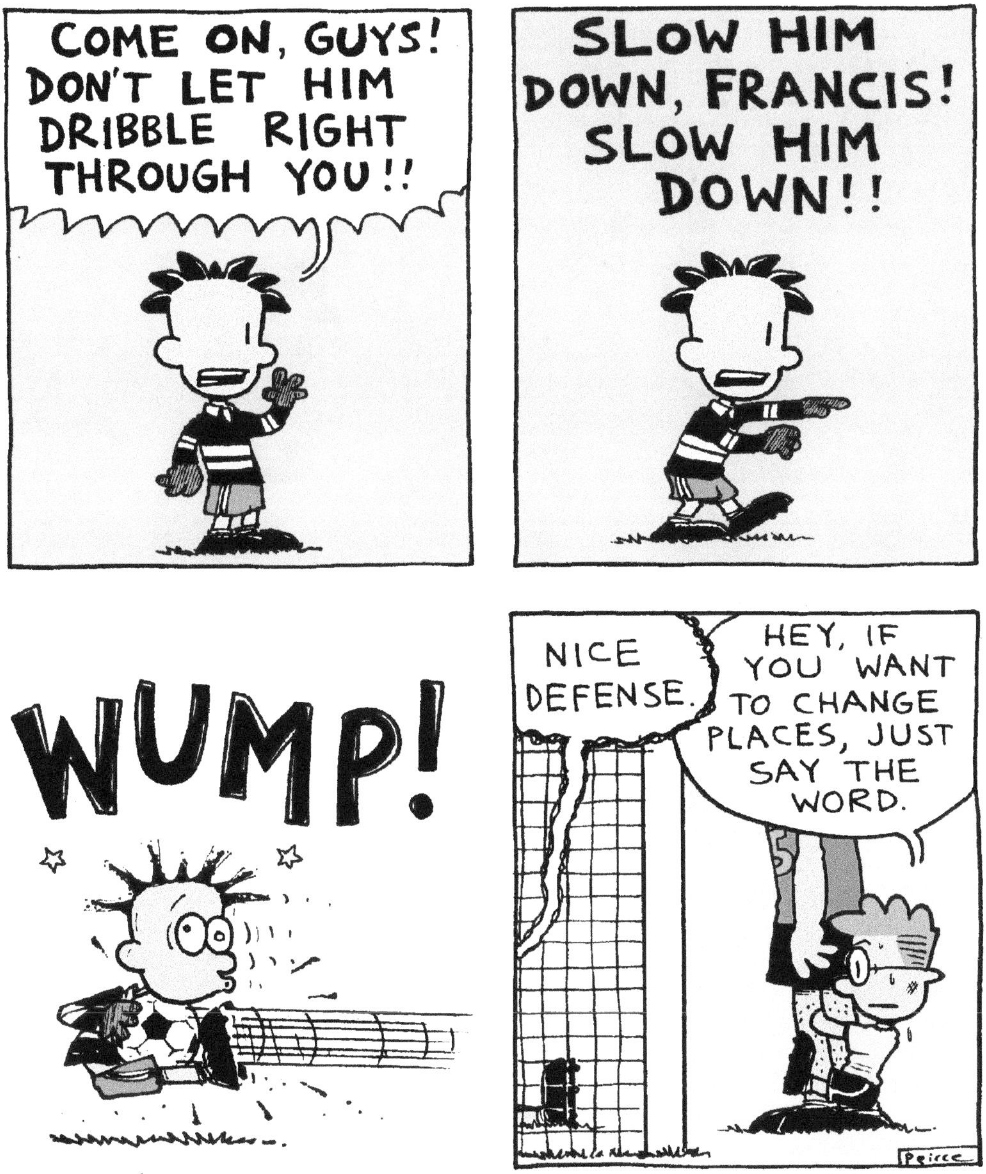
COME ON, GUYS! DON'T LET HIM DRIBBLE RIGHT THROUGH YOU!!
SLOW HIM DOWN, FRANCIS! SLOW HIM DOWN!!
WUMP!
NICE DEFENSE.
HEY, IF YOU WANT TO CHANGE PLACES, JUST SAY THE WORD.
Peirce

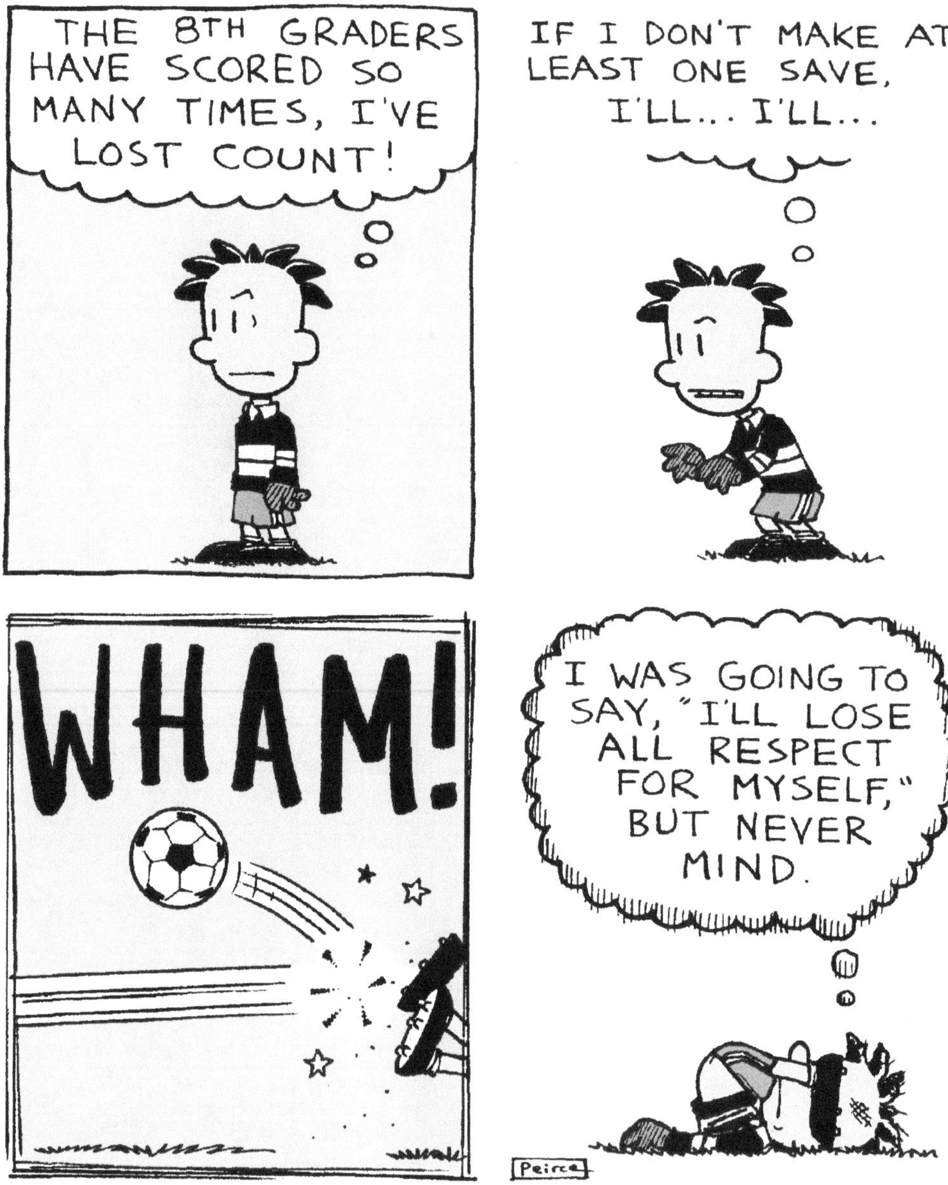
THE 8TH GRADERS HAVE SCORED SO MANY TIMES, I'VE LOST COUNT!
IF I DON'T MAKE AT LEAST ONE SAVE, I'LL... I'LL...
WHAM!
I WAS GOING TO SAY, "I'LL LOSE ALL RESPECT FOR MYSELF," BUT NEVER MIND.
Peirce

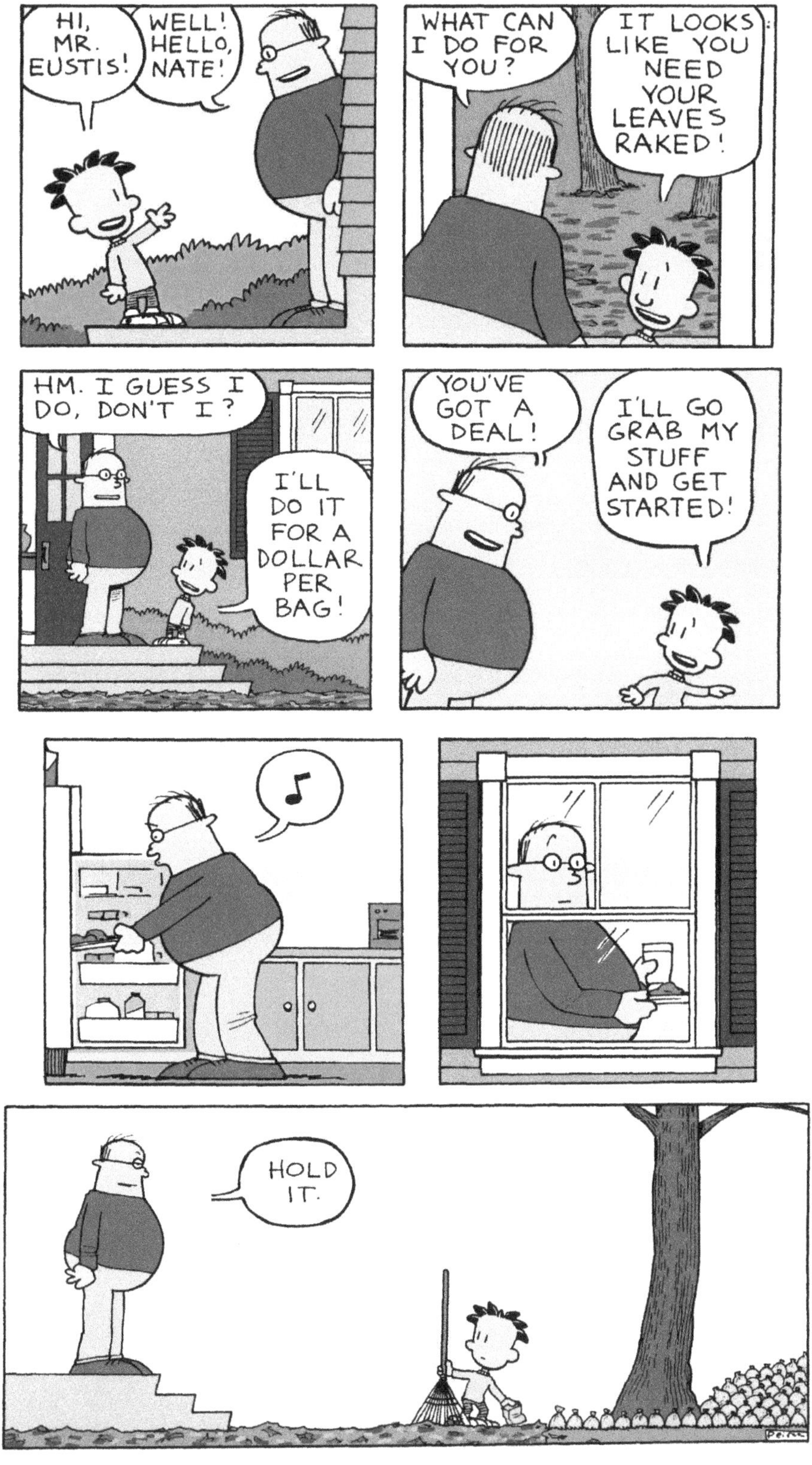
HI, MR. EUSTIS!
WELL! HELLO, NATE!
WHAT CAN I DO FOR YOU?
IT LOOKS LIKE YOU NEED YOUR LEAVES RAKED!
HM. I GUESS I DO, DON'T I?
I'LL DO IT FOR A DOLLAR PER BAG!
YOU'VE GOT A DEAL!
I'LL GO GRAB MY STUFF AND GET STARTED!
HOLD IT.

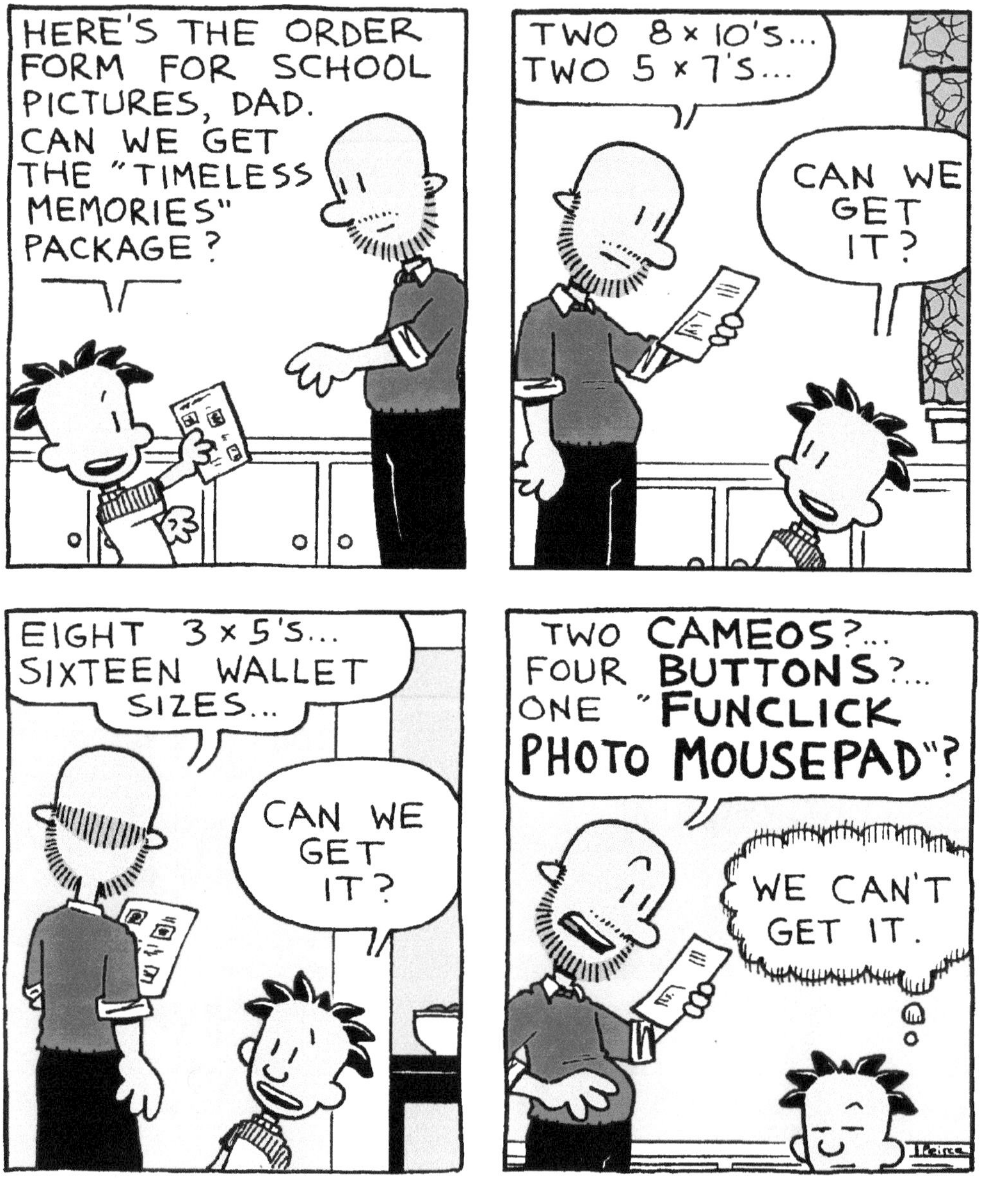
HERE'S THE ORDER FORM FOR SCHOOL PICTURES, DAD. CAN WE GET THE "TIMELESS MEMORIES" PACKAGE?
TWO 8 × 10'S... TWO 5 × 7'S...
CAN WE GET IT?
EIGHT 3 × 5'S... SIXTEEN WALLET SIZES...
CAN WE GET IT?
TWO CAMEOS?... FOUR BUTTONS?... ONE "FUNCLICK PHOTO MOUSEPAD"?
WE CAN'T GET IT.

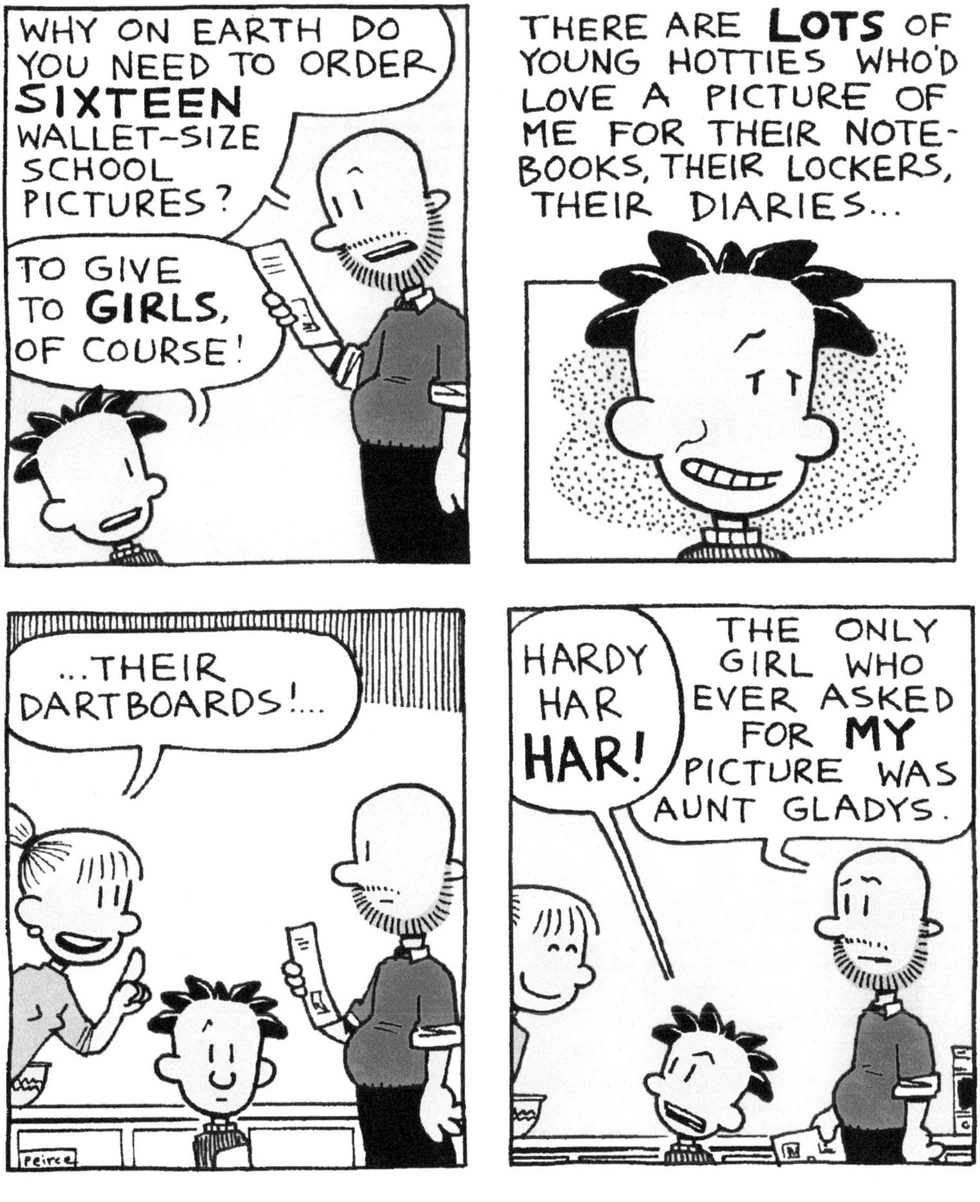
WHY ON EARTH DO YOU NEED TO ORDER **SIXTEEN** WALLET-SIZE SCHOOL PICTURES?
TO GIVE TO **GIRLS**, OF COURSE!
THERE ARE **LOTS** OF YOUNG HOTTIES WHO'D LOVE A PICTURE OF ME FOR THEIR NOTE-BOOKS, THEIR LOCKERS, THEIR DIARIES...
...THEIR DARTBOARDS!...
Peirce
HARDY HAR **HAR!**
THE ONLY GIRL WHO EVER ASKED FOR **MY** PICTURE WAS AUNT GLADYS.

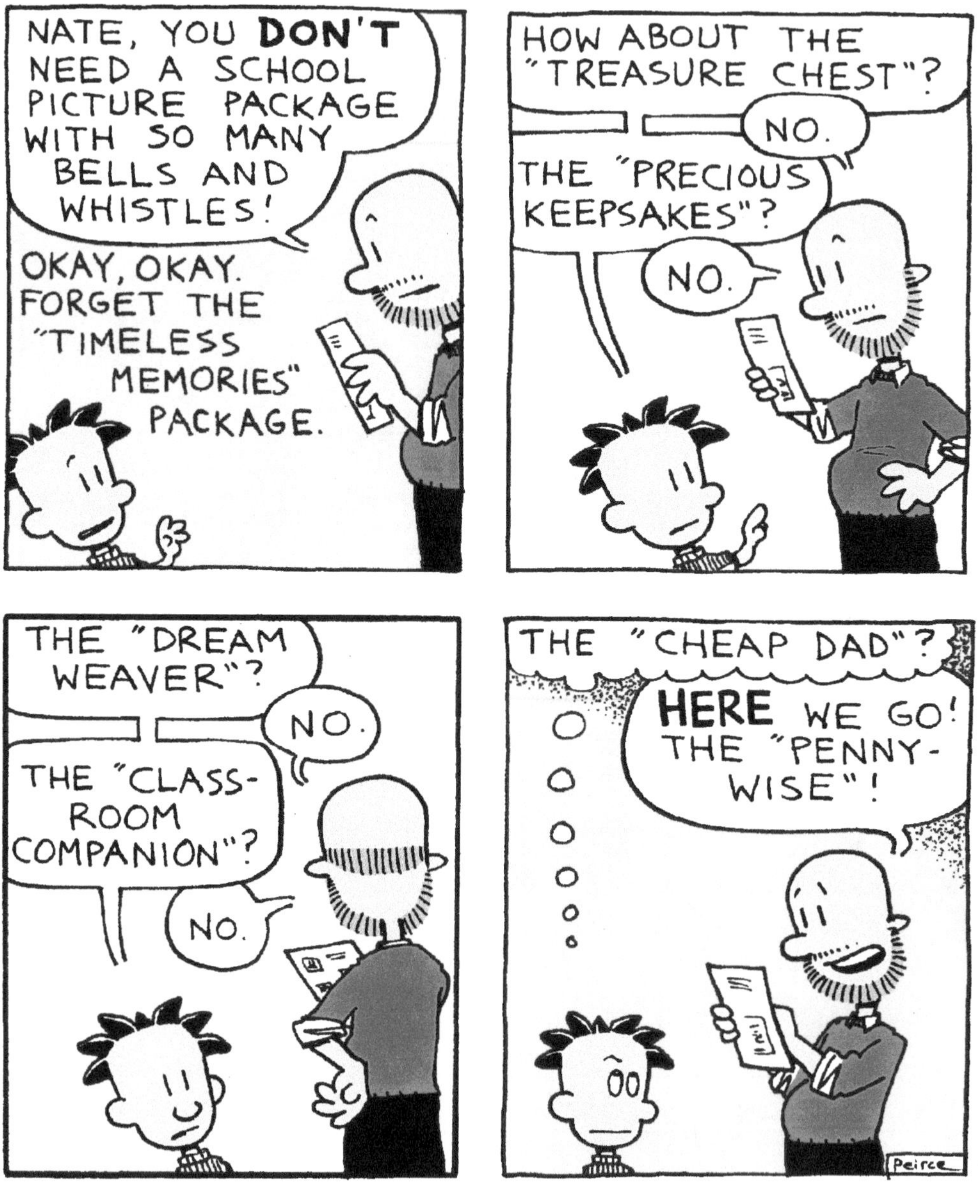
NATE, YOU **DON'T** NEED A SCHOOL PICTURE PACKAGE WITH SO MANY BELLS AND WHISTLES!
OKAY, OKAY. FORGET THE "TIMELESS MEMORIES" PACKAGE.
HOW ABOUT THE "TREASURE CHEST"?
NO.
THE "PRECIOUS KEEPSAKES"?
NO.
THE "DREAM WEAVER"?
NO.
THE "CLASSROOM COMPANION"?
NO.
THE "CHEAP DAD"?
HERE WE GO! THE "PENNY-WISE"!
Peirce

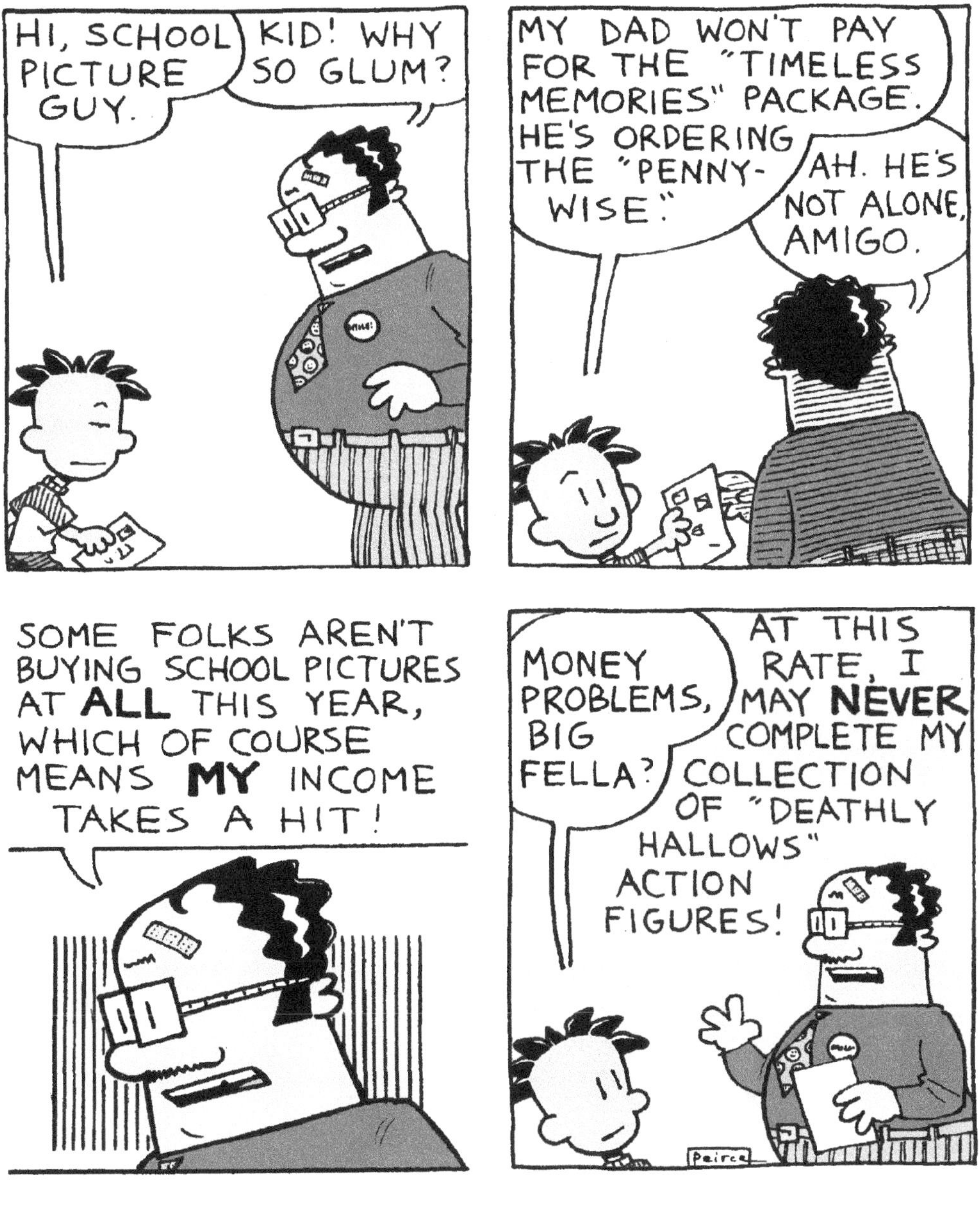
HI, SCHOOL PICTURE GUY.
KID! WHY SO GLUM?
MY DAD WON'T PAY FOR THE "TIMELESS MEMORIES" PACKAGE. HE'S ORDERING THE "PENNY-WISE."
AH. HE'S NOT ALONE, AMIGO.
SOME FOLKS AREN'T BUYING SCHOOL PICTURES AT **ALL** THIS YEAR, WHICH OF COURSE MEANS **MY** INCOME TAKES A HIT!
MONEY PROBLEMS, BIG FELLA?
AT THIS RATE, I MAY **NEVER** COMPLETE MY COLLECTION OF "DEATHLY HALLOWS" ACTION FIGURES!
Peirce

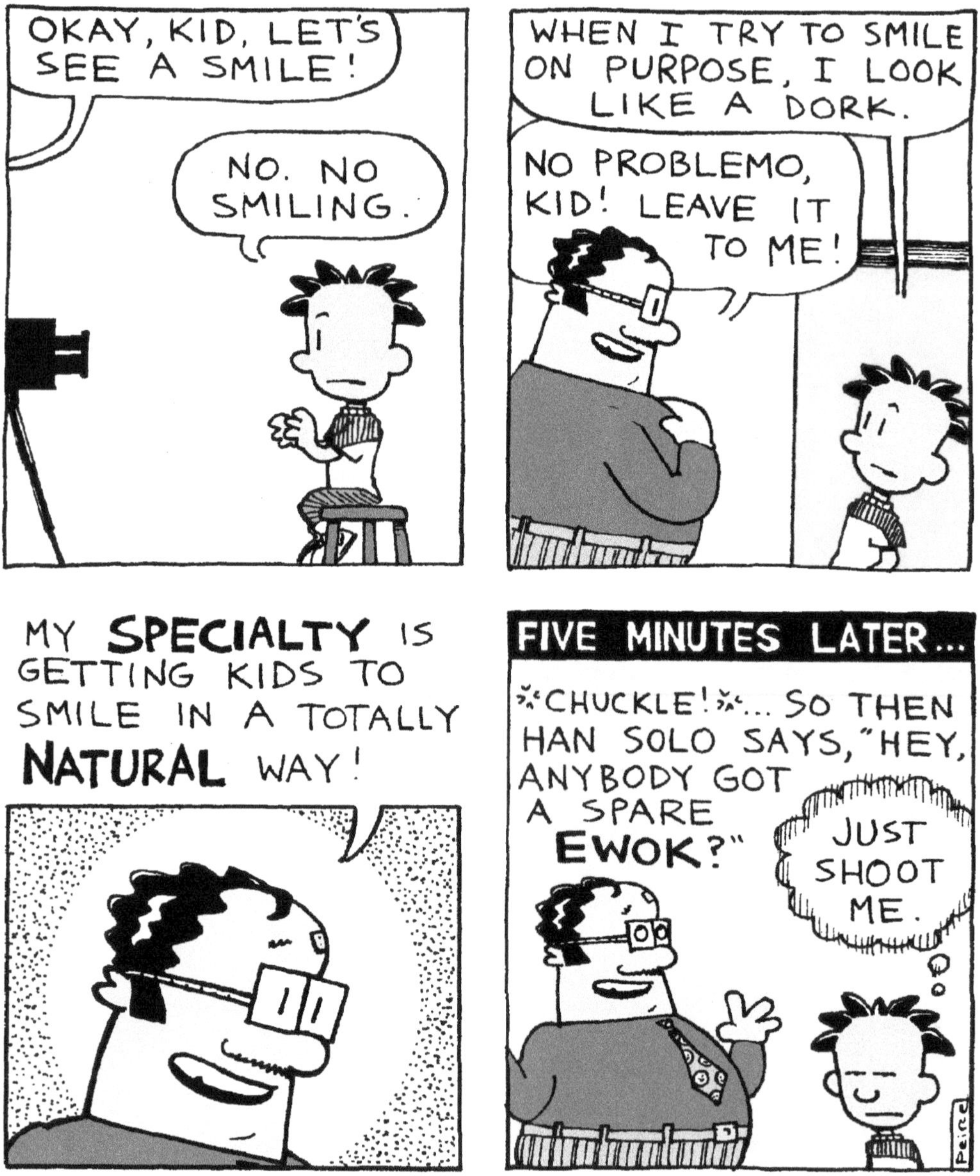
OKAY, KID, LET'S SEE A SMILE!
NO. NO SMILING.
WHEN I TRY TO SMILE ON PURPOSE, I LOOK LIKE A DORK.
NO PROBLEMO, KID! LEAVE IT TO ME!
MY **SPECIALTY** IS GETTING KIDS TO SMILE IN A TOTALLY **NATURAL** WAY!
FIVE MINUTES LATER...
CHUCKLE!... SO THEN HAN SOLO SAYS, "HEY, ANYBODY GOT A SPARE **EWOK**?"
JUST SHOOT ME.
Peirce

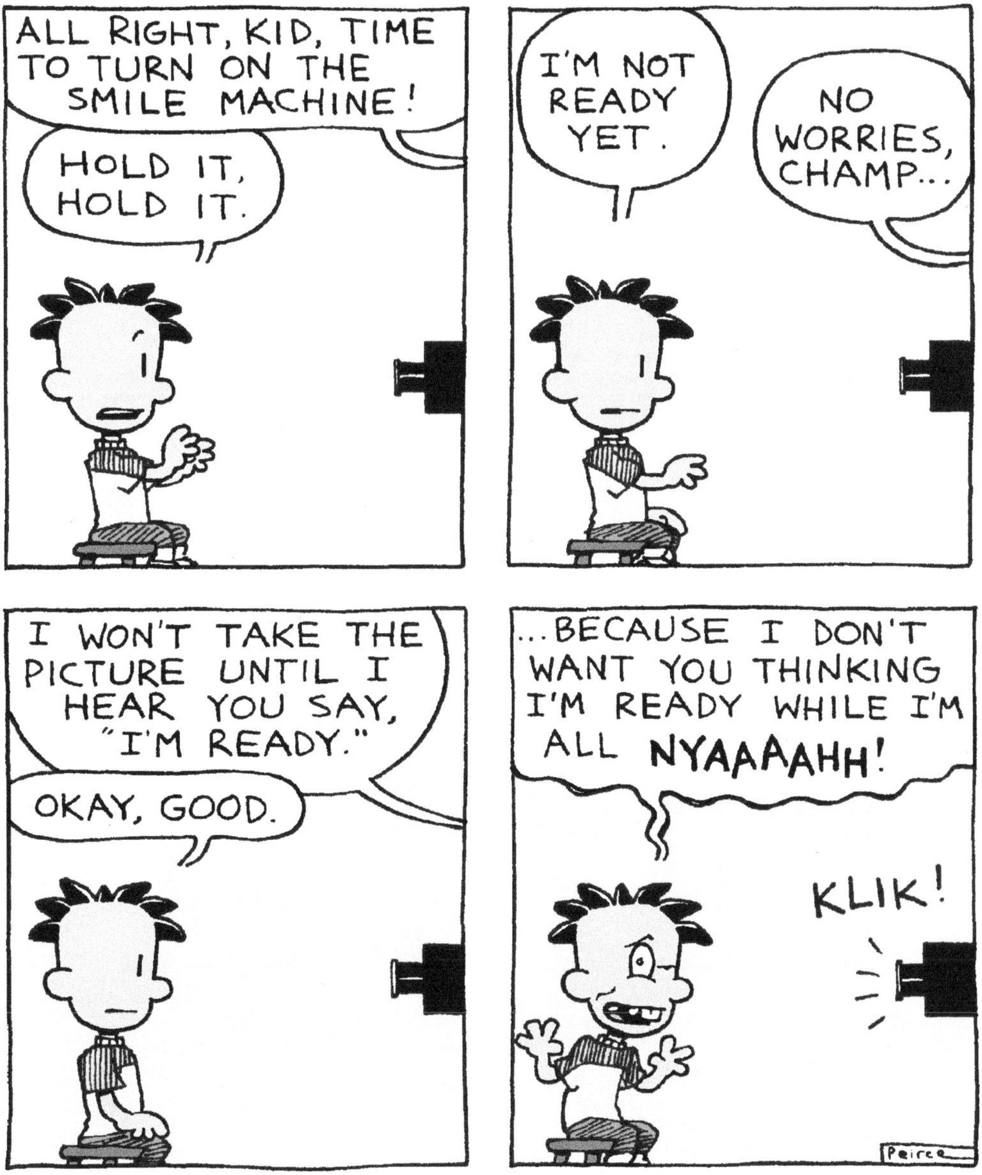
ALL RIGHT, KID, TIME TO TURN ON THE SMILE MACHINE!
HOLD IT, HOLD IT.
I'M NOT READY YET.
NO WORRIES, CHAMP...
I WON'T TAKE THE PICTURE UNTIL I HEAR YOU SAY, "I'M READY."
OKAY, GOOD.
...BECAUSE I DON'T WANT YOU THINKING I'M READY WHILE I'M ALL NYAAAAHH!
KLIK!
Peirce

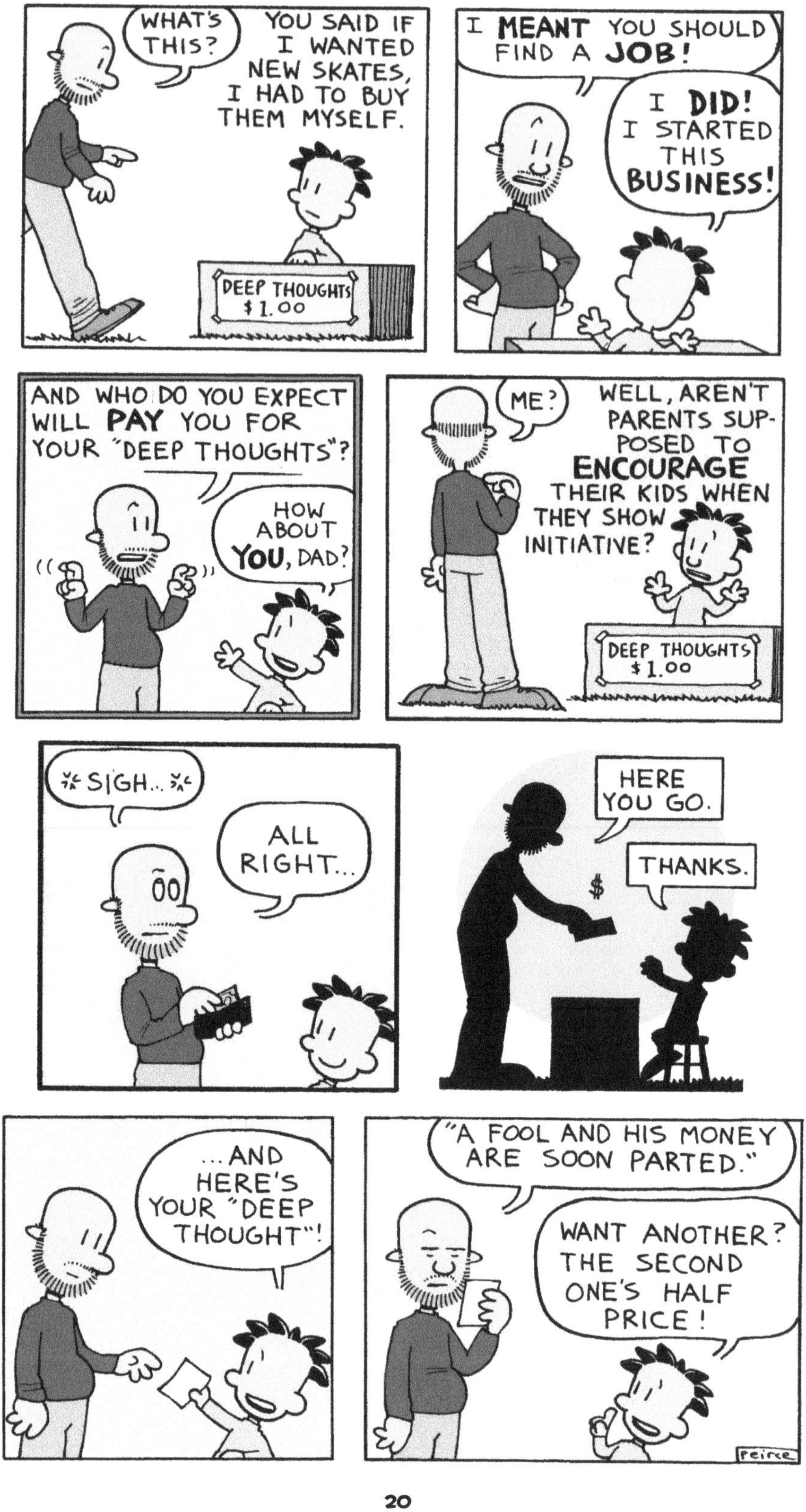
WHAT'S THIS?
YOU SAID IF I WANTED NEW SKATES, I HAD TO BUY THEM MYSELF.
DEEP THOUGHTS $1.00
I MEANT YOU SHOULD FIND A JOB!
I DID! I STARTED THIS BUSINESS!
AND WHO DO YOU EXPECT WILL PAY YOU FOR YOUR "DEEP THOUGHTS"?
HOW ABOUT YOU, DAD?
ME?
WELL, AREN'T PARENTS SUPPOSED TO ENCOURAGE THEIR KIDS WHEN THEY SHOW INITIATIVE?
DEEP THOUGHTS $1.00
SIGH...
ALL RIGHT...
HERE YOU GO.
THANKS.
...AND HERE'S YOUR "DEEP THOUGHT"!
"A FOOL AND HIS MONEY ARE SOON PARTED."
WANT ANOTHER? THE SECOND ONE'S HALF PRICE!
peirce

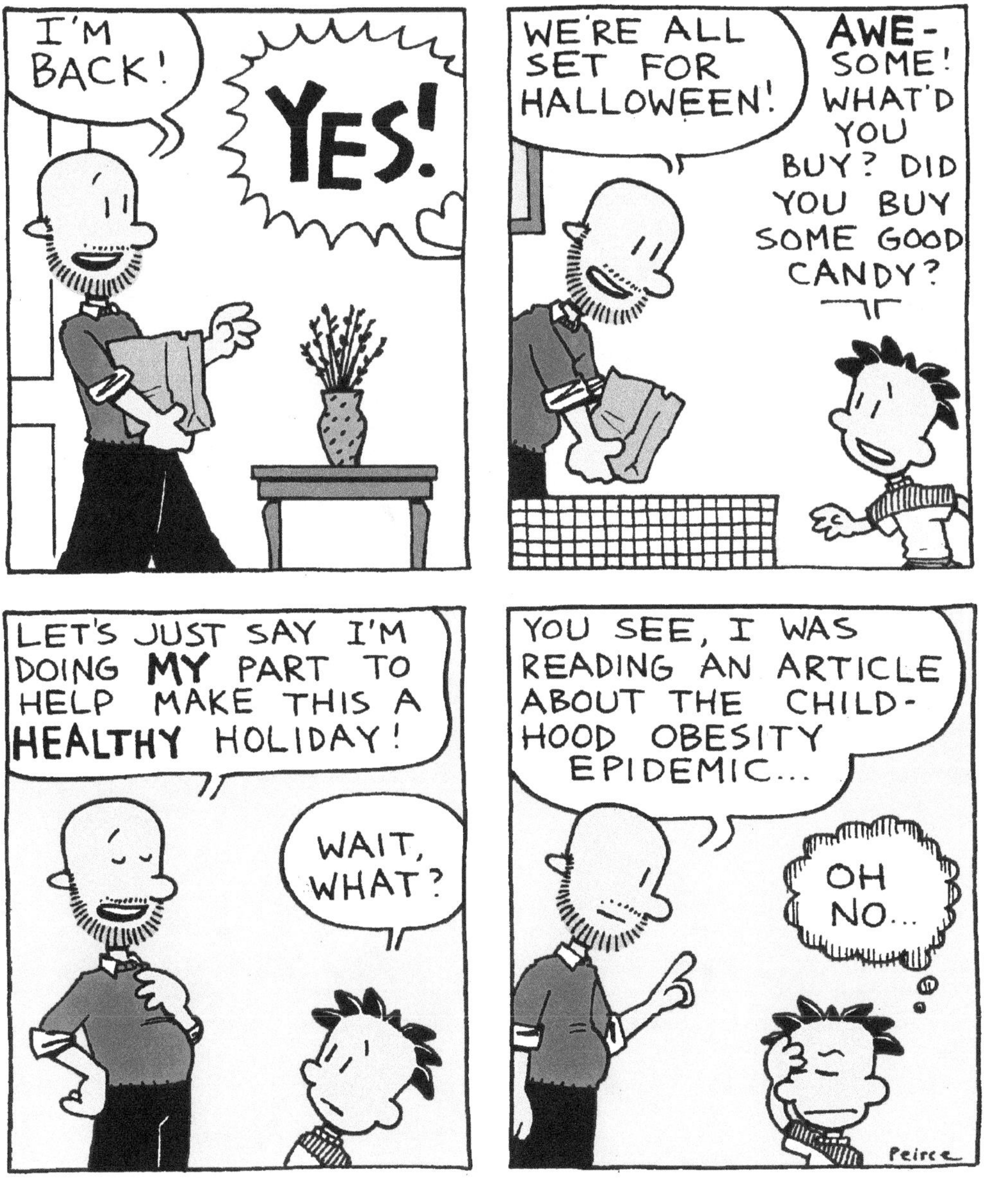
I'M BACK!
YES!
WE'RE ALL SET FOR HALLOWEEN!
AWE-SOME! WHAT'D YOU BUY? DID YOU BUY SOME GOOD CANDY?
LET'S JUST SAY I'M DOING MY PART TO HELP MAKE THIS A HEALTHY HOLIDAY!
WAIT, WHAT?
YOU SEE, I WAS READING AN ARTICLE ABOUT THE CHILD-HOOD OBESITY EPIDEMIC...
OH NO...
Peirce

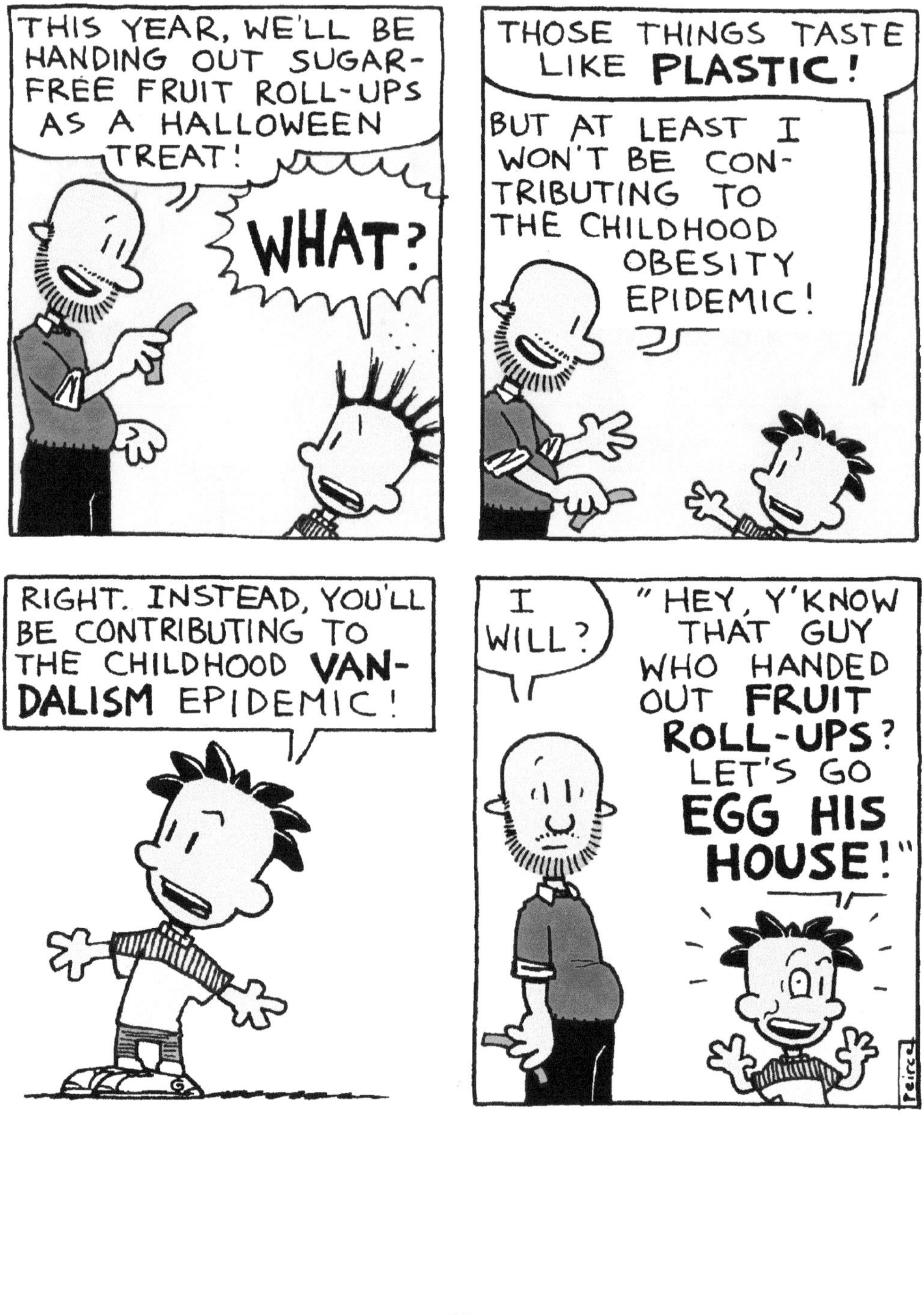
THIS YEAR, WE'LL BE HANDING OUT SUGAR-FREE FRUIT ROLL-UPS AS A HALLOWEEN TREAT!
WHAT?
THOSE THINGS TASTE LIKE **PLASTIC**!
BUT AT LEAST I WON'T BE CONTRIBUTING TO THE CHILDHOOD OBESITY EPIDEMIC!
RIGHT. INSTEAD, YOU'LL BE CONTRIBUTING TO THE CHILDHOOD **VANDALISM** EPIDEMIC!
I WILL?
"HEY, Y'KNOW THAT GUY WHO HANDED OUT **FRUIT ROLL-UPS**? LET'S GO **EGG HIS HOUSE**!"
Peirce

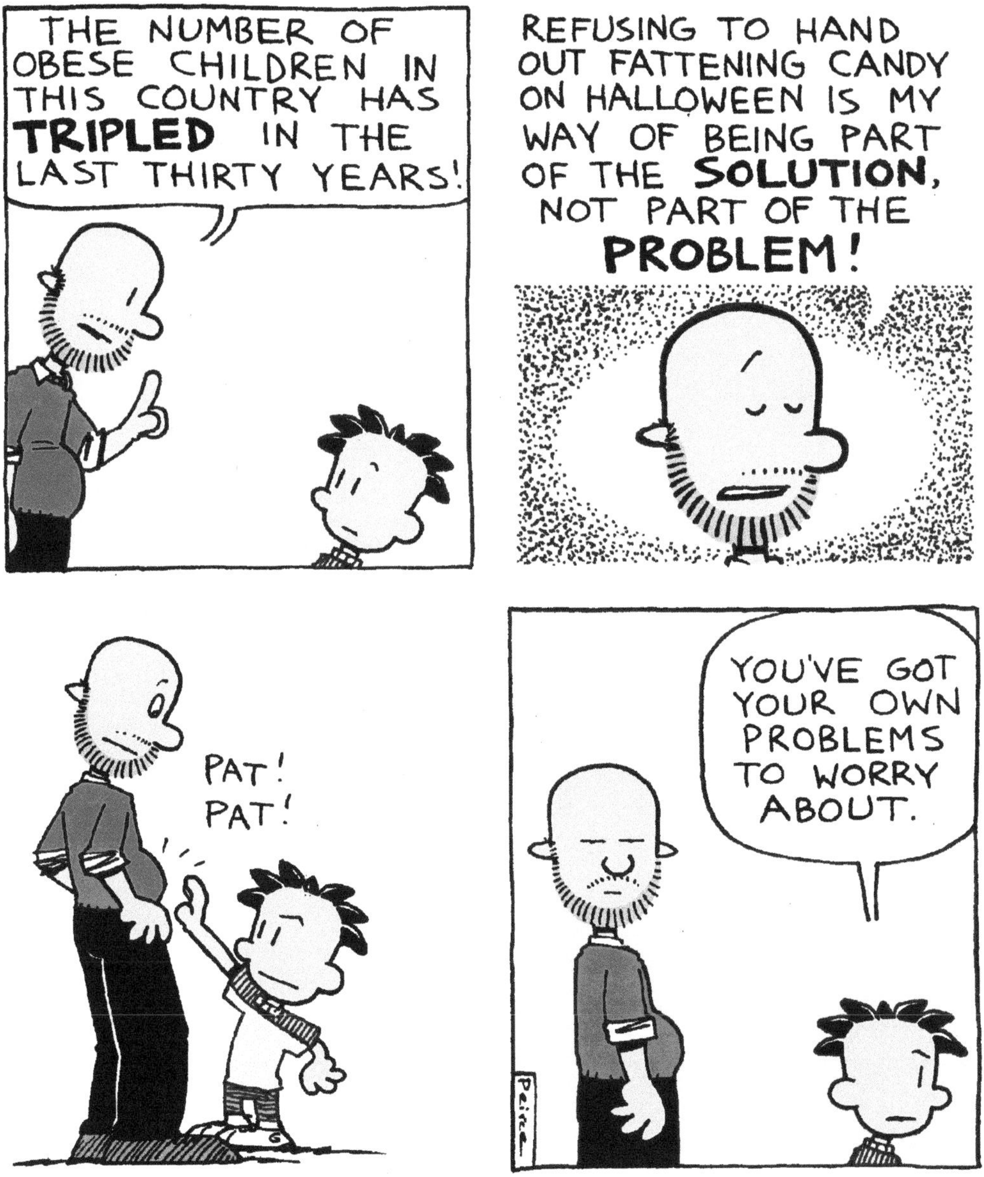
THE NUMBER OF OBESE CHILDREN IN THIS COUNTRY HAS TRIPLED IN THE LAST THIRTY YEARS!
REFUSING TO HAND OUT FATTENING CANDY ON HALLOWEEN IS MY WAY OF BEING PART OF THE SOLUTION, NOT PART OF THE PROBLEM!
PAT! PAT!
YOU'VE GOT YOUR OWN PROBLEMS TO WORRY ABOUT.

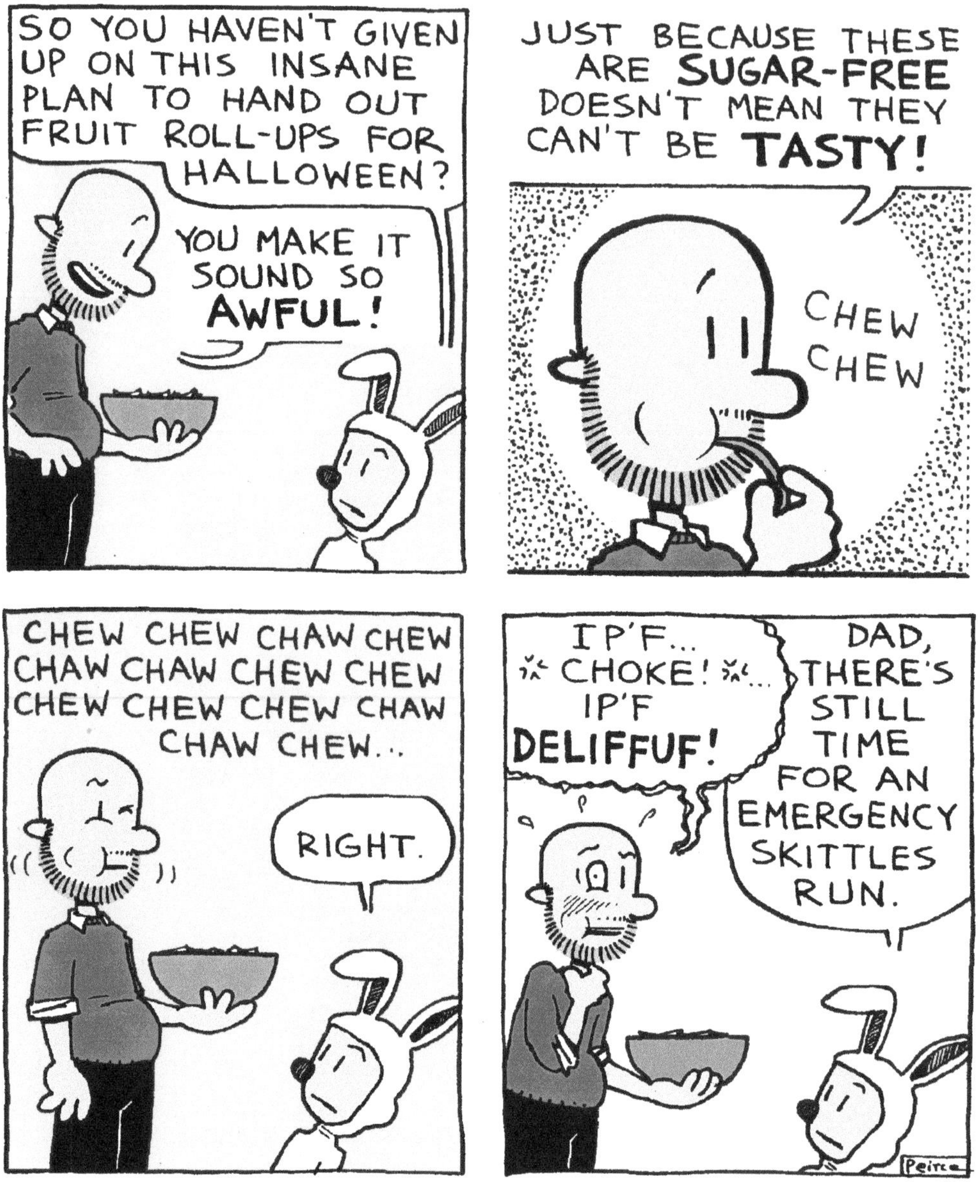
SO YOU HAVEN'T GIVEN UP ON THIS INSANE PLAN TO HAND OUT FRUIT ROLL-UPS FOR HALLOWEEN?
YOU MAKE IT SOUND SO **AWFUL**!
JUST BECAUSE THESE ARE **SUGAR-FREE** DOESN'T MEAN THEY CAN'T BE **TASTY**!
CHEW CHEW
CHEW CHEW CHAW CHEW CHAW CHAW CHEW CHEW CHEW CHEW CHEW CHAW CHAW CHEW...
RIGHT.
IP'F... CHOKE! IP'F **DELIFFUF**!
DAD, THERE'S STILL TIME FOR AN EMERGENCY SKITTLES RUN.
Peirce

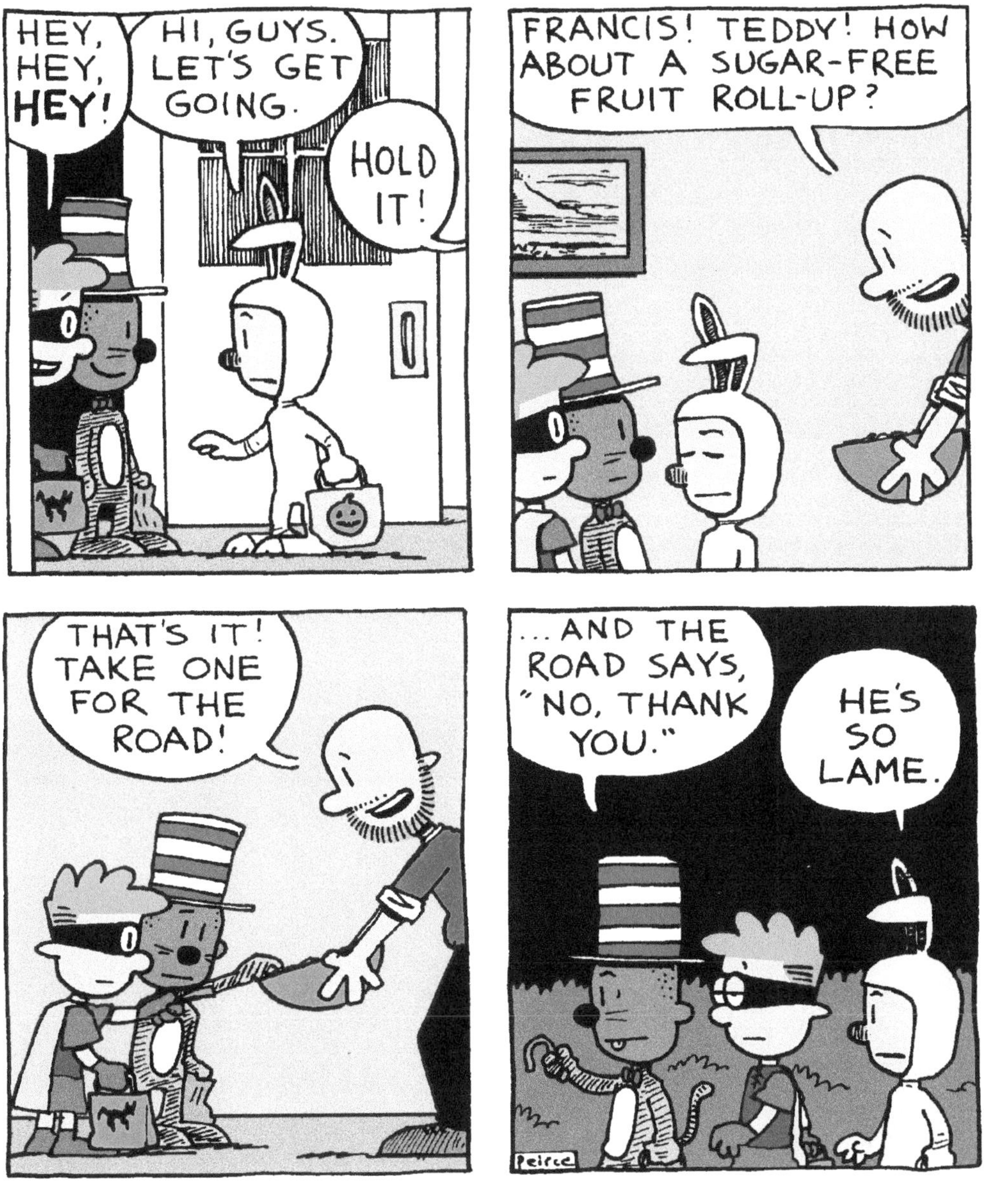
HEY, HEY, HEY!
HI, GUYS. LET'S GET GOING.
HOLD IT!
FRANCIS! TEDDY! HOW ABOUT A SUGAR-FREE FRUIT ROLL-UP?
THAT'S IT! TAKE ONE FOR THE ROAD!
...AND THE ROAD SAYS, "NO, THANK YOU."
HE'S SO LAME.
Peirce

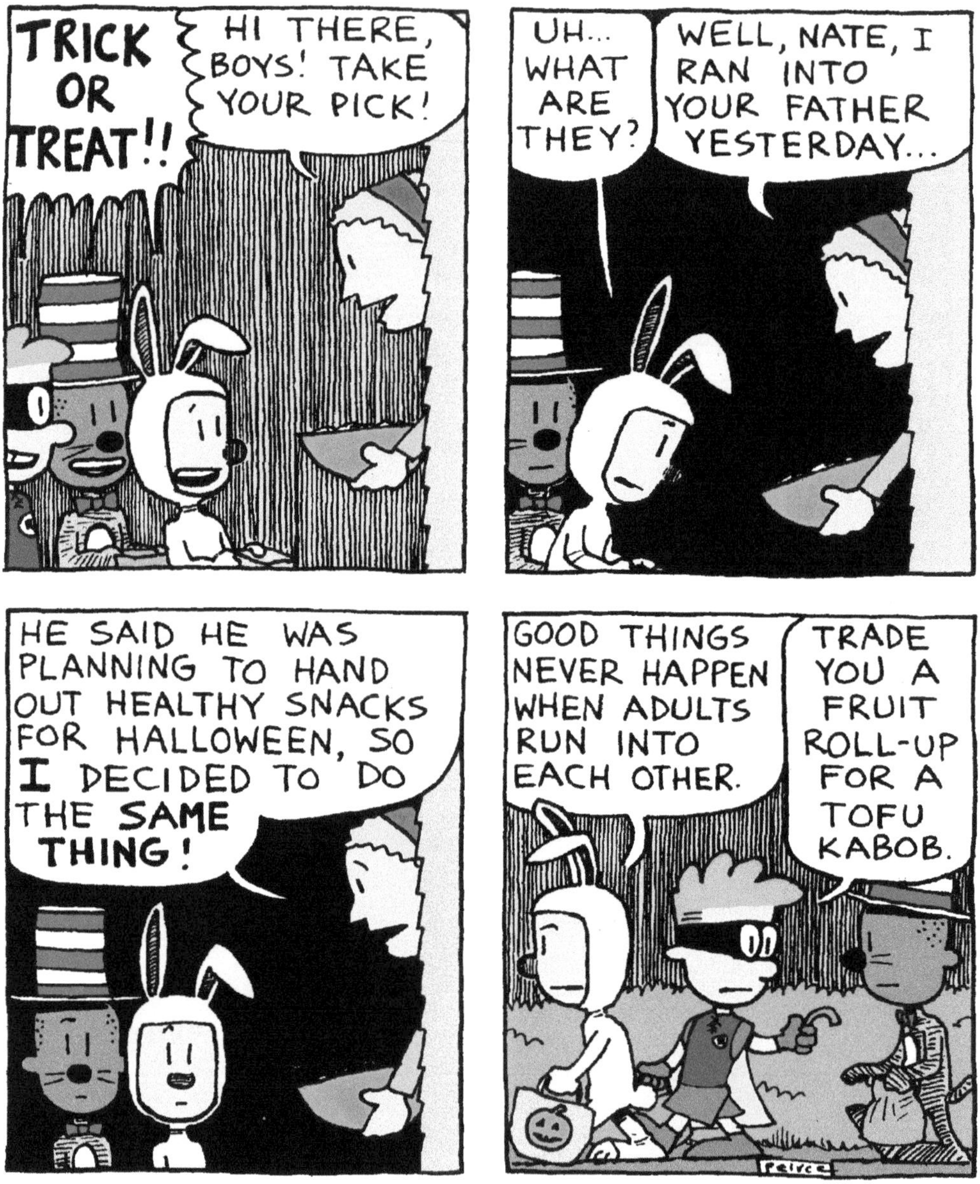
TRICK OR TREAT!!
HI THERE, BOYS! TAKE YOUR PICK!
UH... WHAT ARE THEY?
WELL, NATE, I RAN INTO YOUR FATHER YESTERDAY...
HE SAID HE WAS PLANNING TO HAND OUT HEALTHY SNACKS FOR HALLOWEEN, SO I DECIDED TO DO THE SAME THING!
GOOD THINGS NEVER HAPPEN WHEN ADULTS RUN INTO EACH OTHER.
TRADE YOU A FRUIT ROLL-UP FOR A TOFU KABOB.
peirce

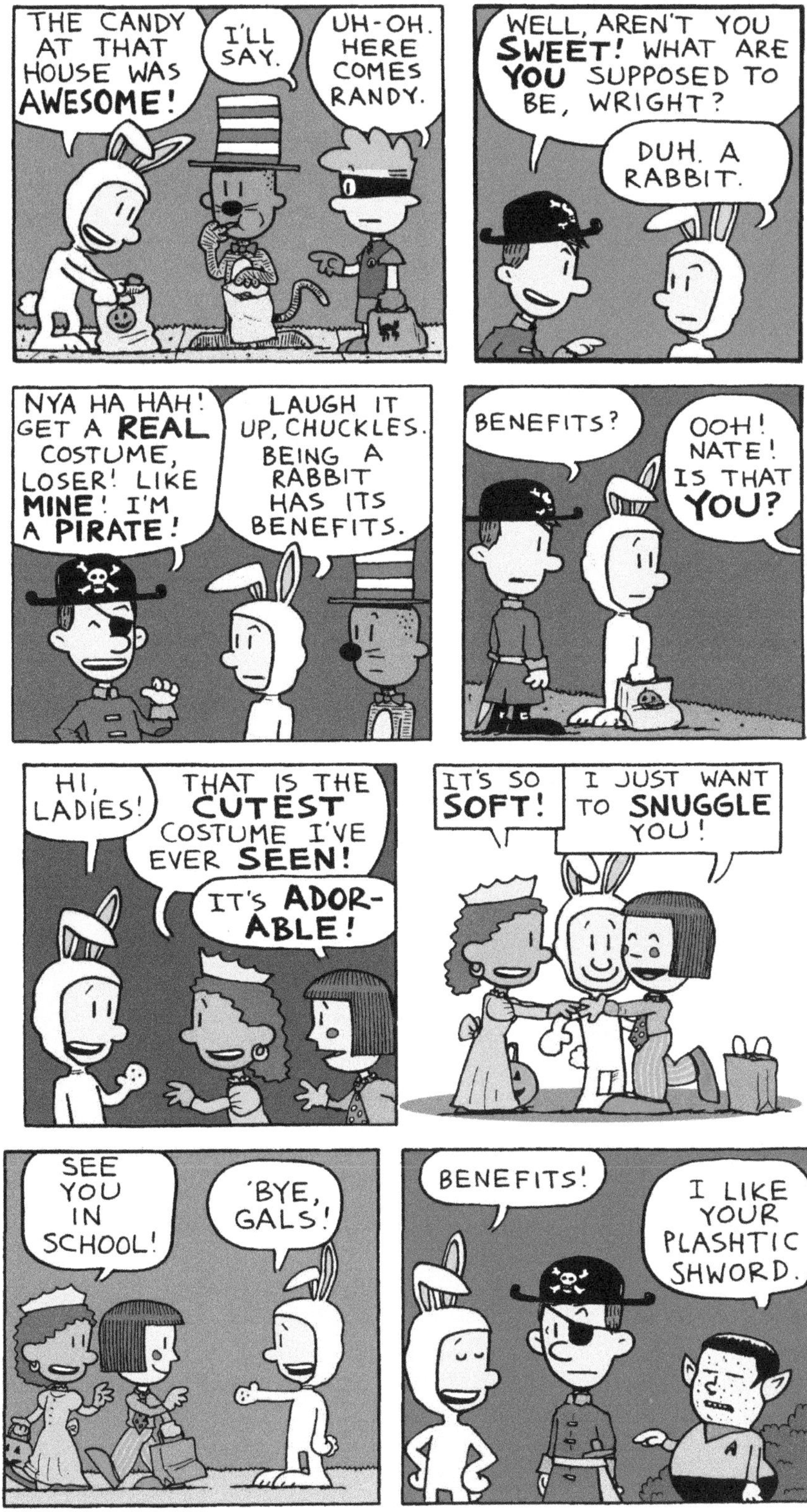
THE CANDY AT THAT HOUSE WAS AWESOME!
I'LL SAY.
UH-OH. HERE COMES RANDY.
WELL, AREN'T YOU SWEET! WHAT ARE YOU SUPPOSED TO BE, WRIGHT?
DUH. A RABBIT.
NYA HA HAH! GET A REAL COSTUME, LOSER! LIKE MINE! I'M A PIRATE!
LAUGH IT UP, CHUCKLES. BEING A RABBIT HAS ITS BENEFITS.
BENEFITS?
OOH! NATE! IS THAT YOU?
HI, LADIES!
THAT IS THE CUTEST COSTUME I'VE EVER SEEN!
IT'S ADOR-ABLE!
IT'S SO SOFT!
I JUST WANT TO SNUGGLE YOU!
SEE YOU IN SCHOOL!
'BYE, GALS!
BENEFITS!
I LIKE YOUR PLASHTIC SHWORD.
Peirce

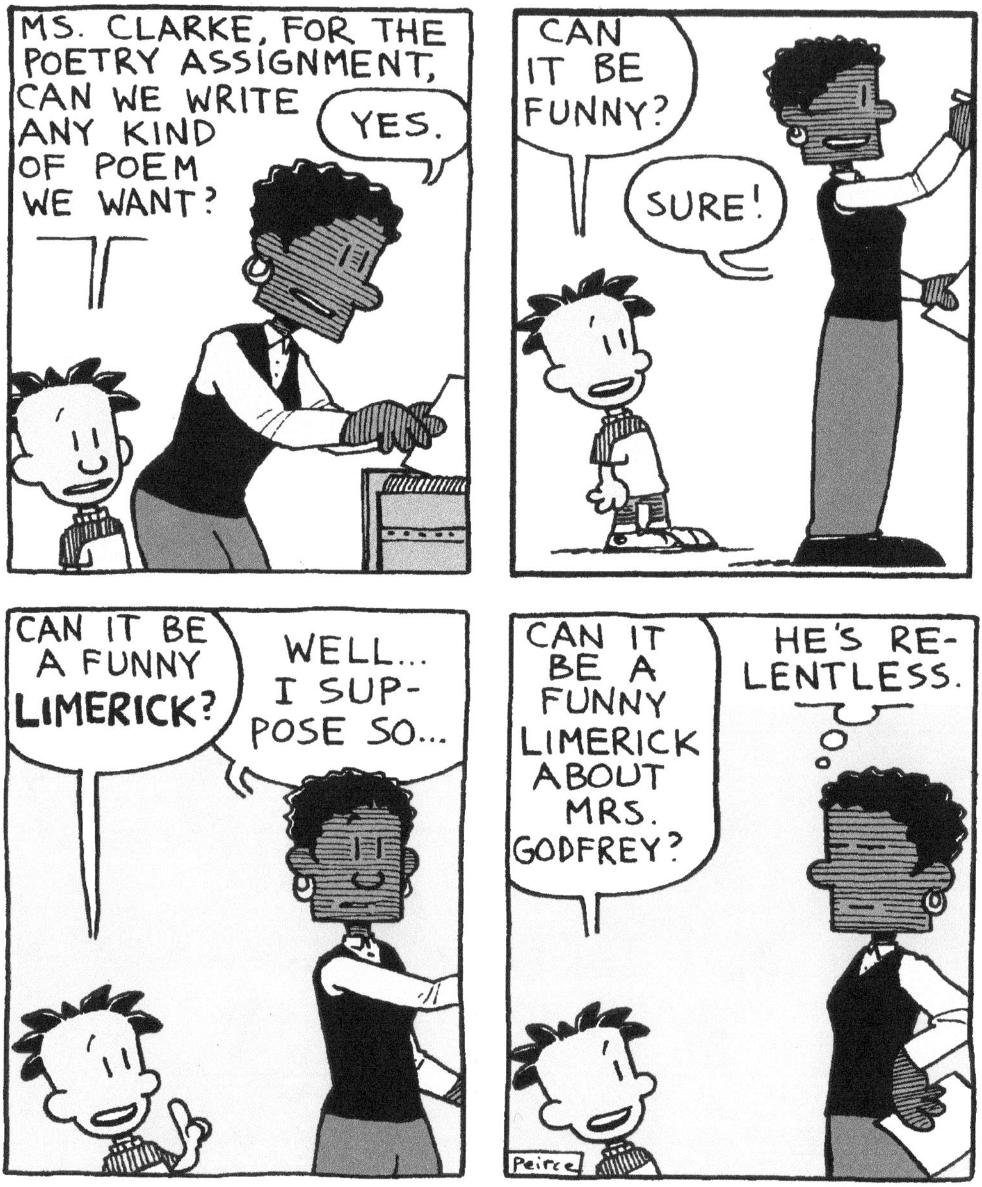
MS. CLARKE, FOR THE POETRY ASSIGNMENT, CAN WE WRITE ANY KIND OF POEM WE WANT?
YES.
CAN IT BE FUNNY?
SURE!
CAN IT BE A FUNNY **LIMERICK**?
WELL... I SUPPOSE SO...
CAN IT BE A FUNNY LIMERICK ABOUT MRS. GODFREY?
HE'S RELENTLESS.
Peirce

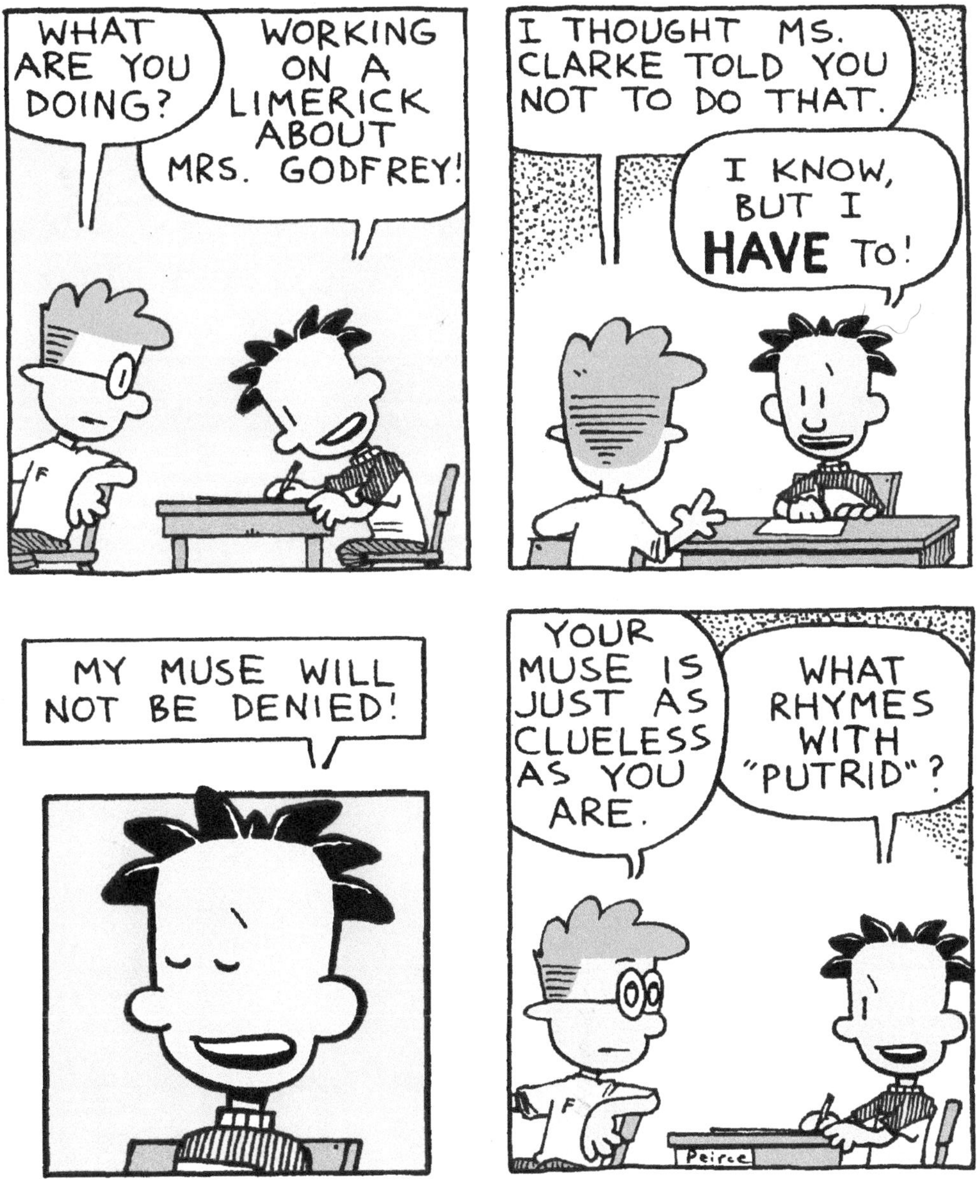

WHAT ARE YOU DOING?
WORKING ON A LIMERICK ABOUT MRS. GODFREY!
I THOUGHT MS. CLARKE TOLD YOU NOT TO DO THAT.
I KNOW, BUT I HAVE TO!
MY MUSE WILL NOT BE DENIED!
YOUR MUSE IS JUST AS CLUELESS AS YOU ARE.
WHAT RHYMES WITH "PUTRID"?
Peirce

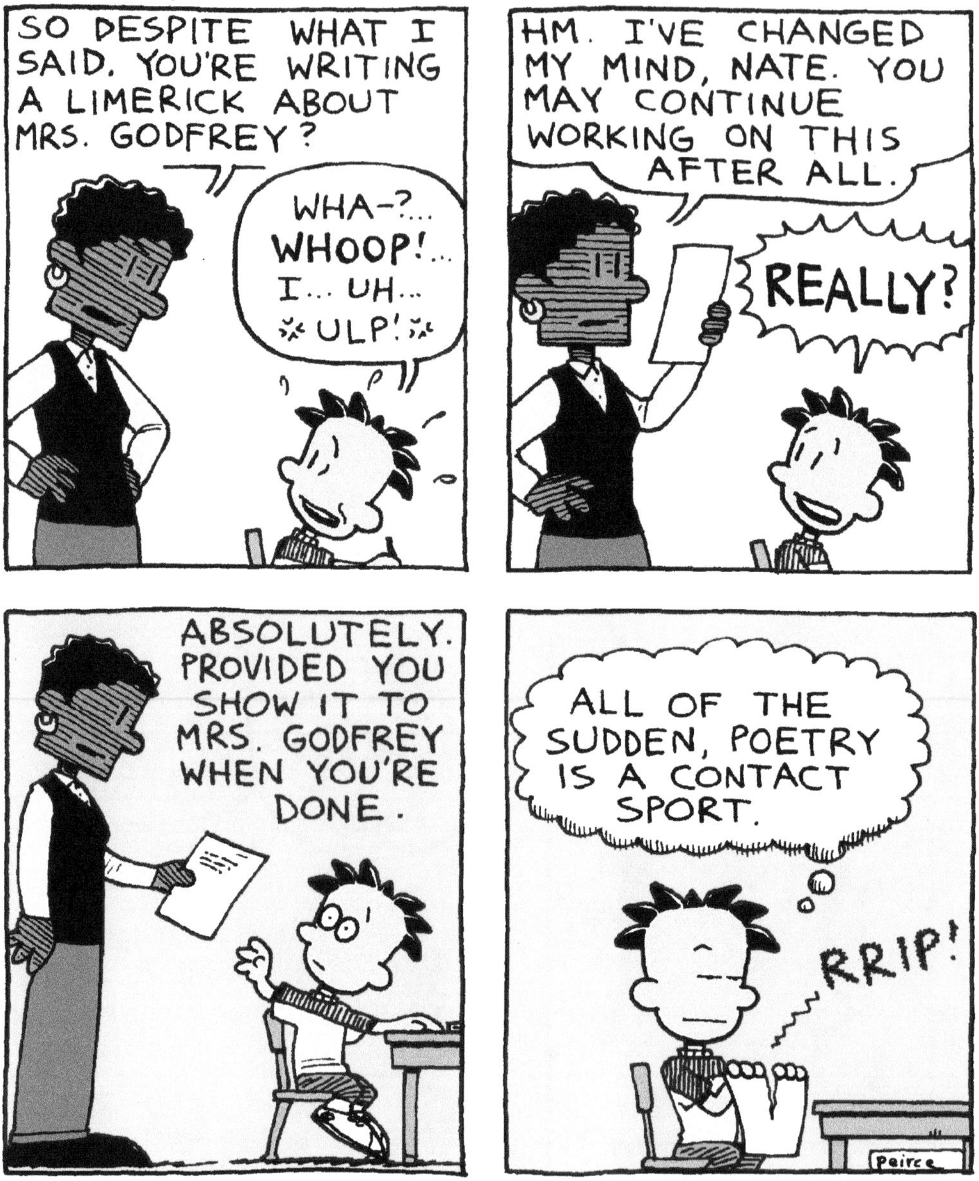
SO DESPITE WHAT I SAID, YOU'RE WRITING A LIMERICK ABOUT MRS. GODFREY?
WHA-?... WHOOP!... I... UH... ULP!
HM. I'VE CHANGED MY MIND, NATE. YOU MAY CONTINUE WORKING ON THIS AFTER ALL.
REALLY?
ABSOLUTELY. PROVIDED YOU SHOW IT TO MRS. GODFREY WHEN YOU'RE DONE.
ALL OF THE SUDDEN, POETRY IS A CONTACT SPORT.
RRIP!
Peirce

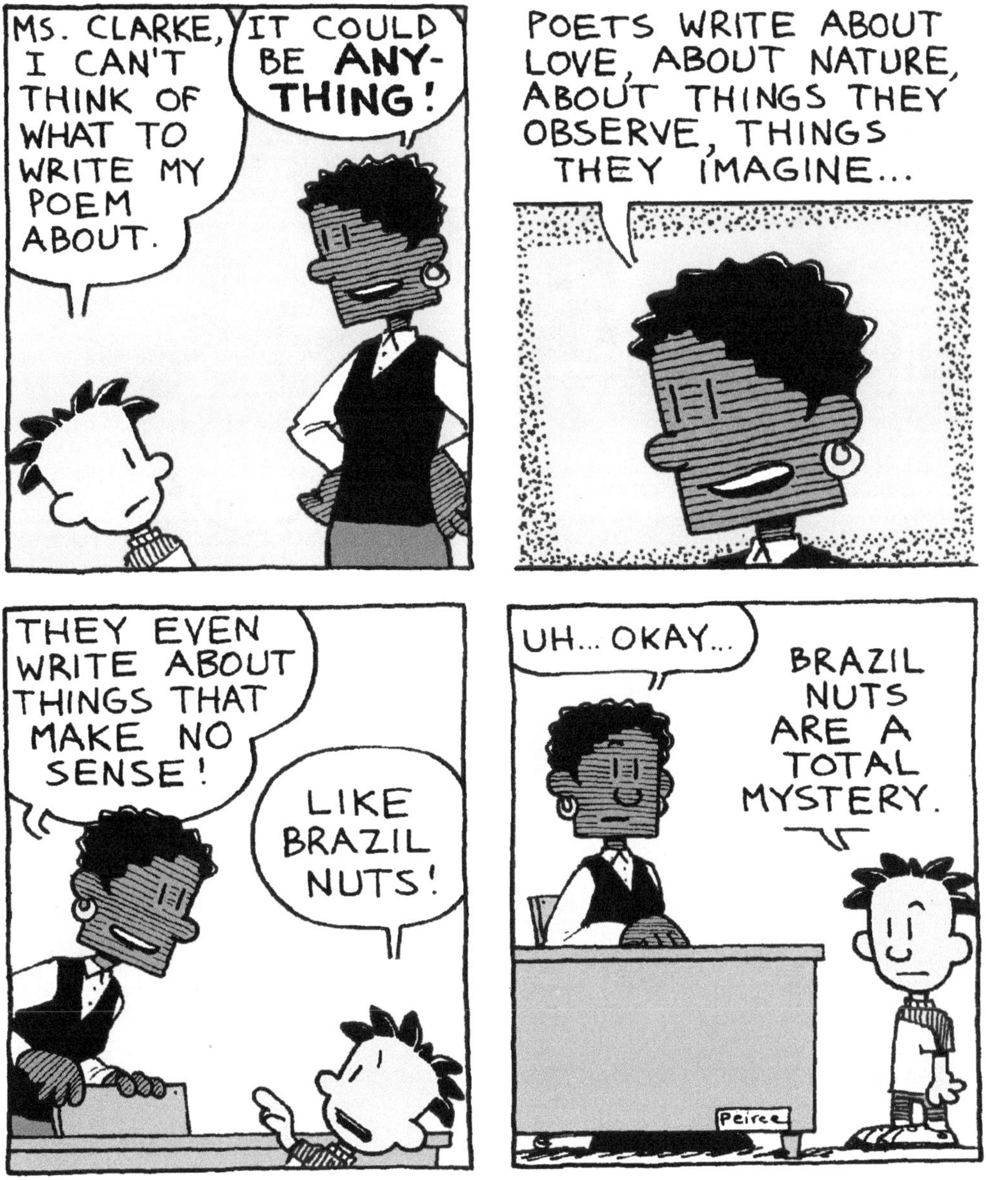
MS. CLARKE, I CAN'T THINK OF WHAT TO WRITE MY POEM ABOUT.
IT COULD BE **ANY-THING**!
POETS WRITE ABOUT LOVE, ABOUT NATURE, ABOUT THINGS THEY OBSERVE, THINGS THEY IMAGINE...
THEY EVEN WRITE ABOUT THINGS THAT MAKE NO SENSE!
LIKE BRAZIL NUTS!
UH... OKAY...
BRAZIL NUTS ARE A TOTAL MYSTERY.
Peirce

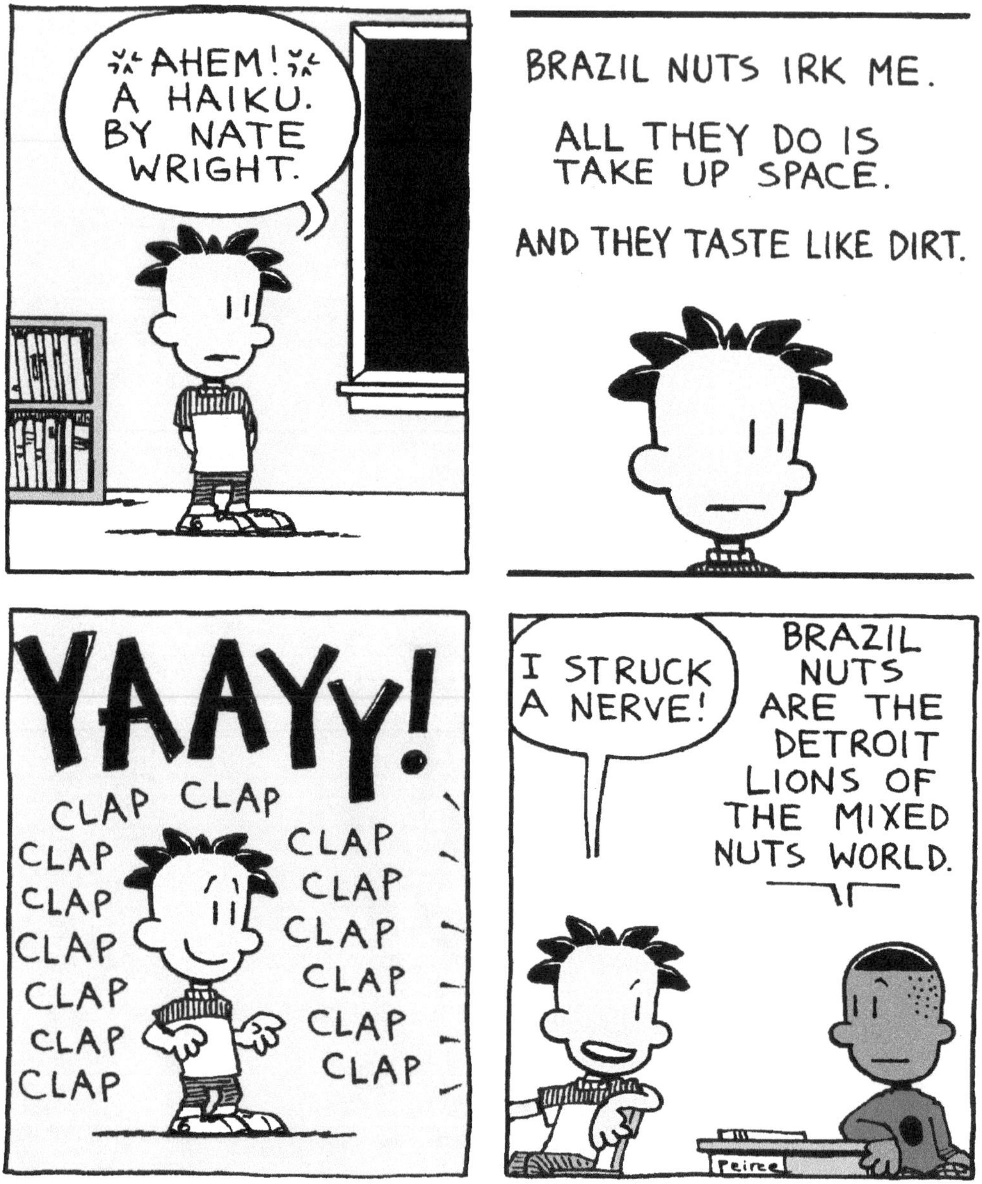
AHEM! A HAIKU. BY NATE WRIGHT.
BRAZIL NUTS IRK ME.
ALL THEY DO IS TAKE UP SPACE.
AND THEY TASTE LIKE DIRT.
YAAYY!
CLAP CLAP CLAP CLAP CLAP CLAP CLAP CLAP CLAP CLAP CLAP CLAP CLAP CLAP
I STRUCK A NERVE!
BRAZIL NUTS ARE THE DETROIT LIONS OF THE MIXED NUTS WORLD.
Peirce

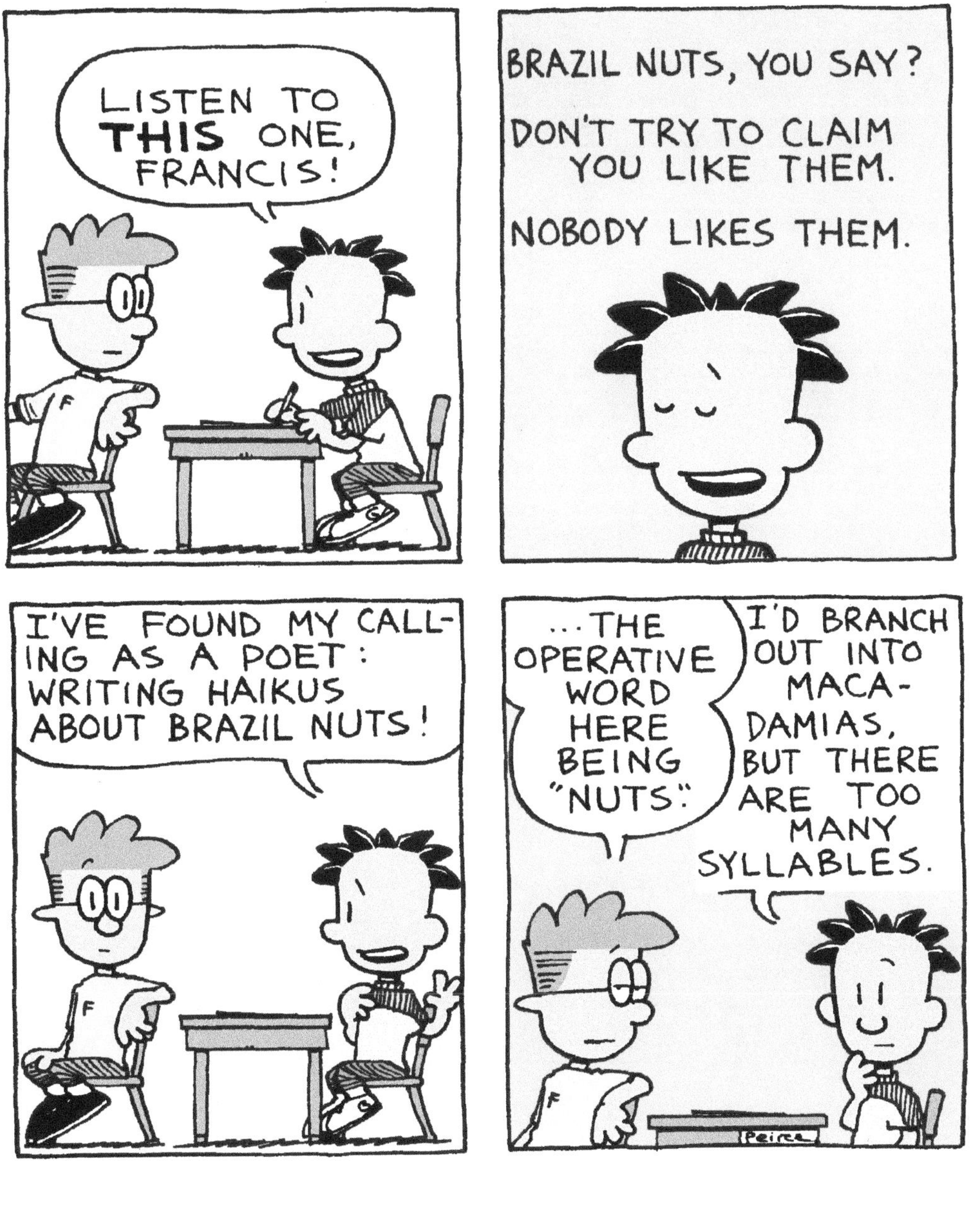
LISTEN TO **THIS** ONE, FRANCIS!
BRAZIL NUTS, YOU SAY?
DON'T TRY TO CLAIM YOU LIKE THEM.
NOBODY LIKES THEM.
I'VE FOUND MY CALLING AS A POET: WRITING HAIKUS ABOUT BRAZIL NUTS!
...THE OPERATIVE WORD HERE BEING "NUTS."
I'D BRANCH OUT INTO MACADAMIAS, BUT THERE ARE TOO MANY SYLLABLES.
Peirce

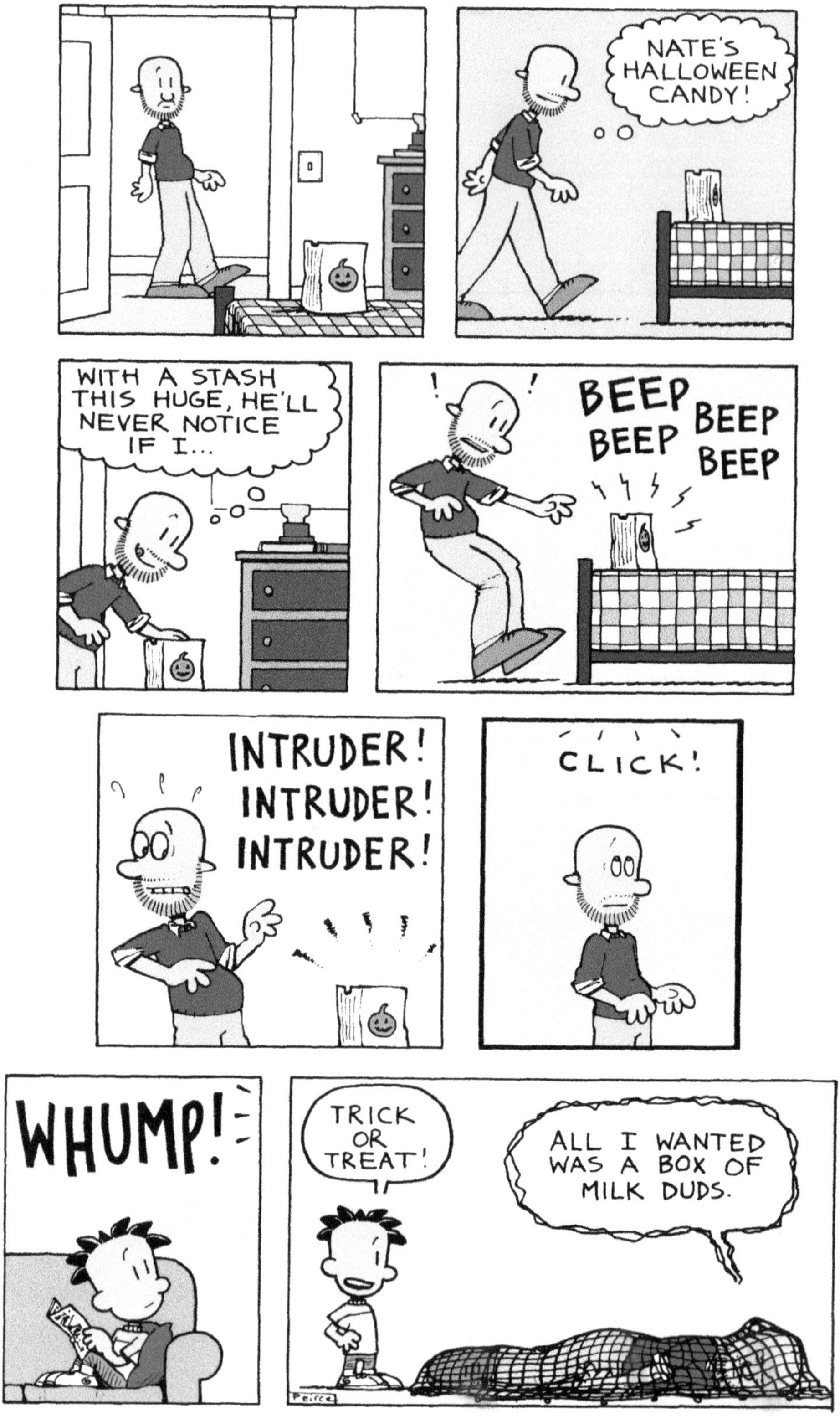
NATE'S HALLOWEEN CANDY!
WITH A STASH THIS HUGE, HE'LL NEVER NOTICE IF I...
! !
BEEP BEEP BEEP BEEP
INTRUDER! INTRUDER! INTRUDER!
CLICK!
WHUMP!
TRICK OR TREAT!
ALL I WANTED WAS A BOX OF MILK DUDS.
Peirce

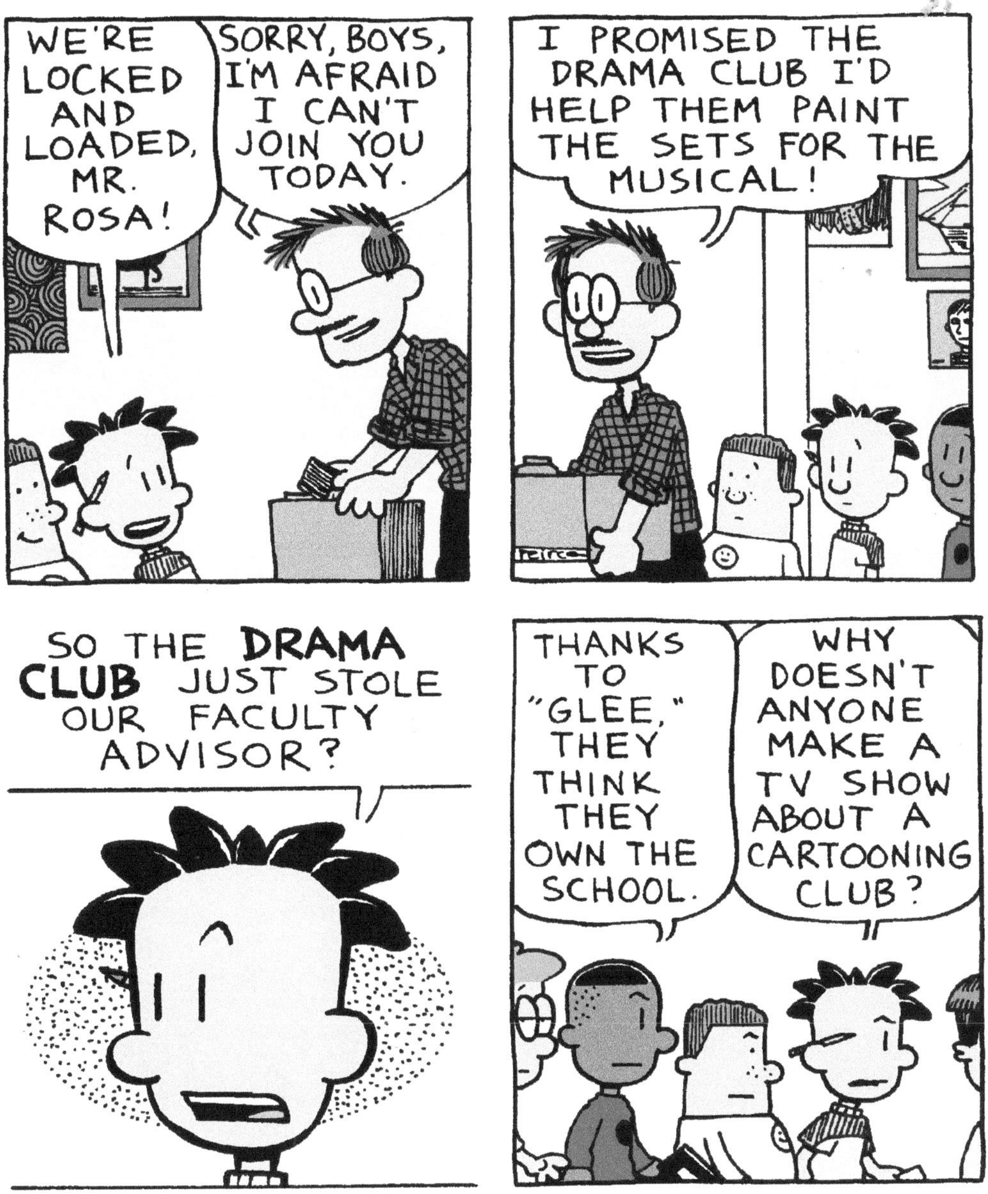
WE'RE LOCKED AND LOADED, MR. ROSA!
SORRY, BOYS, I'M AFRAID I CAN'T JOIN YOU TODAY.
I PROMISED THE DRAMA CLUB I'D HELP THEM PAINT THE SETS FOR THE MUSICAL!
SO THE **DRAMA CLUB** JUST STOLE OUR FACULTY ADVISOR?
THANKS TO "GLEE," THEY THINK THEY OWN THE SCHOOL.
WHY DOESN'T ANYONE MAKE A TV SHOW ABOUT A CARTOONING CLUB?

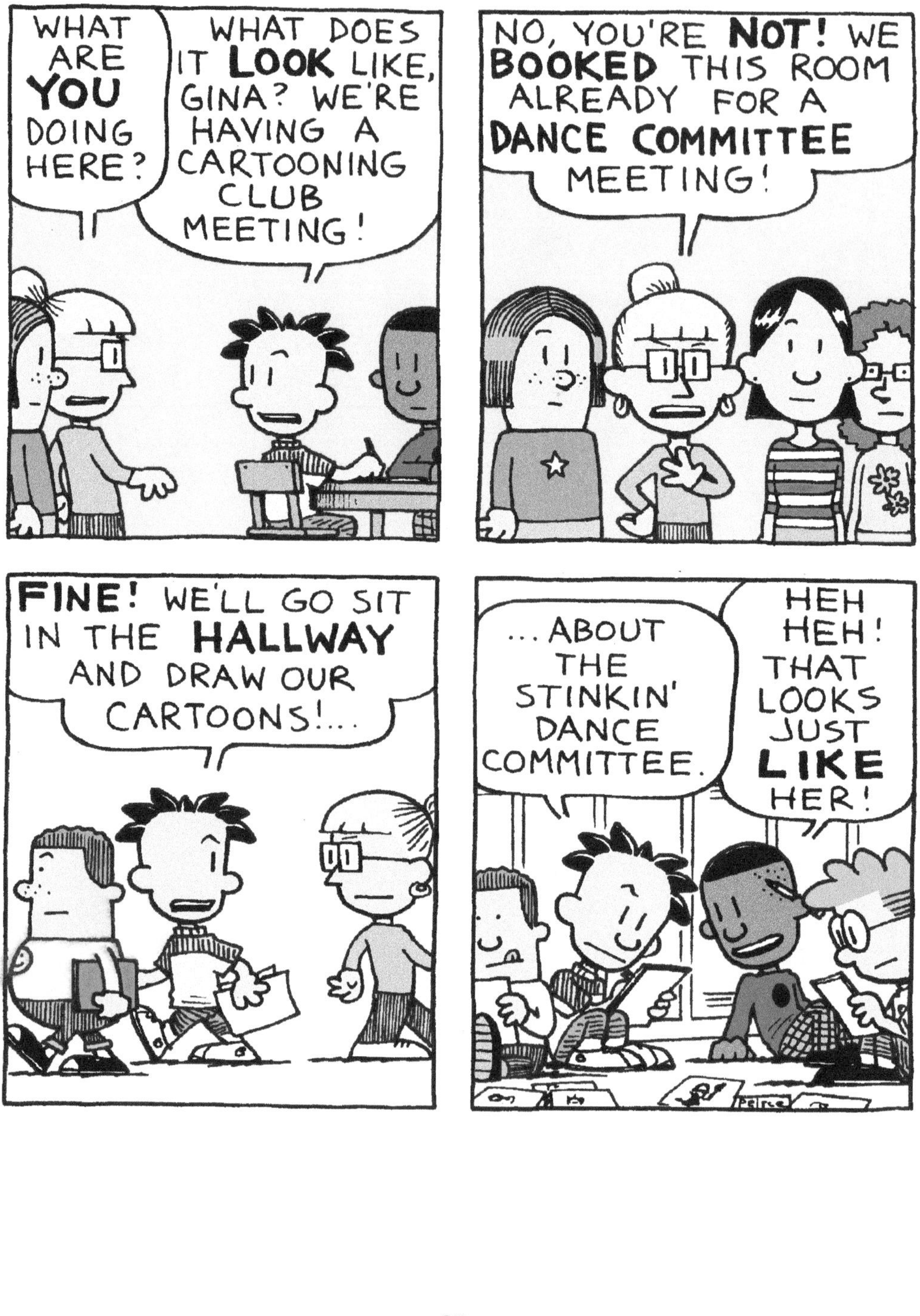
WHAT ARE YOU DOING HERE?
WHAT DOES IT LOOK LIKE, GINA? WE'RE HAVING A CARTOONING CLUB MEETING!
NO, YOU'RE NOT! WE BOOKED THIS ROOM ALREADY FOR A DANCE COMMITTEE MEETING!
FINE! WE'LL GO SIT IN THE HALLWAY AND DRAW OUR CARTOONS!...
...ABOUT THE STINKIN' DANCE COMMITTEE.
HEH HEH! THAT LOOKS JUST LIKE HER!

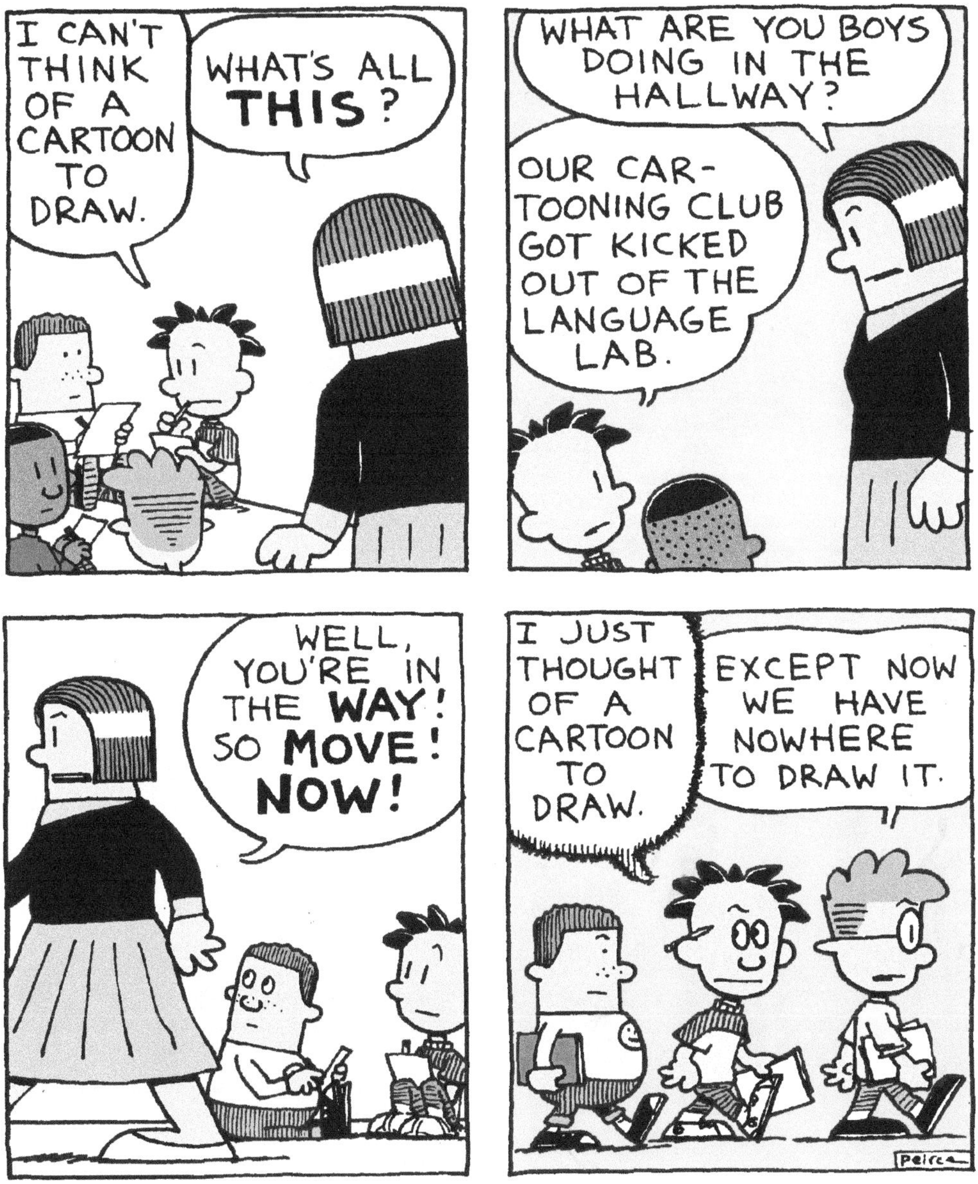
I CAN'T THINK OF A CARTOON TO DRAW.
WHAT'S ALL **THIS**?
WHAT ARE YOU BOYS DOING IN THE HALLWAY?
OUR CARTOONING CLUB GOT KICKED OUT OF THE LANGUAGE LAB.
WELL, YOU'RE IN THE **WAY**! SO **MOVE**! **NOW**!
I JUST THOUGHT OF A CARTOON TO DRAW.
EXCEPT NOW WE HAVE NOWHERE TO DRAW IT.
Peirce

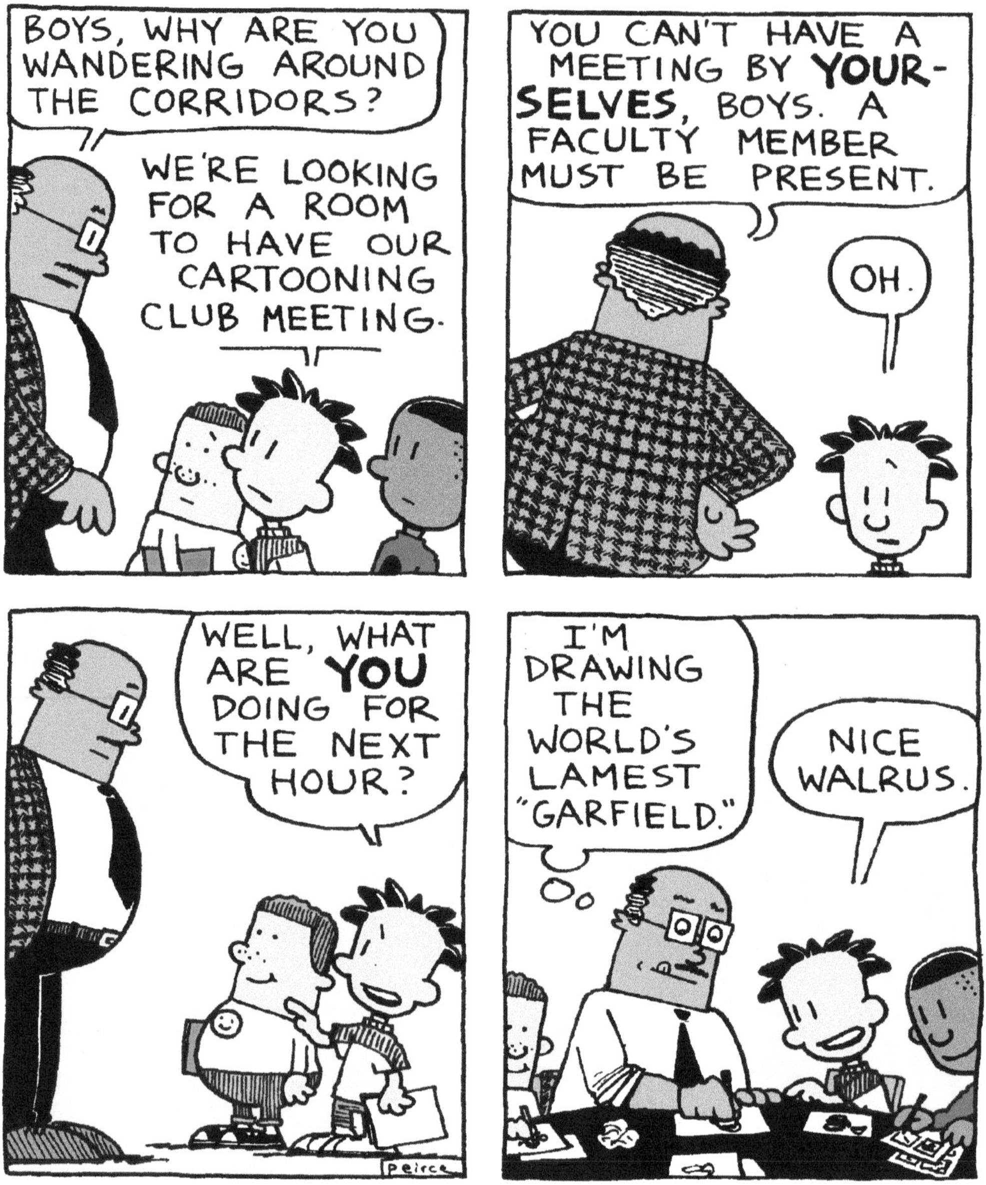
BOYS, WHY ARE YOU WANDERING AROUND THE CORRIDORS?
WE'RE LOOKING FOR A ROOM TO HAVE OUR CARTOONING CLUB MEETING.
YOU CAN'T HAVE A MEETING BY **YOURSELVES**, BOYS. A FACULTY MEMBER MUST BE PRESENT.
OH.
WELL, WHAT ARE **YOU** DOING FOR THE NEXT HOUR?
peirce
I'M DRAWING THE WORLD'S LAMEST "GARFIELD."
NICE WALRUS.

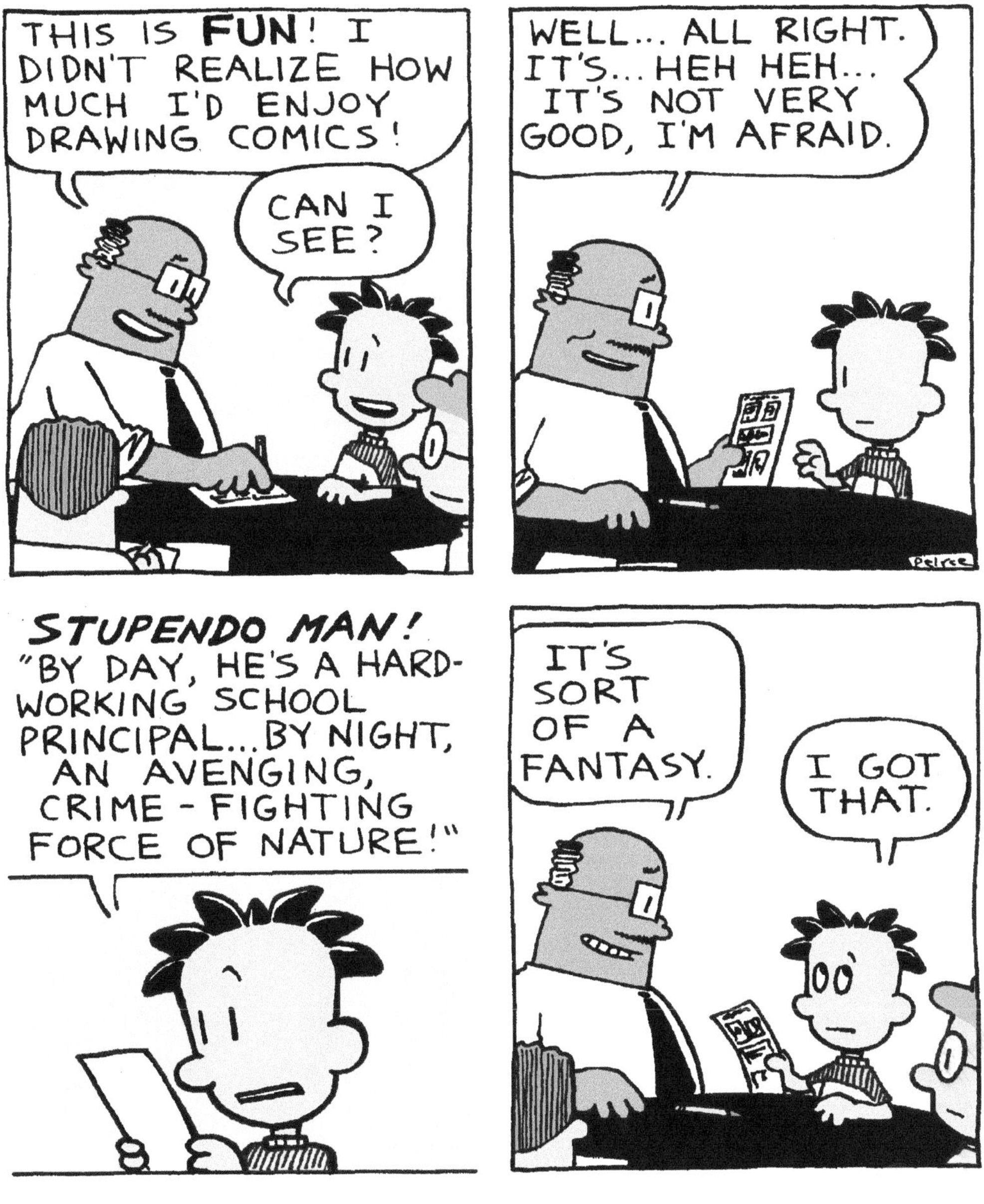
THIS IS **FUN**! I DIDN'T REALIZE HOW MUCH I'D ENJOY DRAWING COMICS!
CAN I SEE?
WELL... ALL RIGHT. IT'S... HEH HEH... IT'S NOT VERY GOOD, I'M AFRAID.
Peirce
STUPENDO MAN! "BY DAY, HE'S A HARD-WORKING SCHOOL PRINCIPAL... BY NIGHT, AN AVENGING, CRIME-FIGHTING FORCE OF NATURE!"
IT'S SORT OF A FANTASY.
I GOT THAT.

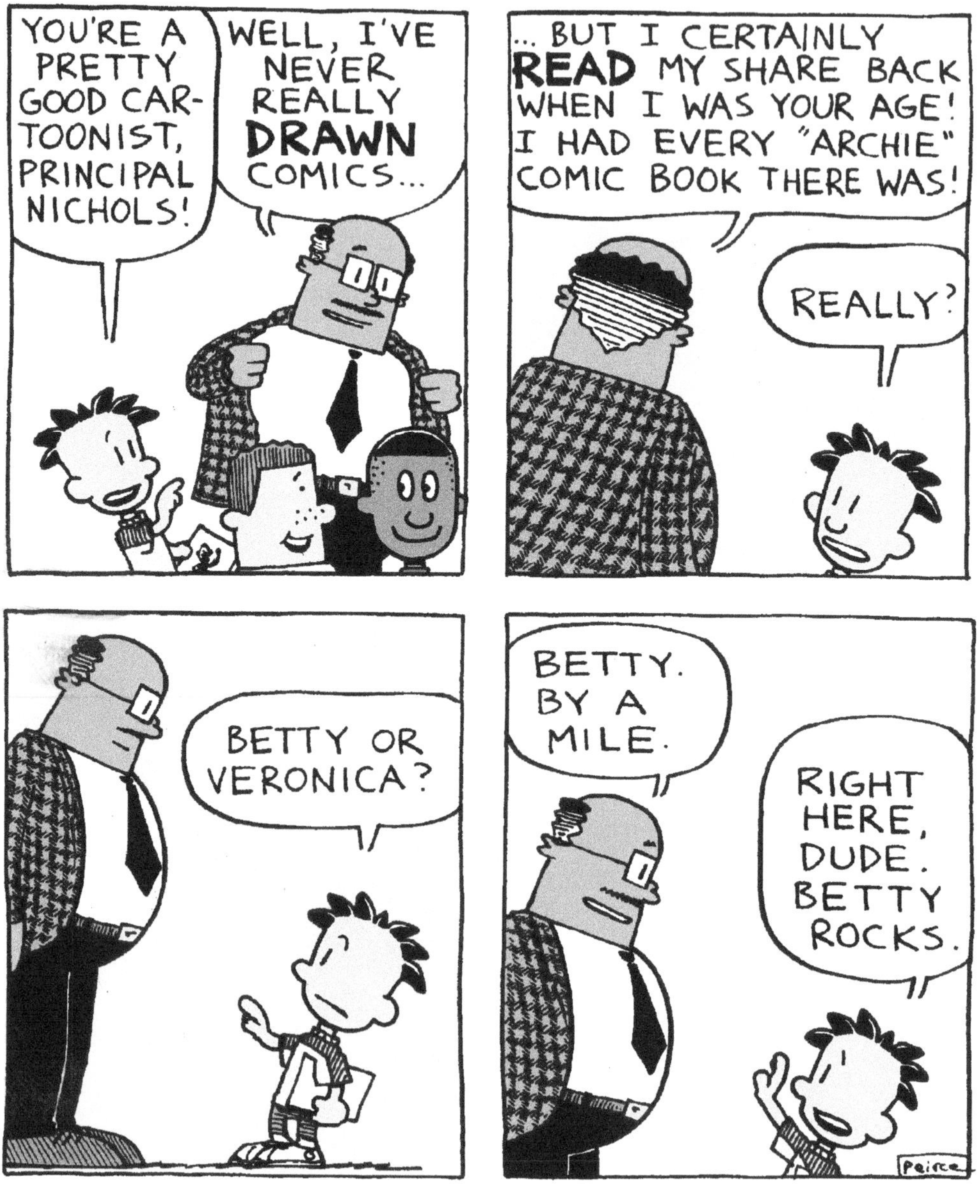

YOU'RE A PRETTY GOOD CARTOONIST, PRINCIPAL NICHOLS!
WELL, I'VE NEVER REALLY **DRAWN** COMICS...
... BUT I CERTAINLY **READ** MY SHARE BACK WHEN I WAS YOUR AGE! I HAD EVERY "ARCHIE" COMIC BOOK THERE WAS!
REALLY?
BETTY OR VERONICA?
BETTY. BY A MILE.
RIGHT HERE, DUDE. BETTY ROCKS.
Peirce

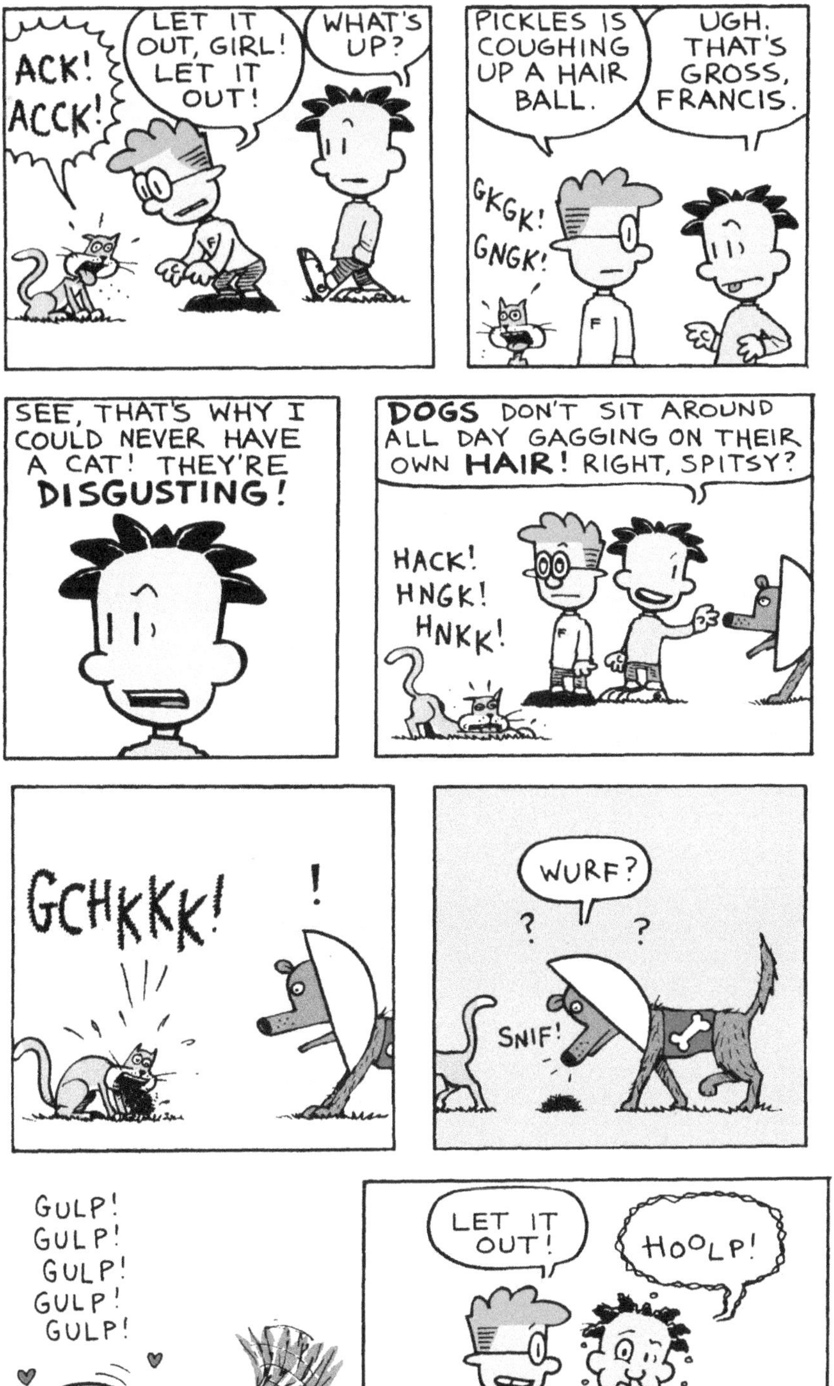
ACK! ACCK!
LET IT OUT, GIRL! LET IT OUT!
WHAT'S UP?
PICKLES IS COUGHING UP A HAIR BALL.
UGH. THAT'S GROSS, FRANCIS.
GKGK! GNGK!
SEE, THAT'S WHY I COULD NEVER HAVE A CAT! THEY'RE DISGUSTING!
DOGS DON'T SIT AROUND ALL DAY GAGGING ON THEIR OWN HAIR! RIGHT, SPITSY?
HACK! HNGK! HNKK!
GCHKKK!
!
WURF?
? ?
SNIF!
GULP! GULP! GULP! GULP! GULP!
LET IT OUT!
HOOLP!
Peirce

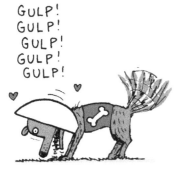

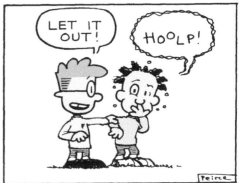

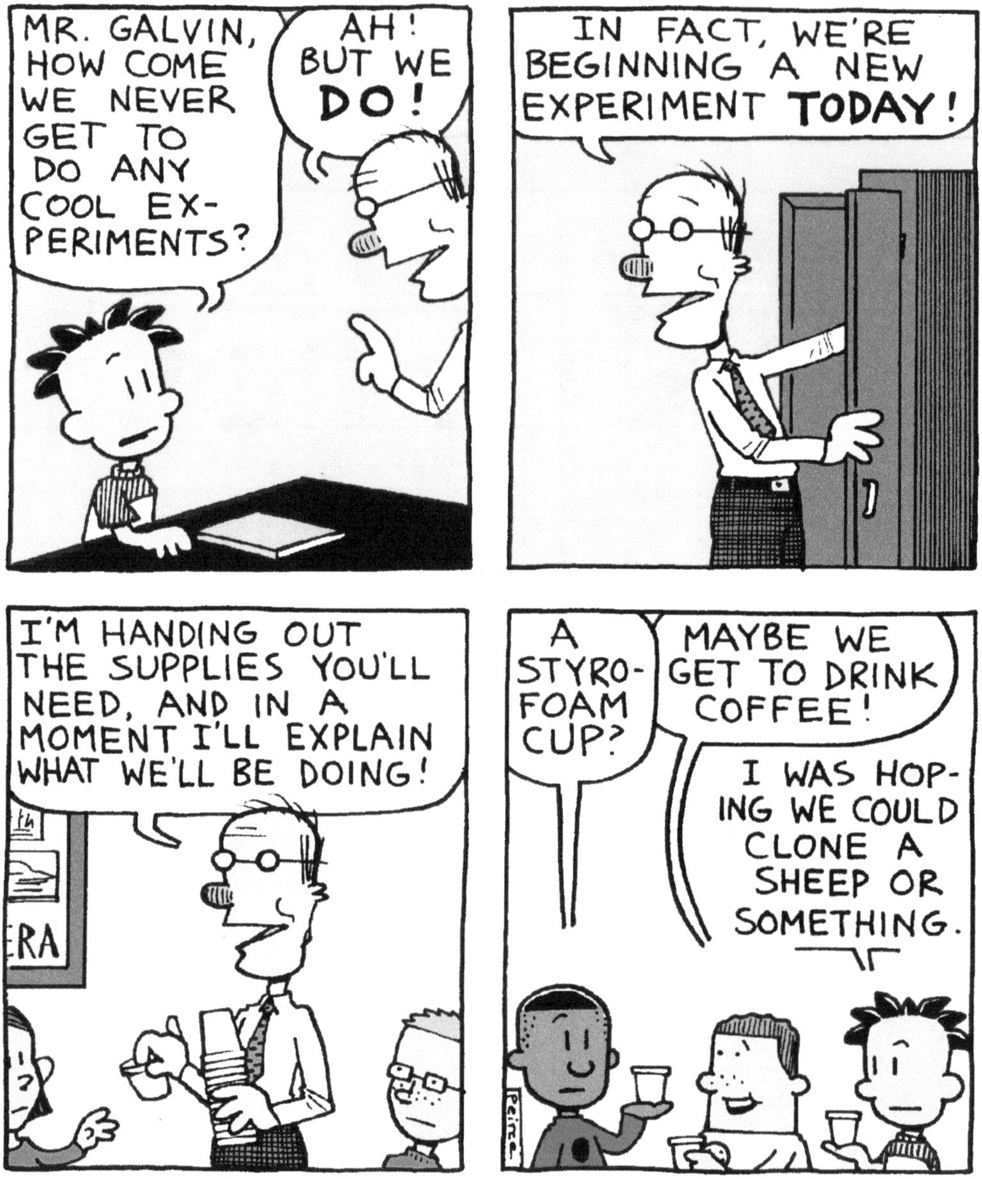
MR. GALVIN, HOW COME WE NEVER GET TO DO ANY COOL EXPERIMENTS?
AH! BUT WE **DO**!
IN FACT, WE'RE BEGINNING A NEW EXPERIMENT **TODAY**!
I'M HANDING OUT THE SUPPLIES YOU'LL NEED, AND IN A MOMENT I'LL EXPLAIN WHAT WE'LL BE DOING!
A STYRO-FOAM CUP?
MAYBE WE GET TO DRINK COFFEE!
I WAS HOPING WE COULD CLONE A SHEEP OR SOMETHING.

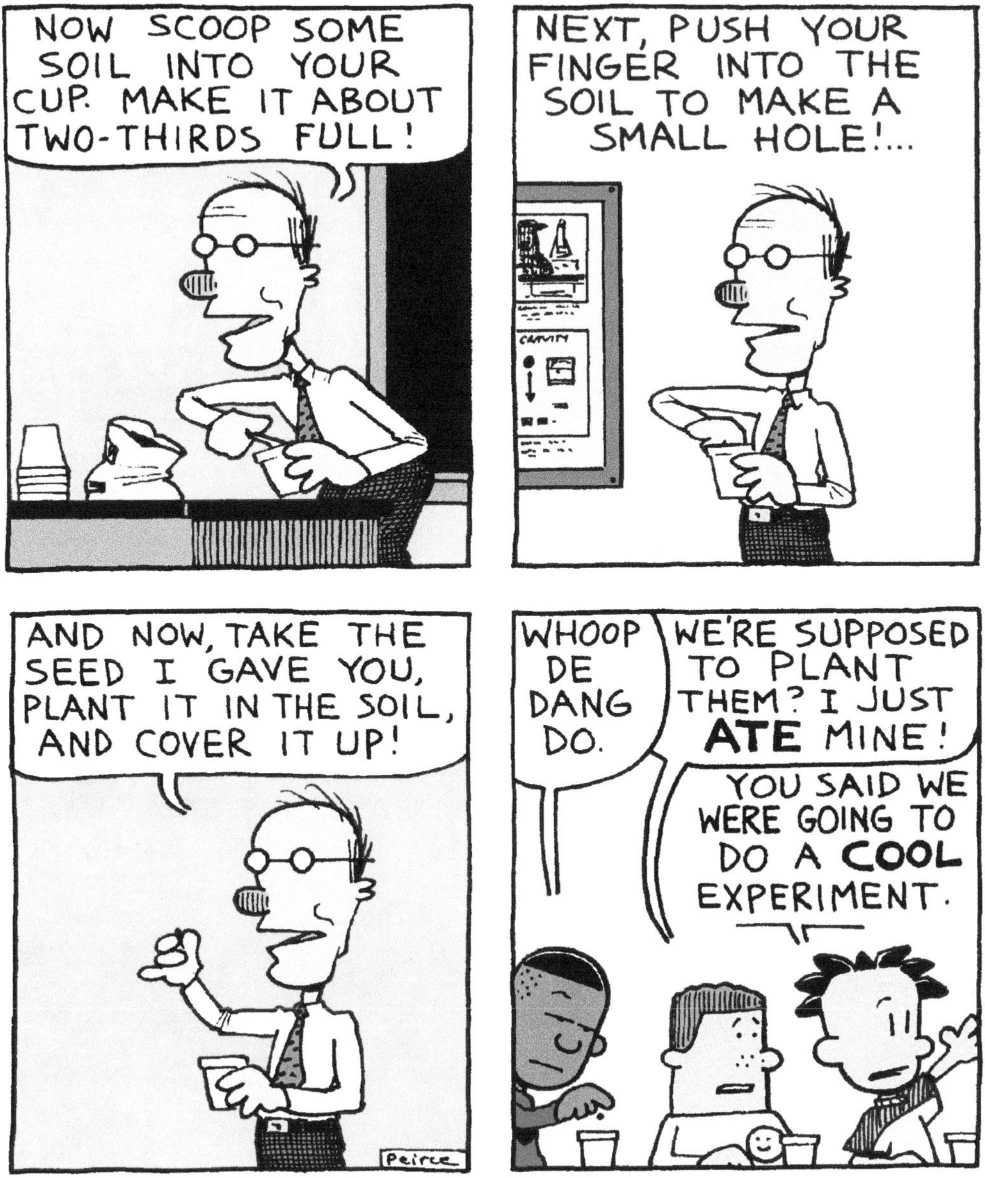
NOW SCOOP SOME SOIL INTO YOUR CUP. MAKE IT ABOUT TWO-THIRDS FULL!
NEXT, PUSH YOUR FINGER INTO THE SOIL TO MAKE A SMALL HOLE!...
AND NOW, TAKE THE SEED I GAVE YOU, PLANT IT IN THE SOIL, AND COVER IT UP!
Peirce
WHOOP DE DANG DO.
WE'RE SUPPOSED TO PLANT THEM? I JUST **ATE** MINE!
YOU SAID WE WERE GOING TO DO A **COOL** EXPERIMENT.

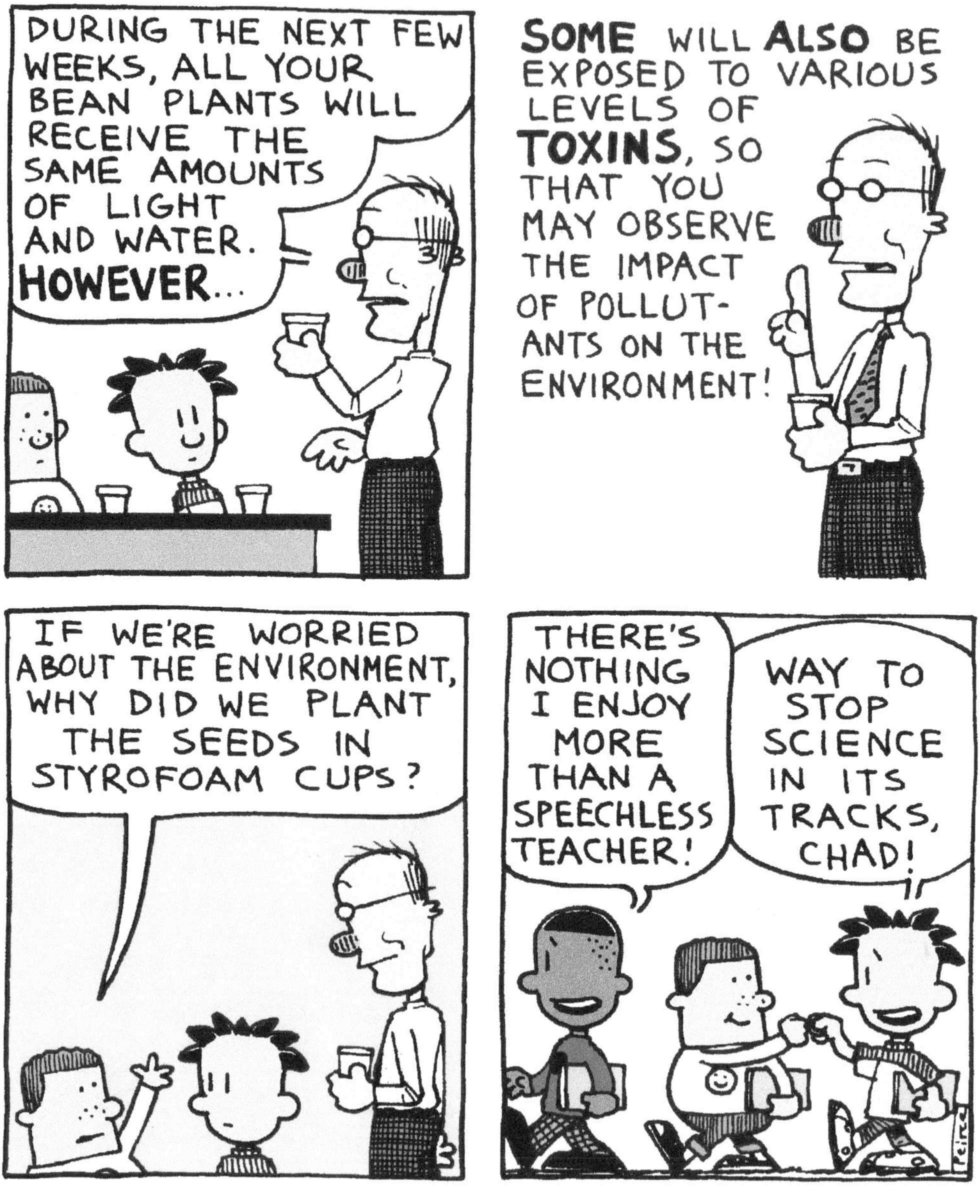
DURING THE NEXT FEW WEEKS, ALL YOUR BEAN PLANTS WILL RECEIVE THE SAME AMOUNTS OF LIGHT AND WATER. HOWEVER...
SOME WILL ALSO BE EXPOSED TO VARIOUS LEVELS OF TOXINS, SO THAT YOU MAY OBSERVE THE IMPACT OF POLLUT-ANTS ON THE ENVIRONMENT!
IF WE'RE WORRIED ABOUT THE ENVIRONMENT, WHY DID WE PLANT THE SEEDS IN STYROFOAM CUPS?
THERE'S NOTHING I ENJOY MORE THAN A SPEECHLESS TEACHER!
WAY TO STOP SCIENCE IN ITS TRACKS, CHAD!
Peirce

...AND AFTER YOU'VE COVERED THE SEED WITH SOIL, POUR A LITTLE WATER INTO THE CUP.

NOTHING'S HAPPENING.

MR. GALVIN? MY SEED'S NOT SPROUTING.

THEY'RE BEAN PLANTS, SON, NOT SEA MONKEYS.

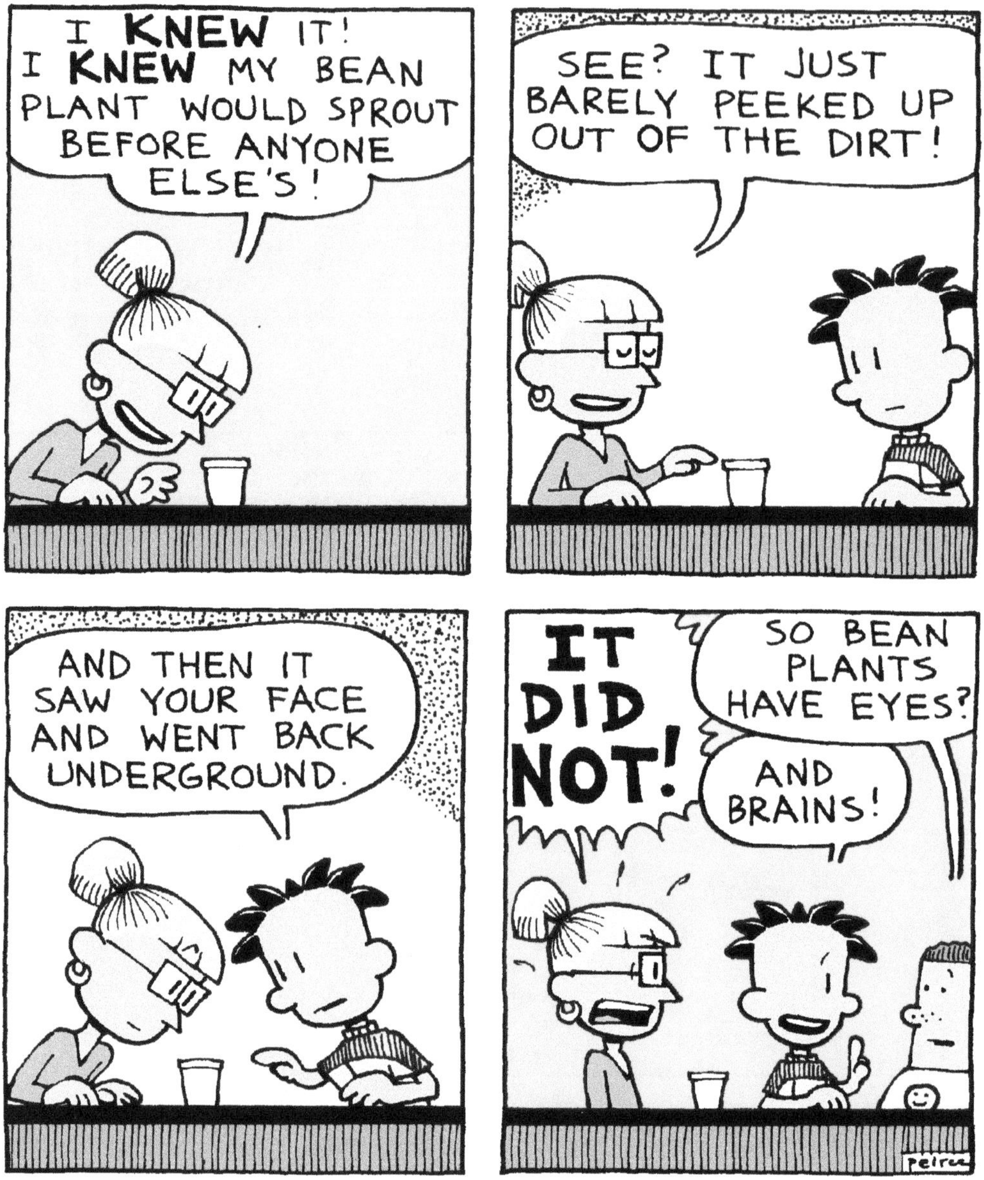
I **KNEW** IT! I **KNEW** MY BEAN PLANT WOULD SPROUT BEFORE ANYONE ELSE'S!
SEE? IT JUST BARELY PEEKED UP OUT OF THE DIRT!
AND THEN IT SAW YOUR FACE AND WENT BACK UNDERGROUND.
IT DID NOT!
SO BEAN PLANTS HAVE EYES?
AND BRAINS!
peirce

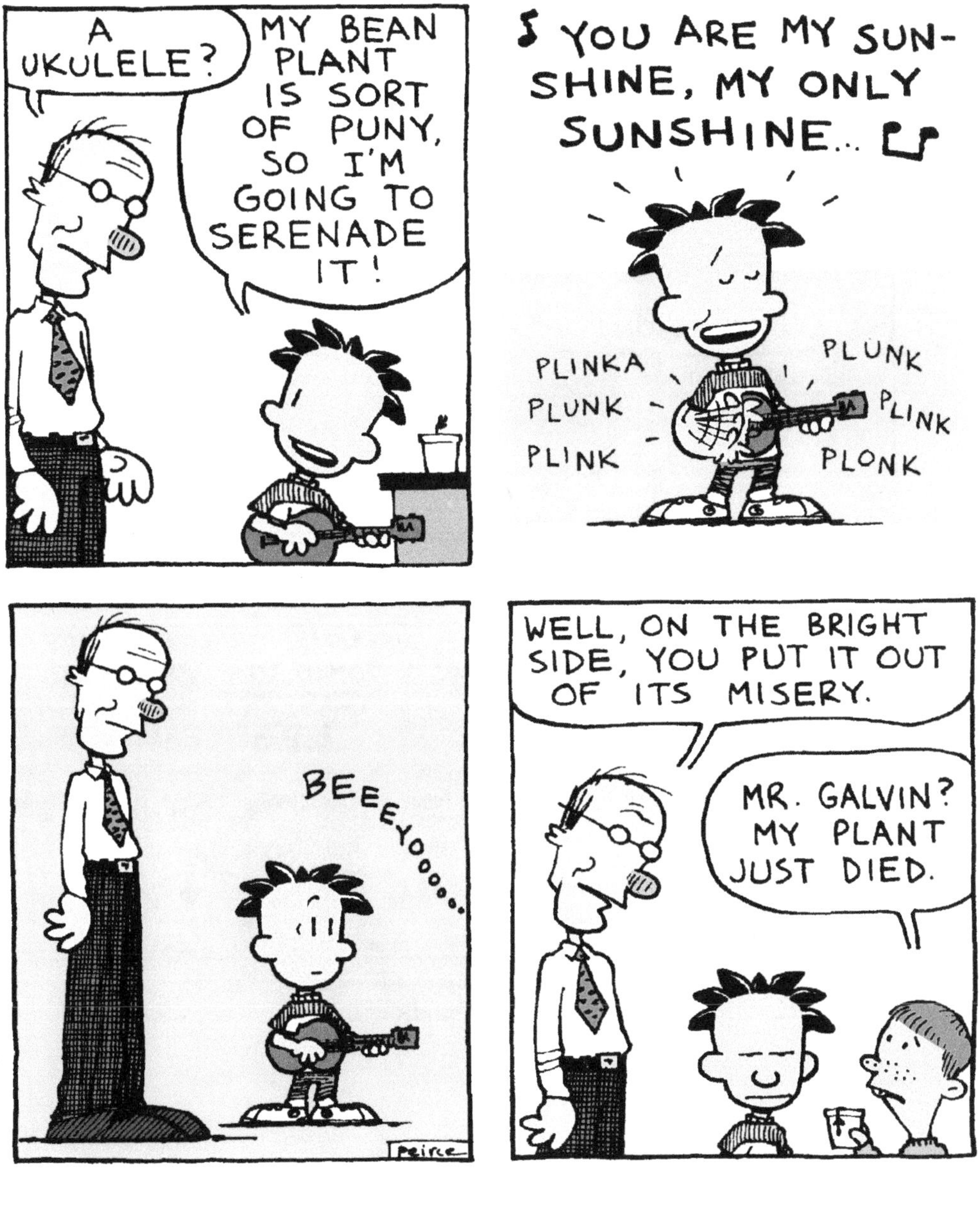
A UKULELE?
MY BEAN PLANT IS SORT OF PUNY, SO I'M GOING TO SERENADE IT!
YOU ARE MY SUNSHINE, MY ONLY SUNSHINE...
PLINKA
PLUNK
PLINK
PLUNK
PLINK
PLONK
BEEEEYOOOOO
WELL, ON THE BRIGHT SIDE, YOU PUT IT OUT OF ITS MISERY.
MR. GALVIN? MY PLANT JUST DIED.

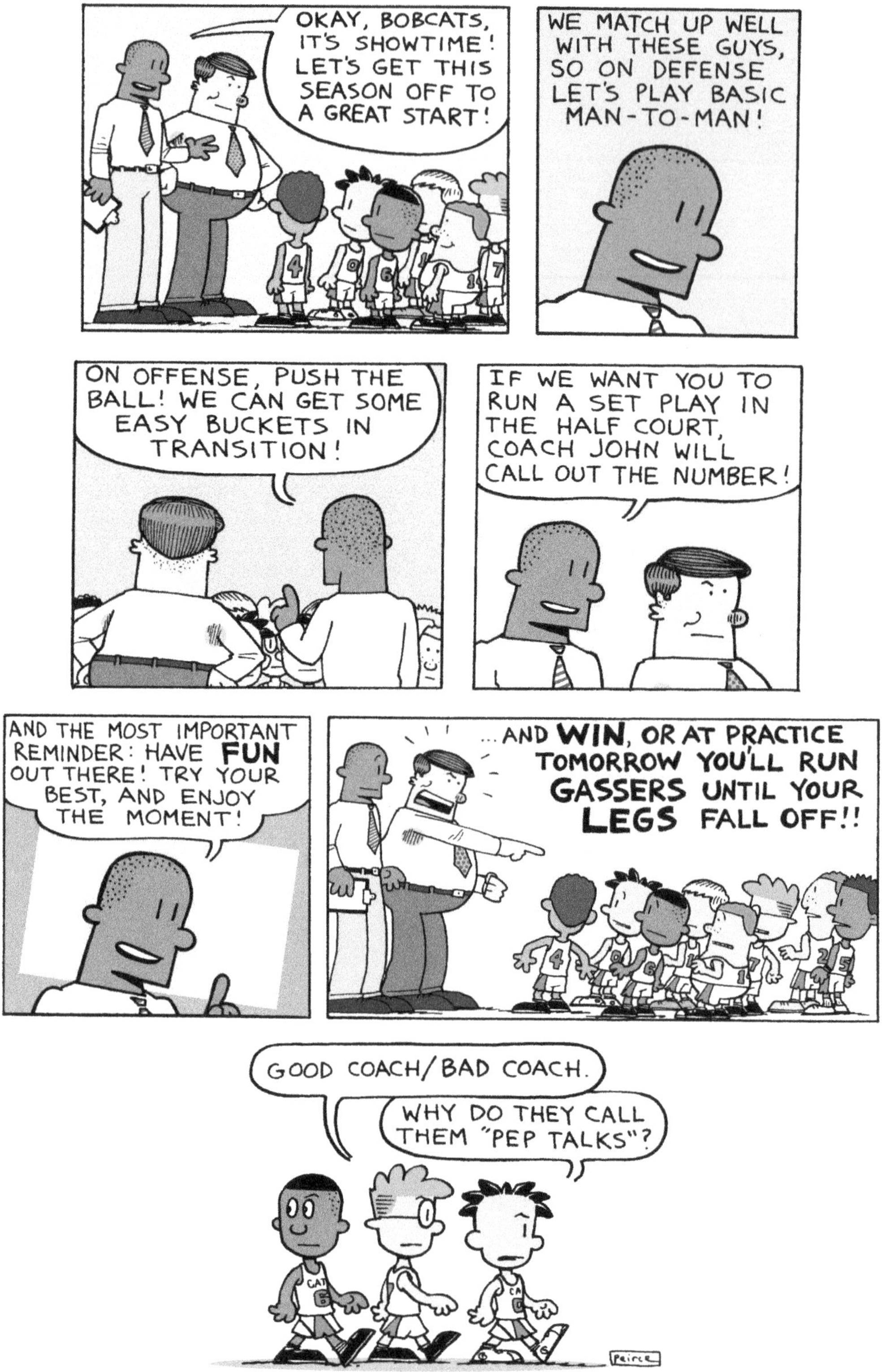

OKAY, BOBCATS, IT'S SHOWTIME! LET'S GET THIS SEASON OFF TO A GREAT START!
WE MATCH UP WELL WITH THESE GUYS, SO ON DEFENSE LET'S PLAY BASIC MAN-TO-MAN!
ON OFFENSE, PUSH THE BALL! WE CAN GET SOME EASY BUCKETS IN TRANSITION!
IF WE WANT YOU TO RUN A SET PLAY IN THE HALF COURT, COACH JOHN WILL CALL OUT THE NUMBER!
AND THE MOST IMPORTANT REMINDER: HAVE FUN OUT THERE! TRY YOUR BEST, AND ENJOY THE MOMENT!
...AND WIN, OR AT PRACTICE TOMORROW YOU'LL RUN GASSERS UNTIL YOUR LEGS FALL OFF!!
GOOD COACH/BAD COACH.
WHY DO THEY CALL THEM "PEP TALKS"?
peirce

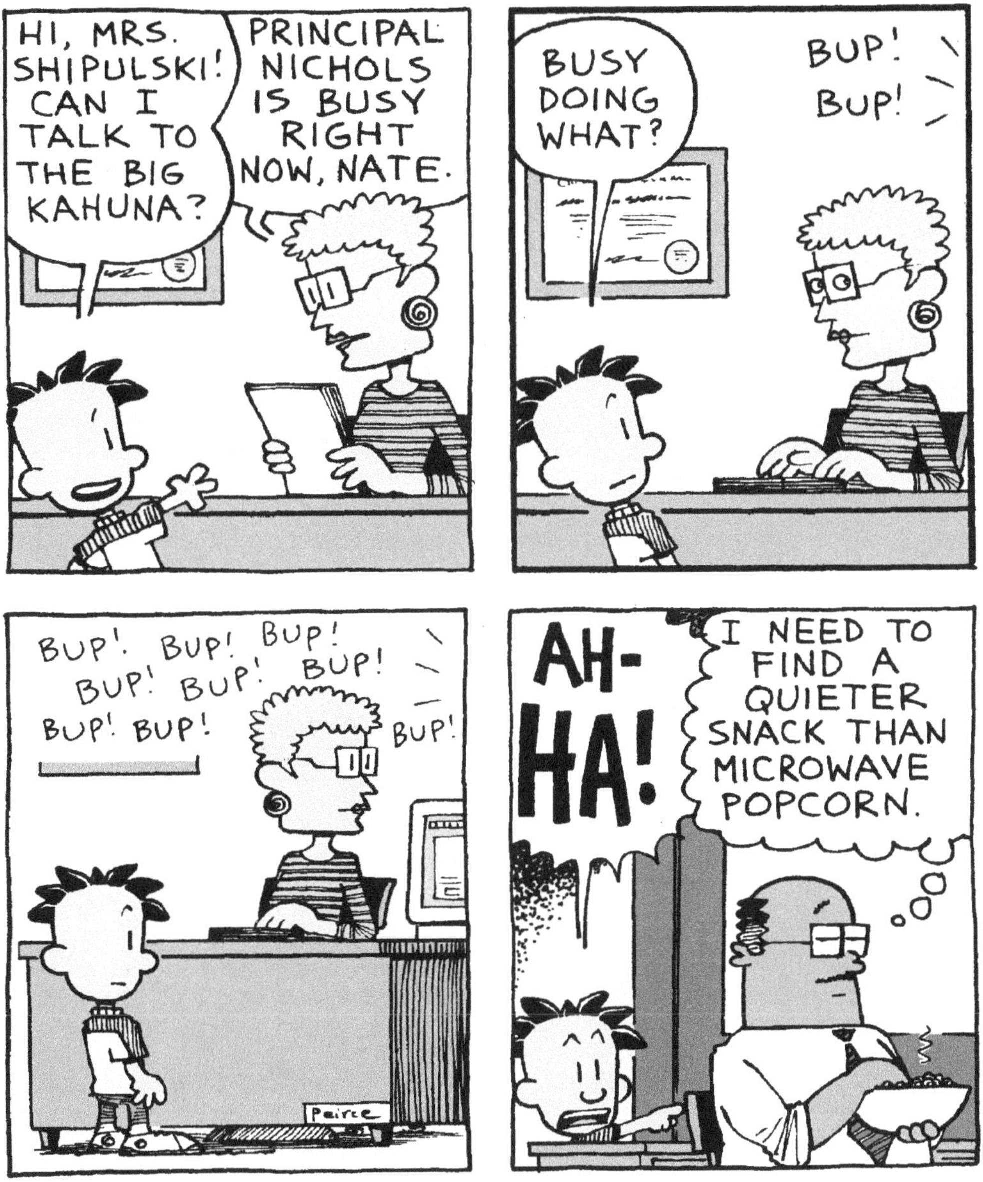
HI, MRS. SHIPULSKI! CAN I TALK TO THE BIG KAHUNA?
PRINCIPAL NICHOLS IS BUSY RIGHT NOW, NATE.
BUSY DOING WHAT?
BUP! BUP!
BUP! BUP! BUP! BUP! BUP! BUP! BUP! BUP! BUP!
AH-HA!
I NEED TO FIND A QUIETER SNACK THAN MICROWAVE POPCORN.

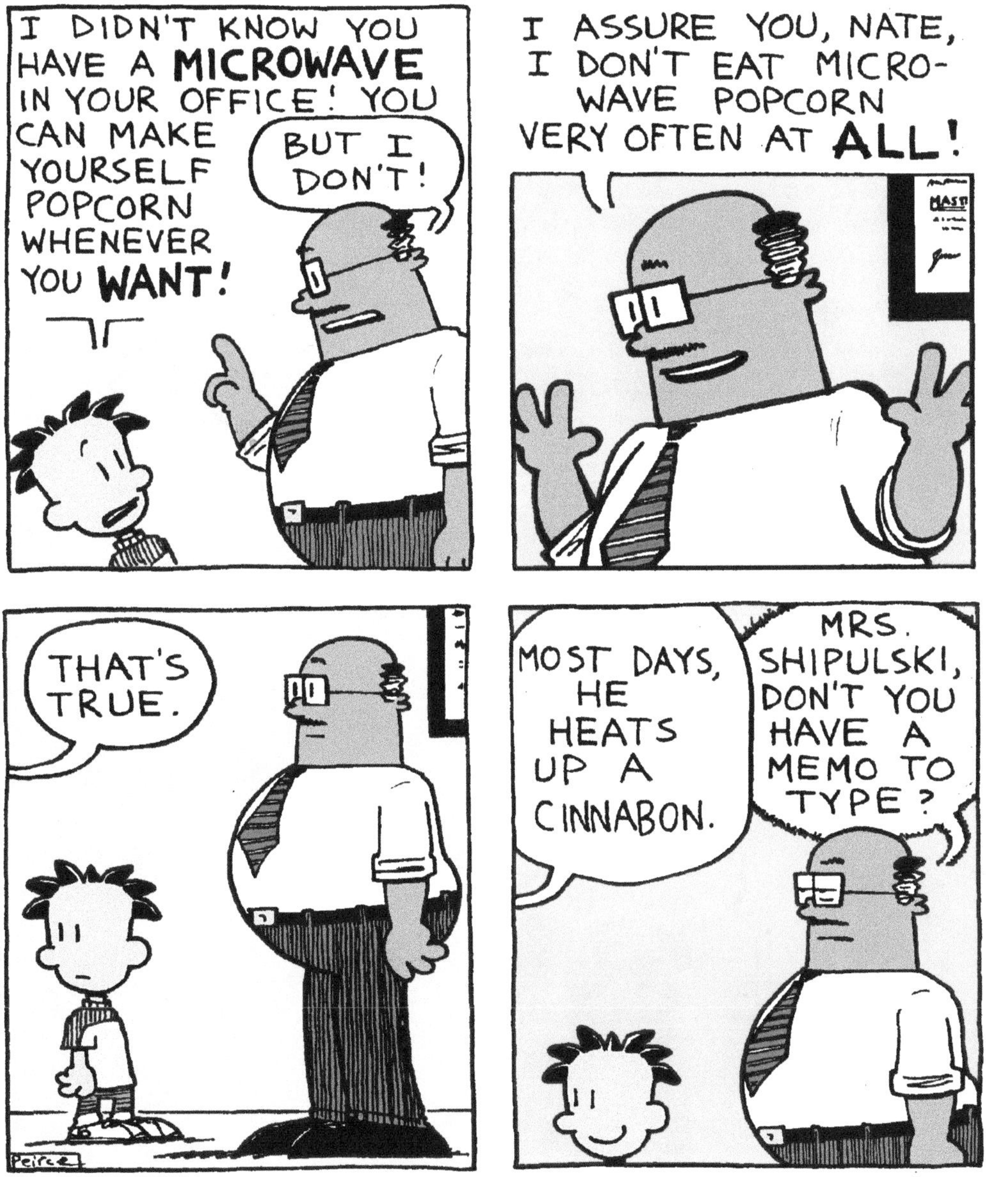
I DIDN'T KNOW YOU HAVE A **MICROWAVE** IN YOUR OFFICE! YOU CAN MAKE YOURSELF POPCORN WHENEVER YOU **WANT**!
BUT I DON'T!
I ASSURE YOU, NATE, I DON'T EAT MICRO-WAVE POPCORN VERY OFTEN AT **ALL**!
THAT'S TRUE.
MOST DAYS, HE HEATS UP A CINNABON.
MRS. SHIPULSKI, DON'T YOU HAVE A MEMO TO TYPE?
Peirce

LOOK, NATE, IT'S NOT AS IF I SIT AROUND EATING SNACKS ALL DAY! I HAPPENED TO SKIP BREAKFAST THIS MORNING, AND I NEEDED SOMETHING TO KEEP ME GOING!
I HAVE A VERY DEMANDING JOB, NATE! IT'S CONSTANT STRESS, CONSTANT WORK! IT'S...
IS THAT A COT?
I DO LIKE MY POWER NAPS.
Peirce

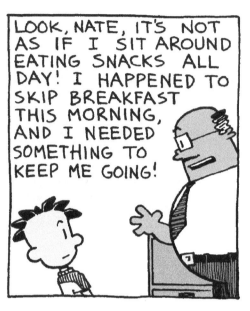

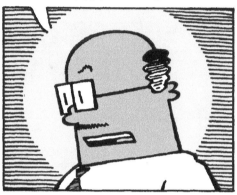

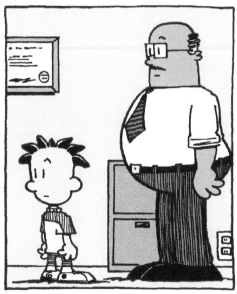

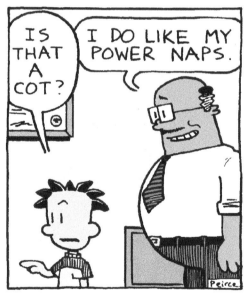

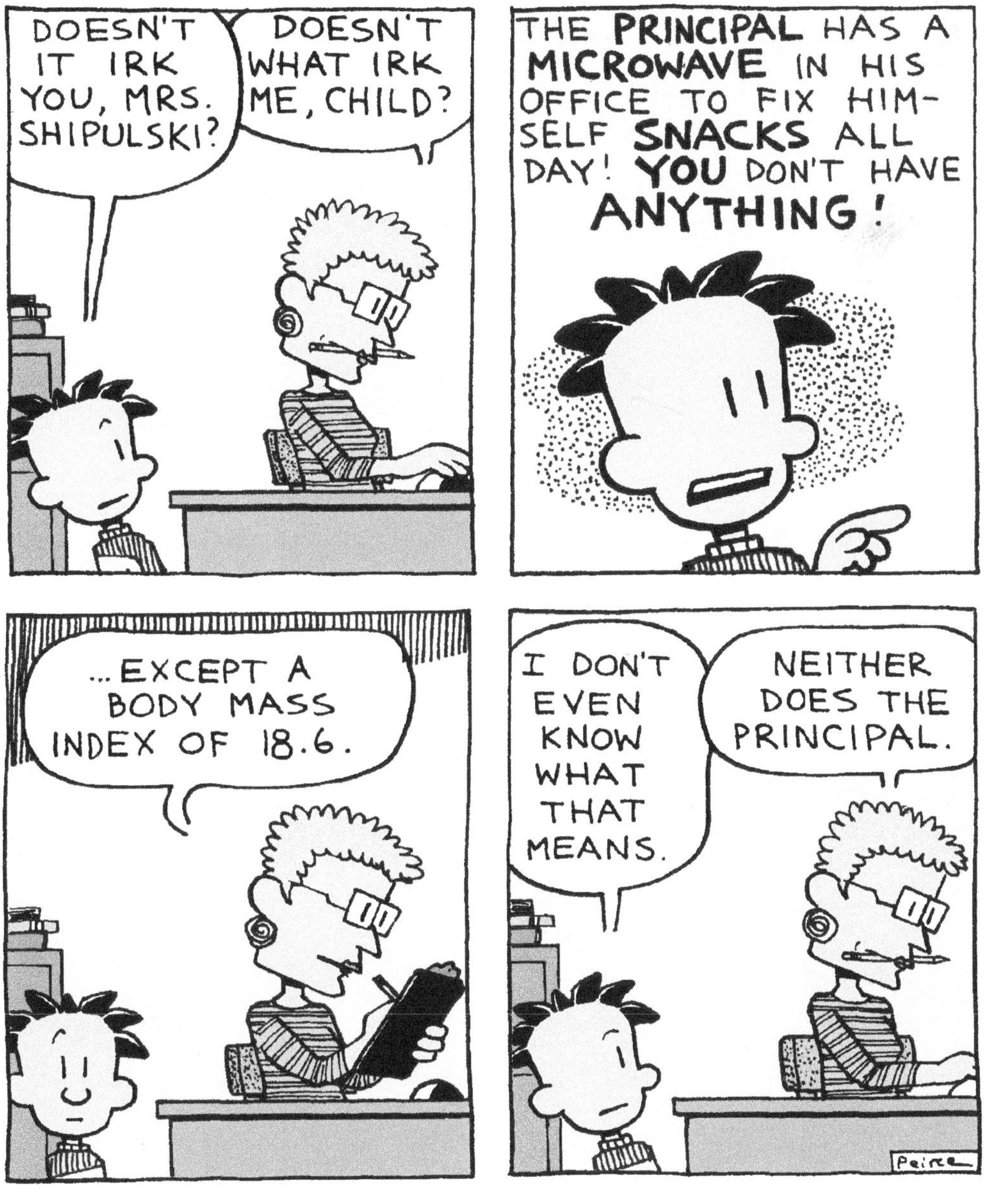
DOESN'T IT IRK YOU, MRS. SHIPULSKI?
DOESN'T WHAT IRK ME, CHILD?
THE **PRINCIPAL** HAS A **MICROWAVE** IN HIS OFFICE TO FIX HIMSELF **SNACKS** ALL DAY! **YOU** DON'T HAVE **ANYTHING**!
...EXCEPT A BODY MASS INDEX OF 18.6.
I DON'T EVEN KNOW WHAT THAT MEANS.
NEITHER DOES THE PRINCIPAL.
Peirce

I'M TAKING A SURVEY, ARTUR.

IF YOU COULD HAVE LUNCH WITH THREE PEOPLE, LIVING OR DEAD, WHO WOULD YOU CHOOSE?

AH! YOU, FRANCIS AND TEDDY!

LIVING OR DEAD, ARTUR! YOU CAN TALK TO **ANYBODY IN HISTORY!** JULIUS CAESAR! ABE LINCOLN!

LEONARDO DA VINCI! THE GREATEST MIND OF **ALL TIME!**

YES! GOOD!

BUT WAIT. LEONARDO DA VINCI COULD NOT EATING LUNCH. BECAUSE HE IS DEAD.

IT'S **HYPOTHETICAL,** ARTUR! JUST **PRETEND HE'S ALIVE!**

AH! HOKAY!

THEN I AM SAY: YOU, FRANCIS, AND LEONARDO DA VINCI!

EXCEPT HOLD EVERYTHING. WHAT IS GOING TO BE FOR LUNCH?

I'LL JUST PUT "UNDECIDED."

BECAUSE I AM ALLERGY TO SPAGHETTI SAUCE.

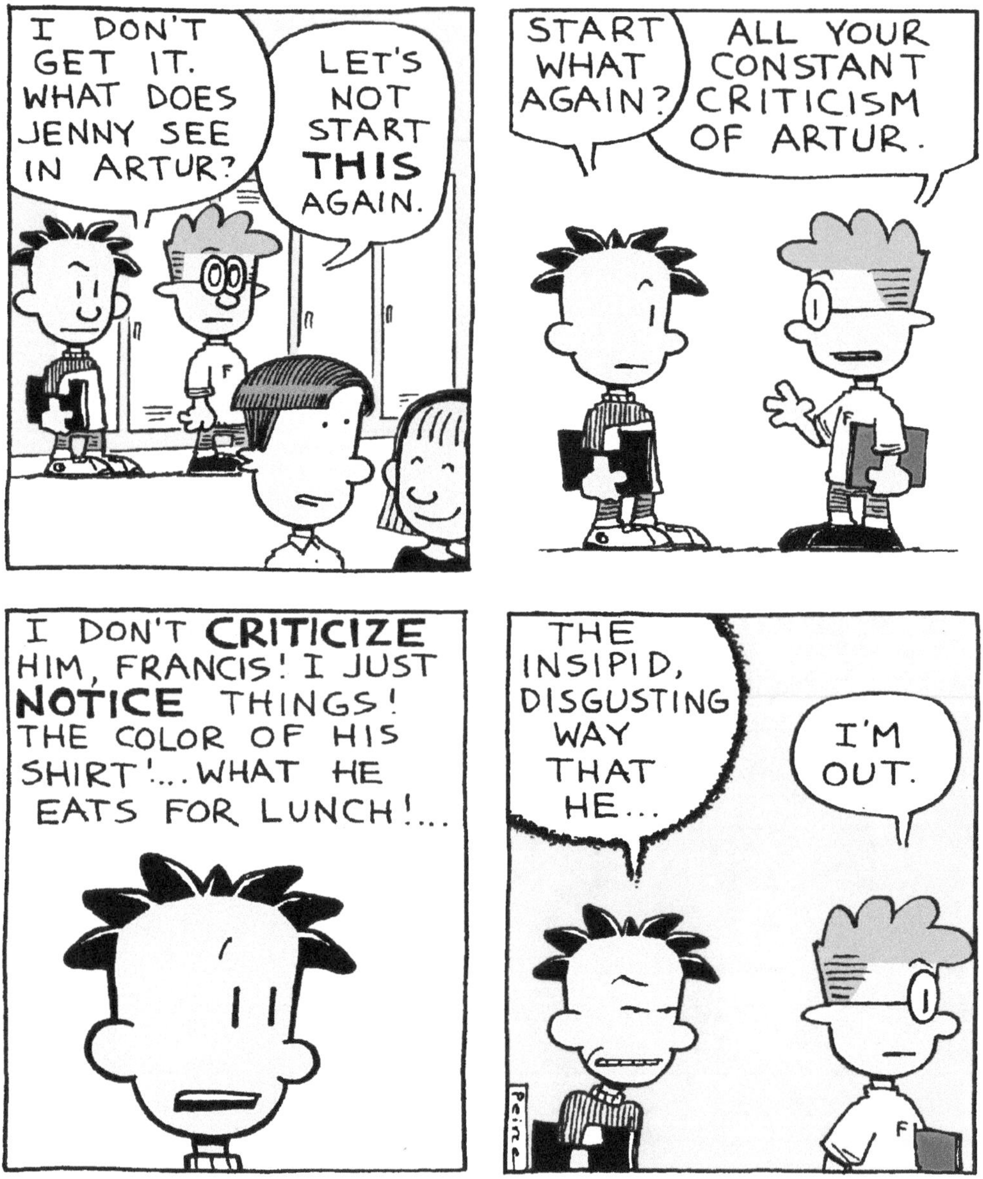
I DON'T GET IT. WHAT DOES JENNY SEE IN ARTUR?
LET'S NOT START **THIS** AGAIN.
START WHAT AGAIN?
ALL YOUR CONSTANT CRITICISM OF ARTUR.
I DON'T **CRITICIZE** HIM, FRANCIS! I JUST **NOTICE** THINGS! THE COLOR OF HIS SHIRT!... WHAT HE EATS FOR LUNCH!...
THE INSIPID, DISGUSTING WAY THAT HE...
I'M OUT.
Peirce

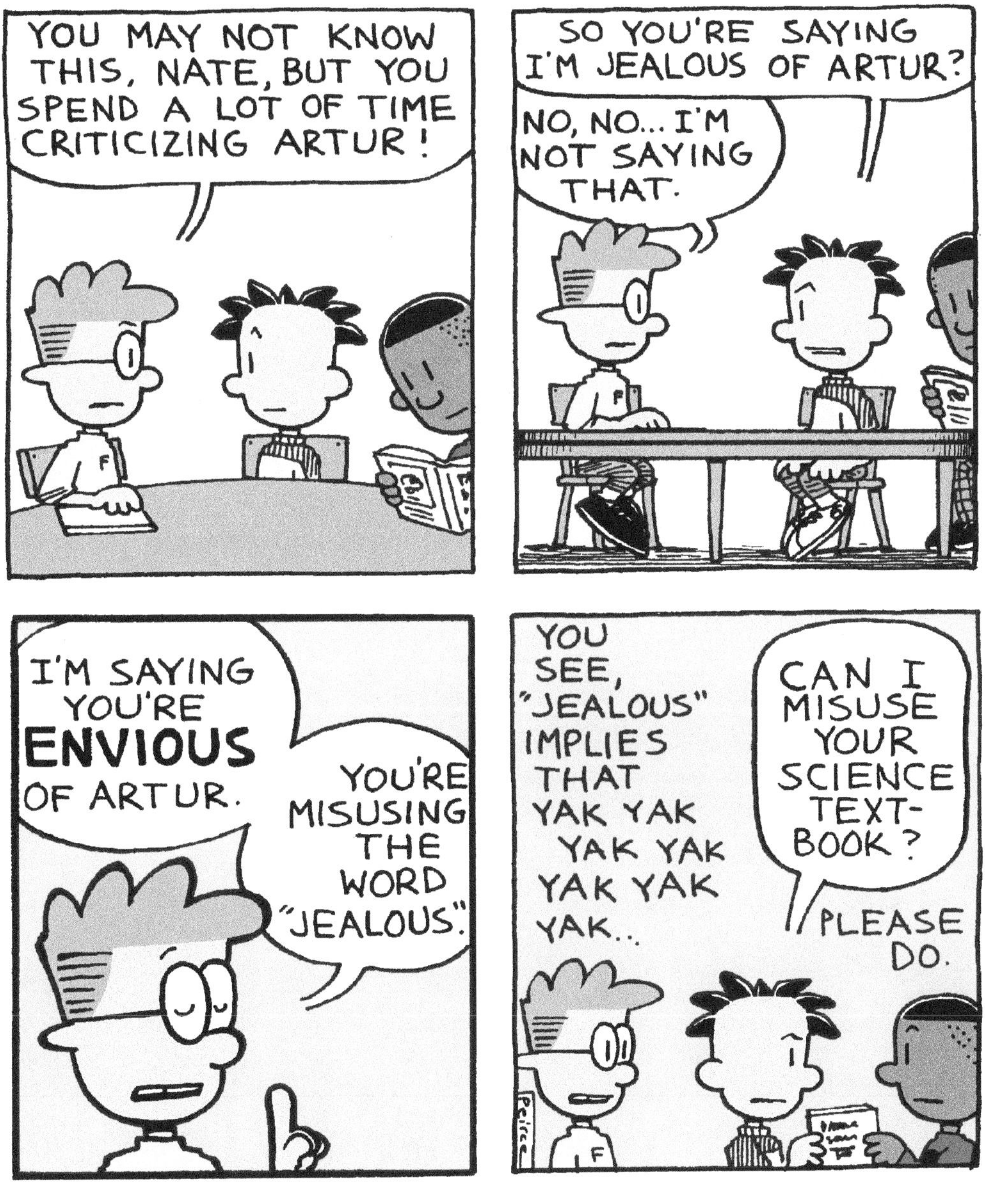
YOU MAY NOT KNOW THIS, NATE, BUT YOU SPEND A LOT OF TIME CRITICIZING ARTUR!
SO YOU'RE SAYING I'M JEALOUS OF ARTUR?
NO, NO... I'M NOT SAYING THAT.
I'M SAYING YOU'RE **ENVIOUS** OF ARTUR.
YOU'RE MISUSING THE WORD "JEALOUS".
YOU SEE, "JEALOUS" IMPLIES THAT YAK YAK YAK YAK YAK YAK YAK...
CAN I MISUSE YOUR SCIENCE TEXT-BOOK?
PLEASE DO.
Peirce

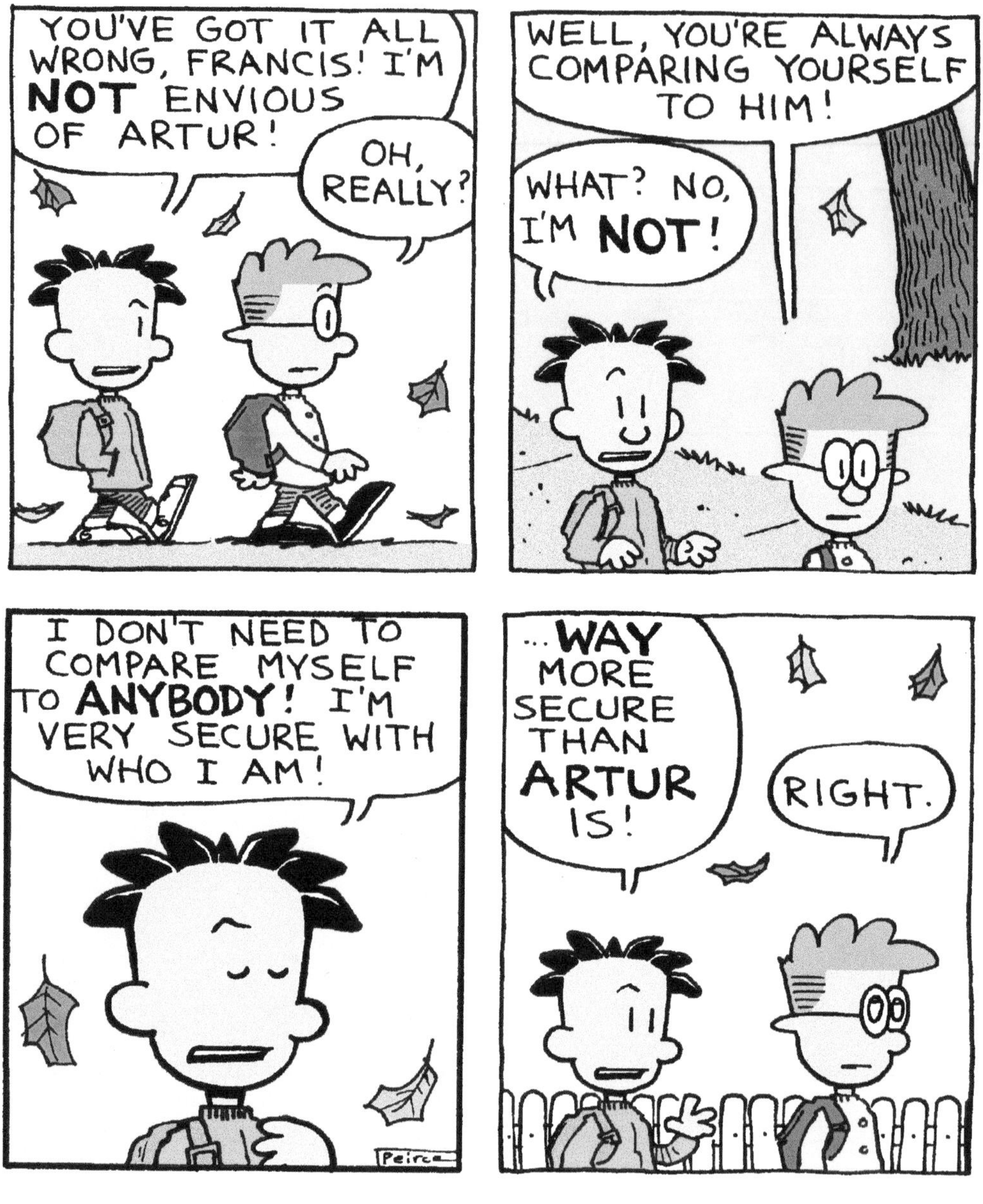
YOU'VE GOT IT ALL WRONG, FRANCIS! I'M NOT ENVIOUS OF ARTUR!
OH, REALLY?
WELL, YOU'RE ALWAYS COMPARING YOURSELF TO HIM!
WHAT? NO, I'M NOT!
I DON'T NEED TO COMPARE MYSELF TO ANYBODY! I'M VERY SECURE WITH WHO I AM!
Peirce
...WAY MORE SECURE THAN ARTUR IS!
RIGHT.

NATE, OPEN YOUR EYES. CAN'T YOU SEE THAT ARTUR'S A REALLY NICE KID?
OF **COURSE** I CAN SEE IT!
I KNOW WHAT A GREAT GUY ARTUR IS! HOW COULD I **NOT** KNOW IT? **EVERY**ONE KNOWS IT! IT'S **OBVIOUS**!
THAT'S WHY I CAN'T **STAND** HIM!
♪
I DON'T GET IT.
I'VE STOPPED TRYING.
Peirce

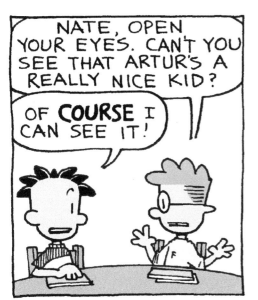

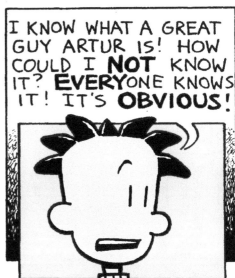

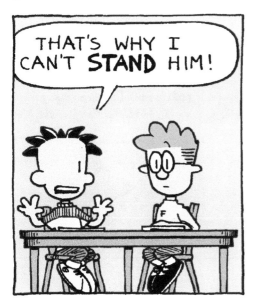

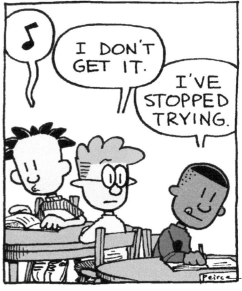

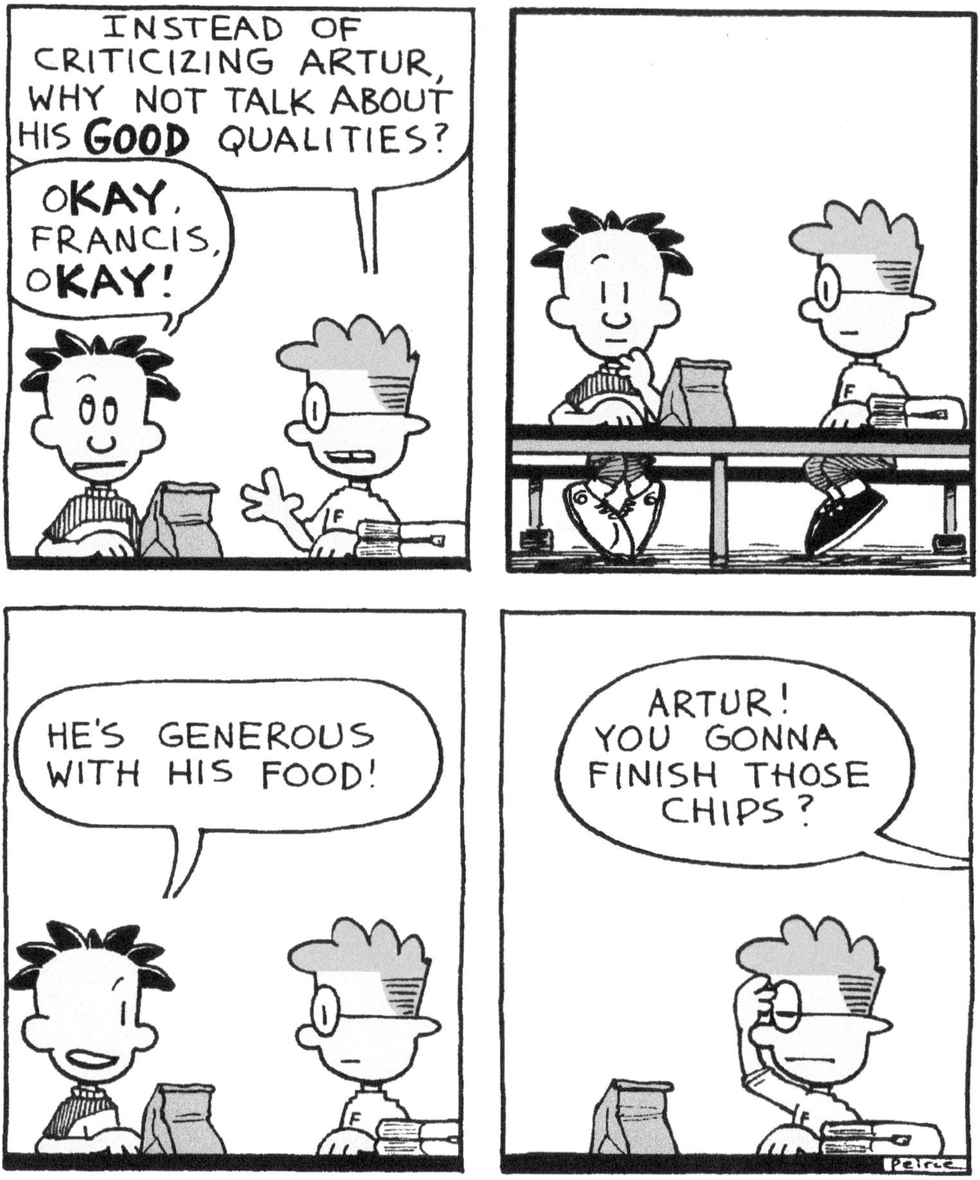
INSTEAD OF CRITICIZING ARTUR, WHY NOT TALK ABOUT HIS **GOOD** QUALITIES?
O**KAY**, FRANCIS, O**KAY**!
HE'S GENEROUS WITH HIS FOOD!
ARTUR! YOU GONNA FINISH THOSE CHIPS?
Peirce

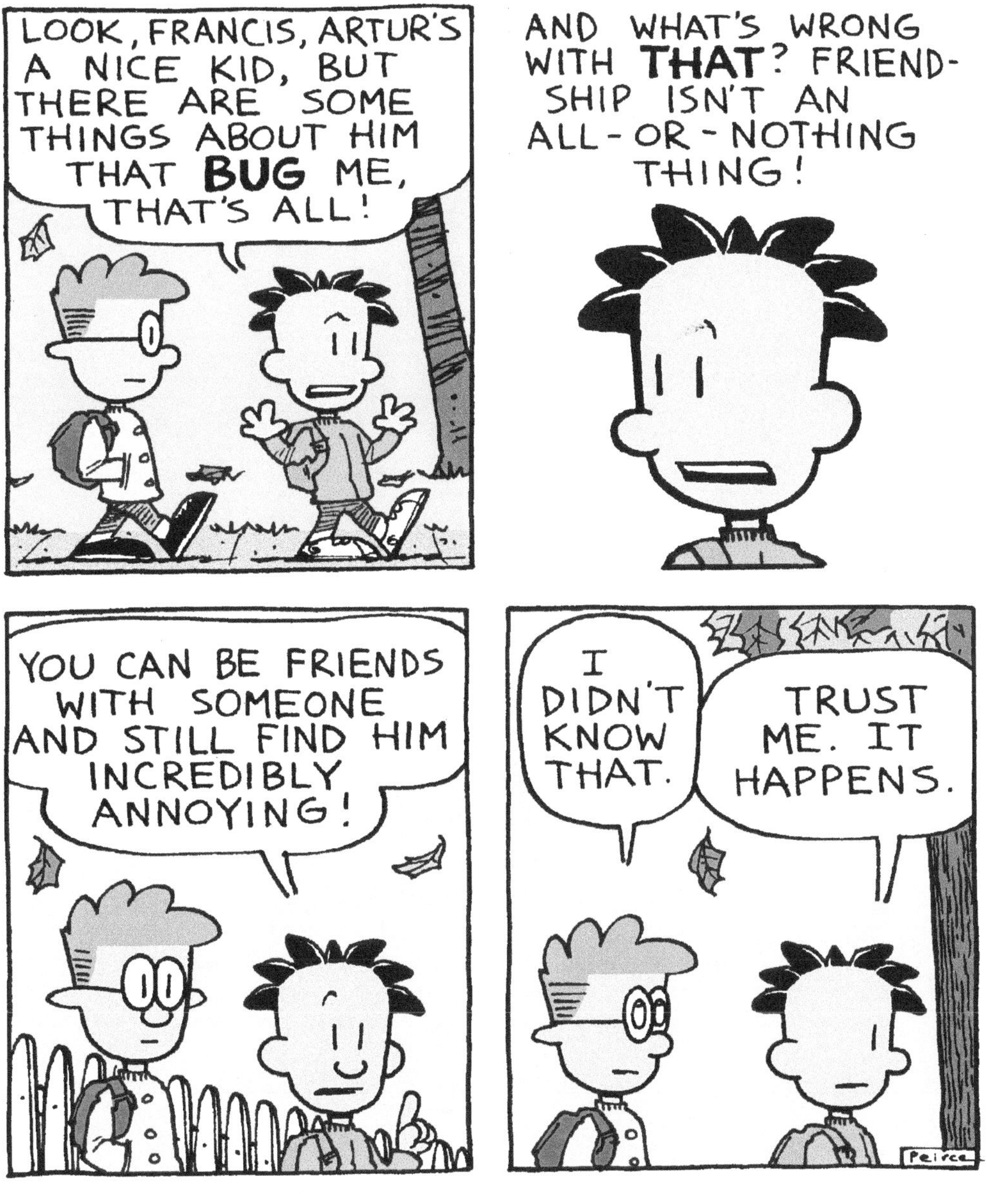
LOOK, FRANCIS, ARTUR'S A NICE KID, BUT THERE ARE SOME THINGS ABOUT HIM THAT **BUG** ME, THAT'S ALL!
AND WHAT'S WRONG WITH **THAT**? FRIENDSHIP ISN'T AN ALL-OR-NOTHING THING!
YOU CAN BE FRIENDS WITH SOMEONE AND STILL FIND HIM INCREDIBLY ANNOYING!
I DIDN'T KNOW THAT.
TRUST ME. IT HAPPENS.
Peirce

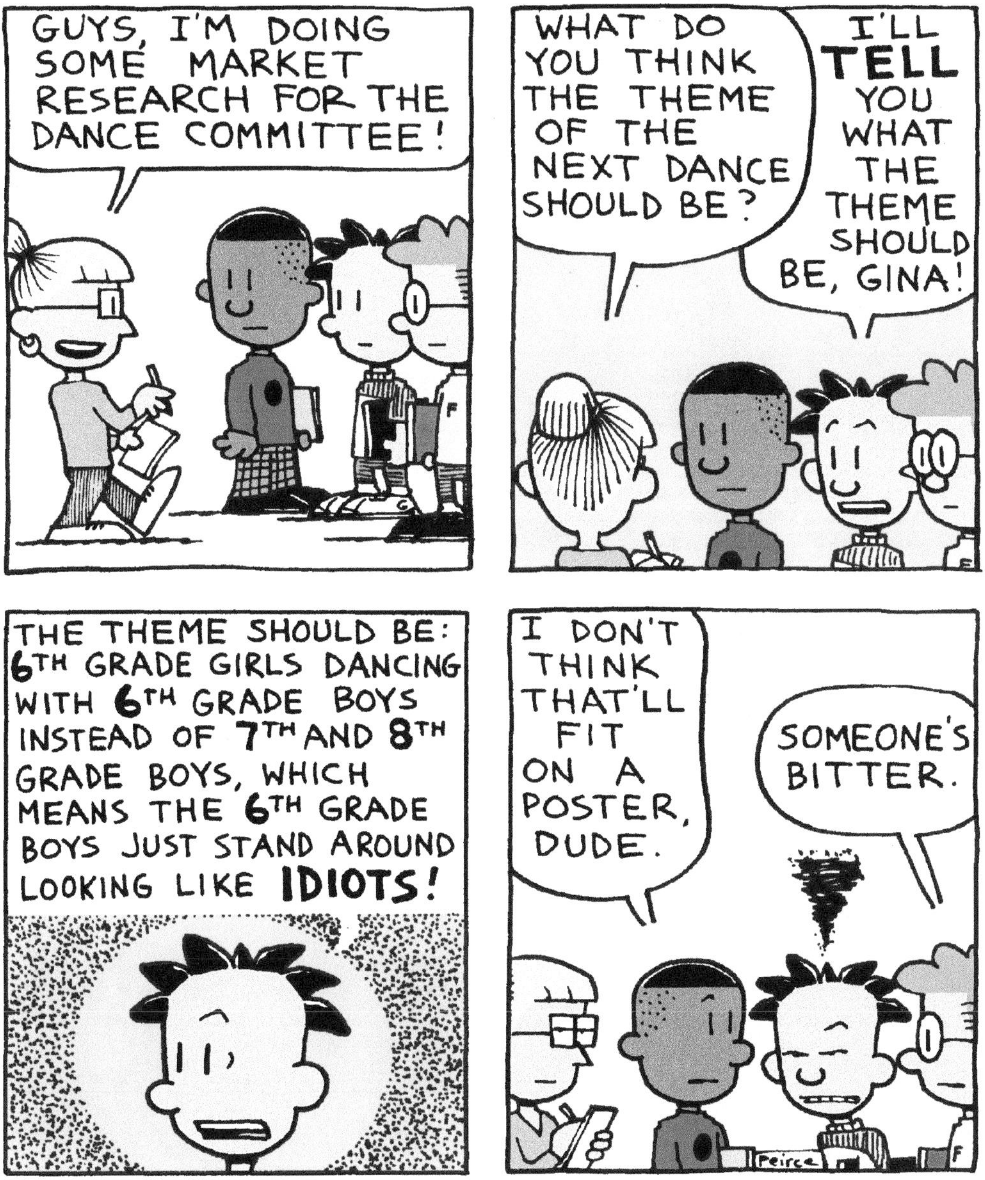
GUYS, I'M DOING SOME MARKET RESEARCH FOR THE DANCE COMMITTEE!
WHAT DO YOU THINK THE THEME OF THE NEXT DANCE SHOULD BE?
I'LL **TELL** YOU WHAT THE THEME SHOULD BE, GINA!
THE THEME SHOULD BE: 6TH GRADE GIRLS DANCING WITH 6TH GRADE BOYS INSTEAD OF 7TH AND 8TH GRADE BOYS, WHICH MEANS THE 6TH GRADE BOYS JUST STAND AROUND LOOKING LIKE **IDIOTS**!
I DON'T THINK THAT'LL FIT ON A POSTER, DUDE.
SOMEONE'S BITTER.
Peirce

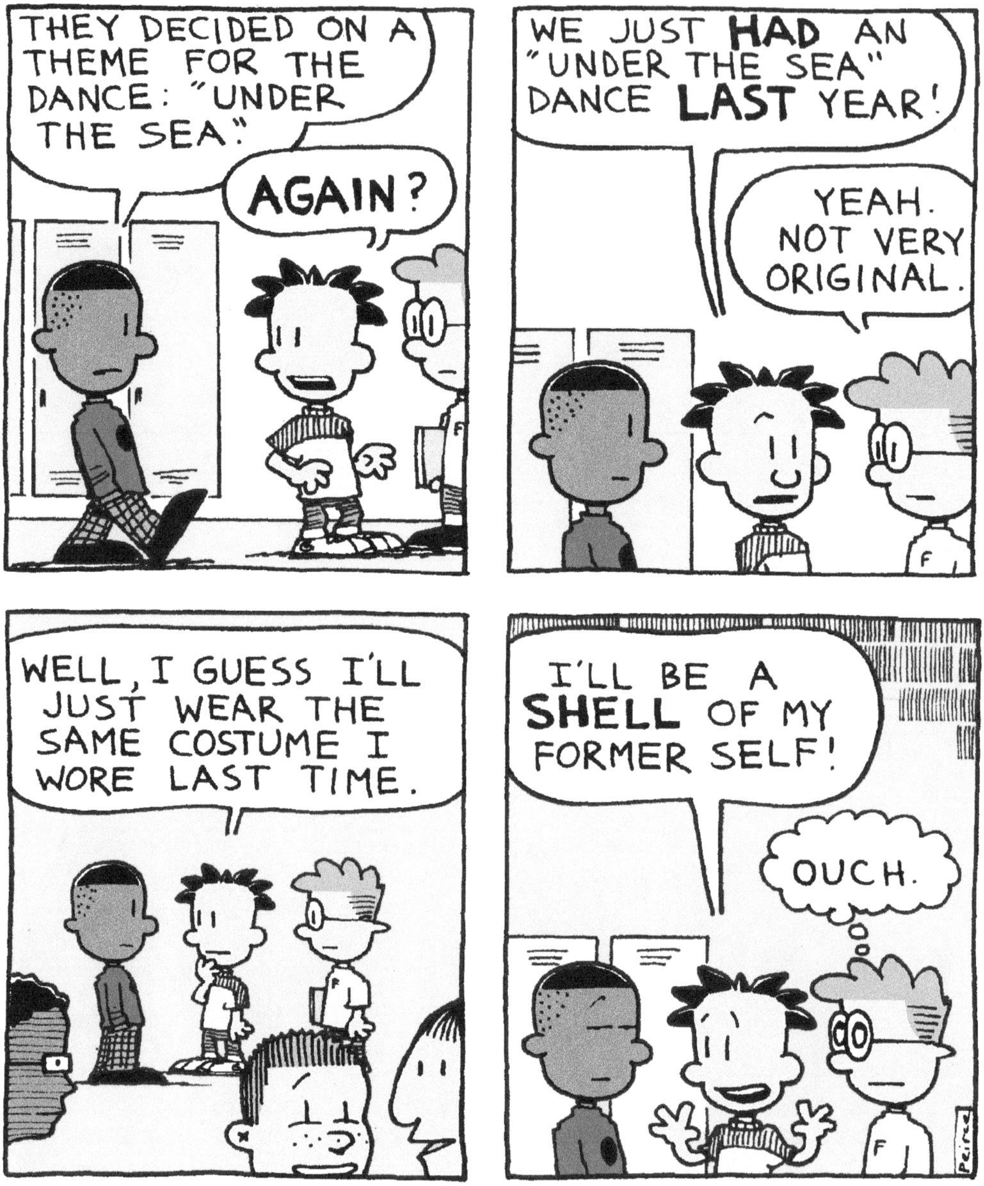
THEY DECIDED ON A THEME FOR THE DANCE: "UNDER THE SEA."
AGAIN?
WE JUST HAD AN "UNDER THE SEA" DANCE LAST YEAR!
YEAH. NOT VERY ORIGINAL.
WELL, I GUESS I'LL JUST WEAR THE SAME COSTUME I WORE LAST TIME.
I'LL BE A SHELL OF MY FORMER SELF!
OUCH.
Peirce

GUYS! I CAN'T BELIEVE WE DIDN'T THINK OF THIS **BEFORE!**

WHAT?

THE THEME OF THE DANCE IS "UNDER THE SEA," RIGHT? IT'S **OBVIOUS** WHO'D BE THE PERFECT BAND TO PERFORM!

"ENSLAVE THE MOLLUSK" WILL ROCK AGAIN!!

BUP! BUP! **BOW!** BUP! B-B-B- **BOW!**

HE'S AIR DRUMMING.

I PREFER THAT TO THE REAL THING.

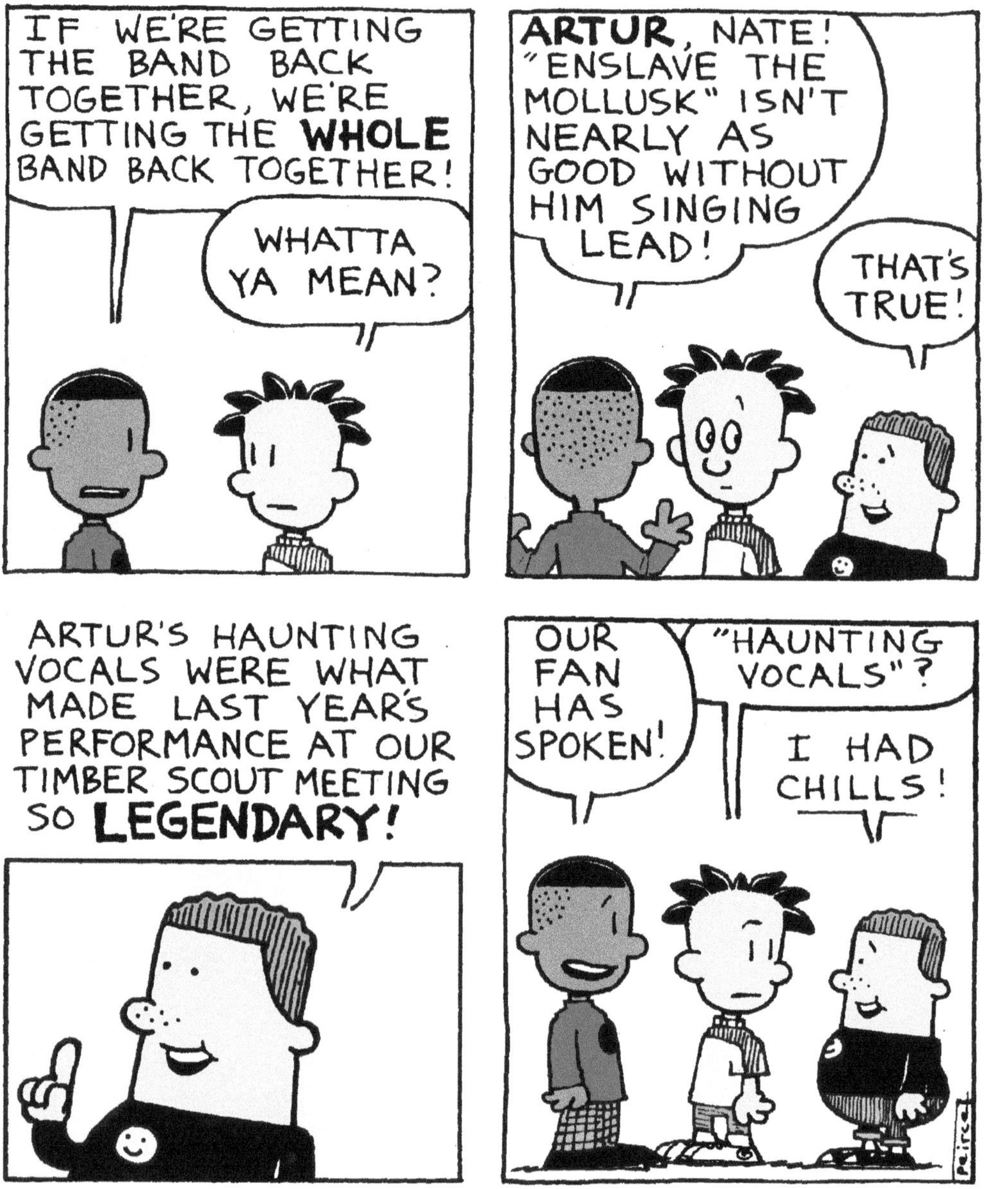
IF WE'RE GETTING THE BAND BACK TOGETHER, WE'RE GETTING THE **WHOLE** BAND BACK TOGETHER!
WHATTA YA MEAN?
ARTUR, NATE! "ENSLAVE THE MOLLUSK" ISN'T NEARLY AS GOOD WITHOUT HIM SINGING LEAD!
THAT'S TRUE!
ARTUR'S HAUNTING VOCALS WERE WHAT MADE LAST YEAR'S PERFORMANCE AT OUR TIMBER SCOUT MEETING SO **LEGENDARY!**
OUR FAN HAS SPOKEN!
"HAUNTING VOCALS"?
I HAD CHILLS!
peirce

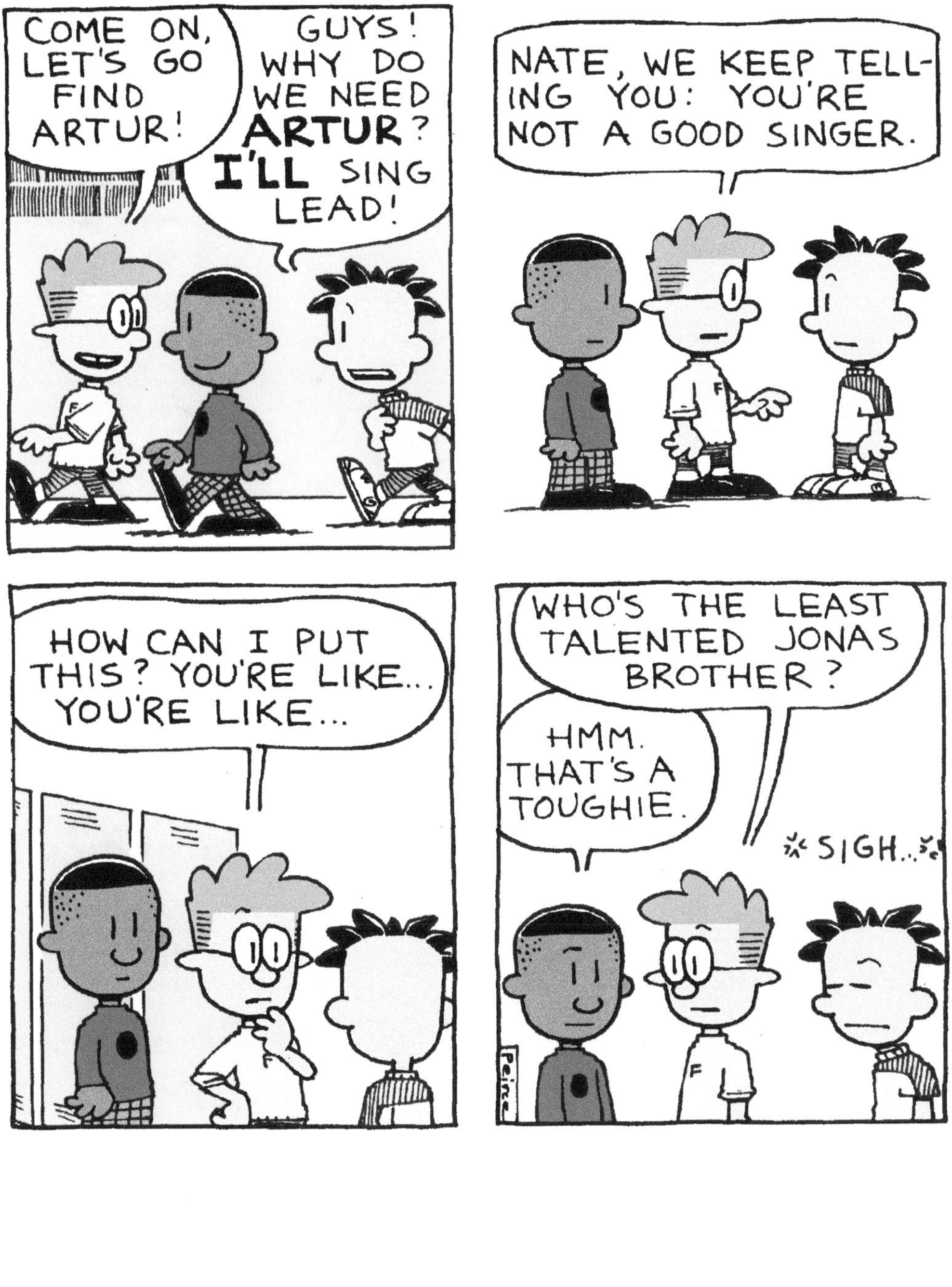
COME ON, LET'S GO FIND ARTUR!
GUYS! WHY DO WE NEED ARTUR? I'LL SING LEAD!
NATE, WE KEEP TELLING YOU: YOU'RE NOT A GOOD SINGER.
HOW CAN I PUT THIS? YOU'RE LIKE... YOU'RE LIKE...
WHO'S THE LEAST TALENTED JONAS BROTHER?
HMM. THAT'S A TOUGHIE.
SIGH...
Peirce

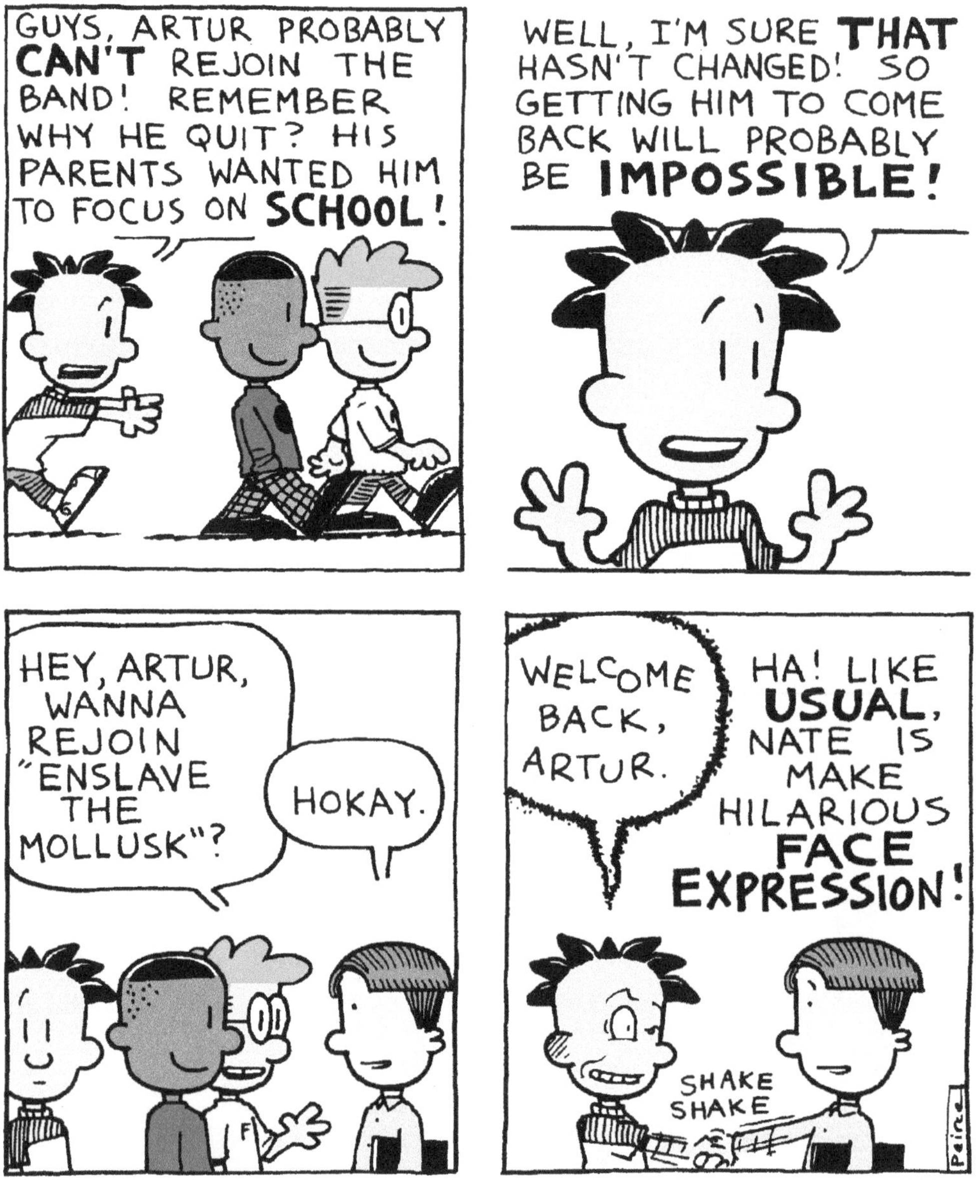
GUYS, ARTUR PROBABLY CAN'T REJOIN THE BAND! REMEMBER WHY HE QUIT? HIS PARENTS WANTED HIM TO FOCUS ON SCHOOL!
WELL, I'M SURE THAT HASN'T CHANGED! SO GETTING HIM TO COME BACK WILL PROBABLY BE IMPOSSIBLE!
HEY, ARTUR, WANNA REJOIN "ENSLAVE THE MOLLUSK"?
HOKAY.
WELCOME BACK, ARTUR.
HA! LIKE USUAL, NATE IS MAKE HILARIOUS FACE EXPRESSION!
SHAKE SHAKE
Peirce

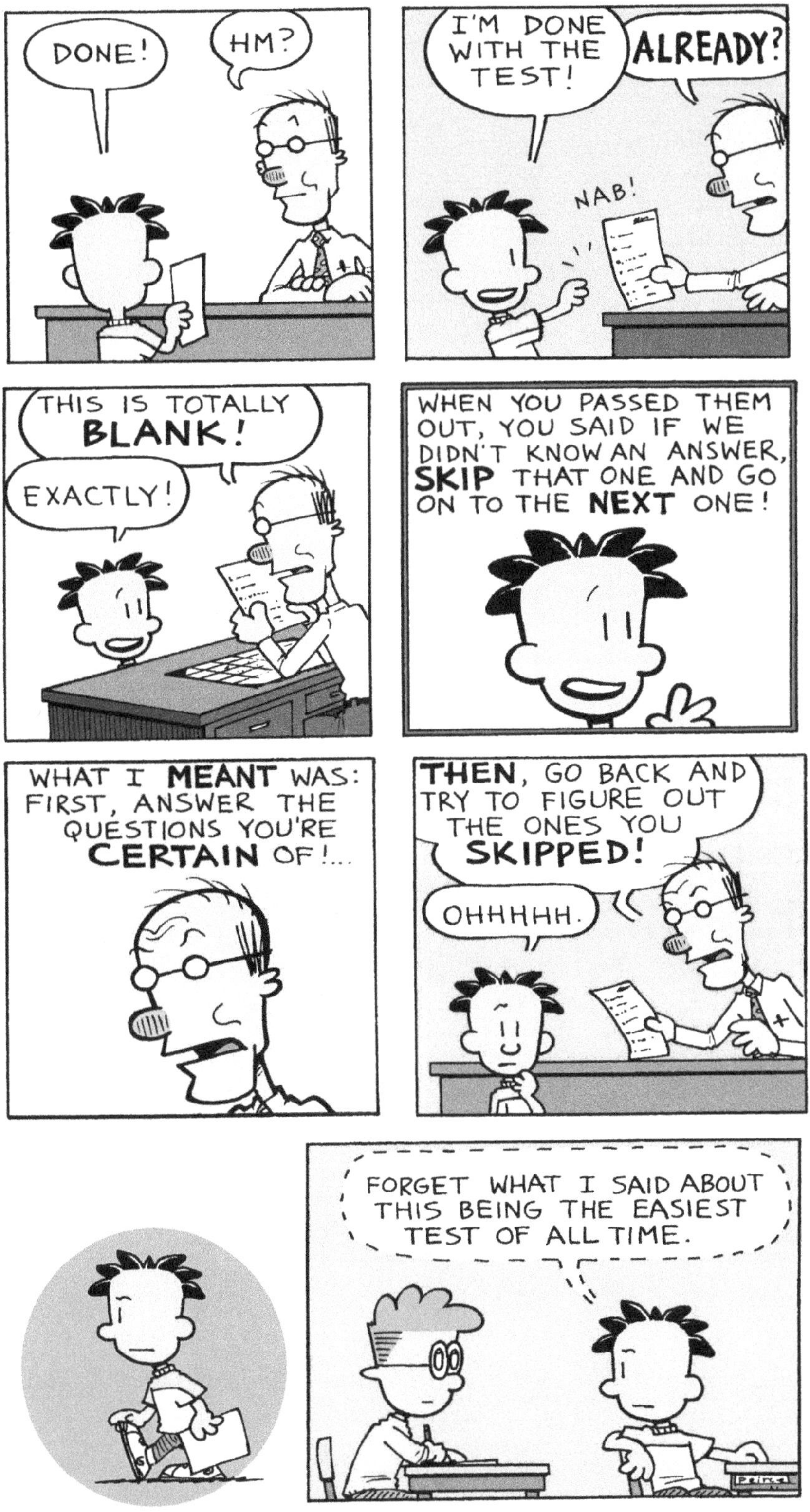
DONE!
HM?
I'M DONE WITH THE TEST!
ALREADY?
NAB!
THIS IS TOTALLY BLANK!
EXACTLY!
WHEN YOU PASSED THEM OUT, YOU SAID IF WE DIDN'T KNOW AN ANSWER, SKIP THAT ONE AND GO ON TO THE NEXT ONE!
WHAT I MEANT WAS: FIRST, ANSWER THE QUESTIONS YOU'RE CERTAIN OF!...
THEN, GO BACK AND TRY TO FIGURE OUT THE ONES YOU SKIPPED!
OHHHHH.
FORGET WHAT I SAID ABOUT THIS BEING THE EASIEST TEST OF ALL TIME.

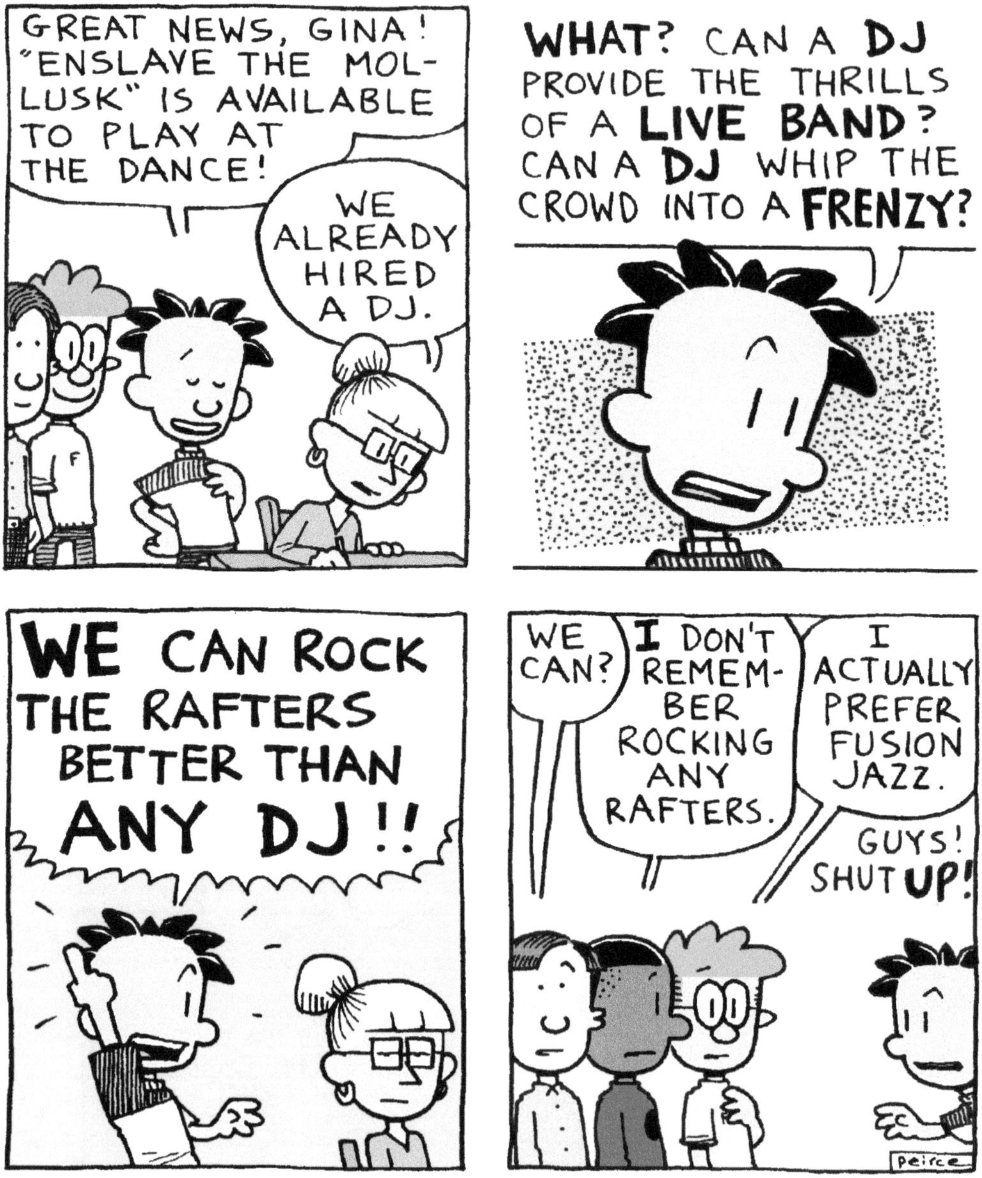
GREAT NEWS, GINA! "ENSLAVE THE MOL-LUSK" IS AVAILABLE TO PLAY AT THE DANCE!
WE ALREADY HIRED A DJ.
WHAT? CAN A DJ PROVIDE THE THRILLS OF A LIVE BAND? CAN A DJ WHIP THE CROWD INTO A FRENZY?
WE CAN ROCK THE RAFTERS BETTER THAN ANY DJ!!
WE CAN?
I DON'T REMEM-BER ROCKING ANY RAFTERS.
I ACTUALLY PREFER FUSION JAZZ.
GUYS! SHUT UP!
peirce

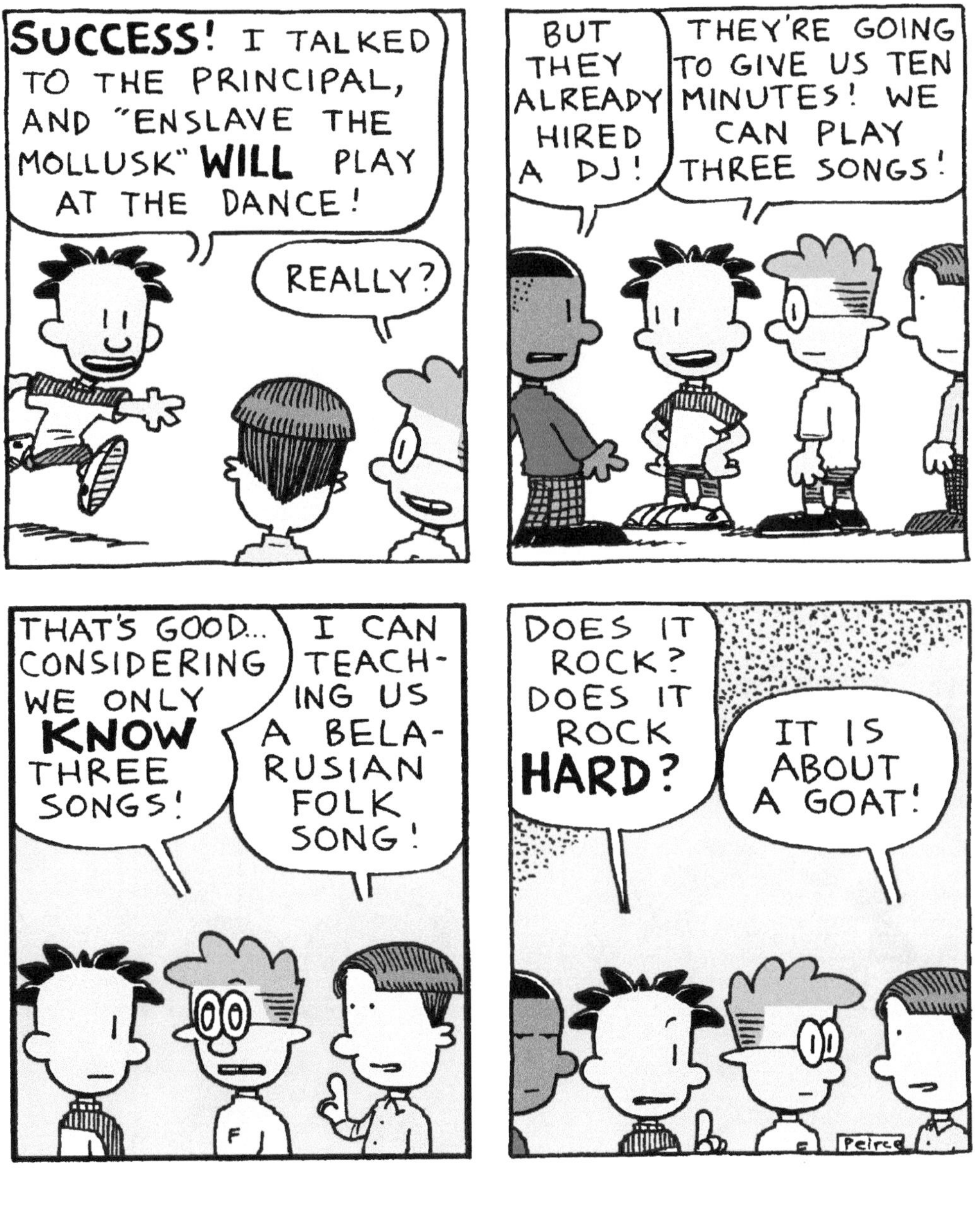
SUCCESS! I TALKED TO THE PRINCIPAL, AND "ENSLAVE THE MOLLUSK" WILL PLAY AT THE DANCE!
REALLY?
BUT THEY ALREADY HIRED A DJ!
THEY'RE GOING TO GIVE US TEN MINUTES! WE CAN PLAY THREE SONGS!
THAT'S GOOD... CONSIDERING WE ONLY KNOW THREE SONGS!
I CAN TEACHING US A BELARUSIAN FOLK SONG!
DOES IT ROCK? DOES IT ROCK HARD?
IT IS ABOUT A GOAT!
Peirce

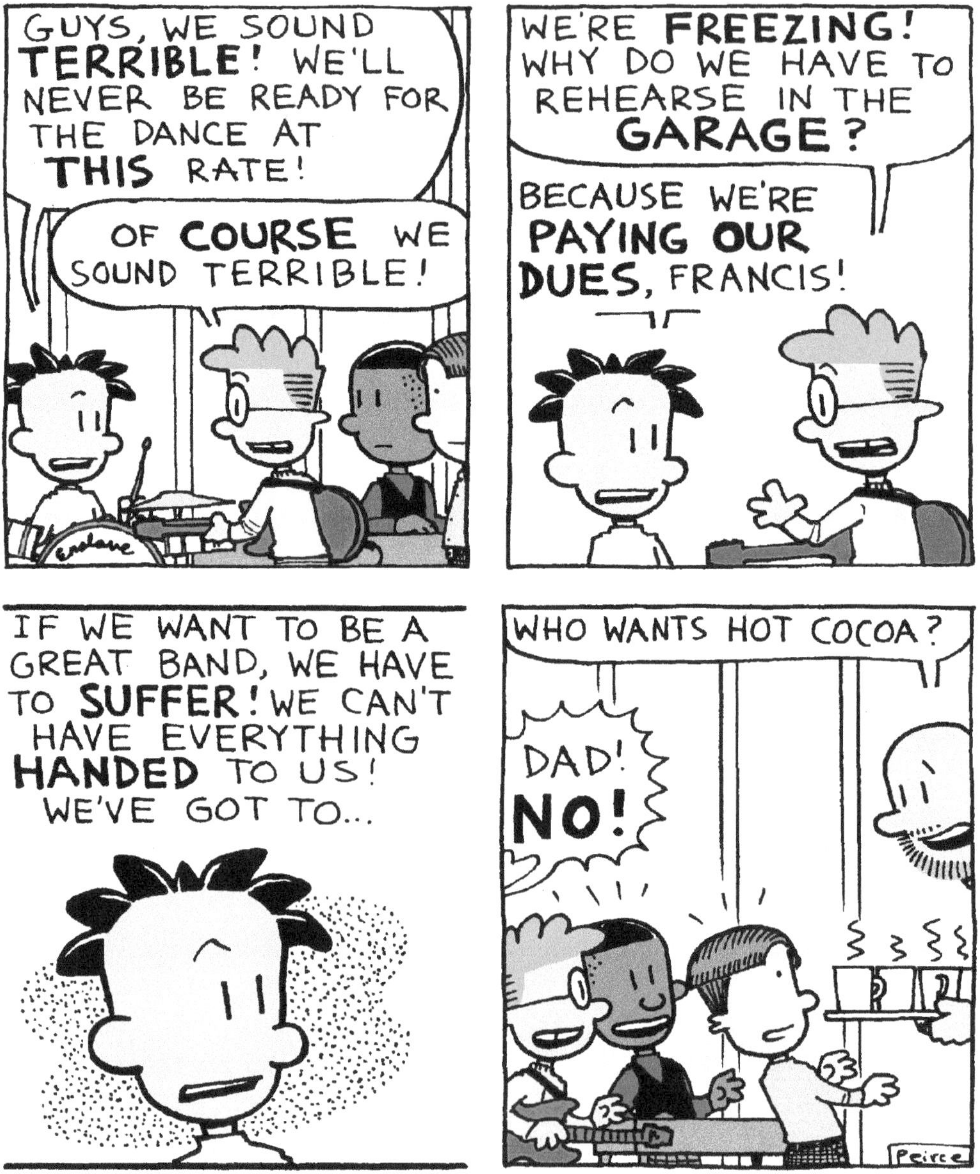
GUYS, WE SOUND TERRIBLE! WE'LL NEVER BE READY FOR THE DANCE AT THIS RATE!
OF COURSE WE SOUND TERRIBLE!
WE'RE FREEZING! WHY DO WE HAVE TO REHEARSE IN THE GARAGE?
BECAUSE WE'RE PAYING OUR DUES, FRANCIS!
IF WE WANT TO BE A GREAT BAND, WE HAVE TO SUFFER! WE CAN'T HAVE EVERYTHING HANDED TO US! WE'VE GOT TO...
WHO WANTS HOT COCOA?
DAD! NO!
Peirce

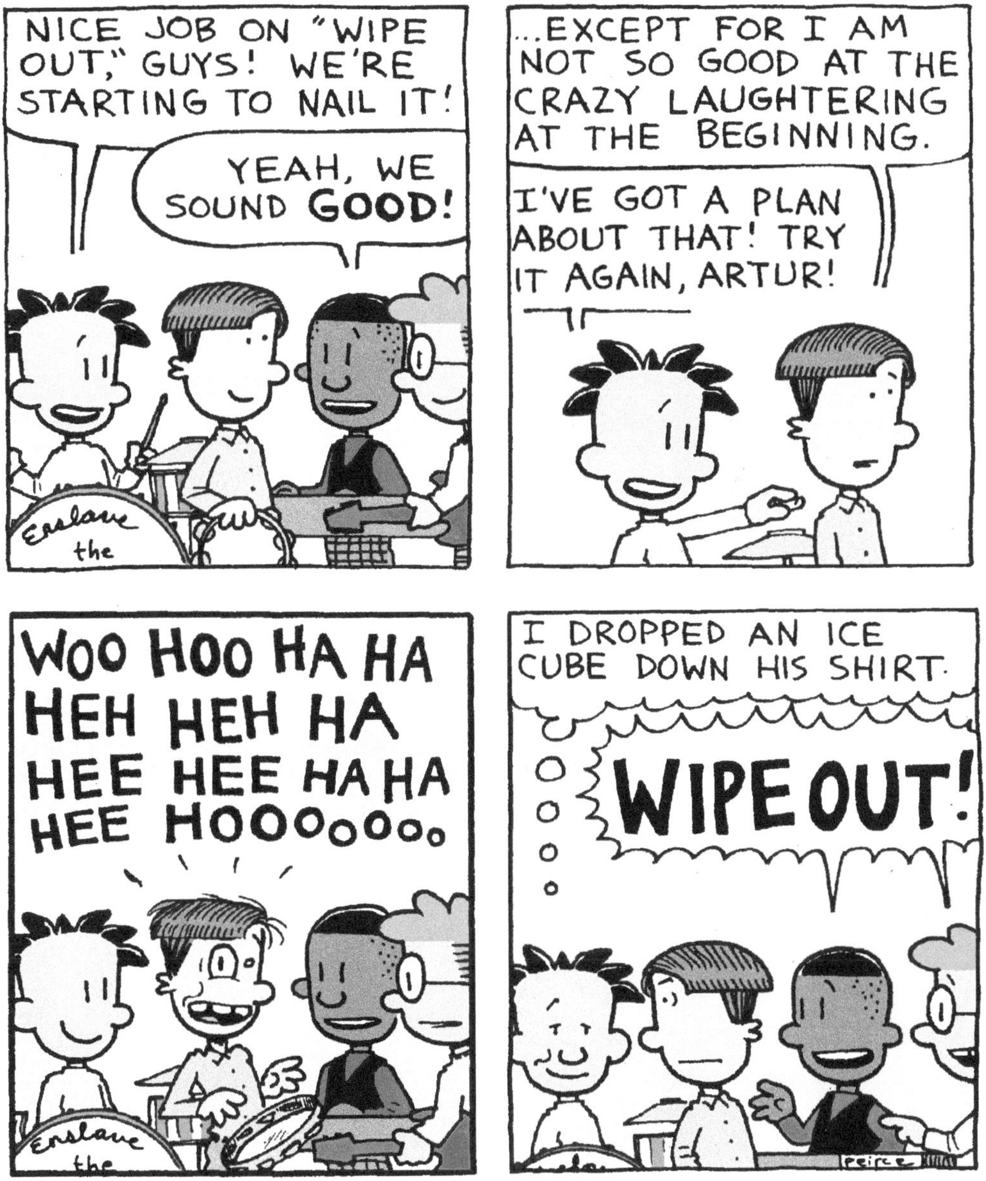
NICE JOB ON "WIPE OUT," GUYS! WE'RE STARTING TO NAIL IT!
YEAH, WE SOUND **GOOD**!
...EXCEPT FOR I AM NOT SO GOOD AT THE CRAZY LAUGHTERING AT THE BEGINNING.
I'VE GOT A PLAN ABOUT THAT! TRY IT AGAIN, ARTUR!
WOO HOO HA HA HEH HEH HA HEE HEE HA HA HEE HOOOoooo
I DROPPED AN ICE CUBE DOWN HIS SHIRT.
WIPE OUT!

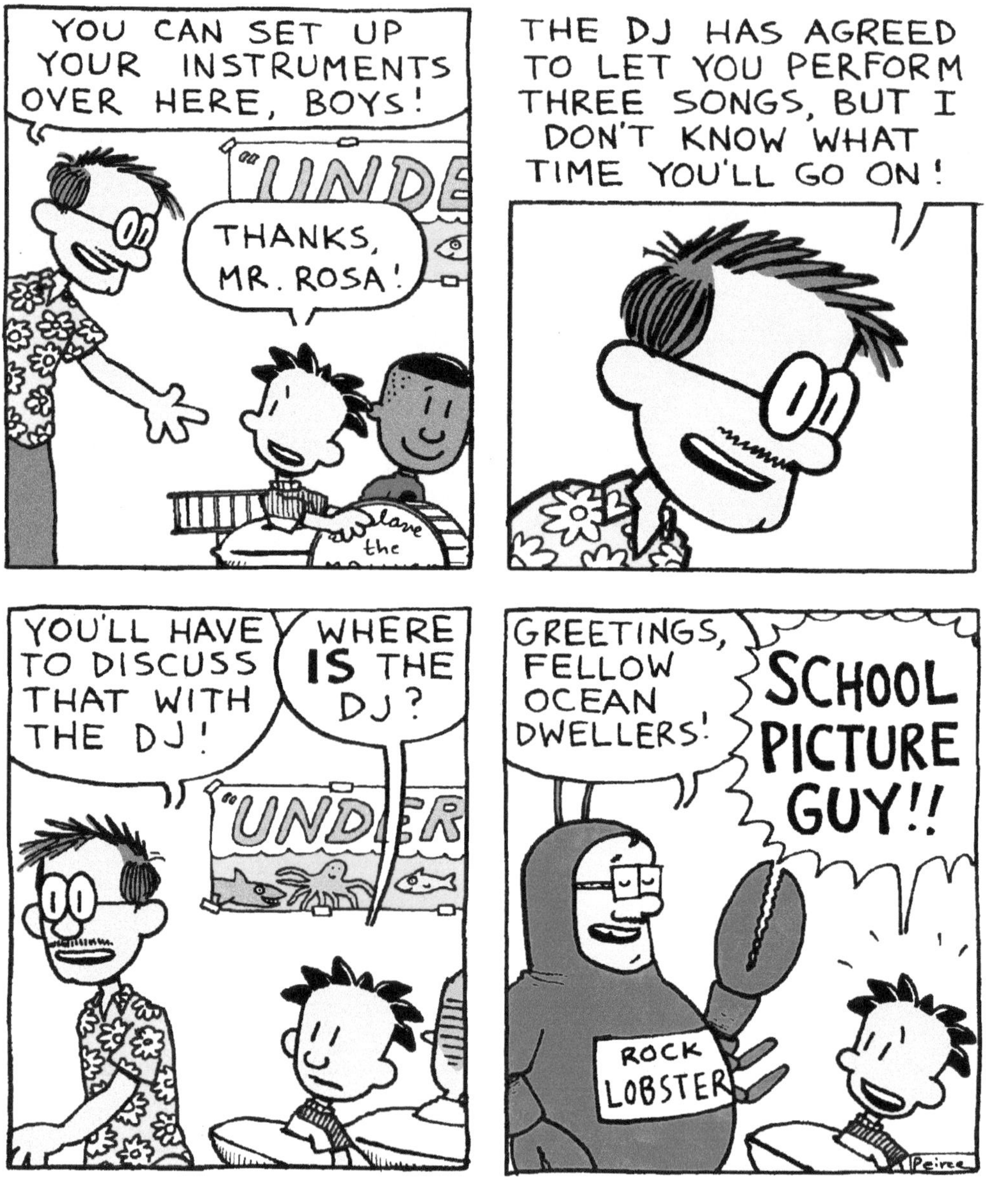
YOU CAN SET UP YOUR INSTRUMENTS OVER HERE, BOYS!
THANKS, MR. ROSA!
THE DJ HAS AGREED TO LET YOU PERFORM THREE SONGS, BUT I DON'T KNOW WHAT TIME YOU'LL GO ON!
YOU'LL HAVE TO DISCUSS THAT WITH THE DJ!
WHERE **IS** THE DJ?
GREETINGS, FELLOW OCEAN DWELLERS!
SCHOOL PICTURE GUY!!
ROCK LOBSTER
Peirce

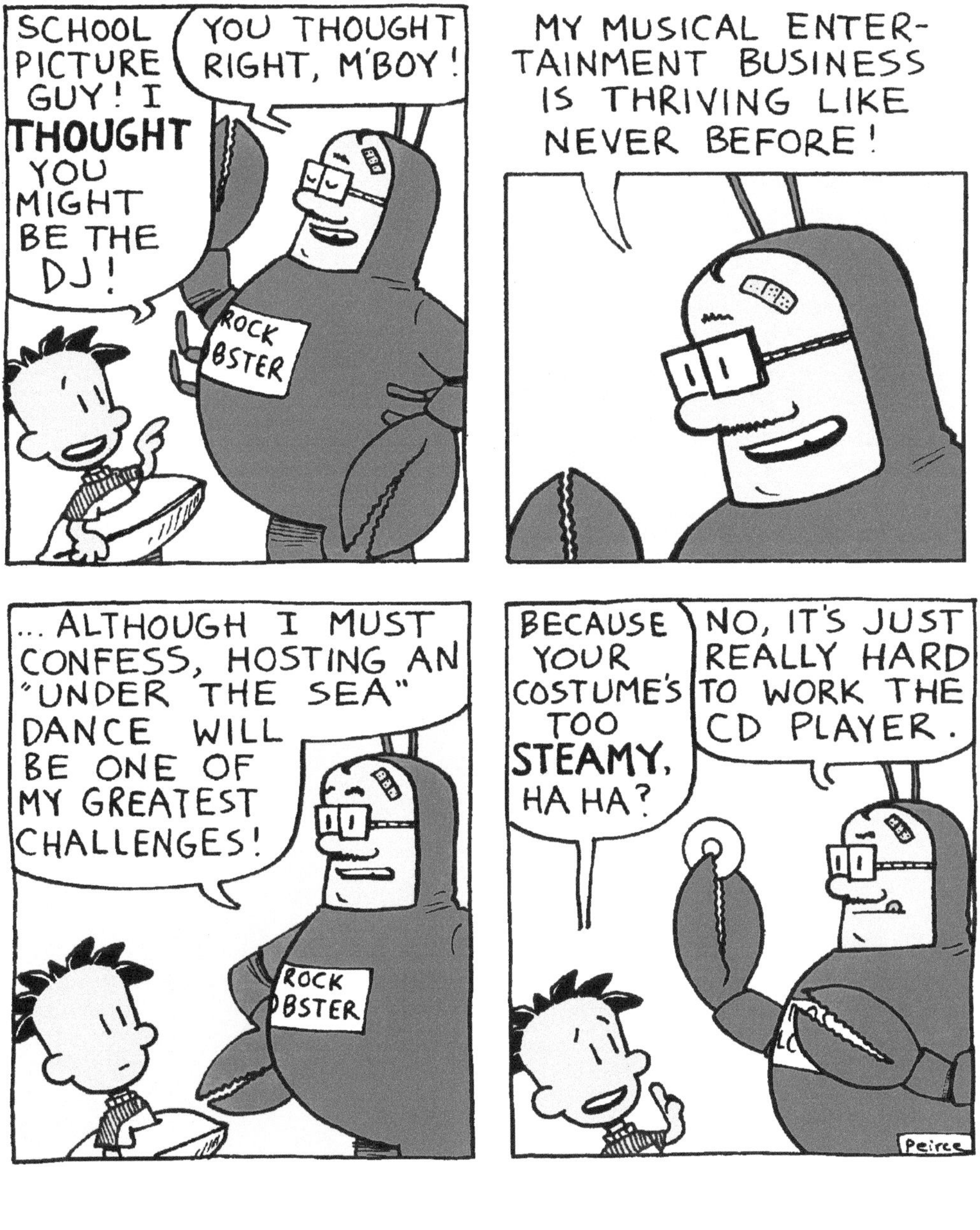
SCHOOL PICTURE GUY! I **THOUGHT** YOU MIGHT BE THE DJ!
YOU THOUGHT RIGHT, M'BOY!
ROCK LOBSTER
MY MUSICAL ENTERTAINMENT BUSINESS IS THRIVING LIKE NEVER BEFORE!
...ALTHOUGH I MUST CONFESS, HOSTING AN "UNDER THE SEA" DANCE WILL BE ONE OF MY GREATEST CHALLENGES!
ROCK LOBSTER
BECAUSE YOUR COSTUME'S TOO **STEAMY**, HA HA?
NO, IT'S JUST REALLY HARD TO WORK THE CD PLAYER.
Peirce

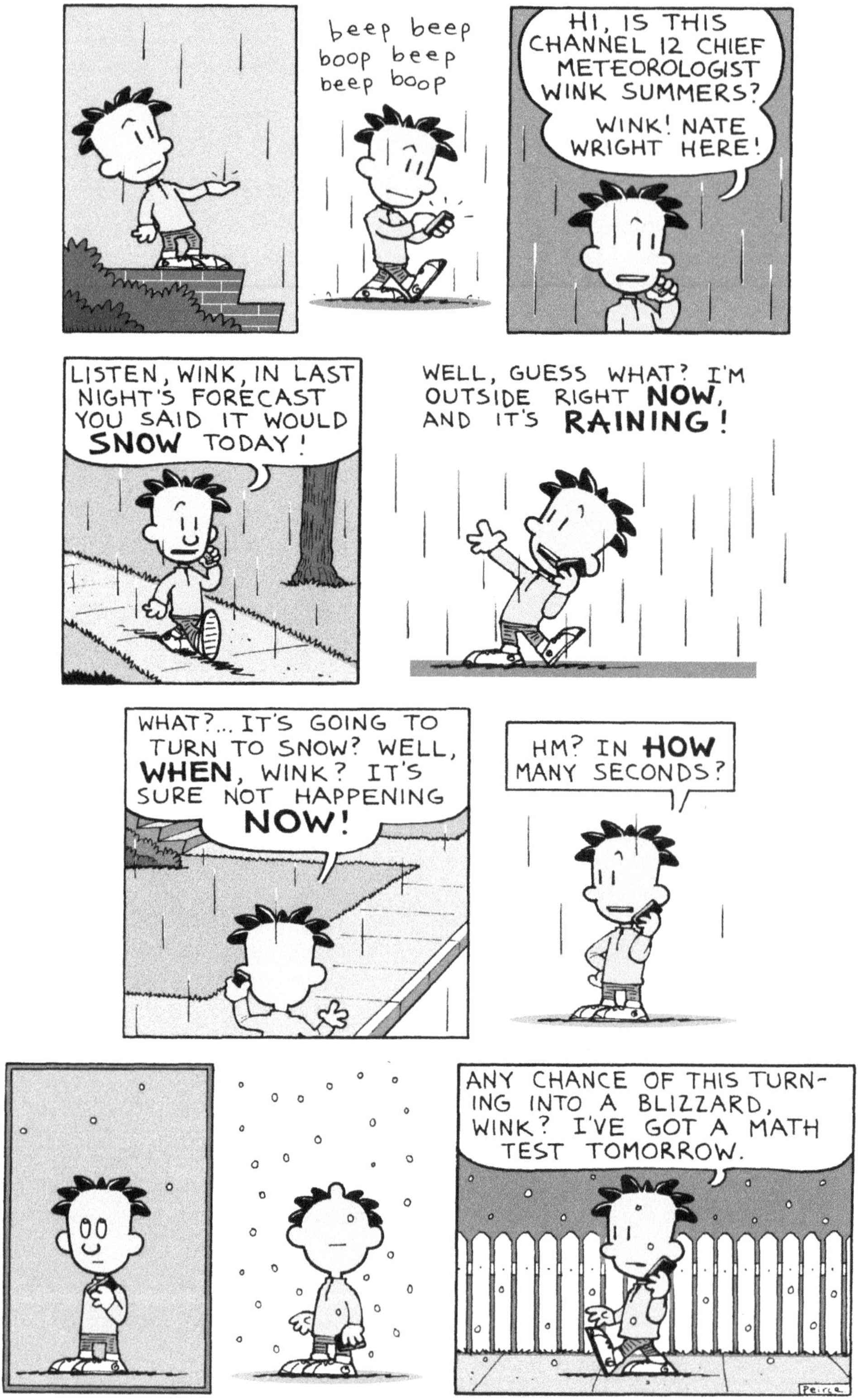
beep beep boop beep beep boop
HI, IS THIS CHANNEL 12 CHIEF METEOROLOGIST WINK SUMMERS?
WINK! NATE WRIGHT HERE!
LISTEN, WINK, IN LAST NIGHT'S FORECAST YOU SAID IT WOULD SNOW TODAY!
WELL, GUESS WHAT? I'M OUTSIDE RIGHT NOW, AND IT'S RAINING!
WHAT?... IT'S GOING TO TURN TO SNOW? WELL, WHEN, WINK? IT'S SURE NOT HAPPENING NOW!
HM? IN HOW MANY SECONDS?
ANY CHANCE OF THIS TURNING INTO A BLIZZARD, WINK? I'VE GOT A MATH TEST TOMORROW.
Peirce

HERE, DUDE. I WROTE THIS SO YOU'LL KNOW WHAT TO SAY WHEN YOU INTRODUCE US.

ROCK LOBST

"LADIES AND GENTLE-MEN... ENGORGE THE MULLET"!

KID, THAT'S THE WORST NAME OF ALL TIME.

IT'S ENSLAVE THE MOLLUSK!

ROCK LOBST

KID, THAT'S THE WORST HANDWRITING OF ALL TIME.

"ENGORGE THE MULLET"? WHO'D NAME A BAND THAT?

ROCK LOBST

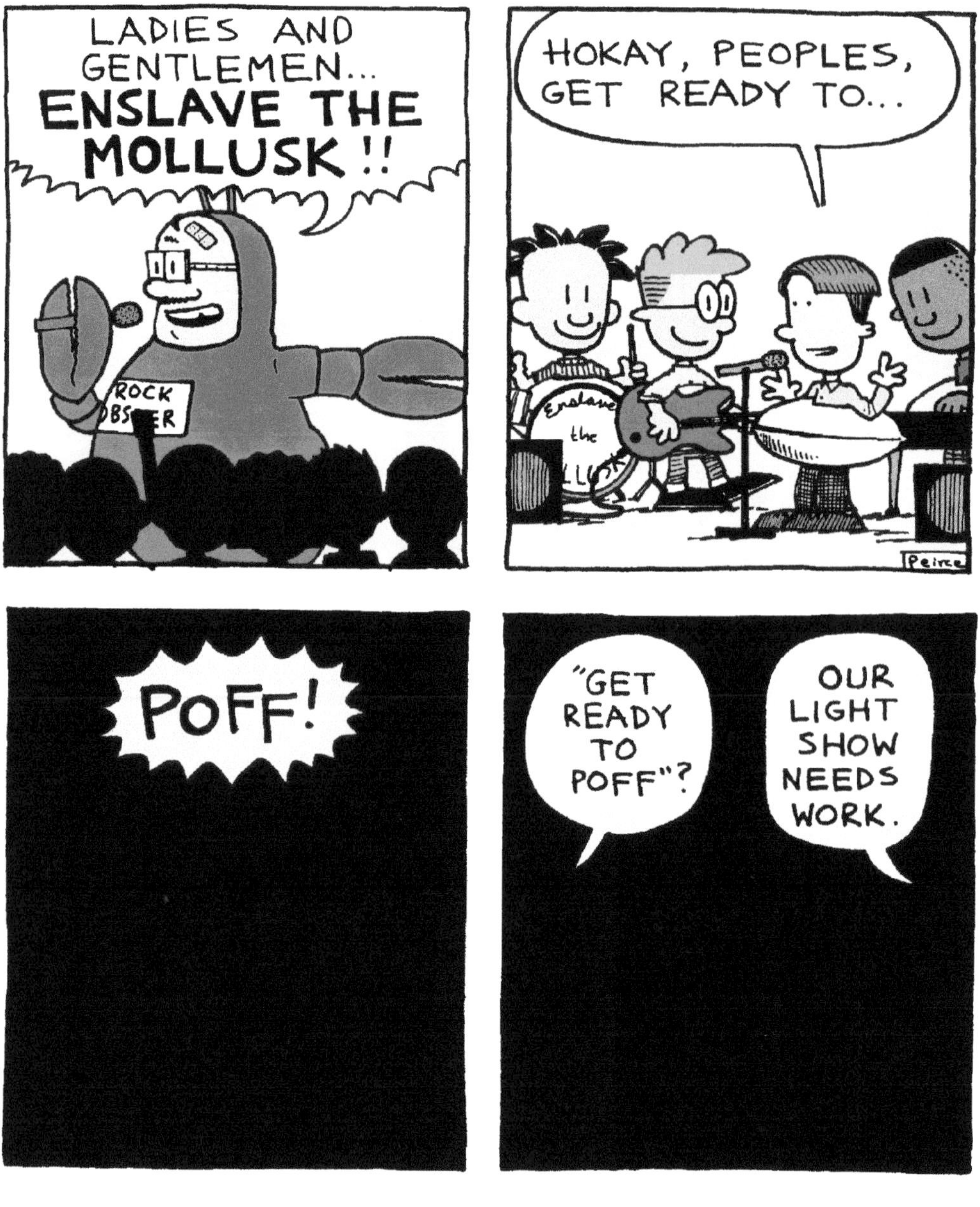
LADIES AND GENTLEMEN... ENSLAVE THE MOLLUSK!!
HOKAY, PEOPLES, GET READY TO...
Peirce
POFF!
"GET READY TO POFF"?
OUR LIGHT SHOW NEEDS WORK.

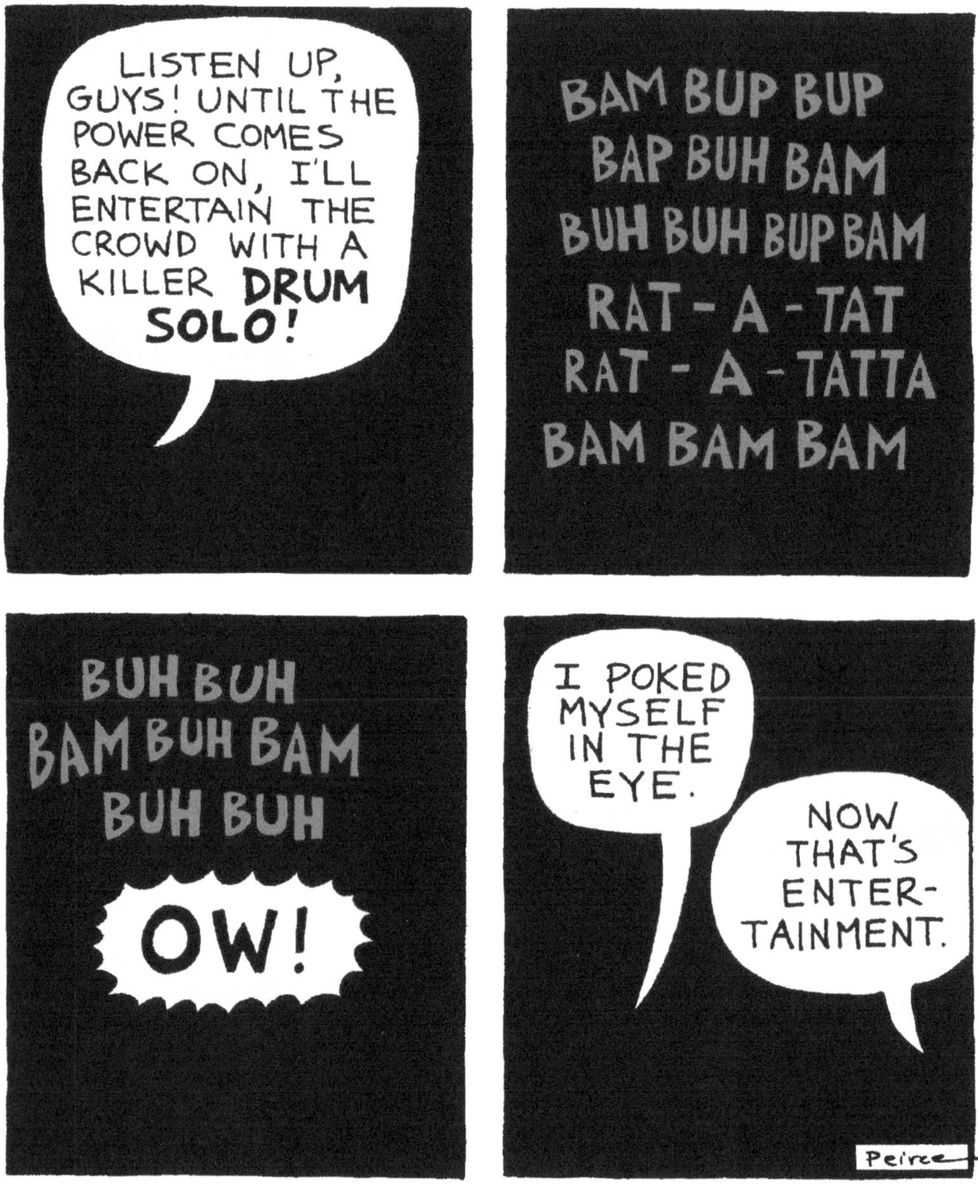
LISTEN UP, GUYS! UNTIL THE POWER COMES BACK ON, I'LL ENTERTAIN THE CROWD WITH A KILLER **DRUM SOLO!**
BAM BUP BUP BAP BUH BAM BUH BUH BUP BAM RAT-A-TAT RAT-A-TATTA BAM BAM BAM
BUH BUH BAM BUH BAM BUH BUH
OW!
I POKED MYSELF IN THE EYE.
NOW THAT'S ENTERTAINMENT.
Peirce

CAN YOU BELIEVE IT? FIVE SECONDS BEFORE OUR PERFORMANCE, THE WHOLE SCHOOL **LOSES POWER!**

OUR BIG MOMENT WAS **RUINED!**

BUT EVEN WITHOUT ELECTRICS, WE WERE ABLE AT LEAST TO PUT ON SOME **ENTERTAININGS!**

THANKS TO GOODNESS I HAD MY KAZOO!

YES, ARTUR, THAT **WAS** LUCKY.

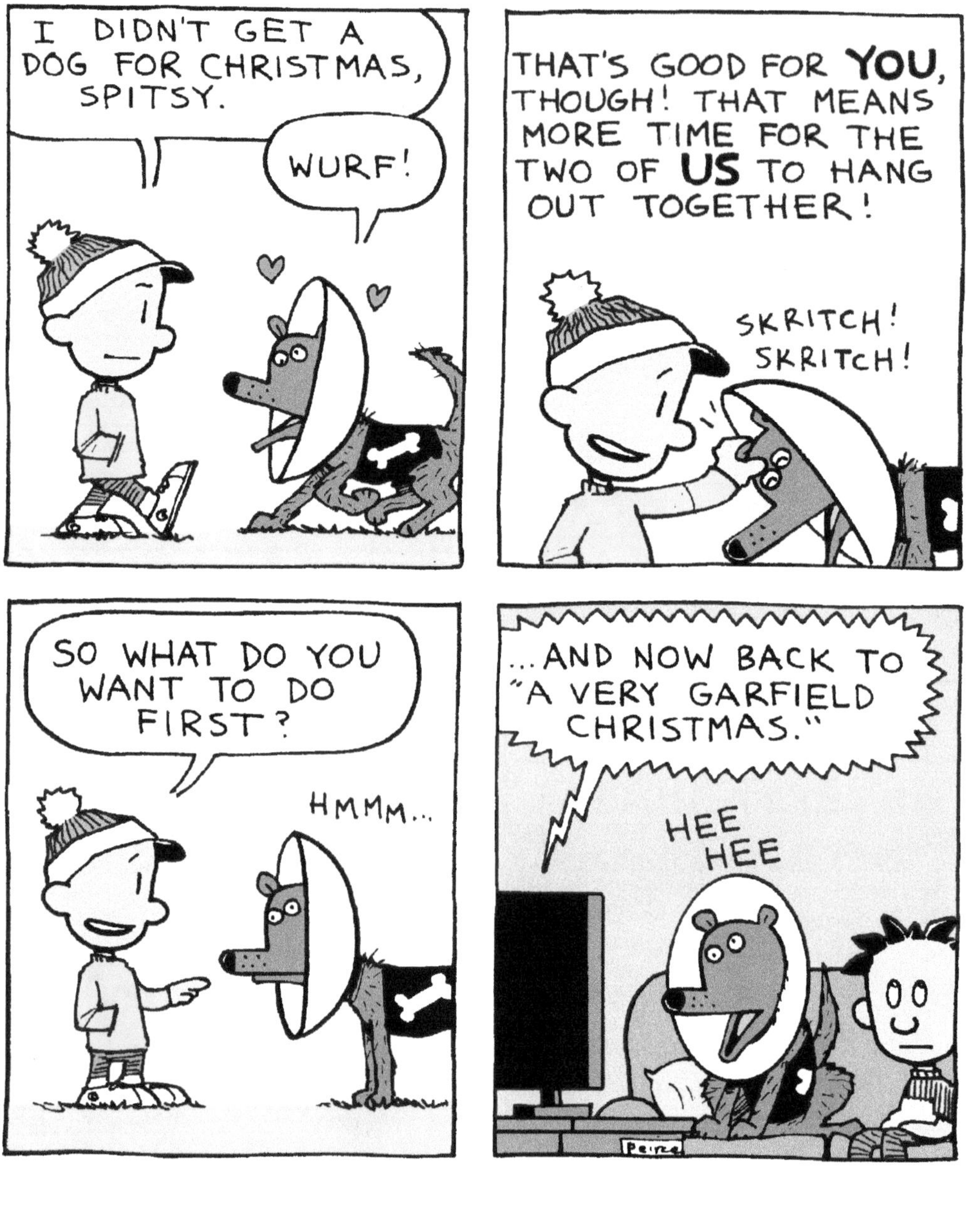
I DIDN'T GET A DOG FOR CHRISTMAS, SPITSY.
WURF!
THAT'S GOOD FOR **YOU**, THOUGH! THAT MEANS MORE TIME FOR THE TWO OF **US** TO HANG OUT TOGETHER!
SKRITCH! SKRITCH!
SO WHAT DO YOU WANT TO DO FIRST?
HMMM...
...AND NOW BACK TO "A VERY GARFIELD CHRISTMAS."
HEE HEE
Peirce

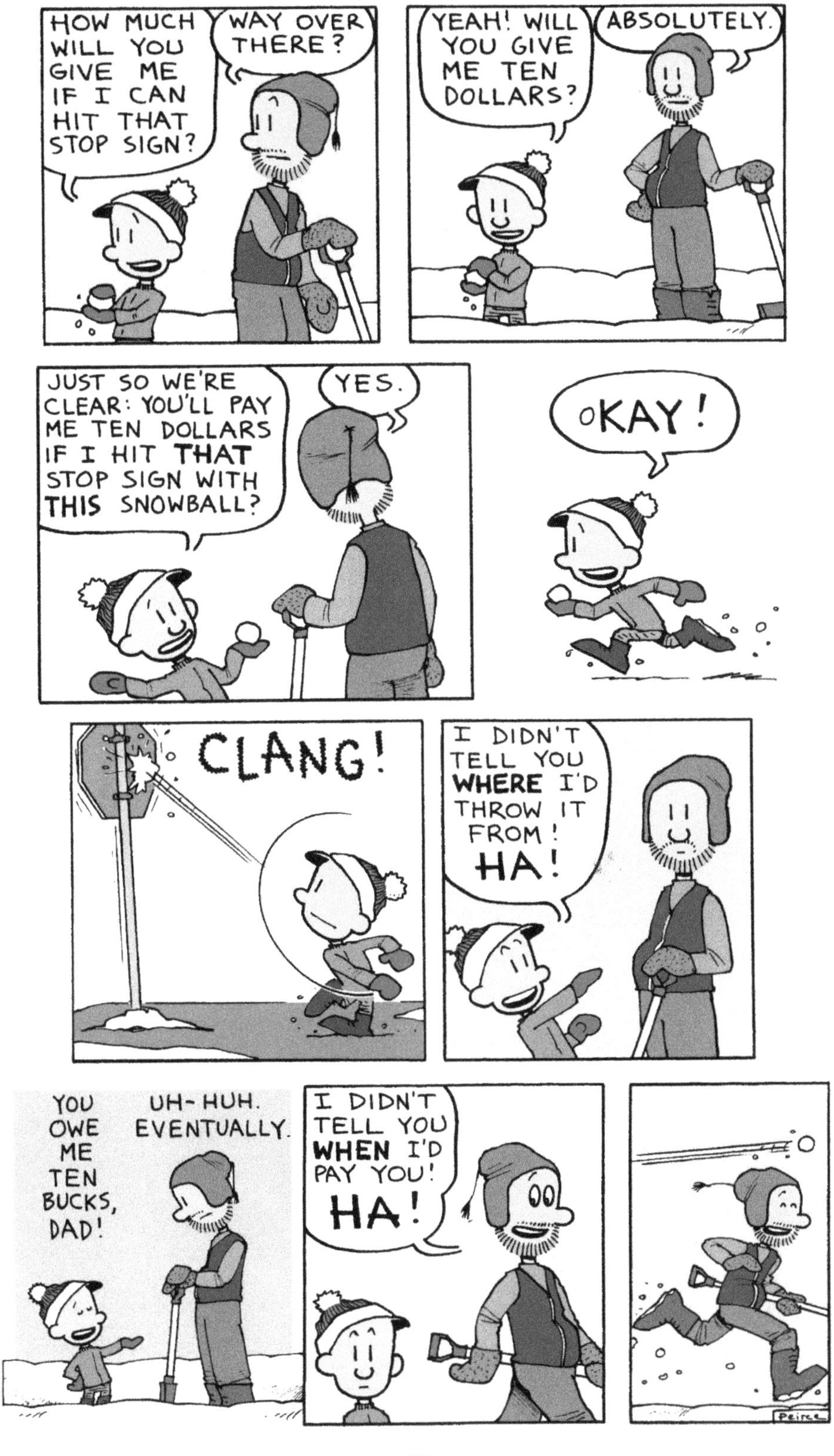
HOW MUCH WILL YOU GIVE ME IF I CAN HIT THAT STOP SIGN?
WAY OVER THERE?
YEAH! WILL YOU GIVE ME TEN DOLLARS?
ABSOLUTELY.
JUST SO WE'RE CLEAR: YOU'LL PAY ME TEN DOLLARS IF I HIT THAT STOP SIGN WITH THIS SNOWBALL?
YES.
OKAY!
CLANG!
I DIDN'T TELL YOU WHERE I'D THROW IT FROM! HA!
YOU OWE ME TEN BUCKS, DAD!
UH-HUH. EVENTUALLY.
I DIDN'T TELL YOU WHEN I'D PAY YOU! HA!
Peirce

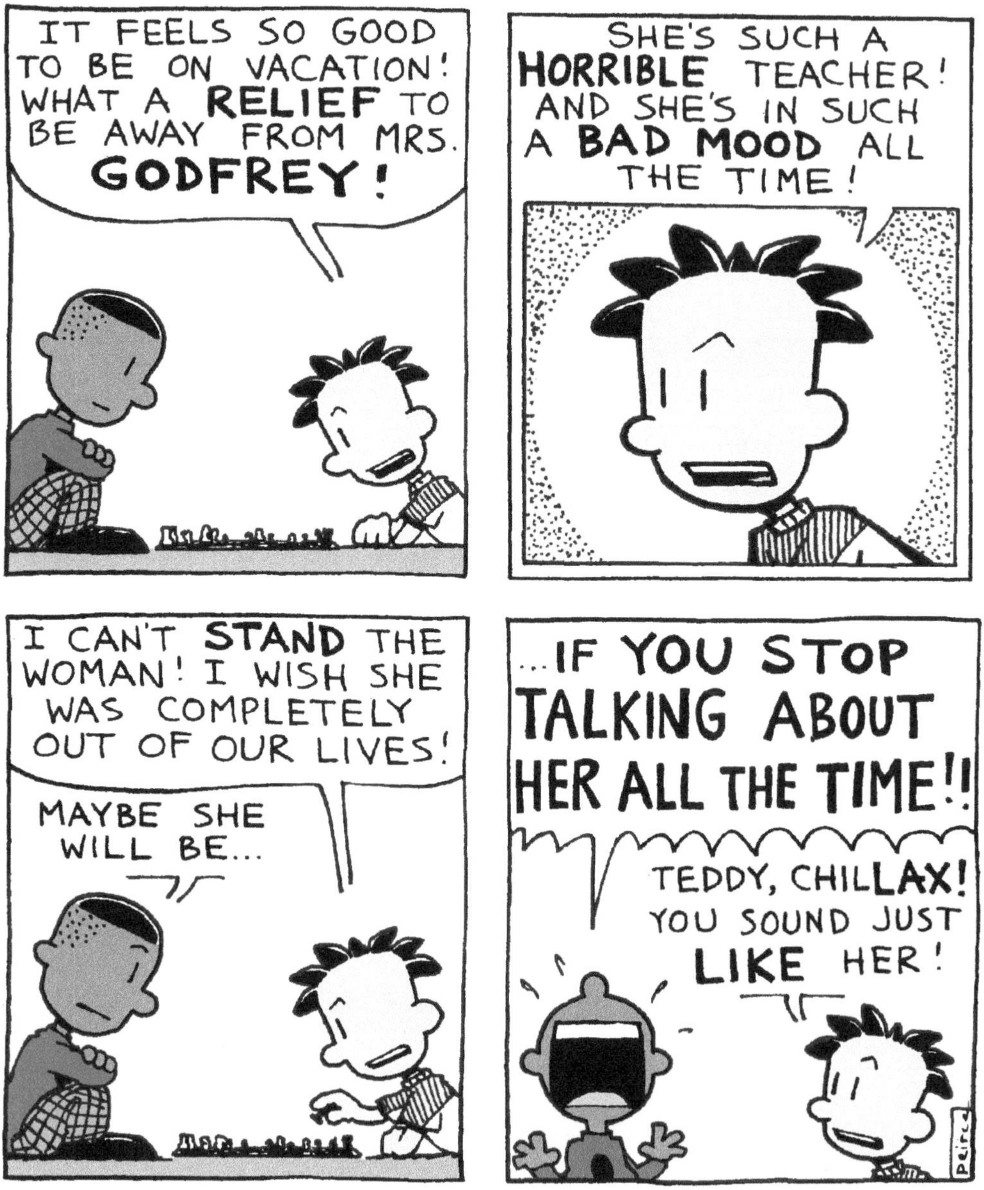
IT FEELS SO GOOD TO BE ON VACATION! WHAT A RELIEF TO BE AWAY FROM MRS. GODFREY!
SHE'S SUCH A HORRIBLE TEACHER! AND SHE'S IN SUCH A BAD MOOD ALL THE TIME!
I CAN'T STAND THE WOMAN! I WISH SHE WAS COMPLETELY OUT OF OUR LIVES!
MAYBE SHE WILL BE...
...IF YOU STOP TALKING ABOUT HER ALL THE TIME!!
TEDDY, CHILLAX! YOU SOUND JUST LIKE HER!
PEIRCE

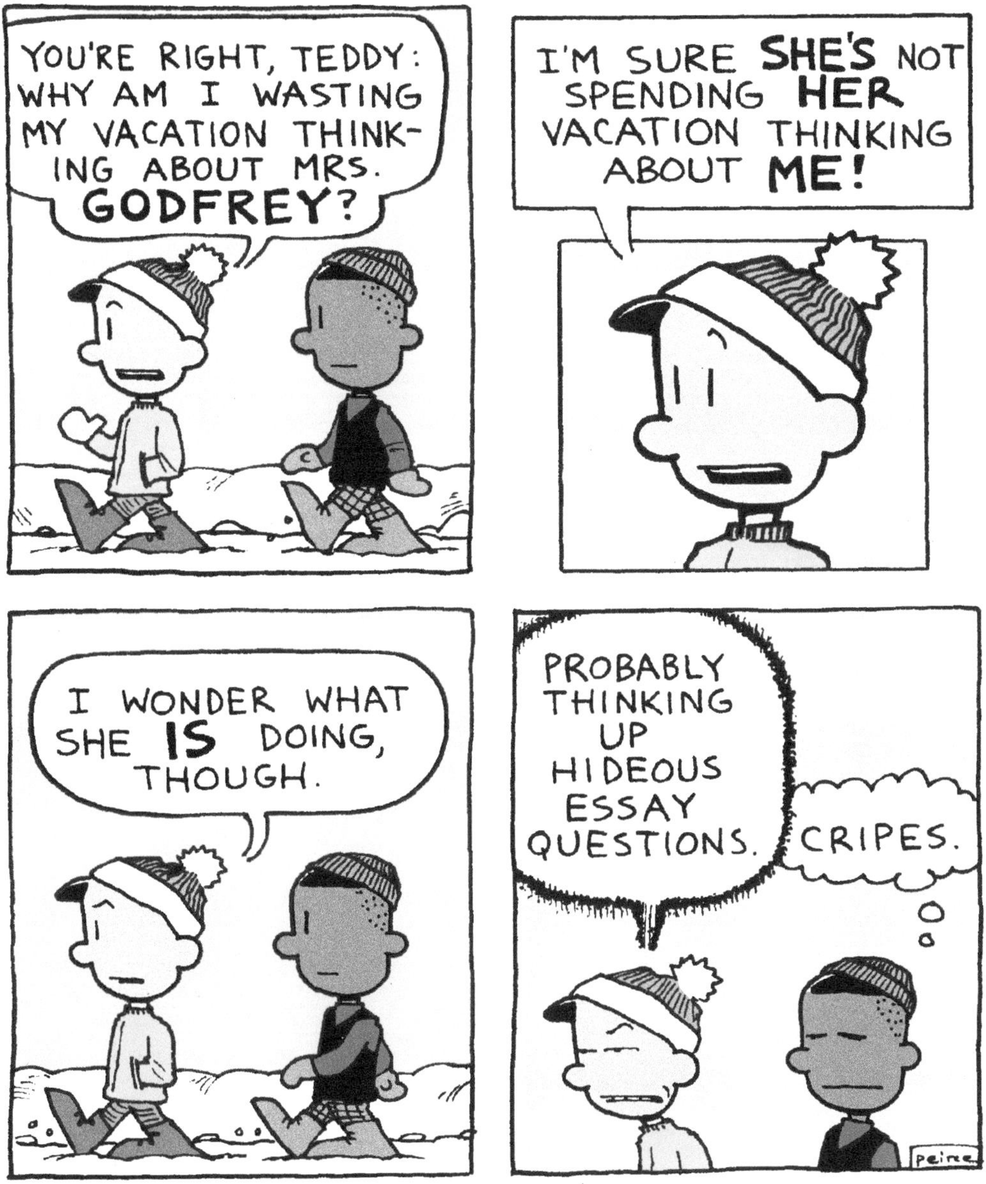
YOU'RE RIGHT, TEDDY: WHY AM I WASTING MY VACATION THINKING ABOUT MRS. GODFREY?
I'M SURE SHE'S NOT SPENDING HER VACATION THINKING ABOUT ME!
I WONDER WHAT SHE IS DOING, THOUGH.
PROBABLY THINKING UP HIDEOUS ESSAY QUESTIONS.
CRIPES.
peirce

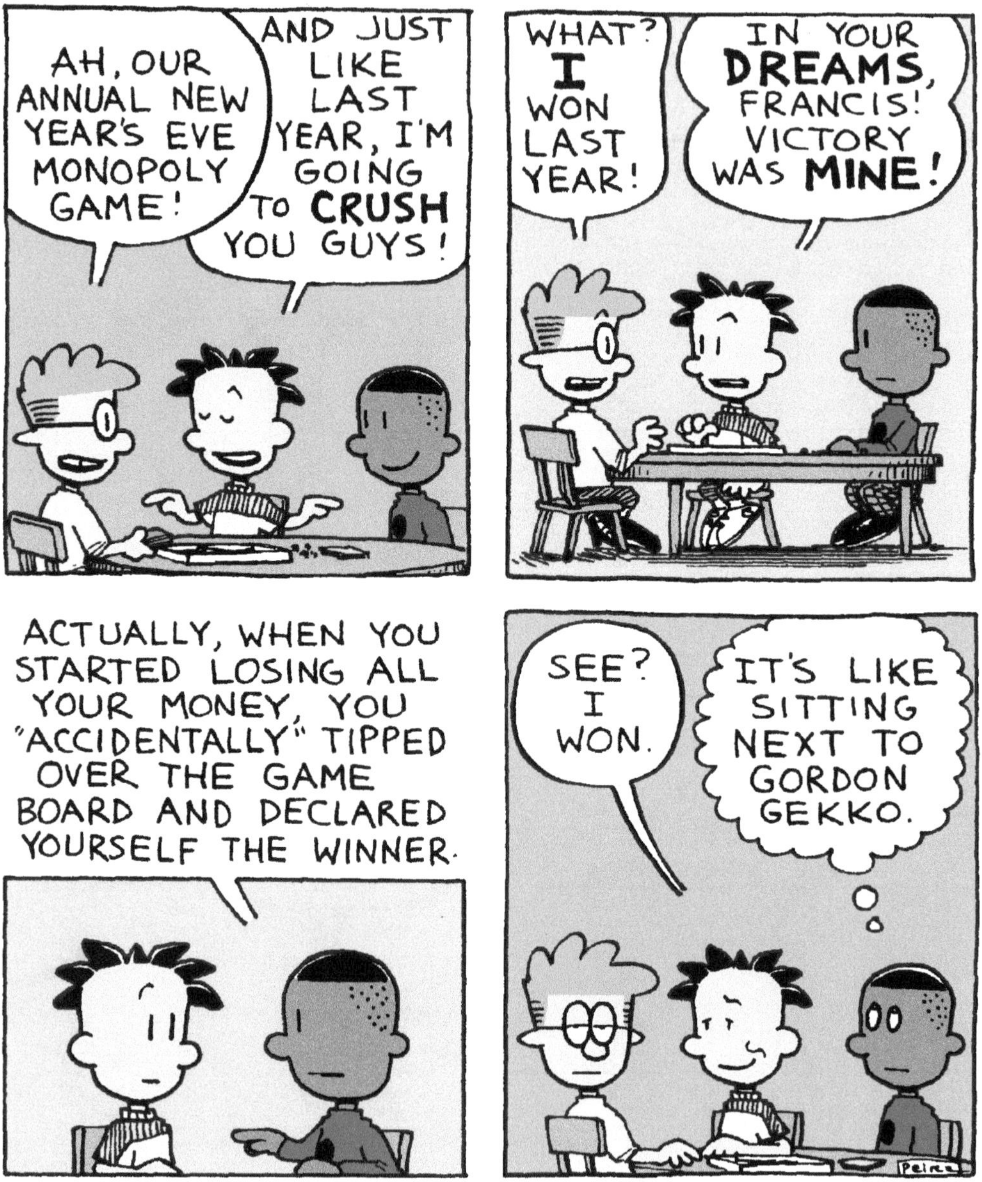
AH, OUR ANNUAL NEW YEAR'S EVE MONOPOLY GAME!
AND JUST LIKE LAST YEAR, I'M GOING TO **CRUSH** YOU GUYS!
WHAT? **I** WON LAST YEAR!
IN YOUR **DREAMS**, FRANCIS! VICTORY WAS **MINE**!
ACTUALLY, WHEN YOU STARTED LOSING ALL YOUR MONEY, YOU "ACCIDENTALLY" TIPPED OVER THE GAME BOARD AND DECLARED YOURSELF THE WINNER.
SEE? I WON.
IT'S LIKE SITTING NEXT TO GORDON GEKKO.
Peirce

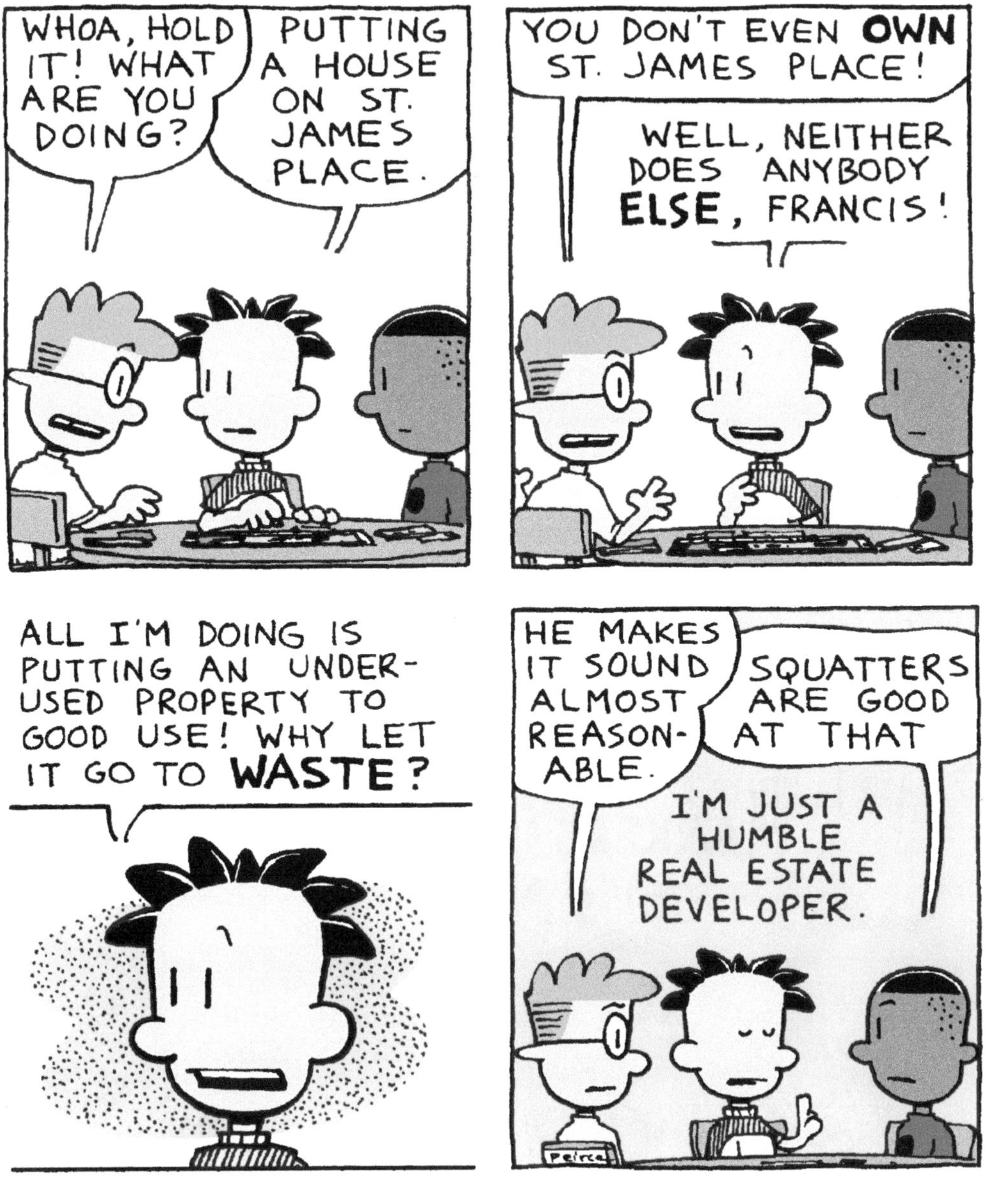
WHOA, HOLD IT! WHAT ARE YOU DOING?
PUTTING A HOUSE ON ST. JAMES PLACE.
YOU DON'T EVEN OWN ST. JAMES PLACE!
WELL, NEITHER DOES ANYBODY ELSE, FRANCIS!
ALL I'M DOING IS PUTTING AN UNDER-USED PROPERTY TO GOOD USE! WHY LET IT GO TO WASTE?
HE MAKES IT SOUND ALMOST REASON-ABLE.
SQUATTERS ARE GOOD AT THAT
I'M JUST A HUMBLE REAL ESTATE DEVELOPER.
Peirce

FIVE... SIX... SEVEN... RATS!
HA! YOU OWE ME 900 DOLLARS!
AND IT LOOKS LIKE YOU'RE ALMOST BROKE!
NOT SO FAST, BOYS! I HAVE A SECRET SAVINGS ACCOUNT!
HERE YOU GO, TEDDY!
WHAT THE...? THAT ISN'T EVEN **REAL**! YOU DREW THAT WITH **MARKERS**!
WAIT, YOU MADE COUNTERFEIT **MONOPOLY MONEY**?
IT GETS WORSE HE DREW HIS OWN FACE ON THE BILLS
Peirce

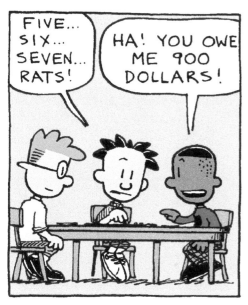

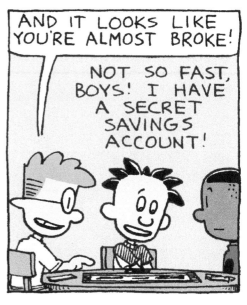

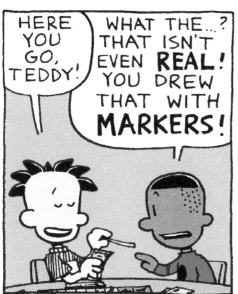

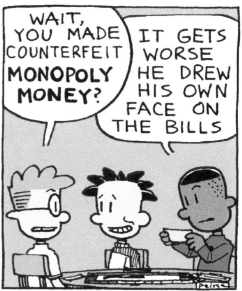

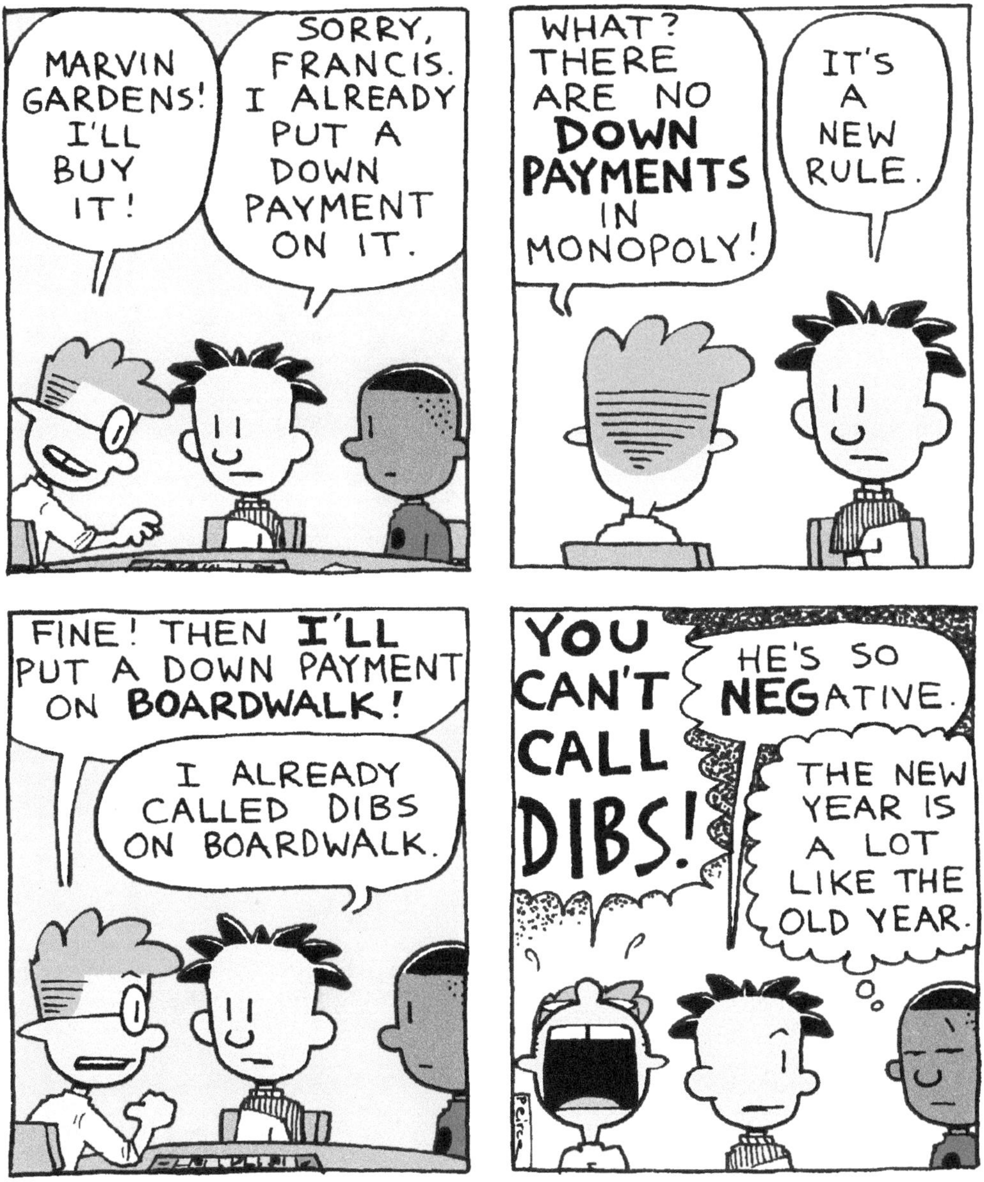
MARVIN GARDENS! I'LL BUY IT!
SORRY, FRANCIS. I ALREADY PUT A DOWN PAYMENT ON IT.
WHAT? THERE ARE NO DOWN PAYMENTS IN MONOPOLY!
IT'S A NEW RULE.
FINE! THEN I'LL PUT A DOWN PAYMENT ON BOARDWALK!
I ALREADY CALLED DIBS ON BOARDWALK.
YOU CAN'T CALL DIBS!
HE'S SO NEGATIVE.
THE NEW YEAR IS A LOT LIKE THE OLD YEAR.
Peirce

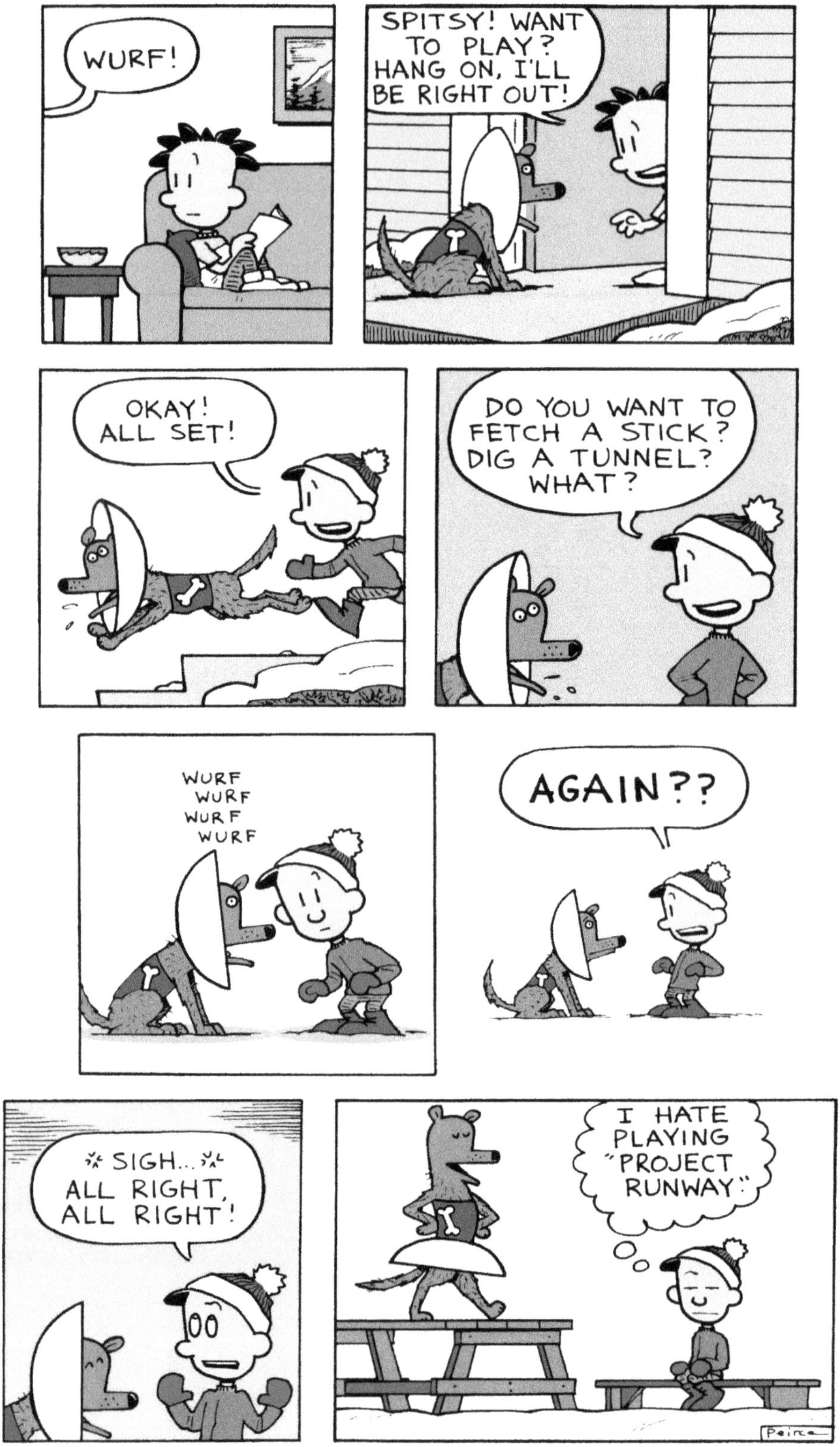
WURF!
SPITSY! WANT TO PLAY? HANG ON, I'LL BE RIGHT OUT!
OKAY! ALL SET!
DO YOU WANT TO FETCH A STICK? DIG A TUNNEL? WHAT?
WURF WURF WURF WURF
AGAIN??
SIGH... ALL RIGHT, ALL RIGHT!
I HATE PLAYING "PROJECT RUNWAY."
Peirce

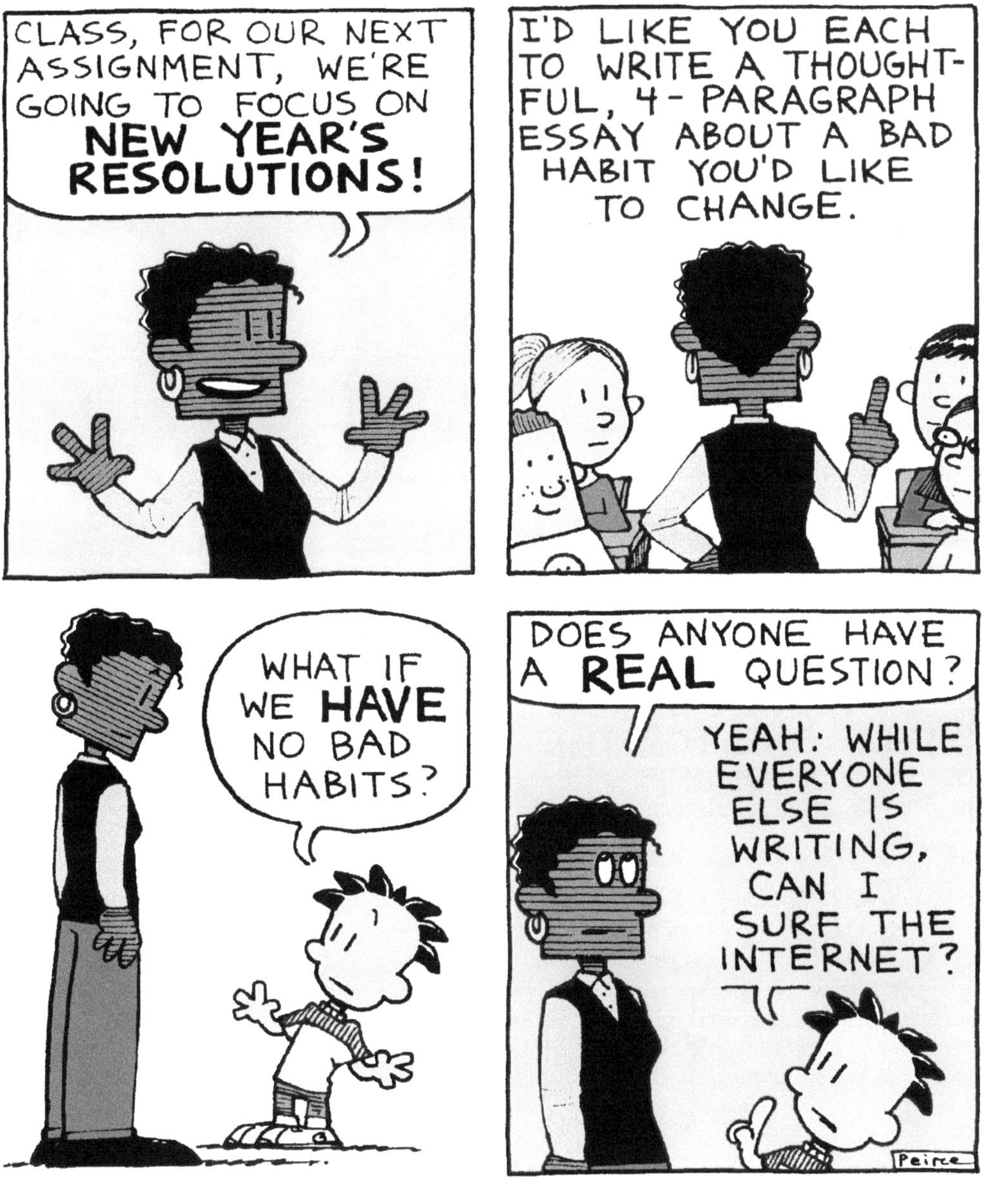
CLASS, FOR OUR NEXT ASSIGNMENT, WE'RE GOING TO FOCUS ON **NEW YEAR'S RESOLUTIONS!**
I'D LIKE YOU EACH TO WRITE A THOUGHTFUL, 4-PARAGRAPH ESSAY ABOUT A BAD HABIT YOU'D LIKE TO CHANGE.
WHAT IF WE **HAVE** NO BAD HABITS?
DOES ANYONE HAVE A **REAL** QUESTION?
YEAH: WHILE EVERYONE ELSE IS WRITING, CAN I SURF THE INTERNET?
Peirce

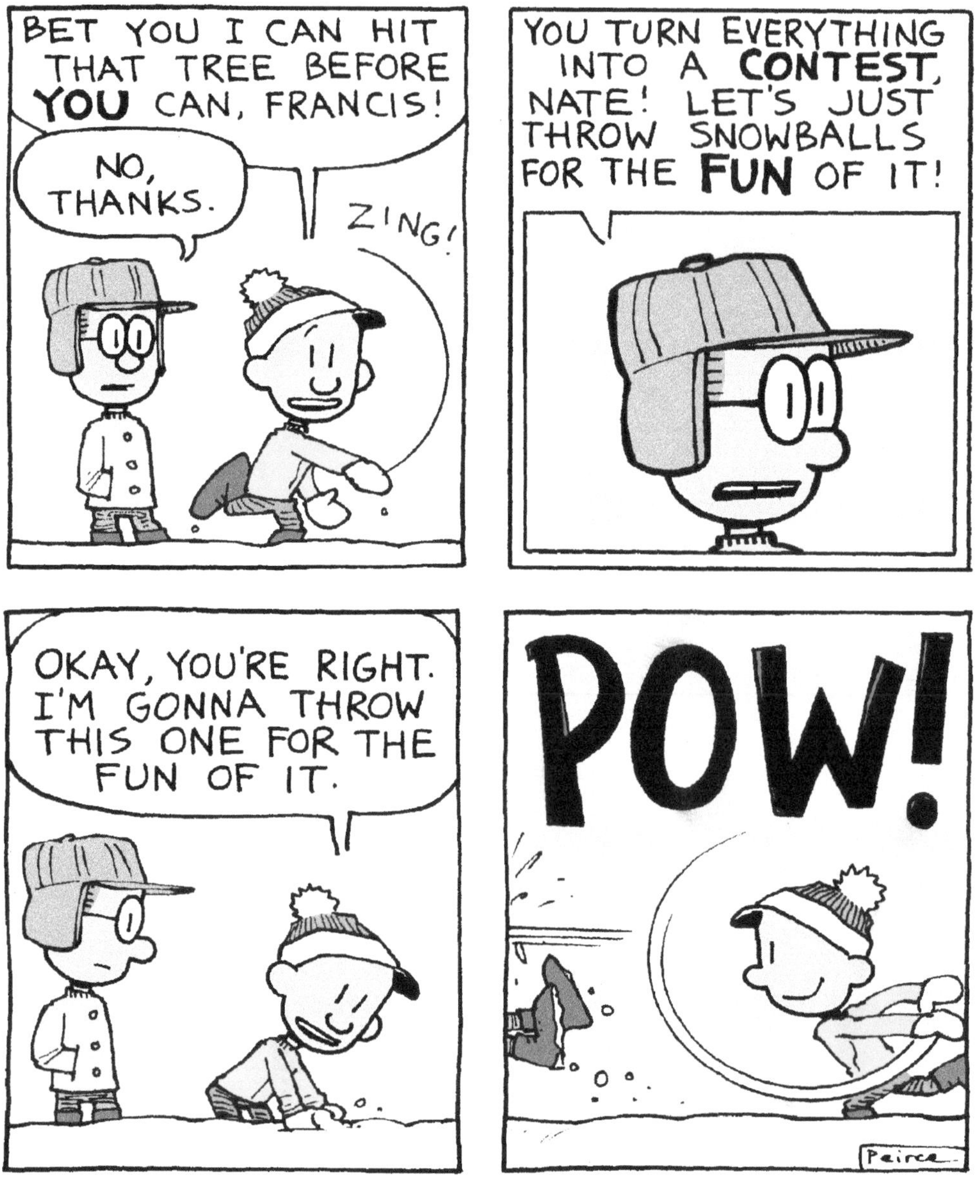
BET YOU I CAN HIT THAT TREE BEFORE **YOU** CAN, FRANCIS!
NO, THANKS.
ZING!
YOU TURN EVERYTHING INTO A **CONTEST**, NATE! LET'S JUST THROW SNOWBALLS FOR THE **FUN** OF IT!
OKAY, YOU'RE RIGHT. I'M GONNA THROW THIS ONE FOR THE FUN OF IT.
POW!
Peirce

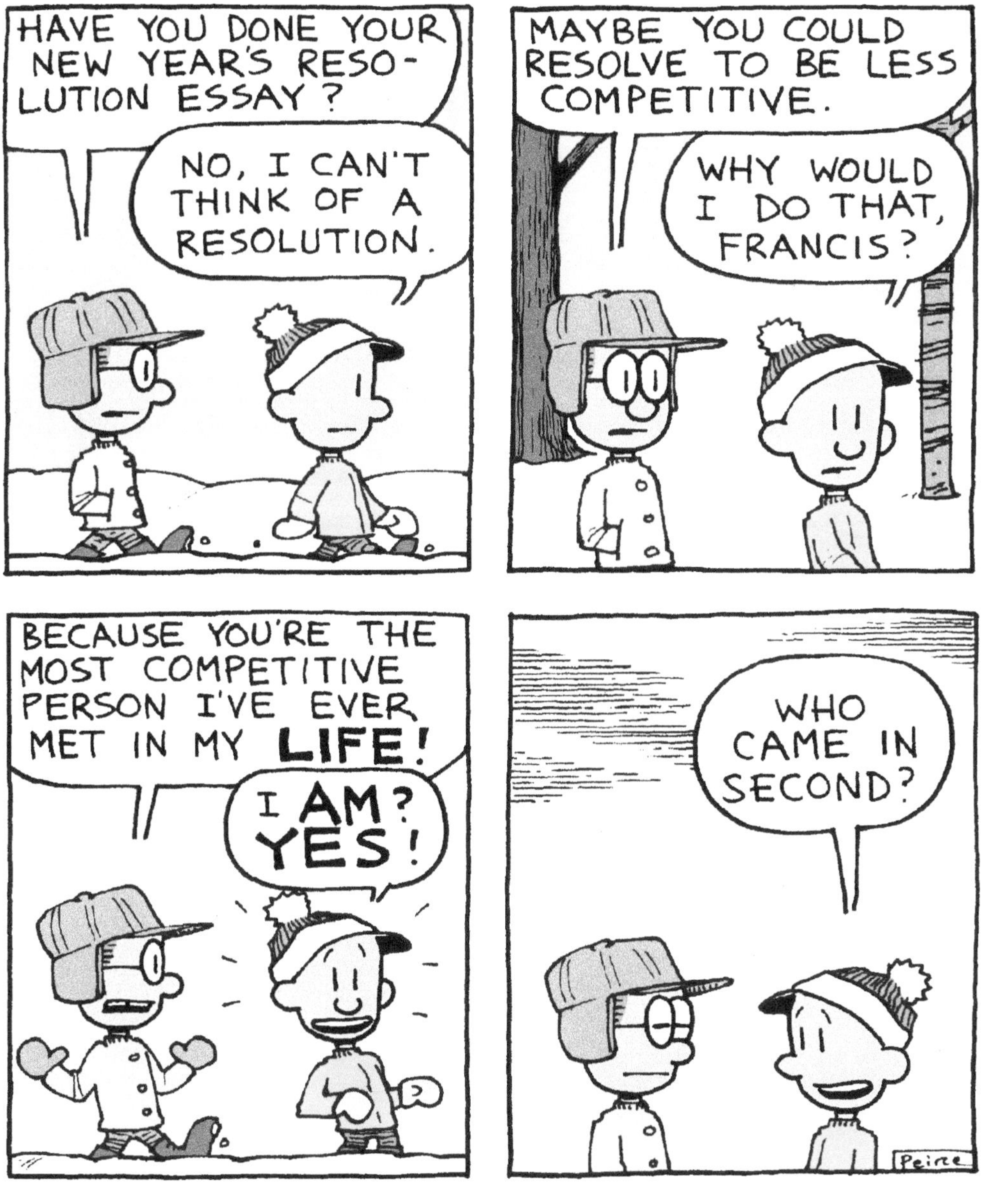
HAVE YOU DONE YOUR NEW YEAR'S RESOLUTION ESSAY?
NO, I CAN'T THINK OF A RESOLUTION.
MAYBE YOU COULD RESOLVE TO BE LESS COMPETITIVE.
WHY WOULD I DO THAT, FRANCIS?
BECAUSE YOU'RE THE MOST COMPETITIVE PERSON I'VE EVER MET IN MY LIFE!
I AM? YES!
WHO CAME IN SECOND?
Peirce

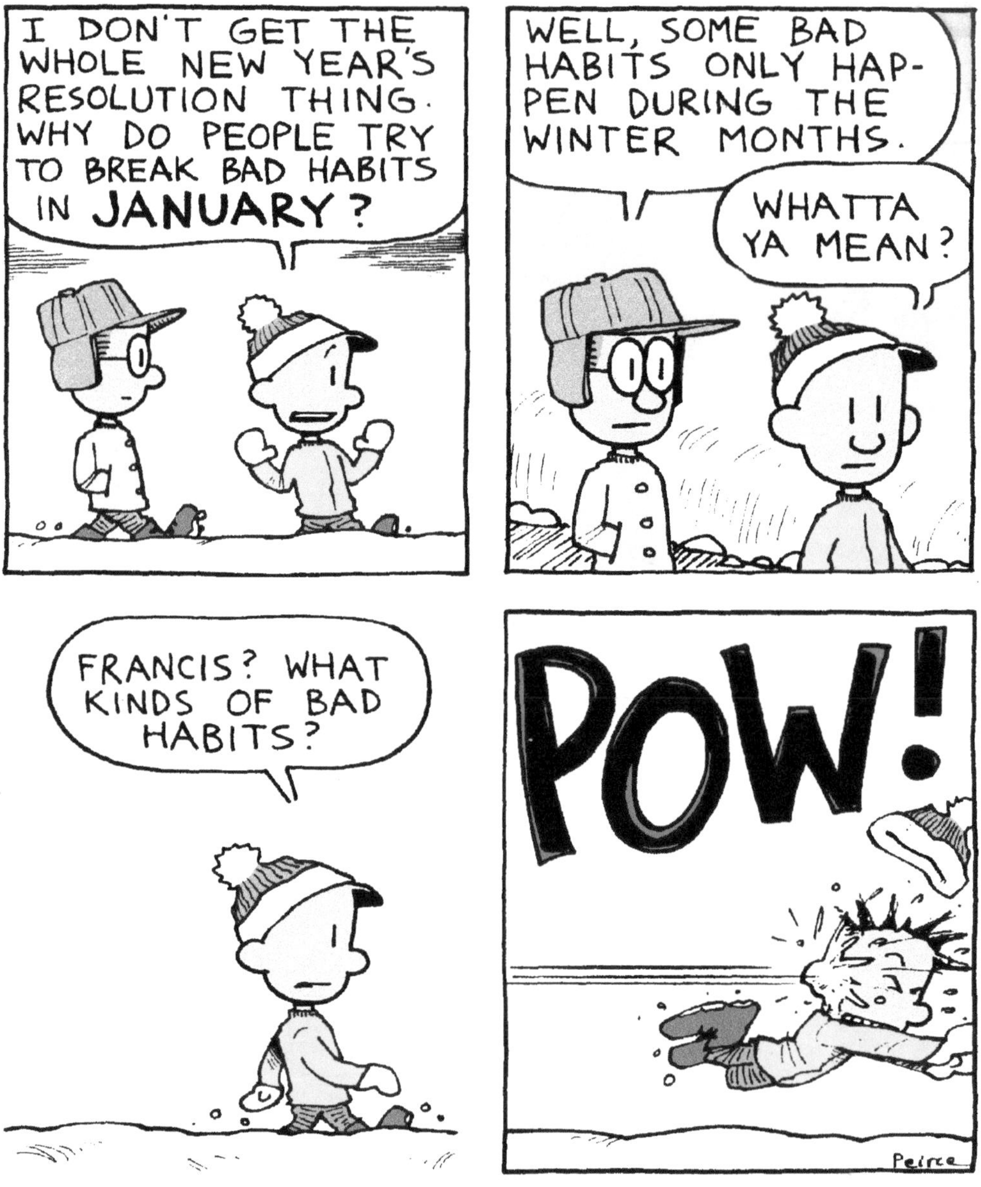
I DON'T GET THE WHOLE NEW YEAR'S RESOLUTION THING. WHY DO PEOPLE TRY TO BREAK BAD HABITS IN **JANUARY**?
WELL, SOME BAD HABITS ONLY HAP-PEN DURING THE WINTER MONTHS.
WHATTA YA MEAN?
FRANCIS? WHAT KINDS OF BAD HABITS?
POW!
Peirce

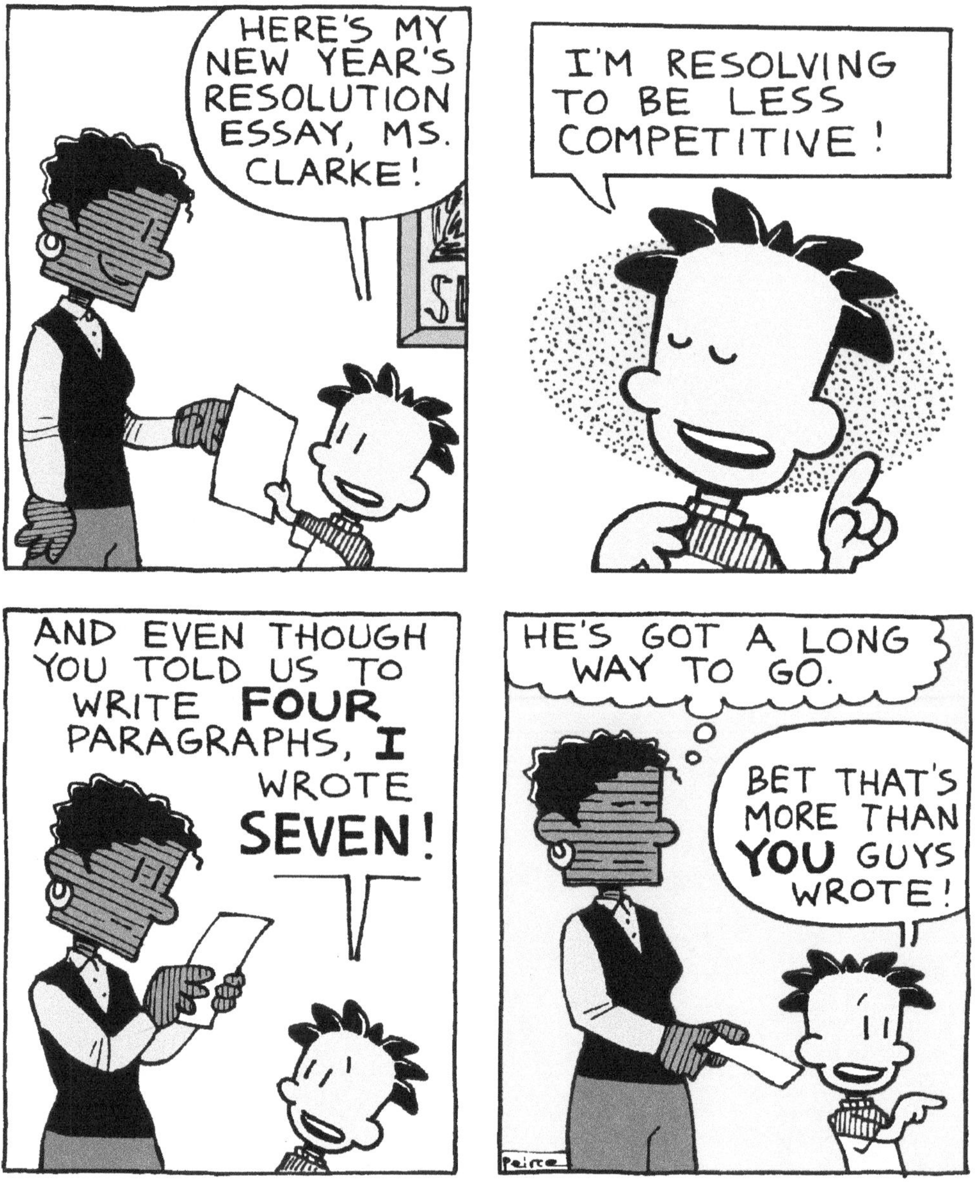
HERE'S MY NEW YEAR'S RESOLUTION ESSAY, MS. CLARKE!
I'M RESOLVING TO BE LESS COMPETITIVE!
AND EVEN THOUGH YOU TOLD US TO WRITE **FOUR** PARAGRAPHS, **I** WROTE **SEVEN**!
HE'S GOT A LONG WAY TO GO.
BET THAT'S MORE THAN **YOU** GUYS WROTE!
Peirce

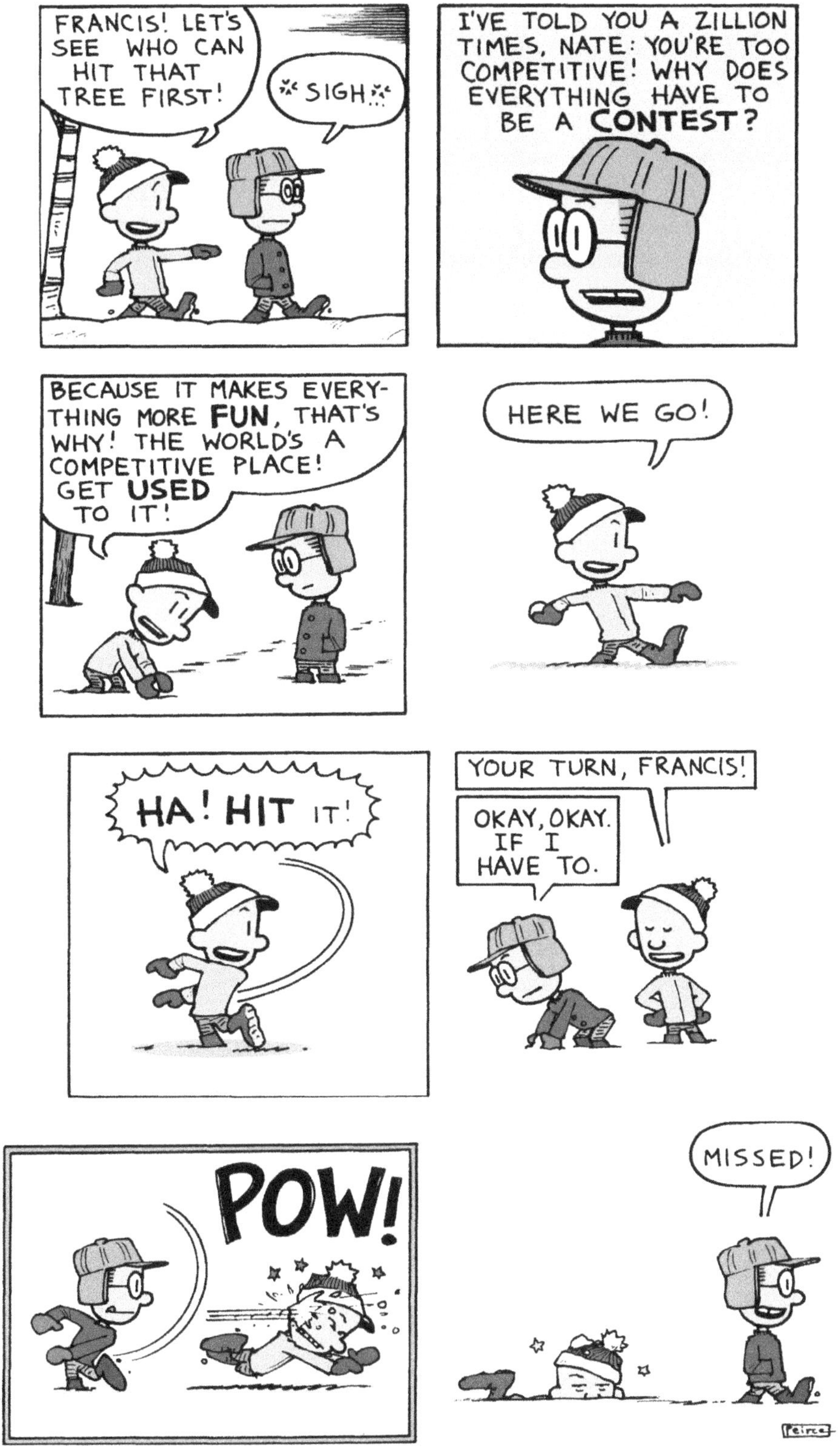
FRANCIS! LET'S SEE WHO CAN HIT THAT TREE FIRST!
SIGH
I'VE TOLD YOU A ZILLION TIMES, NATE: YOU'RE TOO COMPETITIVE! WHY DOES EVERYTHING HAVE TO BE A **CONTEST**?
BECAUSE IT MAKES EVERY-THING MORE **FUN**, THAT'S WHY! THE WORLD'S A COMPETITIVE PLACE! GET **USED** TO IT!
HERE WE GO!
HA! HIT IT!
YOUR TURN, FRANCIS!
OKAY, OKAY. IF I HAVE TO.
POW!
MISSED!
Peirce

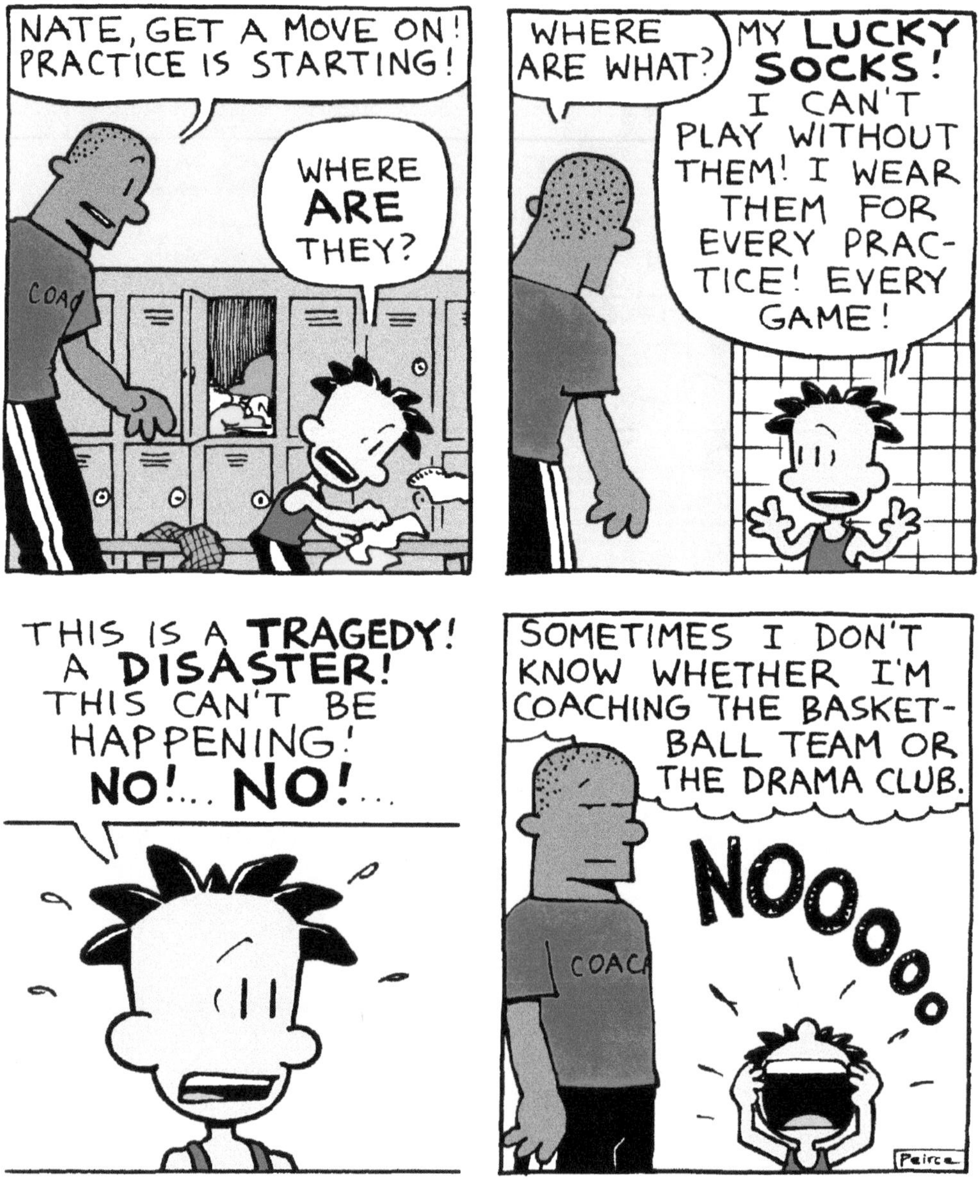
NATE, GET A MOVE ON! PRACTICE IS STARTING!
WHERE ARE THEY?
COACH
WHERE ARE WHAT?
MY LUCKY SOCKS! I CAN'T PLAY WITHOUT THEM! I WEAR THEM FOR EVERY PRACTICE! EVERY GAME!
THIS IS A TRAGEDY! A DISASTER! THIS CAN'T BE HAPPENING! NO!... NO!...
SOMETIMES I DON'T KNOW WHETHER I'M COACHING THE BASKETBALL TEAM OR THE DRAMA CLUB.
NOOOOOO
COACH
Peirce

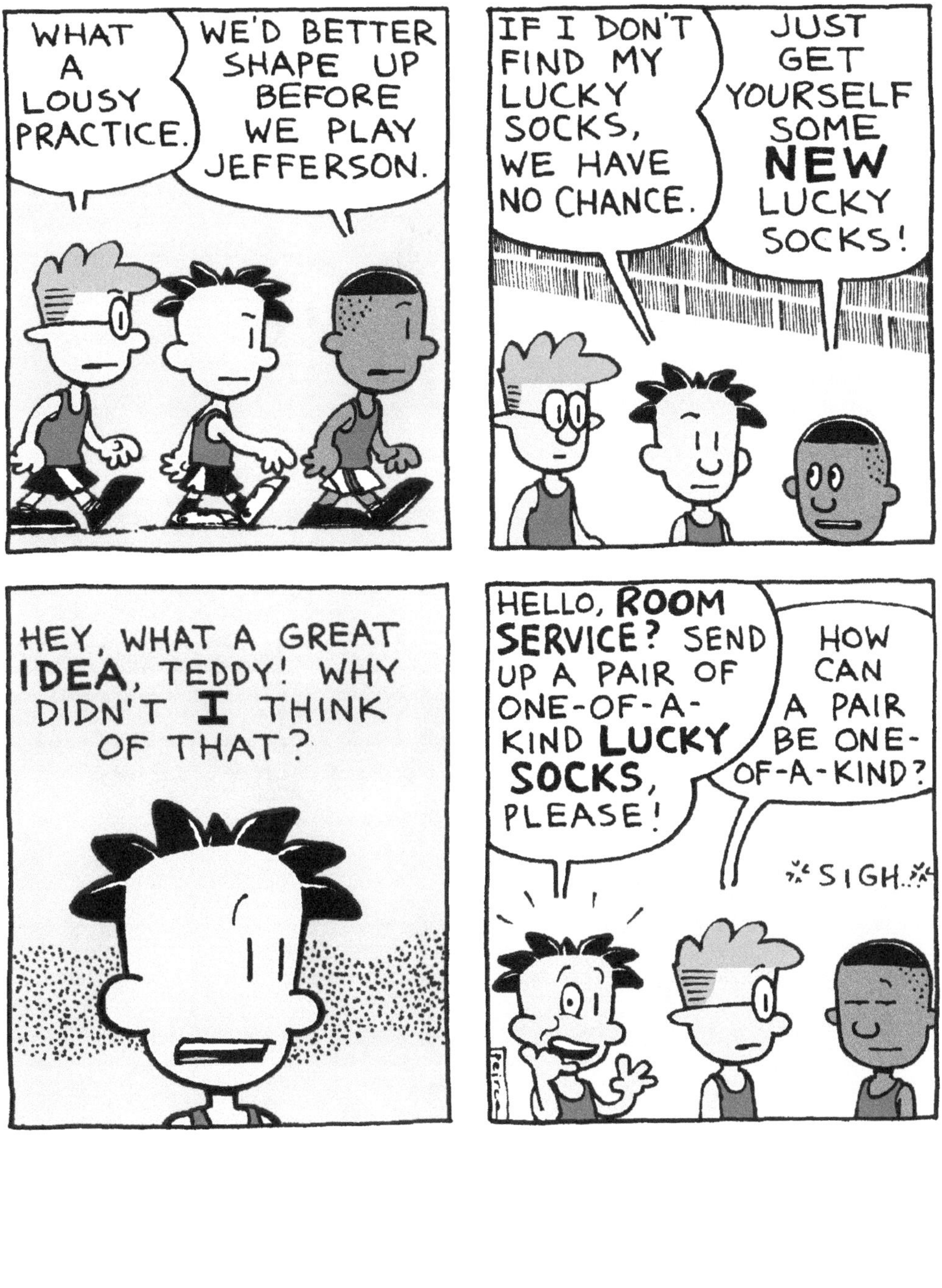
WHAT A LOUSY PRACTICE.
WE'D BETTER SHAPE UP BEFORE WE PLAY JEFFERSON.
IF I DON'T FIND MY LUCKY SOCKS, WE HAVE NO CHANCE.
JUST GET YOURSELF SOME **NEW** LUCKY SOCKS!
HEY, WHAT A GREAT **IDEA**, TEDDY! WHY DIDN'T **I** THINK OF THAT?
HELLO, **ROOM SERVICE?** SEND UP A PAIR OF ONE-OF-A-KIND **LUCKY SOCKS**, PLEASE!
HOW CAN A PAIR BE ONE-OF-A-KIND?
SIGH
Peirce

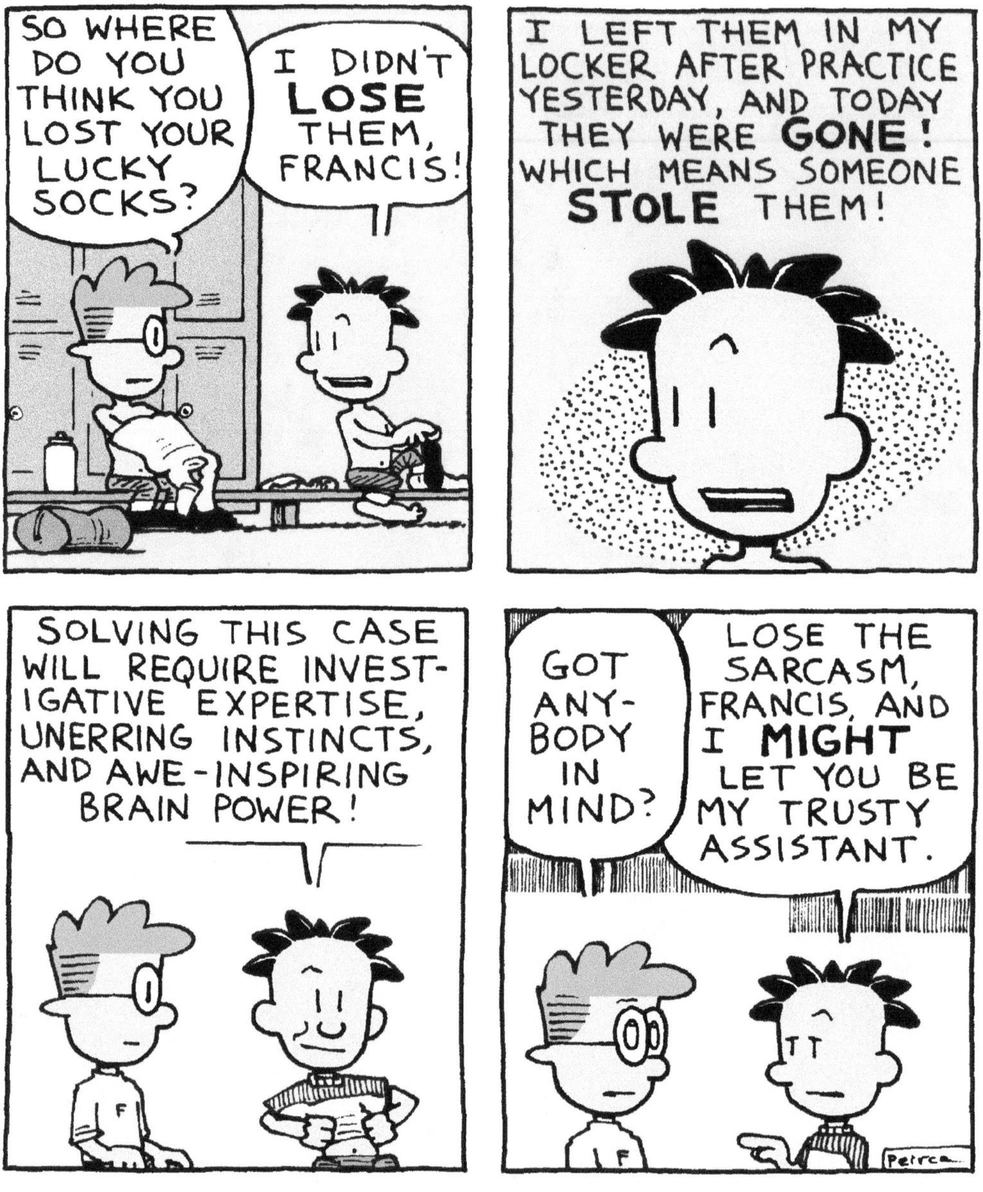
SO WHERE DO YOU THINK YOU LOST YOUR LUCKY SOCKS?
I DIDN'T **LOSE** THEM, FRANCIS!
I LEFT THEM IN MY LOCKER AFTER PRACTICE YESTERDAY, AND TODAY THEY WERE **GONE!** WHICH MEANS SOMEONE **STOLE** THEM!
SOLVING THIS CASE WILL REQUIRE INVESTIGATIVE EXPERTISE, UNERRING INSTINCTS, AND AWE-INSPIRING BRAIN POWER!
GOT ANYBODY IN MIND?
LOSE THE SARCASM, FRANCIS, AND I **MIGHT** LET YOU BE MY TRUSTY ASSISTANT.
F
F
F
Peirce

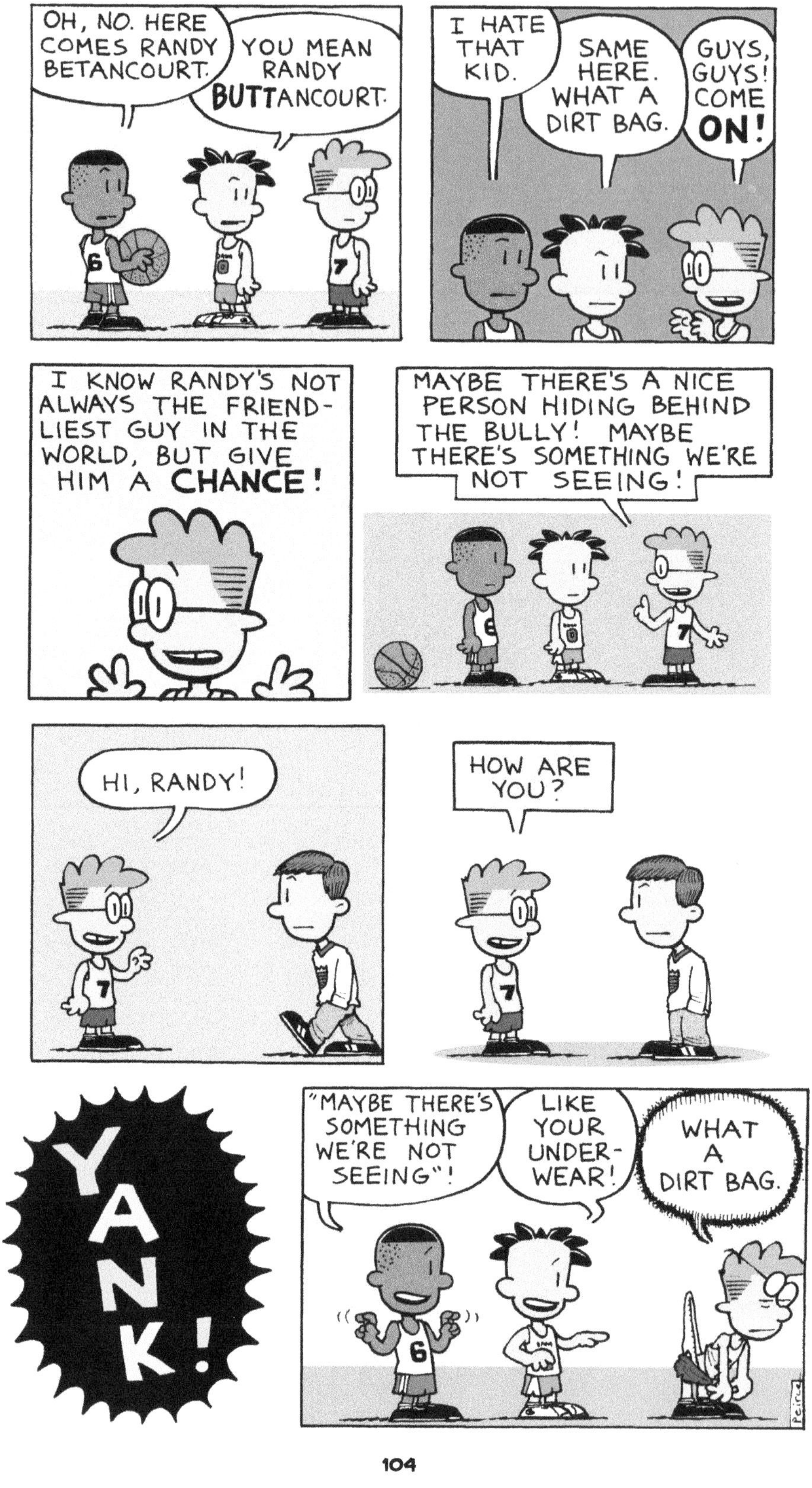
OH, NO. HERE COMES RANDY BETANCOURT.
YOU MEAN RANDY BUTTANCOURT.
I HATE THAT KID.
SAME HERE. WHAT A DIRT BAG.
GUYS, GUYS! COME ON!
I KNOW RANDY'S NOT ALWAYS THE FRIEND-LIEST GUY IN THE WORLD, BUT GIVE HIM A CHANCE!
MAYBE THERE'S A NICE PERSON HIDING BEHIND THE BULLY! MAYBE THERE'S SOMETHING WE'RE NOT SEEING!
HI, RANDY!
HOW ARE YOU?
YANK!
"MAYBE THERE'S SOMETHING WE'RE NOT SEEING"!
LIKE YOUR UNDER-WEAR!
WHAT A DIRT BAG.
Peirce

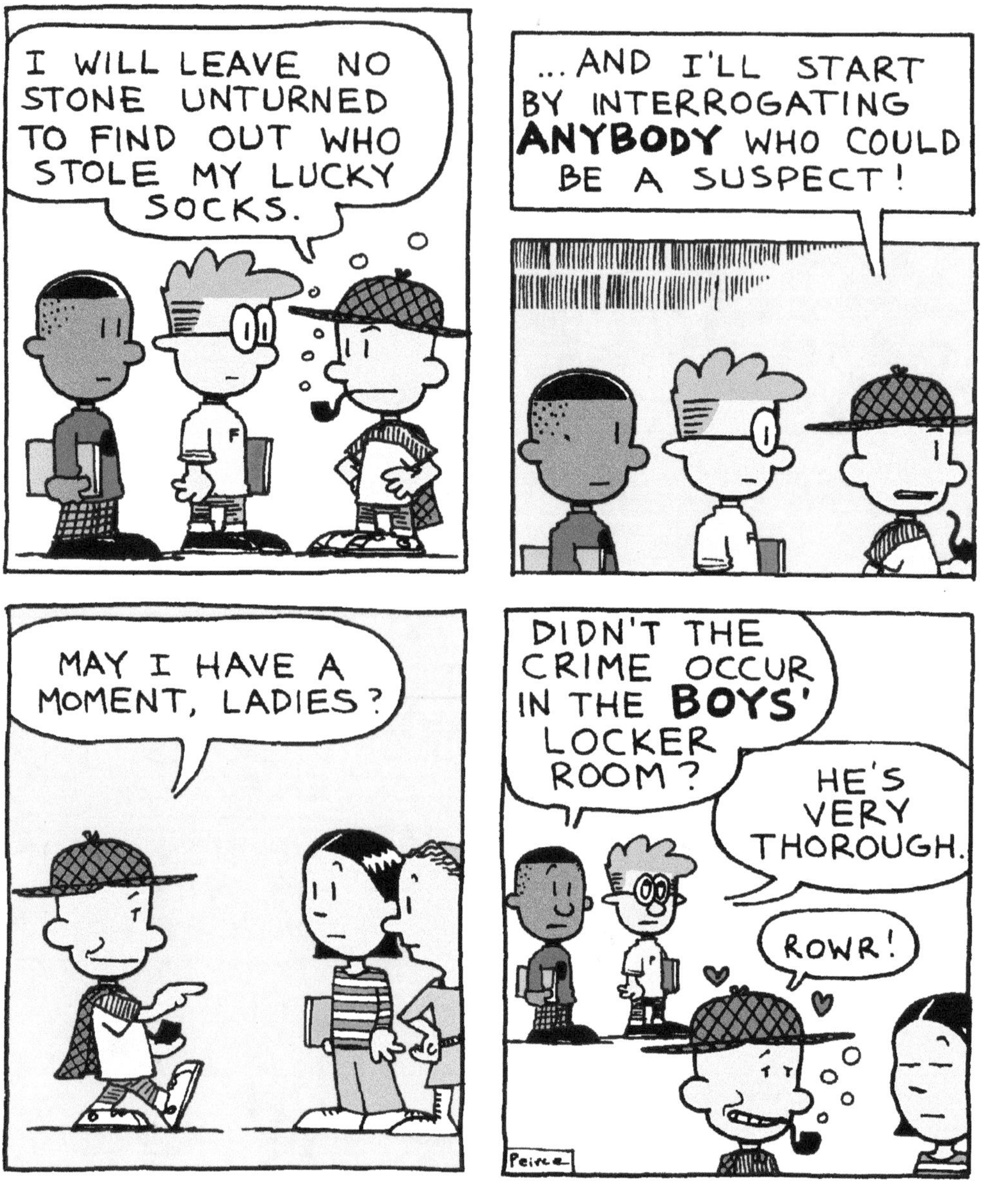
I WILL LEAVE NO STONE UNTURNED TO FIND OUT WHO STOLE MY LUCKY SOCKS.
...AND I'LL START BY INTERROGATING **ANYBODY** WHO COULD BE A SUSPECT!
MAY I HAVE A MOMENT, LADIES?
DIDN'T THE CRIME OCCUR IN THE **BOYS'** LOCKER ROOM?
HE'S VERY THOROUGH.
ROWR!
Peirce

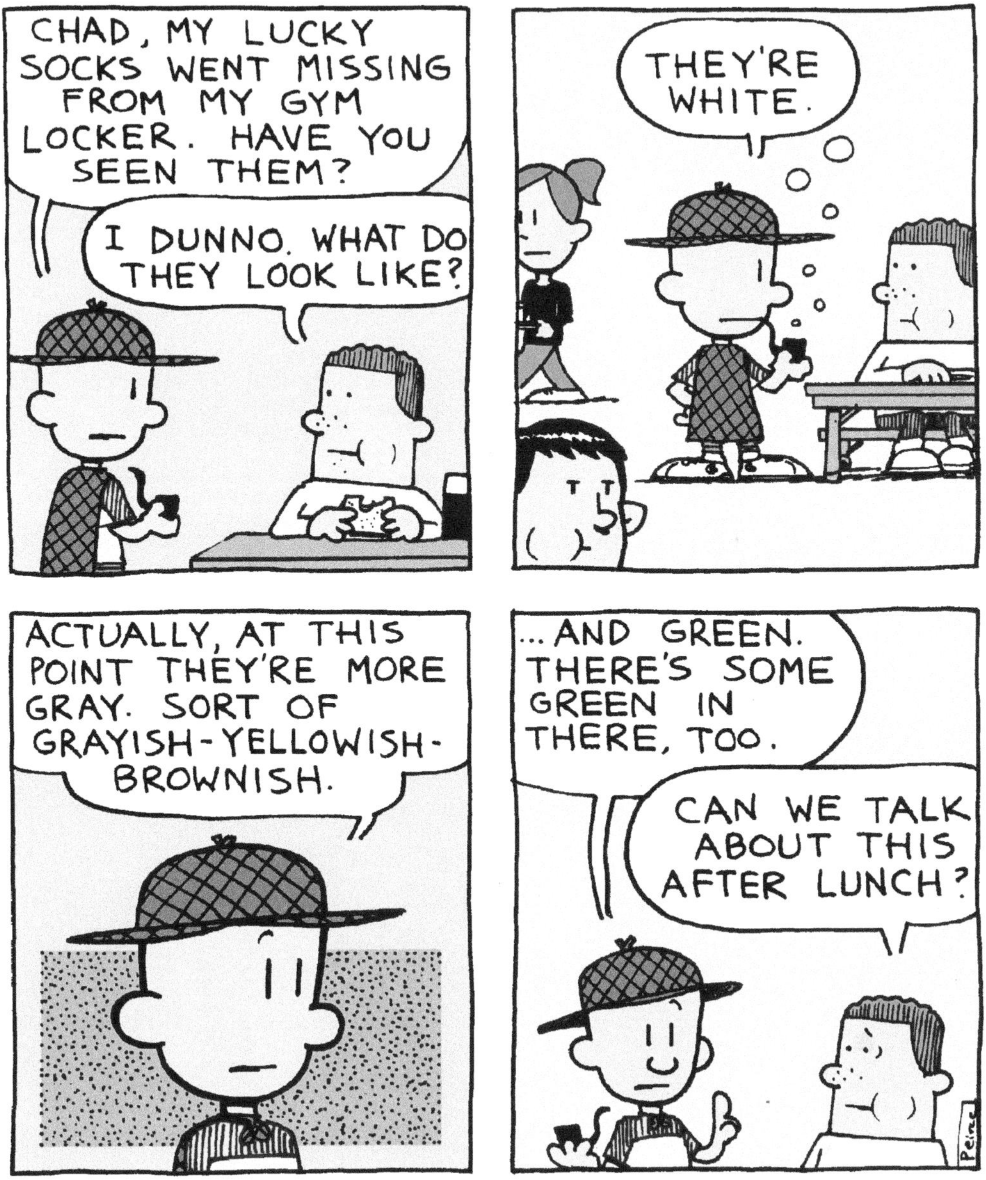
CHAD, MY LUCKY SOCKS WENT MISSING FROM MY GYM LOCKER. HAVE YOU SEEN THEM?
I DUNNO. WHAT DO THEY LOOK LIKE?
THEY'RE WHITE.
ACTUALLY, AT THIS POINT THEY'RE MORE GRAY. SORT OF GRAYISH-YELLOWISH-BROWNISH.
...AND GREEN. THERE'S SOME GREEN IN THERE, TOO.
CAN WE TALK ABOUT THIS AFTER LUNCH?
Peirce

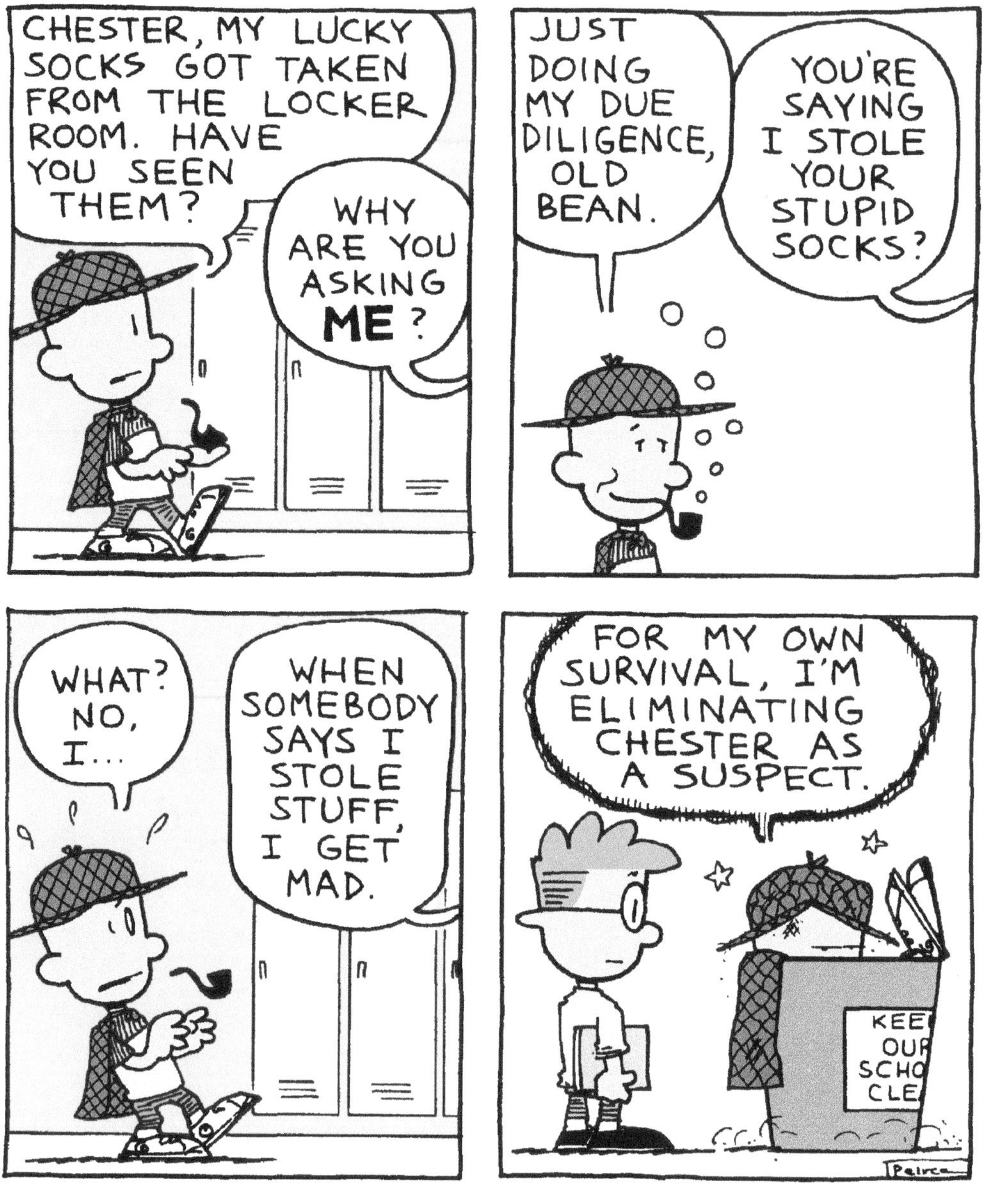
CHESTER, MY LUCKY SOCKS GOT TAKEN FROM THE LOCKER ROOM. HAVE YOU SEEN THEM?
WHY ARE YOU ASKING ME?
JUST DOING MY DUE DILIGENCE, OLD BEAN.
YOU'RE SAYING I STOLE YOUR STUPID SOCKS?
WHAT? NO, I...
WHEN SOMEBODY SAYS I STOLE STUFF, I GET MAD.
FOR MY OWN SURVIVAL, I'M ELIMINATING CHESTER AS A SUSPECT.
KEE
OUR
SCHO
CLE
Peirce

WHOEVER STOLE MY LUCKY SOCKS IS PROBABLY WEARING THEM **RIGHT NOW!**

WHO WOULD **DO** THAT? WHO WOULD SINK TO SUCH NEFARIOUS DEPTHS?

WHAT SORT OF WEIRDO ARE WE **TALKING** ABOUT HERE?

THIS IS WHERE I POINT OUT THAT YOU'VE WORN A HALLOWEEN COSTUME TO SCHOOL ALL WEEK.

EXACTLY. **SOME**ONE'S GOT TO FERRET OUT THE NUT JOBS.

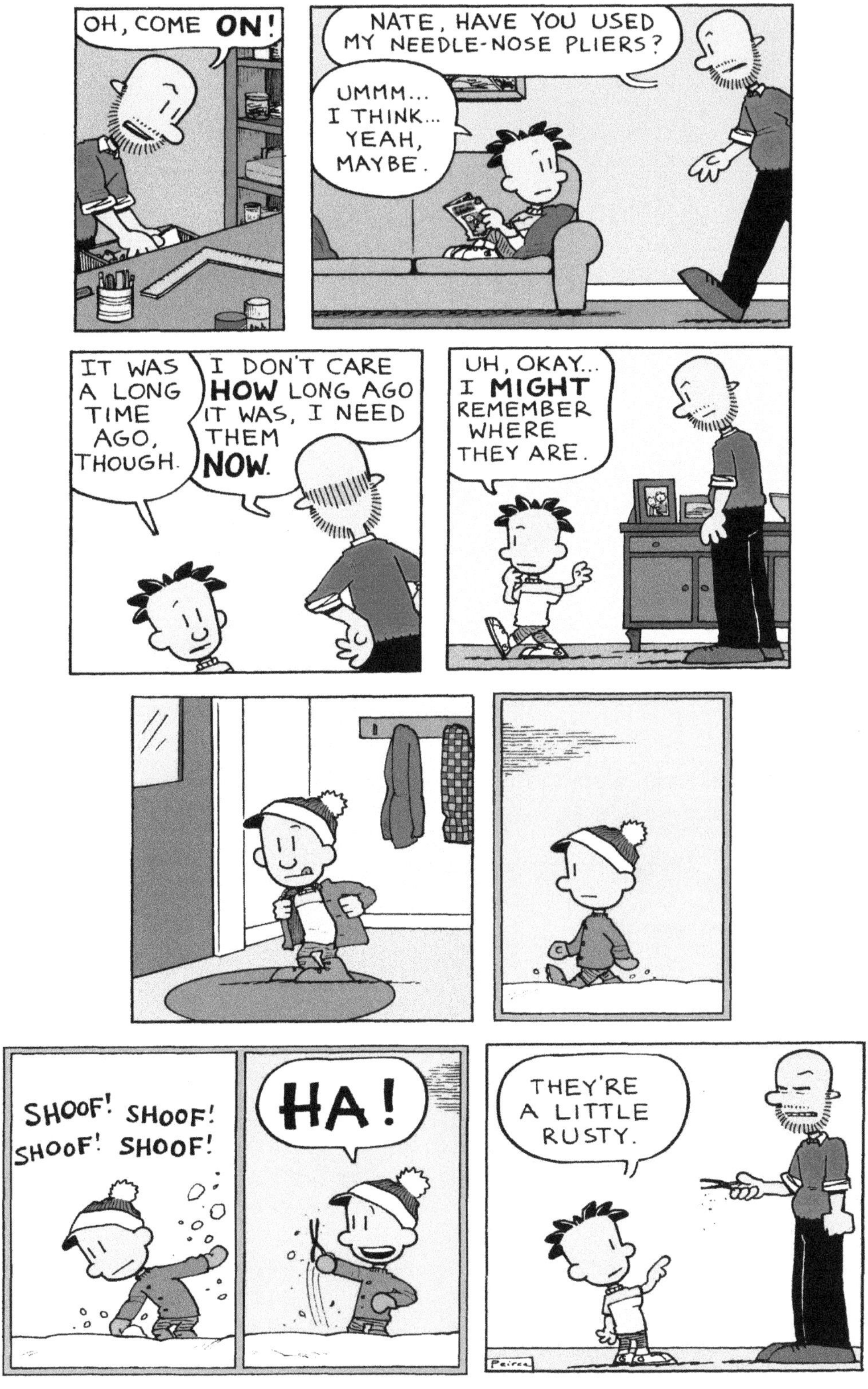
OH, COME **ON**!
NATE, HAVE YOU USED MY NEEDLE-NOSE PLIERS?
UMMM... I THINK... YEAH, MAYBE.
IT WAS A LONG TIME AGO, THOUGH.
I DON'T CARE **HOW** LONG AGO IT WAS, I NEED THEM **NOW**.
UH, OKAY... I **MIGHT** REMEMBER WHERE THEY ARE.
SHOOF! SHOOF! SHOOF! SHOOF!
HA!
THEY'RE A LITTLE RUSTY.
Peirce

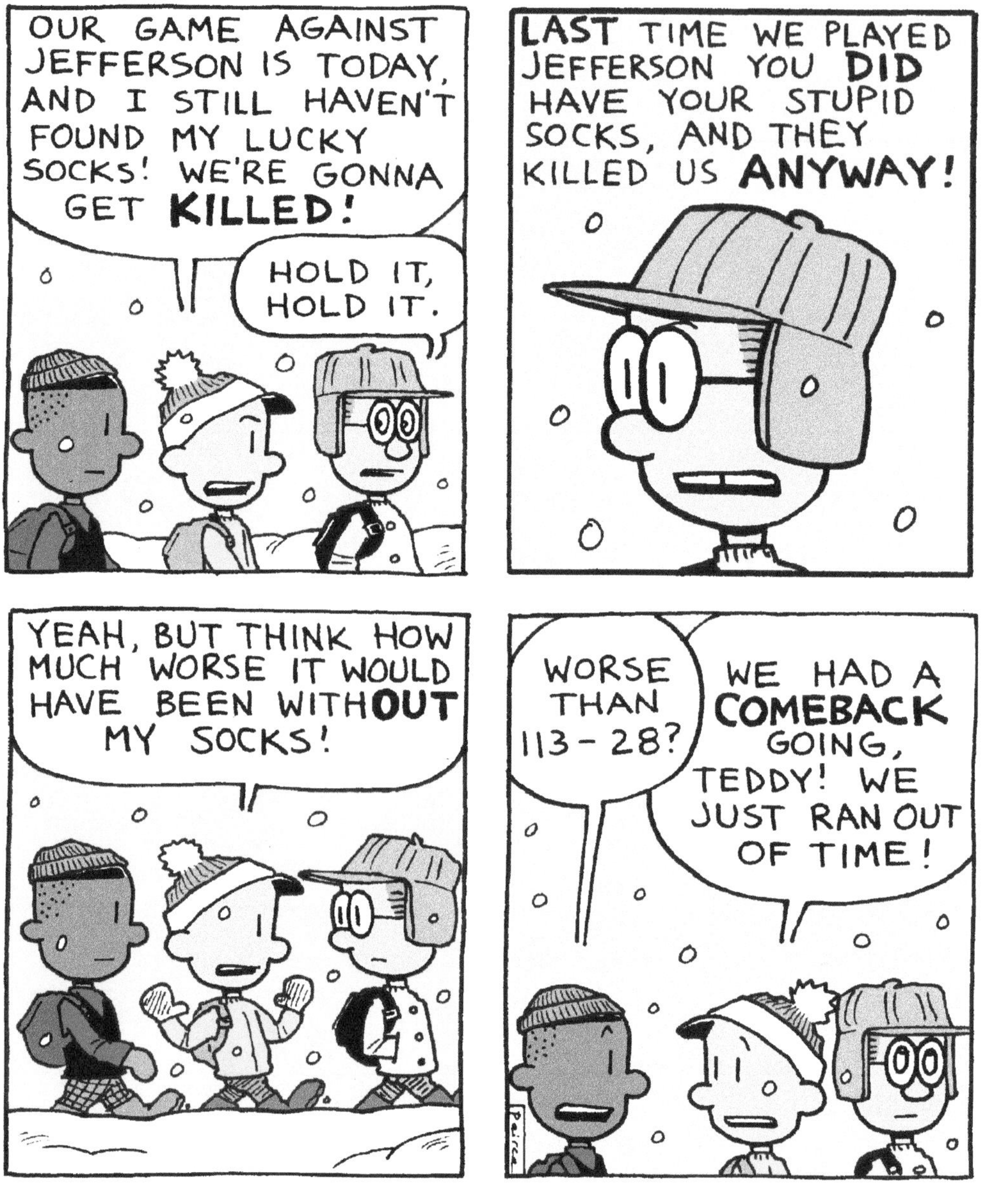
OUR GAME AGAINST JEFFERSON IS TODAY, AND I STILL HAVEN'T FOUND MY LUCKY SOCKS! WE'RE GONNA GET KILLED!
HOLD IT, HOLD IT.
LAST TIME WE PLAYED JEFFERSON YOU DID HAVE YOUR STUPID SOCKS, AND THEY KILLED US ANYWAY!
YEAH, BUT THINK HOW MUCH WORSE IT WOULD HAVE BEEN WITHOUT MY SOCKS!
WORSE THAN 113-28?
WE HAD A COMEBACK GOING, TEDDY! WE JUST RAN OUT OF TIME!

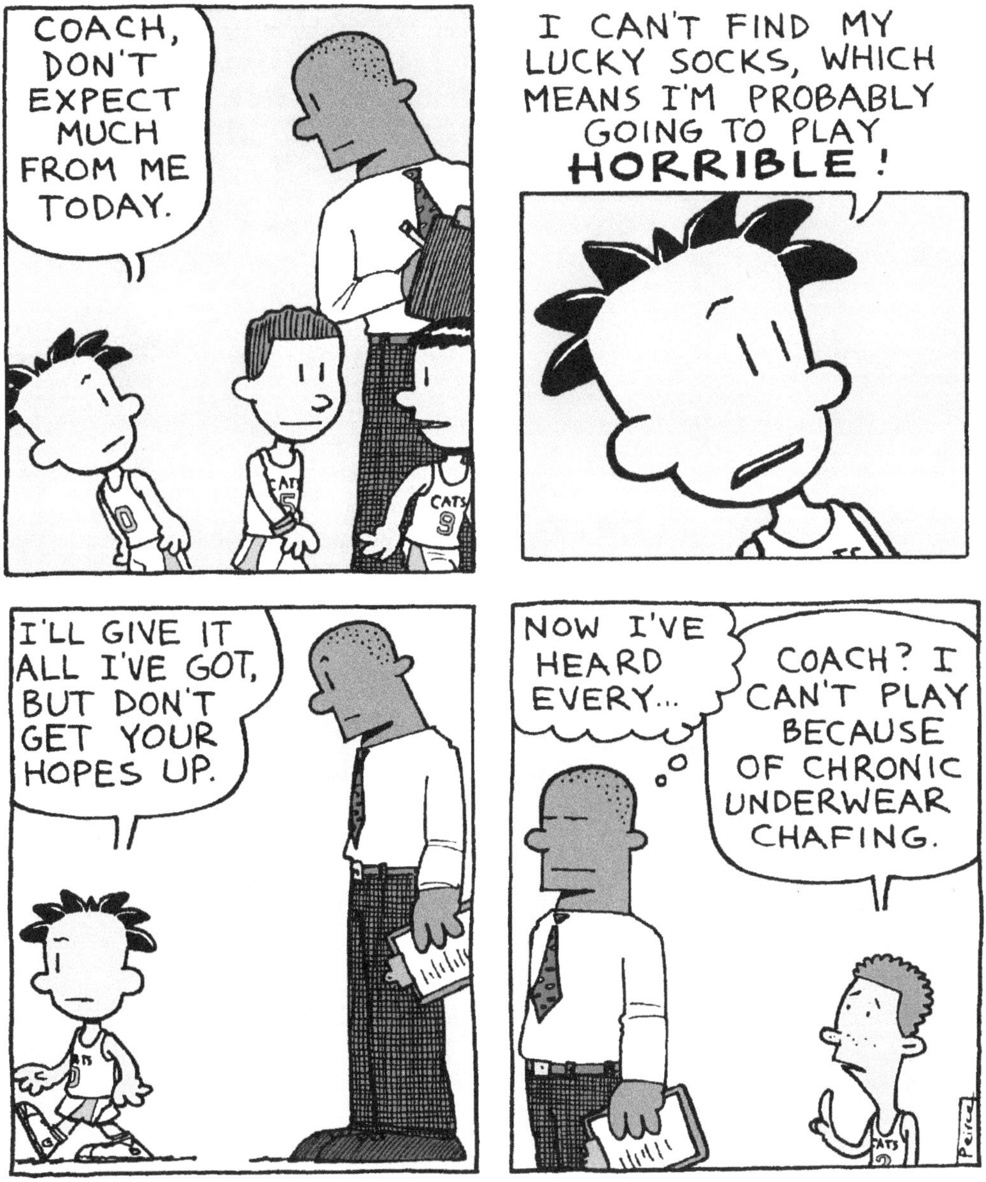
COACH, DON'T EXPECT MUCH FROM ME TODAY.
CATS
CATS 9
I CAN'T FIND MY LUCKY SOCKS, WHICH MEANS I'M PROBABLY GOING TO PLAY **HORRIBLE**!
I'LL GIVE IT ALL I'VE GOT, BUT DON'T GET YOUR HOPES UP.
NOW I'VE HEARD EVERY...
COACH? I CAN'T PLAY BECAUSE OF CHRONIC UNDERWEAR CHAFING.
Peirce

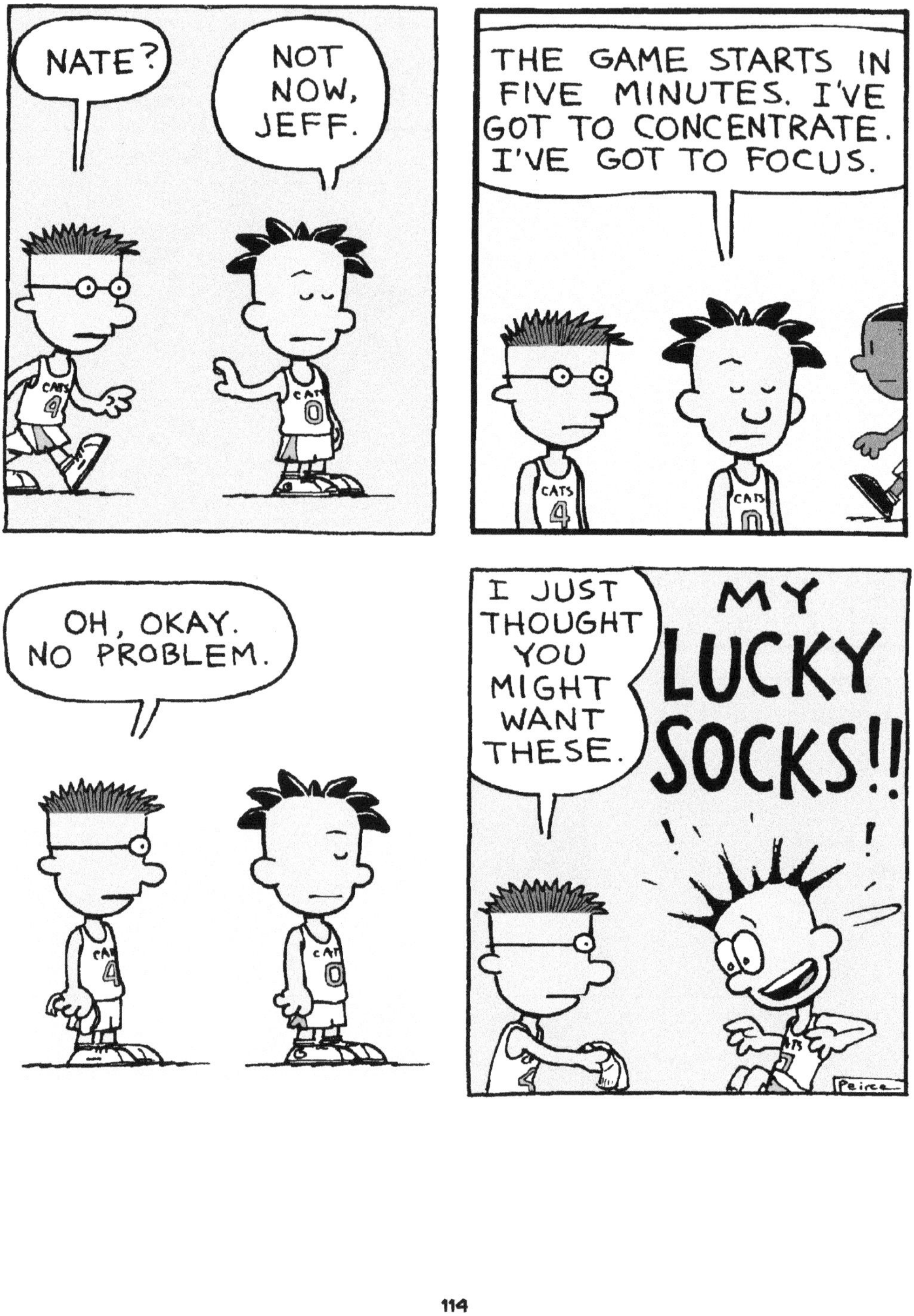
NATE?
NOT NOW, JEFF.
THE GAME STARTS IN FIVE MINUTES. I'VE GOT TO CONCENTRATE. I'VE GOT TO FOCUS.
OH, OKAY. NO PROBLEM.
I JUST THOUGHT YOU MIGHT WANT THESE.
MY LUCKY SOCKS!!
Peirce

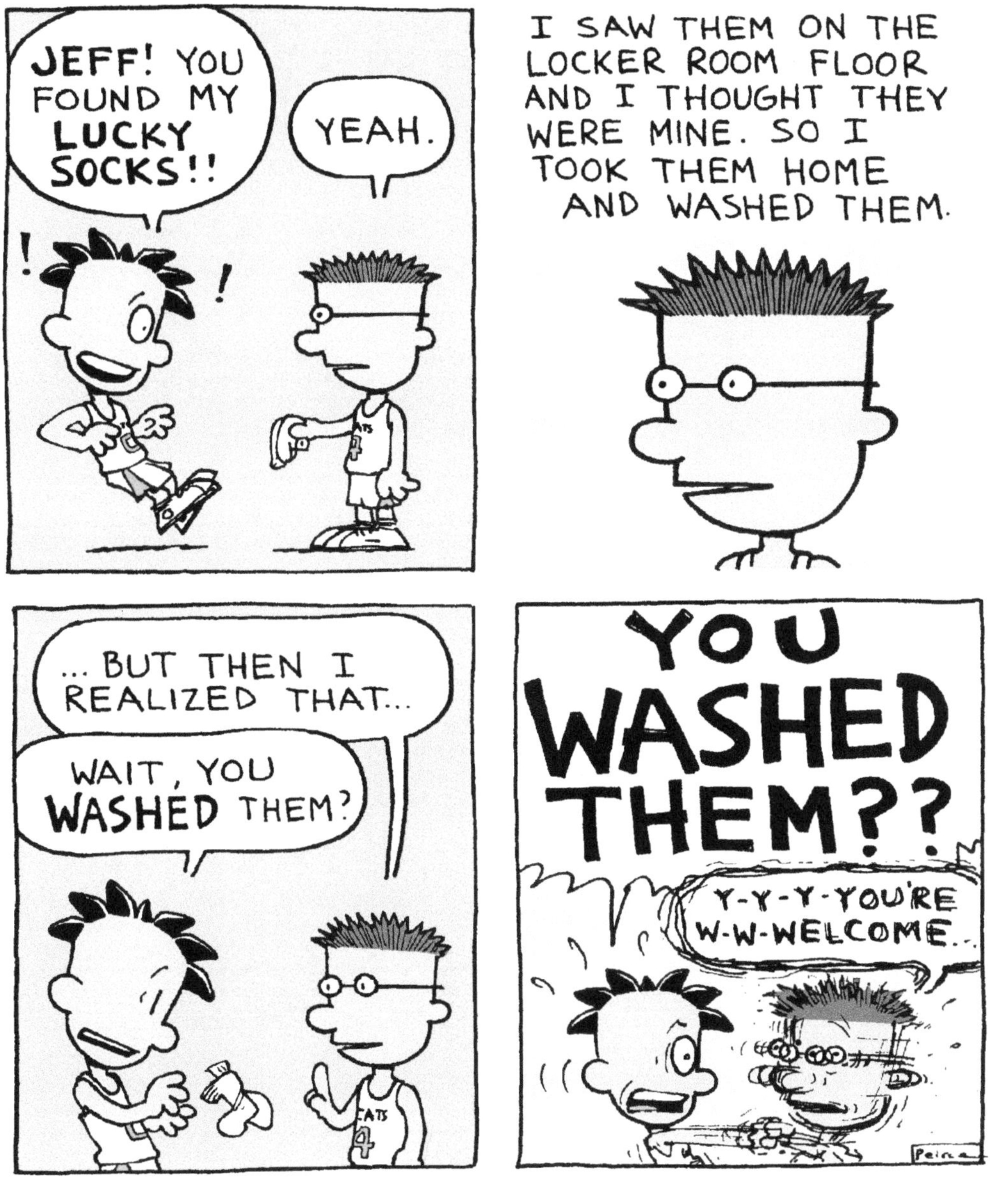
JEFF! YOU FOUND MY LUCKY SOCKS!!
YEAH.
I SAW THEM ON THE LOCKER ROOM FLOOR AND I THOUGHT THEY WERE MINE. SO I TOOK THEM HOME AND WASHED THEM.
... BUT THEN I REALIZED THAT...
WAIT, YOU WASHED THEM?
YOU WASHED THEM??
Y-Y-Y-YOU'RE W-W-WELCOME...

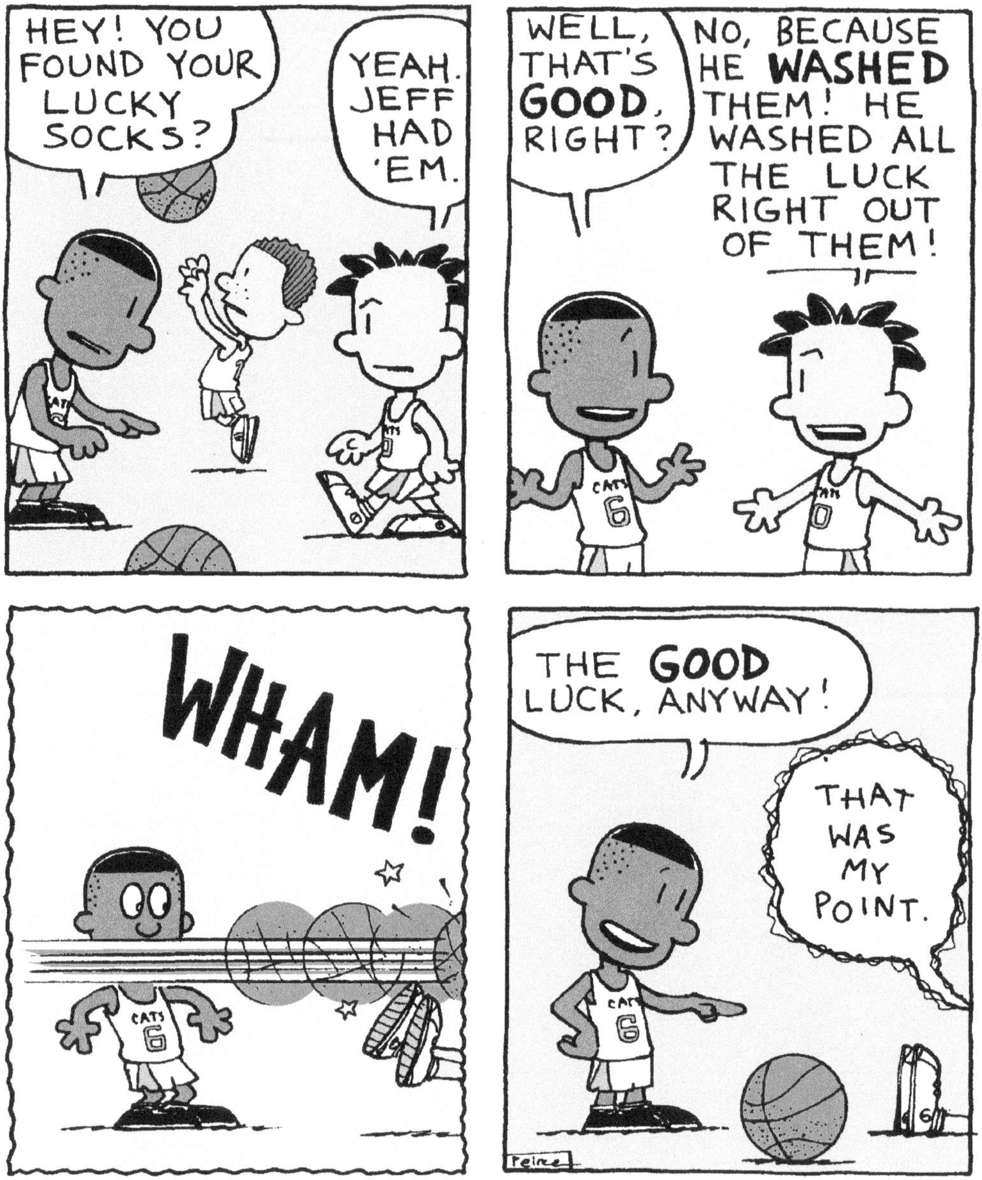
HEY! YOU FOUND YOUR LUCKY SOCKS?
YEAH. JEFF HAD 'EM.
WELL, THAT'S GOOD, RIGHT?
NO, BECAUSE HE WASHED THEM! HE WASHED ALL THE LUCK RIGHT OUT OF THEM!
WHAM!
THE GOOD LUCK, ANYWAY!
THAT WAS MY POINT.
Peirce

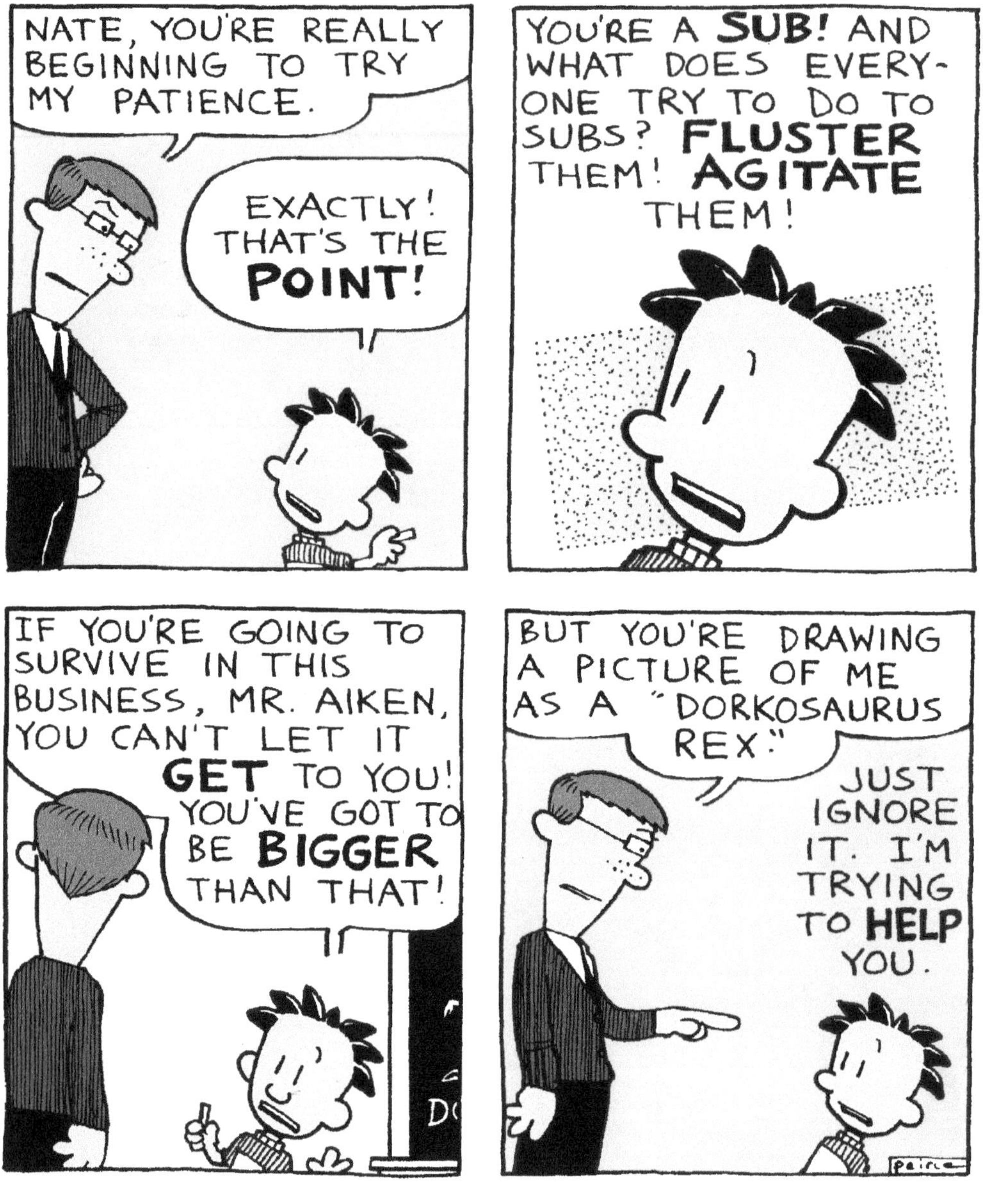
NATE, YOU'RE REALLY BEGINNING TO TRY MY PATIENCE.
EXACTLY! THAT'S THE **POINT**!
YOU'RE A **SUB!** AND WHAT DOES EVERY-ONE TRY TO DO TO SUBS? **FLUSTER** THEM! **AGITATE** THEM!
IF YOU'RE GOING TO SURVIVE IN THIS BUSINESS, MR. AIKEN, YOU CAN'T LET IT **GET** TO YOU! YOU'VE GOT TO BE **BIGGER** THAN THAT!
BUT YOU'RE DRAWING A PICTURE OF ME AS A "DORKOSAURUS REX."
JUST IGNORE IT. I'M TRYING TO **HELP** YOU.
peirce

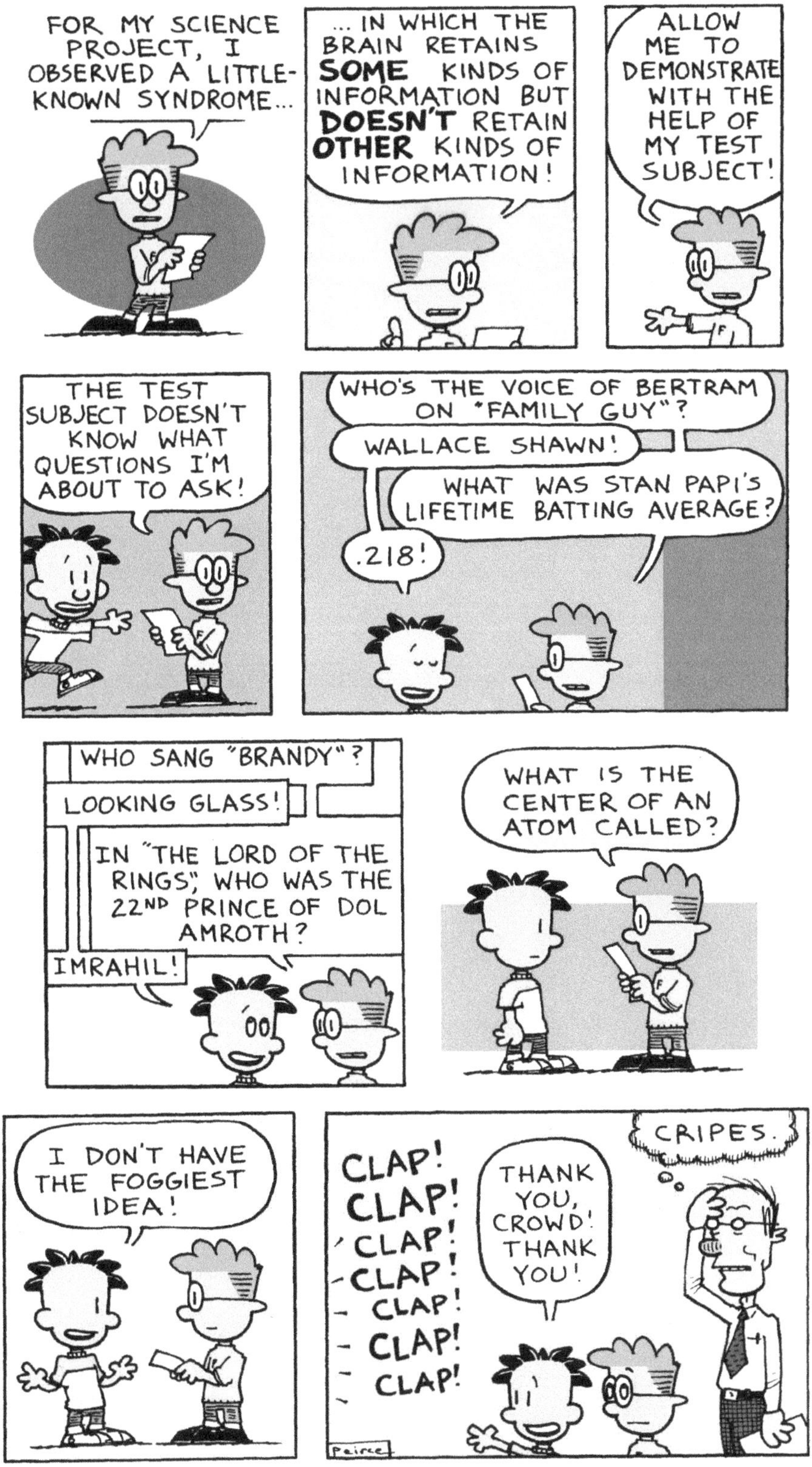
FOR MY SCIENCE PROJECT, I OBSERVED A LITTLE-KNOWN SYNDROME...
... IN WHICH THE BRAIN RETAINS **SOME** KINDS OF INFORMATION BUT **DOESN'T** RETAIN **OTHER** KINDS OF INFORMATION!
ALLOW ME TO DEMONSTRATE WITH THE HELP OF MY TEST SUBJECT!
THE TEST SUBJECT DOESN'T KNOW WHAT QUESTIONS I'M ABOUT TO ASK!
WHO'S THE VOICE OF BERTRAM ON "FAMILY GUY"?
WALLACE SHAWN!
WHAT WAS STAN PAPI'S LIFETIME BATTING AVERAGE?
.218!
WHO SANG "BRANDY"?
LOOKING GLASS!
IN "THE LORD OF THE RINGS," WHO WAS THE 22ND PRINCE OF DOL AMROTH?
IMRAHIL!
WHAT IS THE CENTER OF AN ATOM CALLED?
I DON'T HAVE THE FOGGIEST IDEA!
CLAP! CLAP! CLAP! CLAP! CLAP! CLAP! CLAP!
THANK YOU, CROWD! THANK YOU!
CRIPES.
Peirce

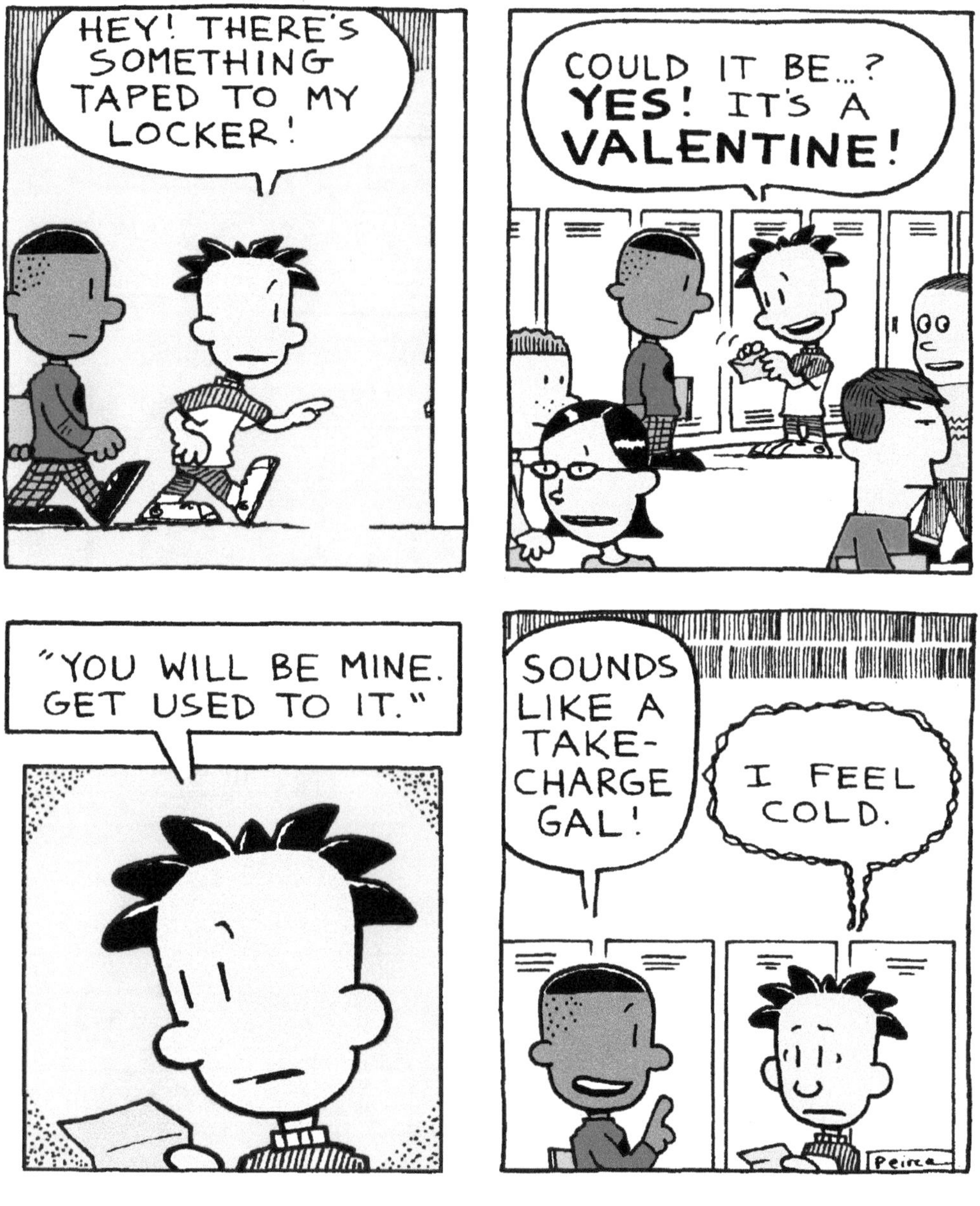
HEY! THERE'S SOMETHING TAPED TO MY LOCKER!
COULD IT BE...? YES! IT'S A VALENTINE!
"YOU WILL BE MINE. GET USED TO IT."
SOUNDS LIKE A TAKE-CHARGE GAL!
I FEEL COLD.
Peirce

130

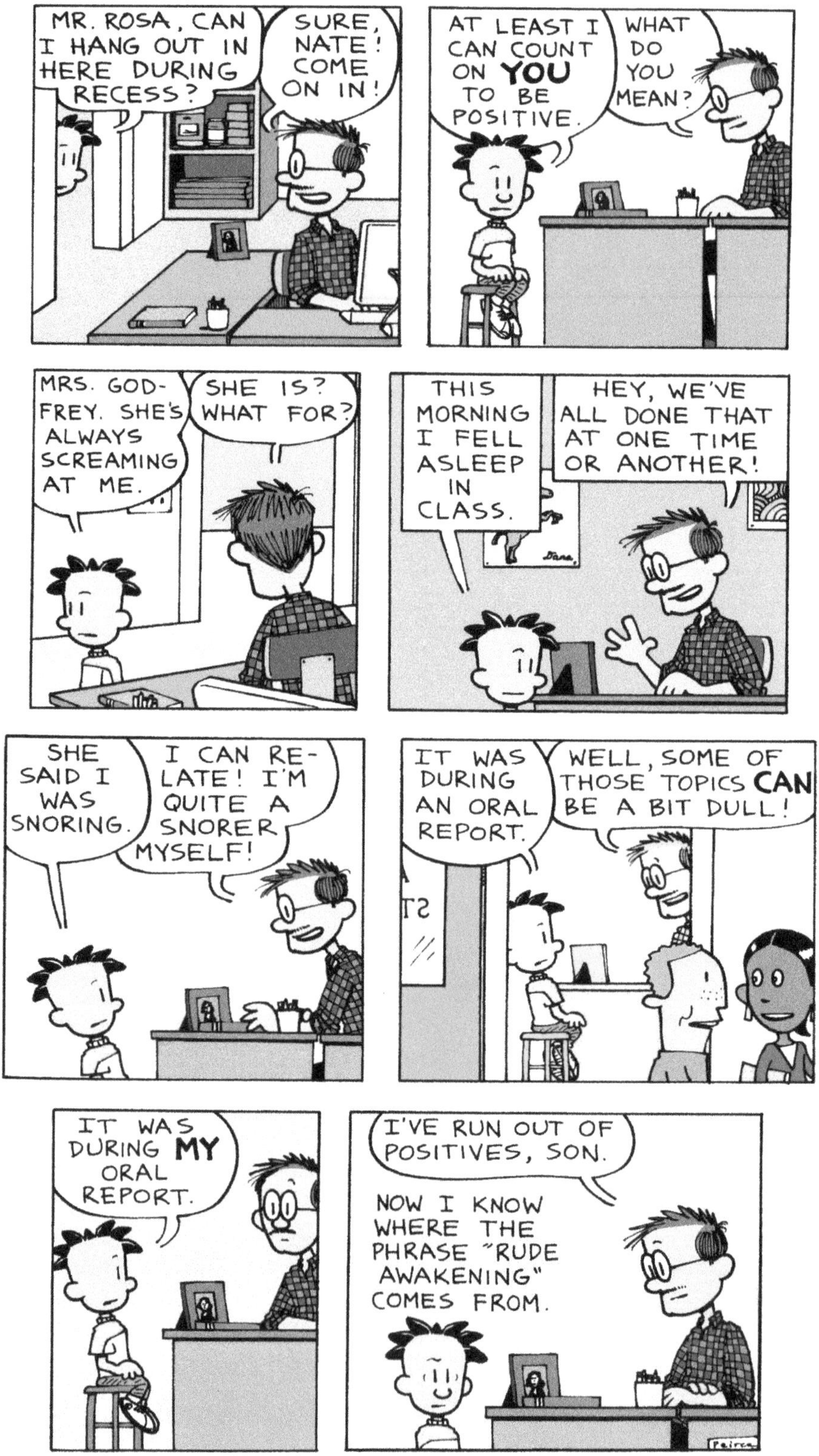
MR. ROSA, CAN I HANG OUT IN HERE DURING RECESS?
SURE, NATE! COME ON IN!
AT LEAST I CAN COUNT ON **YOU** TO BE POSITIVE.
WHAT DO YOU MEAN?
MRS. GODFREY. SHE'S ALWAYS SCREAMING AT ME.
SHE IS? WHAT FOR?
THIS MORNING I FELL ASLEEP IN CLASS.
HEY, WE'VE ALL DONE THAT AT ONE TIME OR ANOTHER!
SHE SAID I WAS SNORING.
I CAN RELATE! I'M QUITE A SNORER MYSELF!
IT WAS DURING AN ORAL REPORT.
WELL, SOME OF THOSE TOPICS **CAN** BE A BIT DULL!
IT WAS DURING **MY** ORAL REPORT.
I'VE RUN OUT OF POSITIVES, SON.
NOW I KNOW WHERE THE PHRASE "RUDE AWAKENING" COMES FROM.
Peirce

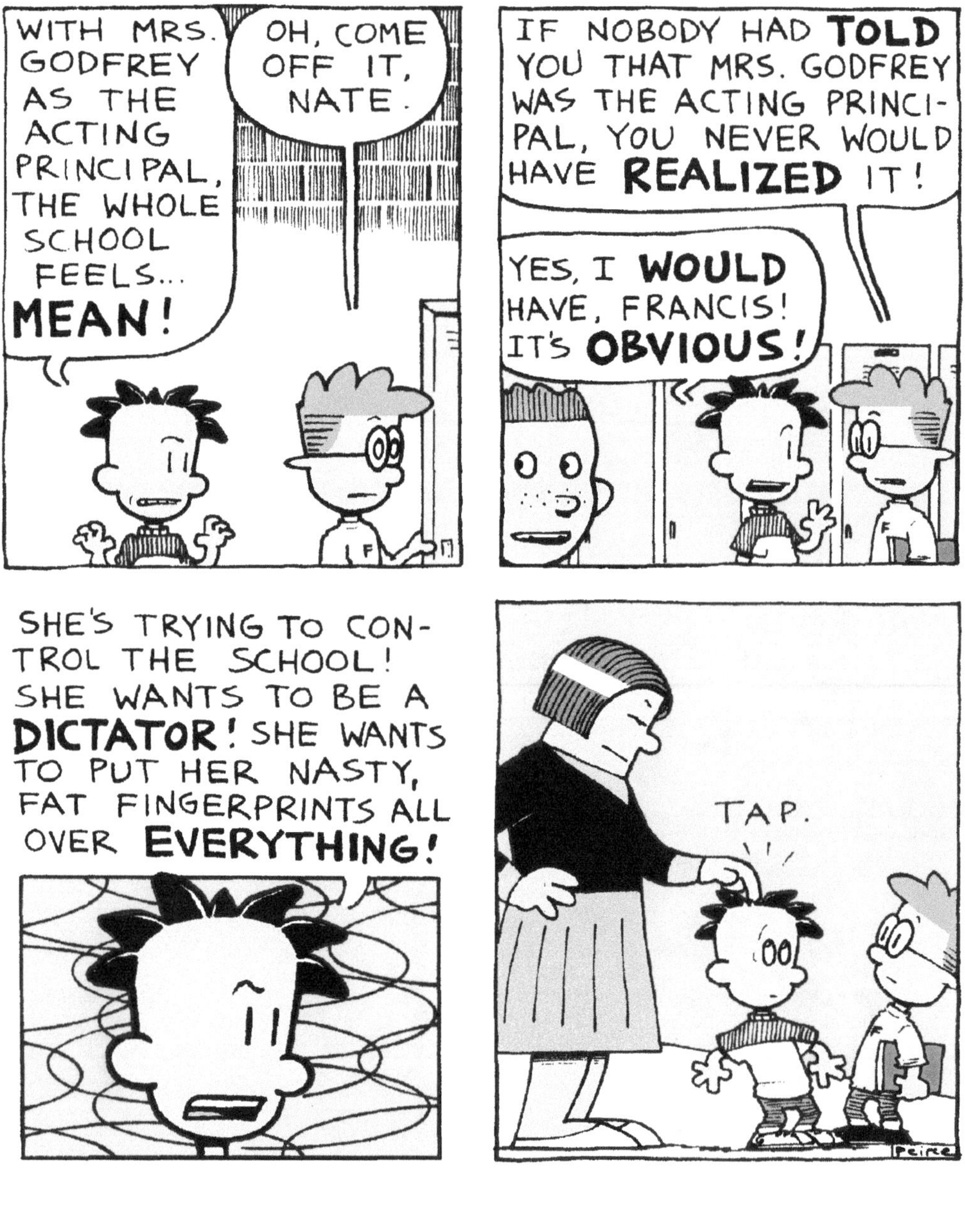
WITH MRS. GODFREY AS THE ACTING PRINCIPAL, THE WHOLE SCHOOL FEELS... **MEAN!**
OH, COME OFF IT, NATE.
IF NOBODY HAD **TOLD** YOU THAT MRS. GODFREY WAS THE ACTING PRINCIPAL, YOU NEVER WOULD HAVE **REALIZED** IT!
YES, I **WOULD** HAVE, FRANCIS! IT'S **OBVIOUS!**
SHE'S TRYING TO CONTROL THE SCHOOL! SHE WANTS TO BE A **DICTATOR!** SHE WANTS TO PUT HER NASTY, FAT FINGERPRINTS ALL OVER **EVERYTHING!**
TAP.
Peirce

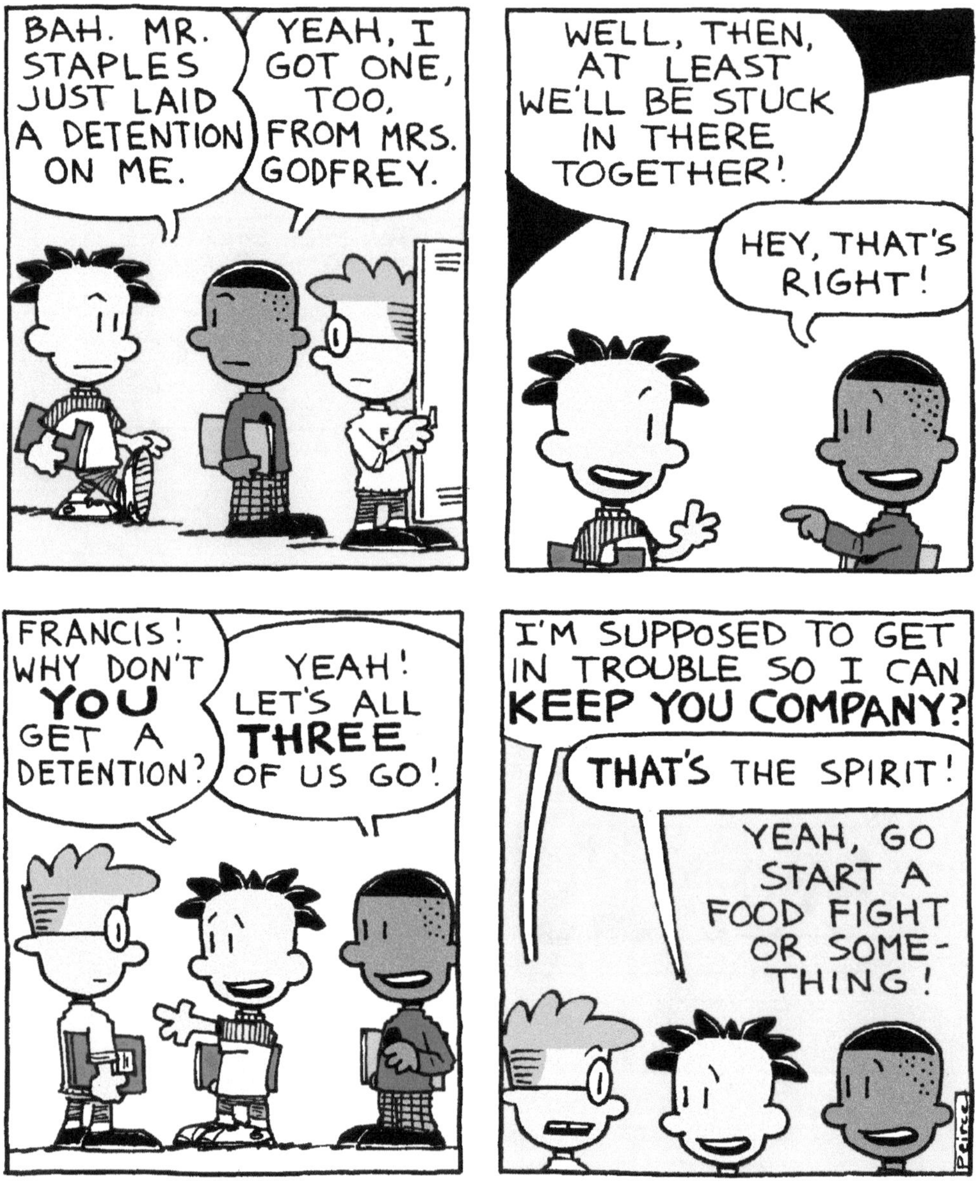
BAH. MR. STAPLES JUST LAID A DETENTION ON ME.
YEAH, I GOT ONE, TOO, FROM MRS. GODFREY.
WELL, THEN, AT LEAST WE'LL BE STUCK IN THERE TOGETHER!
HEY, THAT'S RIGHT!
FRANCIS! WHY DON'T **YOU** GET A DETENTION?
YEAH! LET'S ALL **THREE** OF US GO!
I'M SUPPOSED TO GET IN TROUBLE SO I CAN **KEEP YOU COMPANY?**
THAT'S THE SPIRIT!
YEAH, GO START A FOOD FIGHT OR SOME-THING!
Peirce

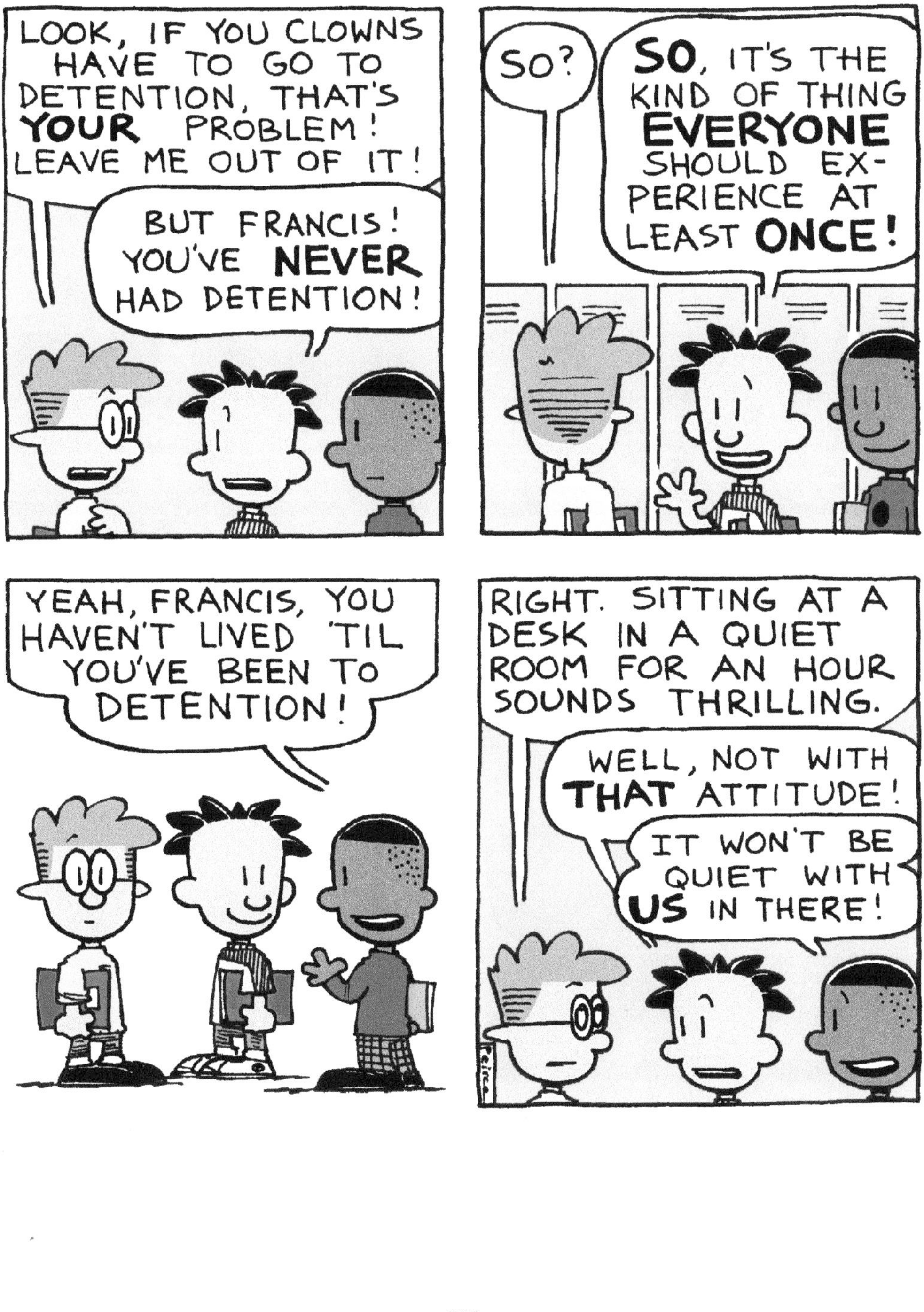
LOOK, IF YOU CLOWNS HAVE TO GO TO DETENTION, THAT'S **YOUR** PROBLEM! LEAVE ME OUT OF IT!
BUT FRANCIS! YOU'VE **NEVER** HAD DETENTION!
SO?
SO, IT'S THE KIND OF THING **EVERYONE** SHOULD EXPERIENCE AT LEAST **ONCE**!
YEAH, FRANCIS, YOU HAVEN'T LIVED 'TIL YOU'VE BEEN TO DETENTION!
RIGHT. SITTING AT A DESK IN A QUIET ROOM FOR AN HOUR SOUNDS THRILLING.
WELL, NOT WITH **THAT** ATTITUDE!
IT WON'T BE QUIET WITH **US** IN THERE!

162

HEY, MARCUS... I WAS JUST...UH... THINKING ABOUT YOUR POSSE. WHAT IF SOMEBODY'S... Y'KNOW... JUST NOT A POSSE KIND OF GUY?

I MEAN...JUST HYPO-THETICALLY... WHAT IF SOMEBODY DECIDED TO... ✳︎KOFF!✳︎... LEAVE THE POSSE?

JUST HYPO-THETICALLY, I'D BREAK HIS FACE.

WHY DO YOU ASK?

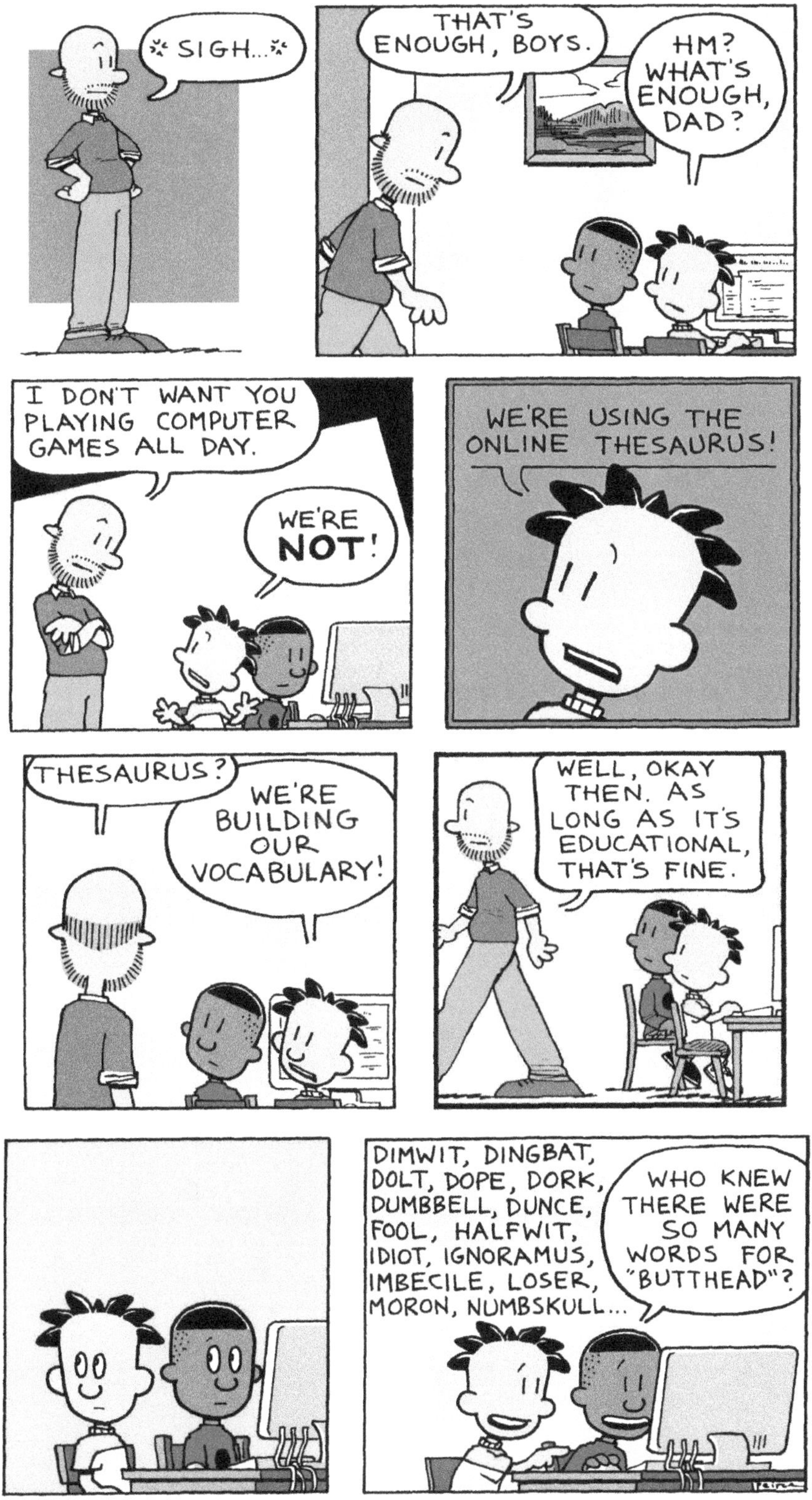
SIGH...
THAT'S ENOUGH, BOYS.
HM? WHAT'S ENOUGH, DAD?
I DON'T WANT YOU PLAYING COMPUTER GAMES ALL DAY.
WE'RE **NOT**!
WE'RE USING THE ONLINE THESAURUS!
THESAURUS?
WE'RE BUILDING OUR VOCABULARY!
WELL, OKAY THEN. AS LONG AS IT'S EDUCATIONAL, THAT'S FINE.
DIMWIT, DINGBAT, DOLT, DOPE, DORK, DUMBBELL, DUNCE, FOOL, HALFWIT, IDIOT, IGNORAMUS, IMBECILE, LOSER, MORON, NUMBSKULL...
WHO KNEW THERE WERE SO MANY WORDS FOR "BUTTHEAD"?

SO JOINING MARCUS' POSSE WASN'T ALL IT WAS CRACKED UP TO BE, HUH?

ZONE

YOU CAN SAY **THAT** AGAIN.

WELL, MAYBE YOU LEARNED SOMETHING FROM THIS LITTLE EXPERIENCE.

DID I EVER.

I LEARNED THAT MARCUS IS A TOTAL... UHH... A TOTAL... HM...

HE'S SO INTRO-SPECTIVE.

WHAT'S ANOTHER WORD FOR "SCUZZ-BUCKET"?

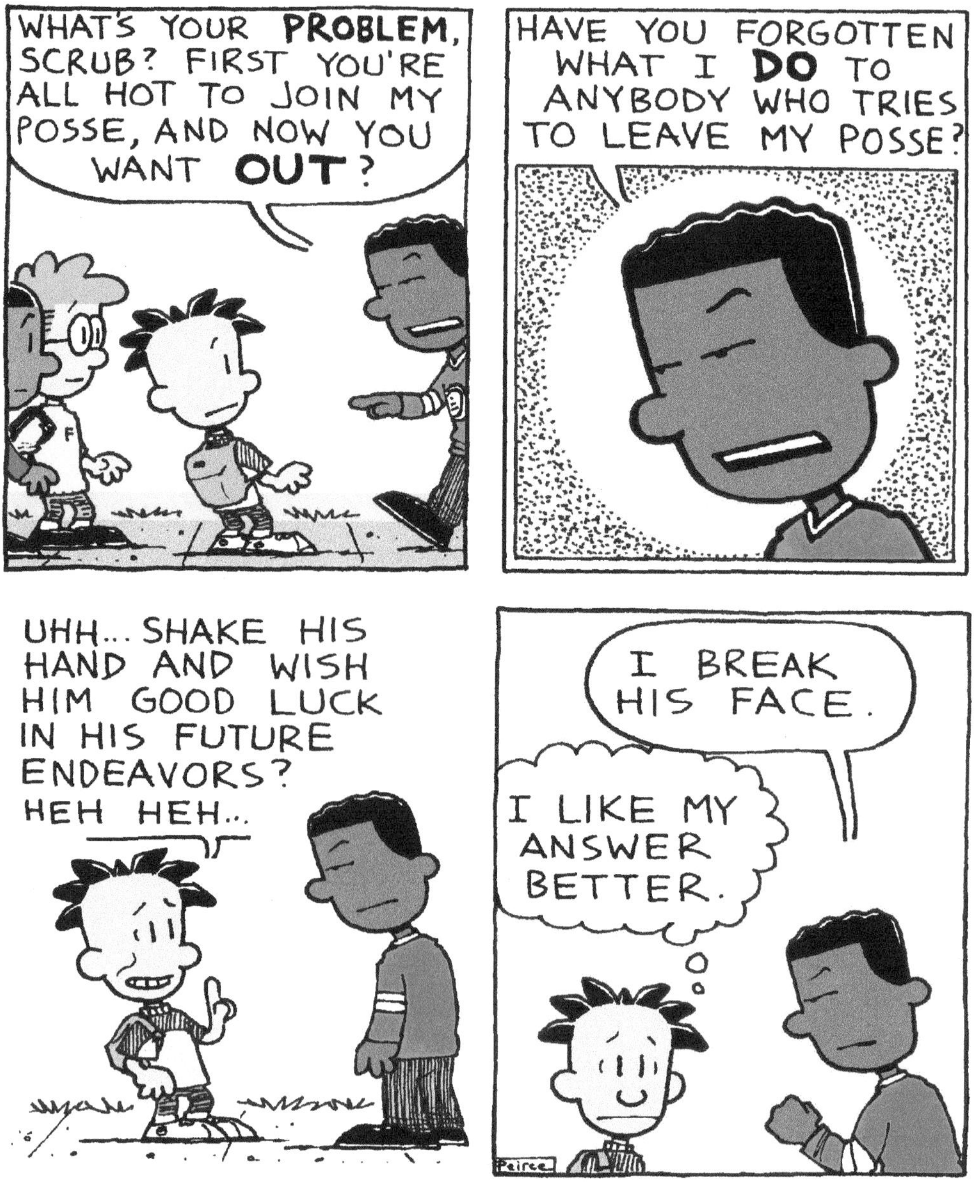
WHAT'S YOUR PROBLEM, SCRUB? FIRST YOU'RE ALL HOT TO JOIN MY POSSE, AND NOW YOU WANT OUT?
HAVE YOU FORGOTTEN WHAT I DO TO ANYBODY WHO TRIES TO LEAVE MY POSSE?
UHH... SHAKE HIS HAND AND WISH HIM GOOD LUCK IN HIS FUTURE ENDEAVORS? HEH HEH...
I BREAK HIS FACE.
I LIKE MY ANSWER BETTER.
Peirce

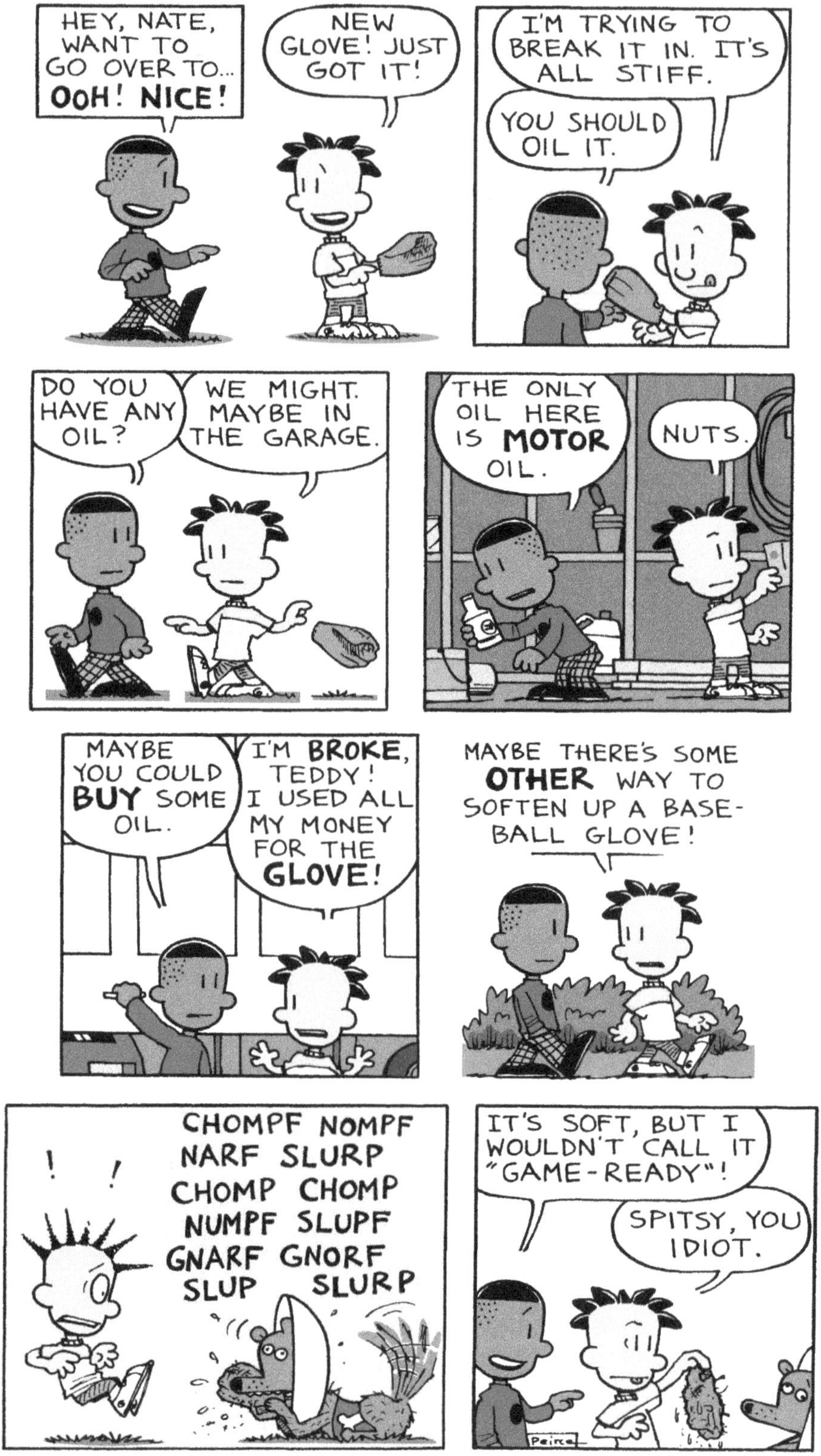
HEY, NATE, WANT TO GO OVER TO... OOH! NICE!
NEW GLOVE! JUST GOT IT!
I'M TRYING TO BREAK IT IN. IT'S ALL STIFF.
YOU SHOULD OIL IT.
DO YOU HAVE ANY OIL?
WE MIGHT. MAYBE IN THE GARAGE.
THE ONLY OIL HERE IS MOTOR OIL.
NUTS.
MAYBE YOU COULD BUY SOME OIL.
I'M BROKE, TEDDY! I USED ALL MY MONEY FOR THE GLOVE!
MAYBE THERE'S SOME OTHER WAY TO SOFTEN UP A BASE-BALL GLOVE!
! !
CHOMPF NOMPF NARF SLURP CHOMP CHOMP NUMPF SLUPF GNARF GNORF SLUP SLURP
IT'S SOFT, BUT I WOULDN'T CALL IT "GAME-READY"!
SPITSY, YOU IDIOT.
Peirce

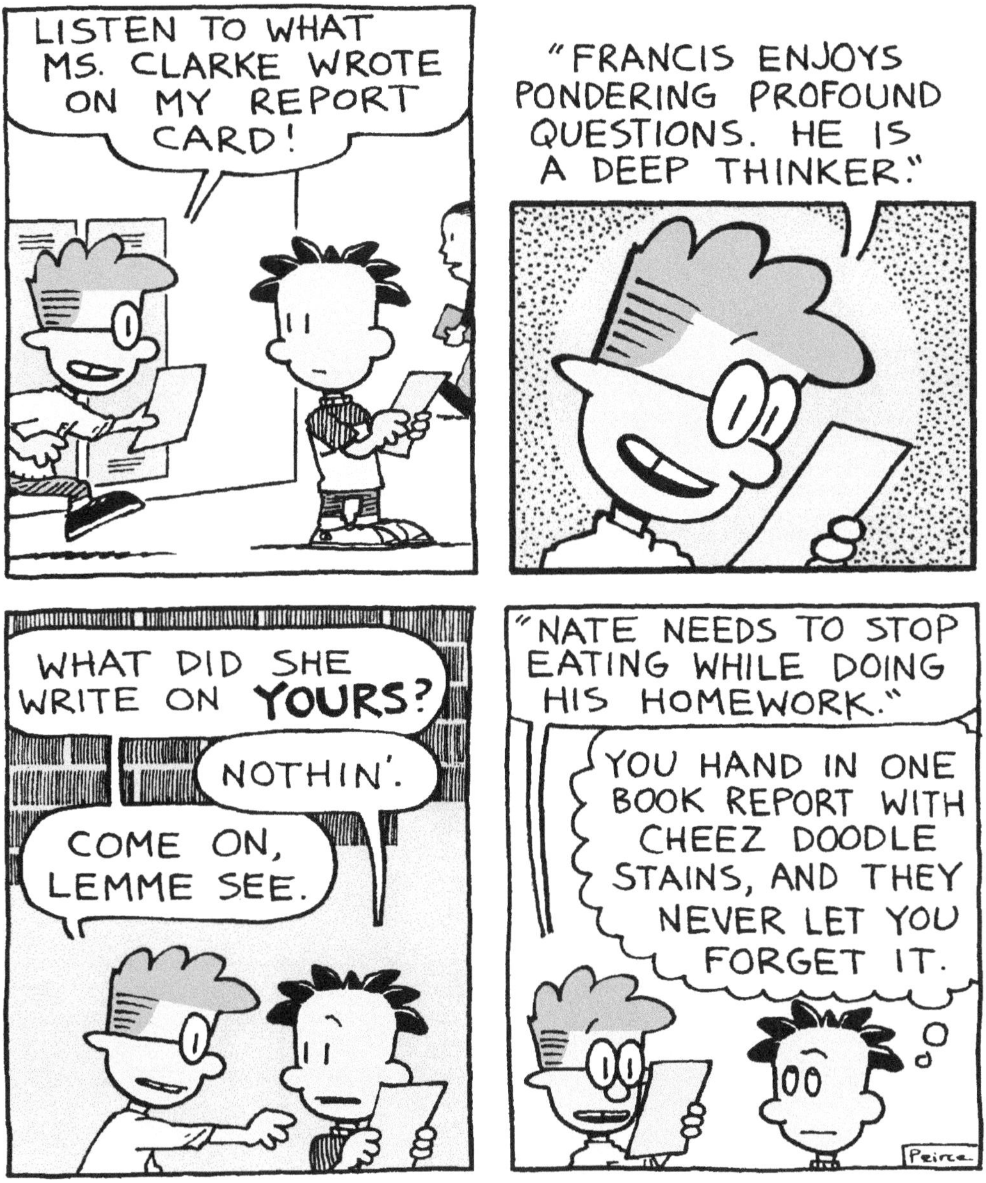
LISTEN TO WHAT MS. CLARKE WROTE ON MY REPORT CARD!
"FRANCIS ENJOYS PONDERING PROFOUND QUESTIONS. HE IS A DEEP THINKER."
WHAT DID SHE WRITE ON **YOURS?**
NOTHIN'.
COME ON, LEMME SEE.
"NATE NEEDS TO STOP EATING WHILE DOING HIS HOMEWORK."
YOU HAND IN ONE BOOK REPORT WITH CHEEZ DOODLE STAINS, AND THEY NEVER LET YOU FORGET IT.
Peirce

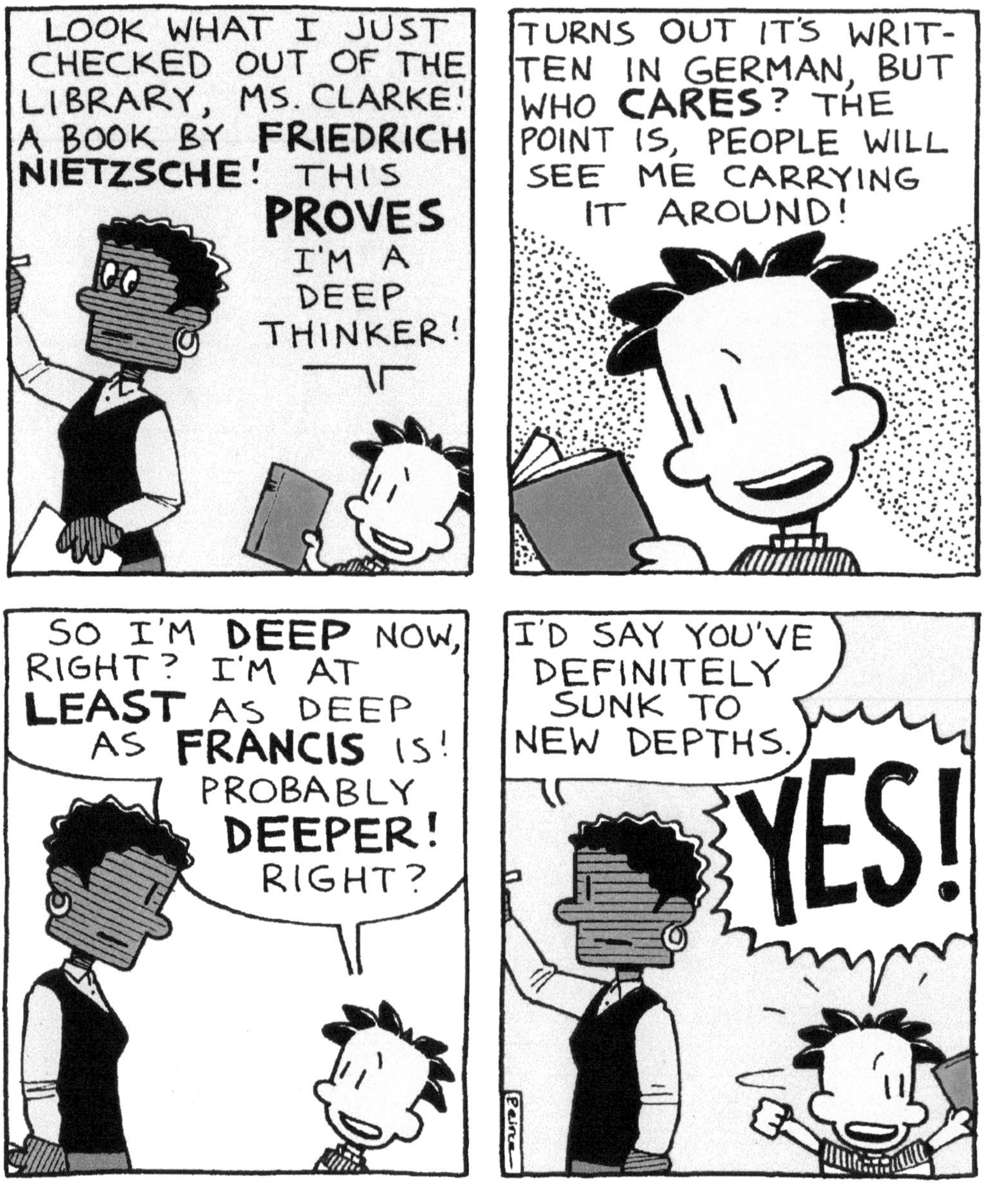
LOOK WHAT I JUST CHECKED OUT OF THE LIBRARY, MS. CLARKE! A BOOK BY FRIEDRICH NIETZSCHE! THIS PROVES I'M A DEEP THINKER!
TURNS OUT IT'S WRITTEN IN GERMAN, BUT WHO CARES? THE POINT IS, PEOPLE WILL SEE ME CARRYING IT AROUND!
SO I'M DEEP NOW, RIGHT? I'M AT LEAST AS DEEP AS FRANCIS IS! PROBABLY DEEPER! RIGHT?
I'D SAY YOU'VE DEFINITELY SUNK TO NEW DEPTHS.
YES!
Peirce

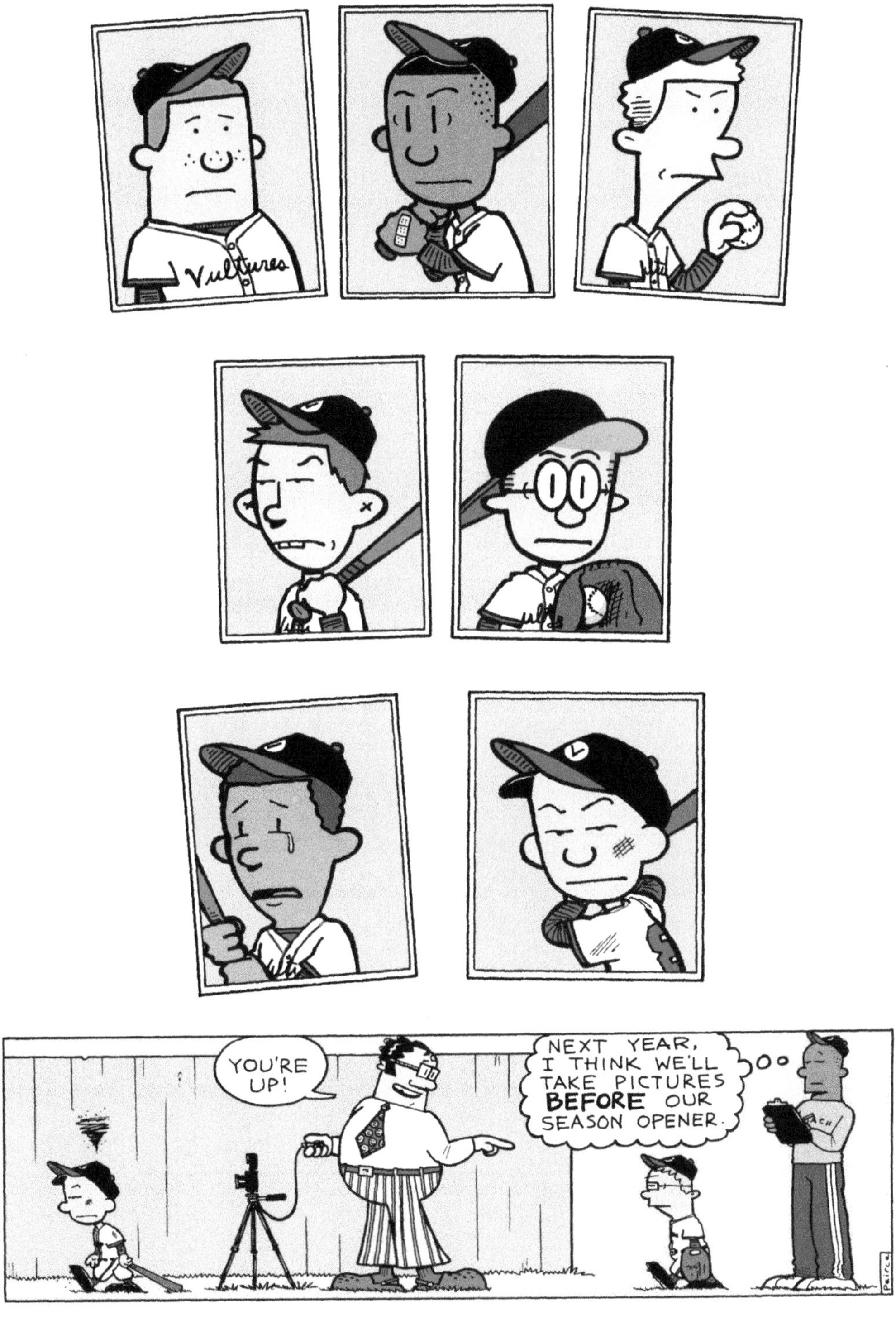
Vultures
YOU'RE UP!
NEXT YEAR, I THINK WE'LL TAKE PICTURES **BEFORE** OUR SEASON OPENER.
Peirce

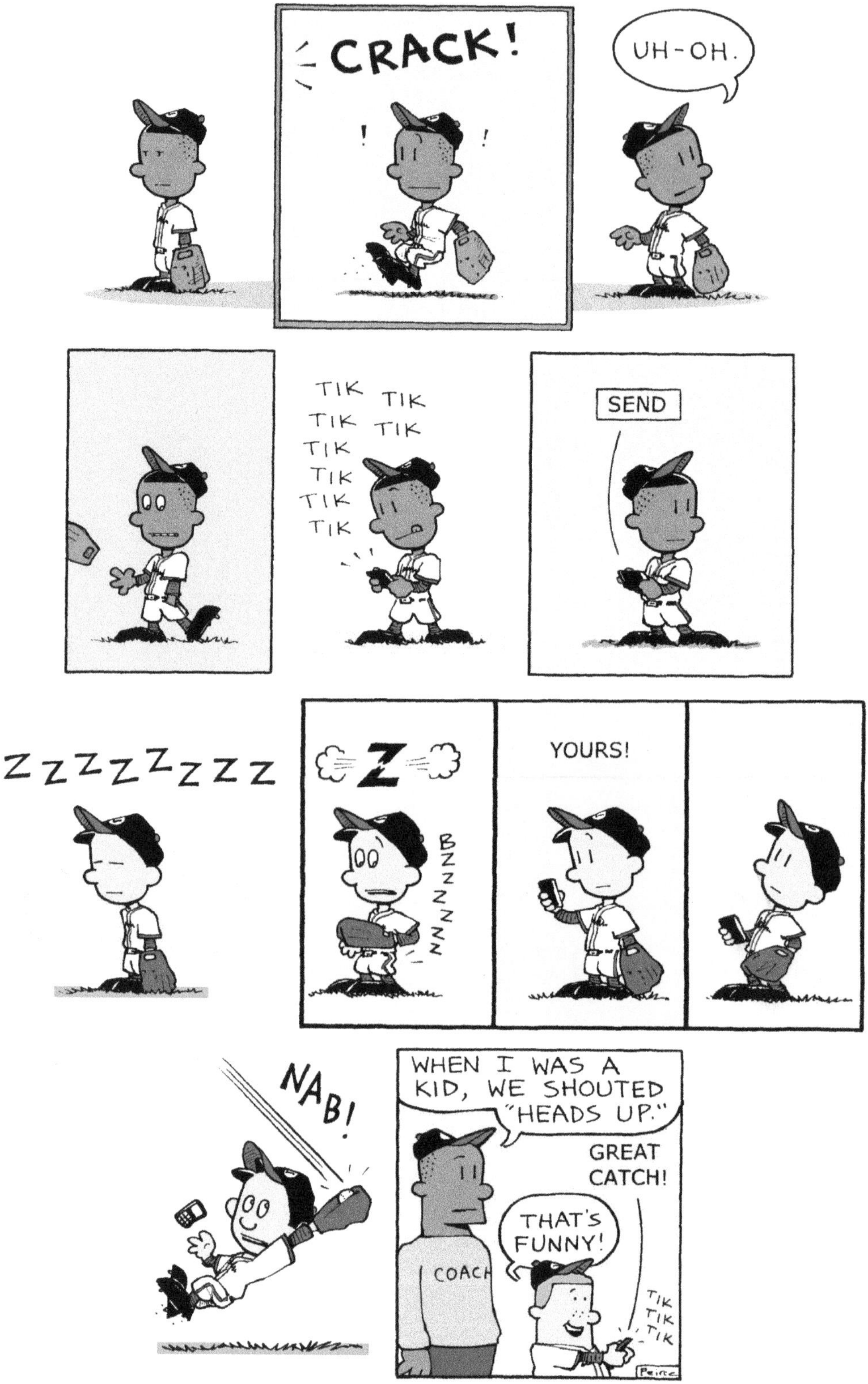
CRACK!
UH-OH.
TIK TIK TIK TIK TIK TIK TIK TIK
SEND
ZZZZZZZZZ
Z
BZZZZZZZ
YOURS!
NAB!
WHEN I WAS A KID, WE SHOUTED "HEADS UP."
GREAT CATCH!
THAT'S FUNNY!
COACH
TIK TIK TIK
Peirce

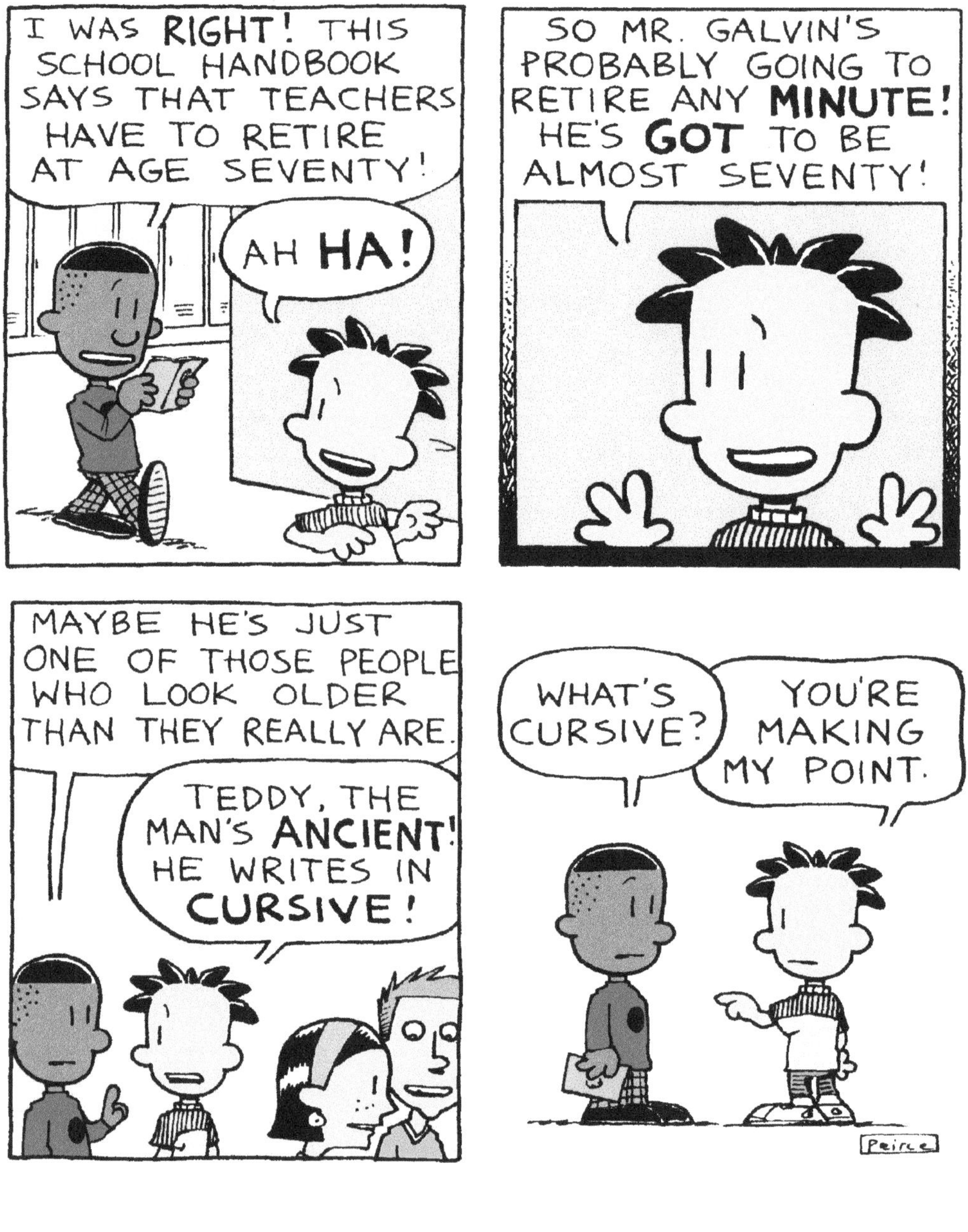
I WAS **RIGHT**! THIS SCHOOL HANDBOOK SAYS THAT TEACHERS HAVE TO RETIRE AT AGE SEVENTY!
AH **HA**!
SO MR. GALVIN'S PROBABLY GOING TO RETIRE ANY **MINUTE**! HE'S **GOT** TO BE ALMOST SEVENTY!
MAYBE HE'S JUST ONE OF THOSE PEOPLE WHO LOOK OLDER THAN THEY REALLY ARE.
TEDDY, THE MAN'S **ANCIENT**! HE WRITES IN **CURSIVE**!
WHAT'S CURSIVE?
YOU'RE MAKING MY POINT.
Peirce

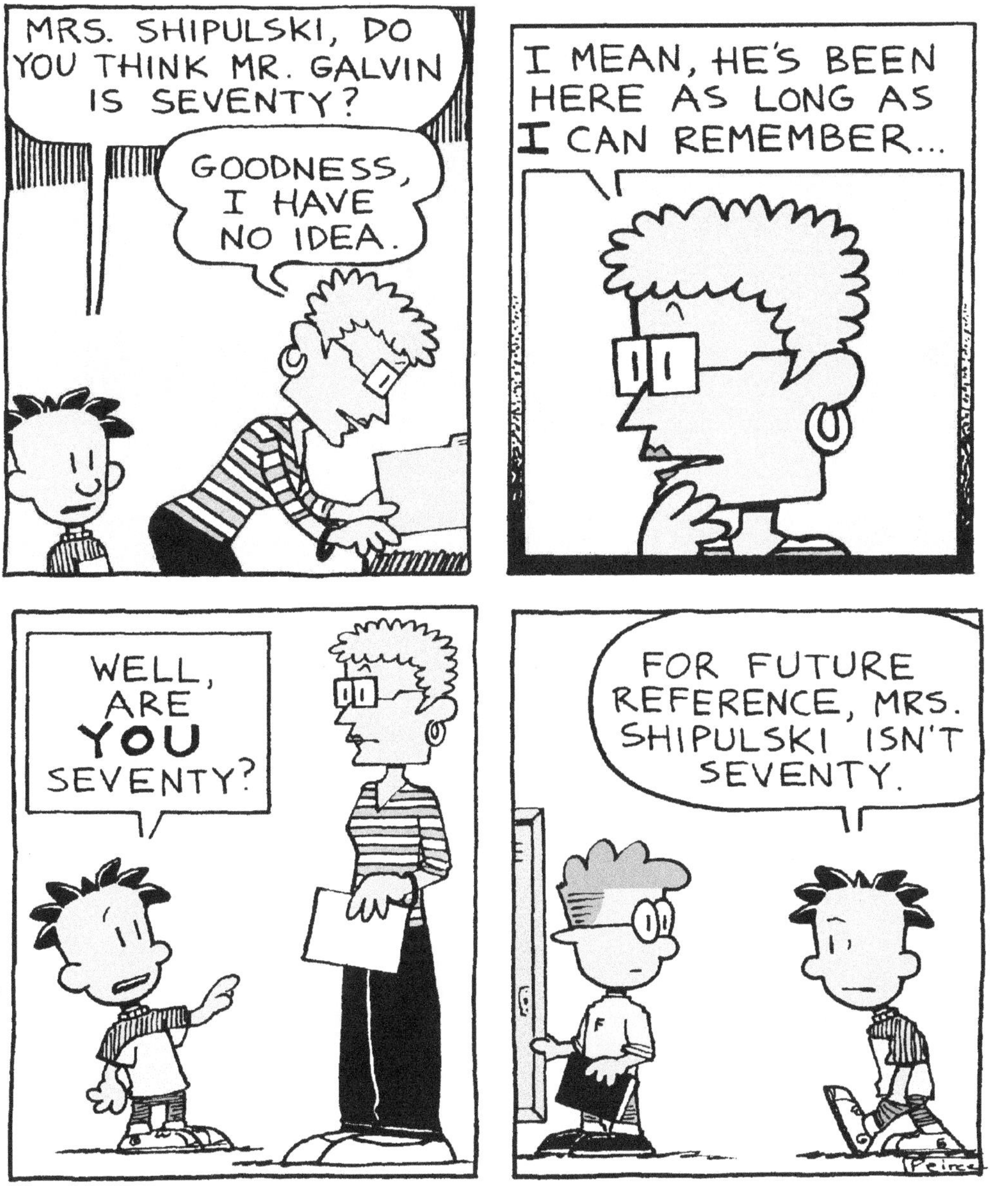
MRS. SHIPULSKI, DO YOU THINK MR. GALVIN IS SEVENTY?
GOODNESS, I HAVE NO IDEA.
I MEAN, HE'S BEEN HERE AS LONG AS I CAN REMEMBER...
WELL, ARE YOU SEVENTY?
FOR FUTURE REFERENCE, MRS. SHIPULSKI ISN'T SEVENTY.
Peirce

Nate: PRINCIPAL NICHOLS! MR. GALVIN HAS TO RETIRE SOON, RIGHT?

Nichols: WHY WOULD HE **HAVE** TO RETIRE?

Nate: IT SAYS IN THE SCHOOL HANDBOOK THAT TEACHERS HAVE TO RETIRE AT AGE SEVENTY.

Nichols: YOU MUST HAVE BEEN LOOKING AT AN OUTDATED HANDBOOK, NATE.

Nichols: THE SCHOOL DID AWAY WITH THAT POLICY A FEW YEARS AGO.

Nate: OH.

Peirce

Nate: SO I GUESS YOU WON'T BE REPLACING HIM WITH A HOT SWEDISH STUDENT TEACHER WHO MOON-LIGHTS AS A BIKINI MODEL.

Nichols: PROBABLY NOT THIS WEEK.

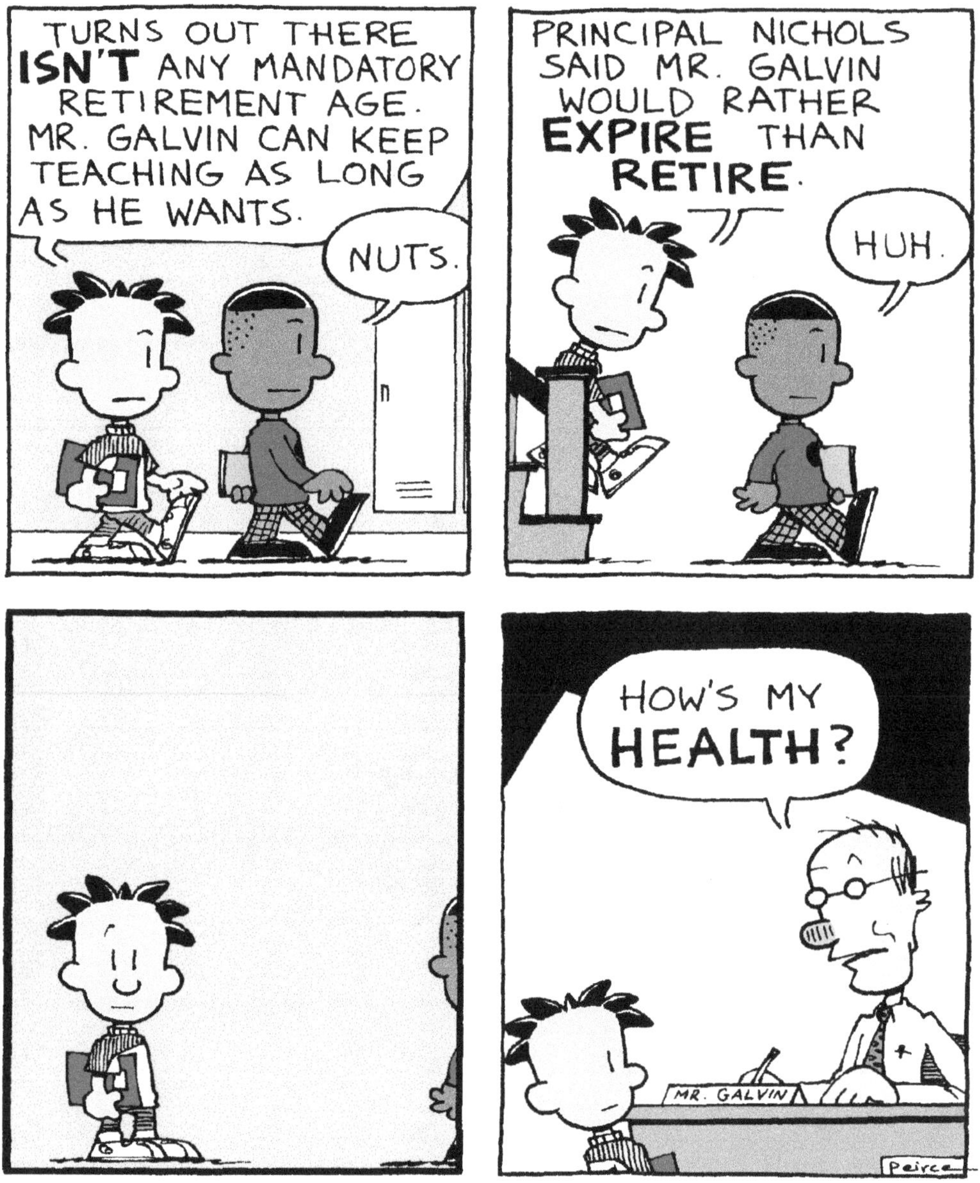
TURNS OUT THERE **ISN'T** ANY MANDATORY RETIREMENT AGE. MR. GALVIN CAN KEEP TEACHING AS LONG AS HE WANTS.
NUTS.
PRINCIPAL NICHOLS SAID MR. GALVIN WOULD RATHER **EXPIRE** THAN **RETIRE**.
HUH.
HOW'S MY **HEALTH**?
MR. GALVIN
Peirce

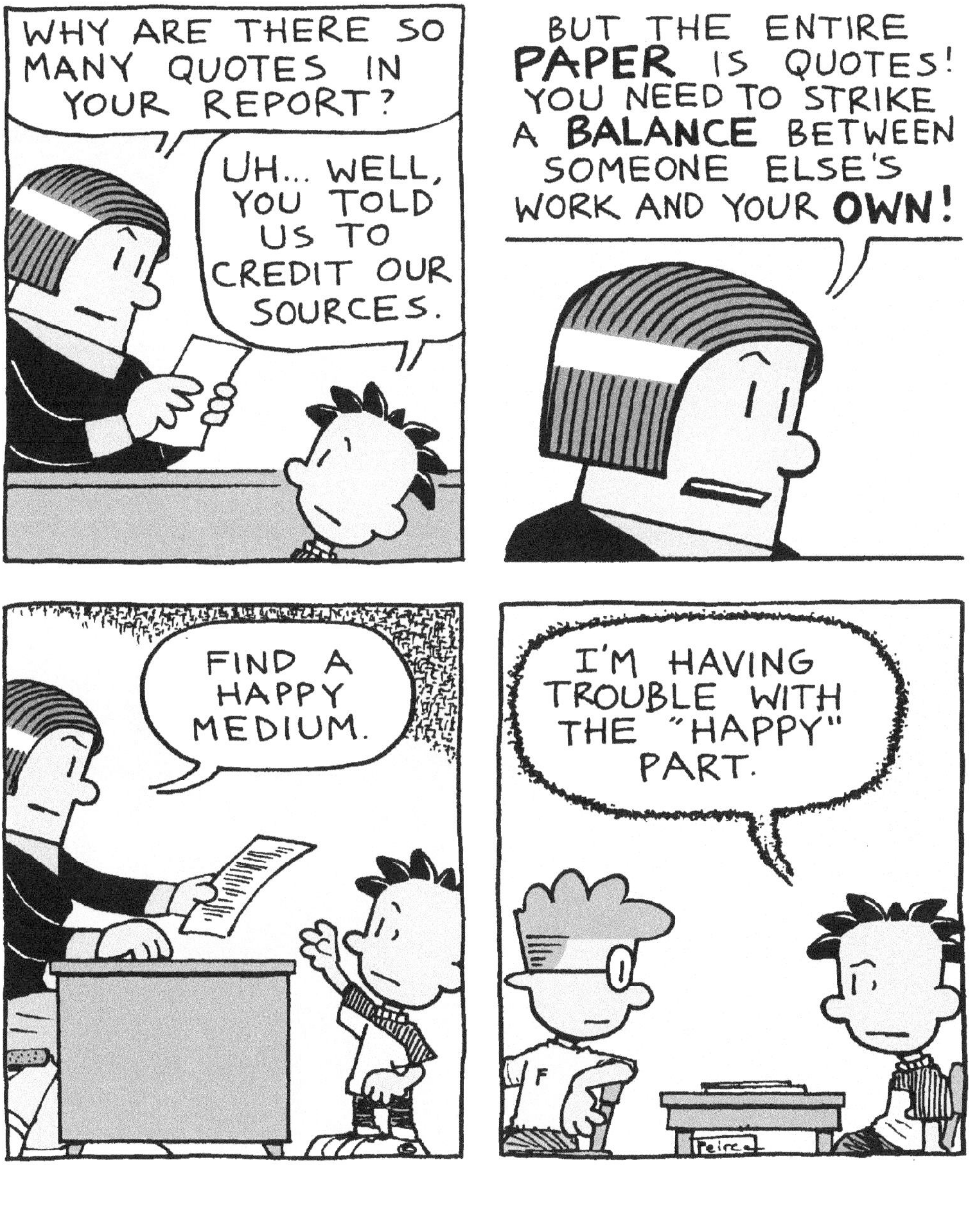
WHY ARE THERE SO MANY QUOTES IN YOUR REPORT?
UH... WELL, YOU TOLD US TO CREDIT OUR SOURCES.
BUT THE ENTIRE **PAPER** IS QUOTES! YOU NEED TO STRIKE A **BALANCE** BETWEEN SOMEONE ELSE'S WORK AND YOUR **OWN**!
FIND A HAPPY MEDIUM.
I'M HAVING TROUBLE WITH THE "HAPPY" PART.
F
Peirce

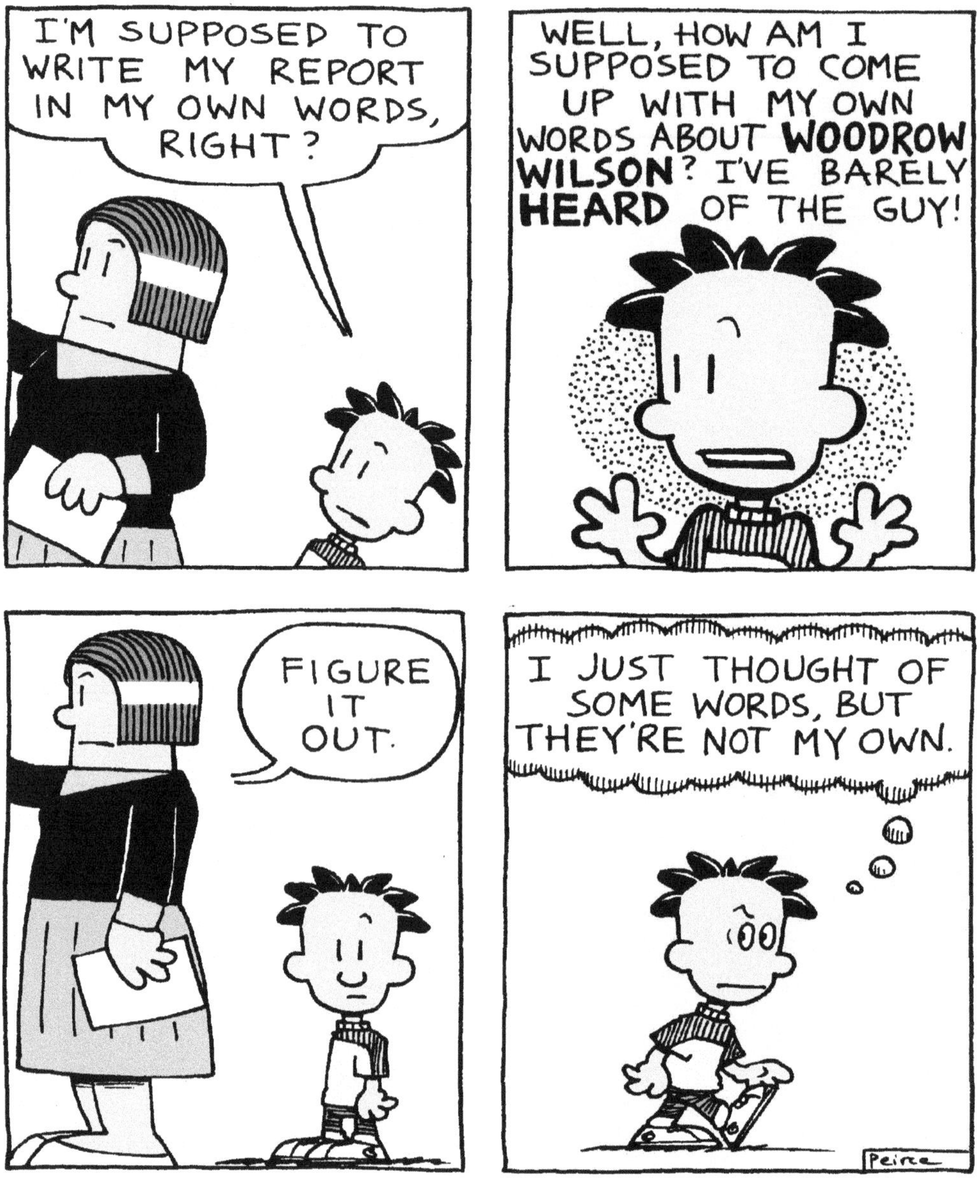
I'M SUPPOSED TO WRITE MY REPORT IN MY OWN WORDS, RIGHT?
WELL, HOW AM I SUPPOSED TO COME UP WITH MY OWN WORDS ABOUT **WOODROW WILSON**? I'VE BARELY **HEARD** OF THE GUY!
FIGURE IT OUT.
I JUST THOUGHT OF SOME WORDS, BUT THEY'RE NOT MY OWN.
Peirce

MRS. GODFREY'S MAKING ME REWRITE MY WOODROW WILSON PAPER!

SHE TOLD ME TO FIND A BALANCE BETWEEN FACT AND OPINION... WHATEVER **THAT** MEANS.

IT PROBABLY MEANS JUST WHAT IT SOUNDS LIKE.

SO EVERY TIME I WRITE SOMETHING FACTUAL, I WRITE AN OPINION IN THE VERY SAME SENTENCE?

RIGHT.

Woodrow Wilson was the twenty-eighth president of the United States, but who really cares?

"WOODROW WILSON OVERSAW THE CREATION OF THE FEDERAL RESERVE SYSTEM, CUT THE TARIFF, AND..." BLAH, BLAH, **BLAH!** HOW AM I SUPPOSED TO PUT THIS IN MY OWN WORDS?

I'M SURE IF YOU GIVE IT SOME THOUGHT, YOU'LL BE ABLE TO RE-INTERPRET WHAT YOU'VE READ.

Woodrow Wilson led a very boring life.

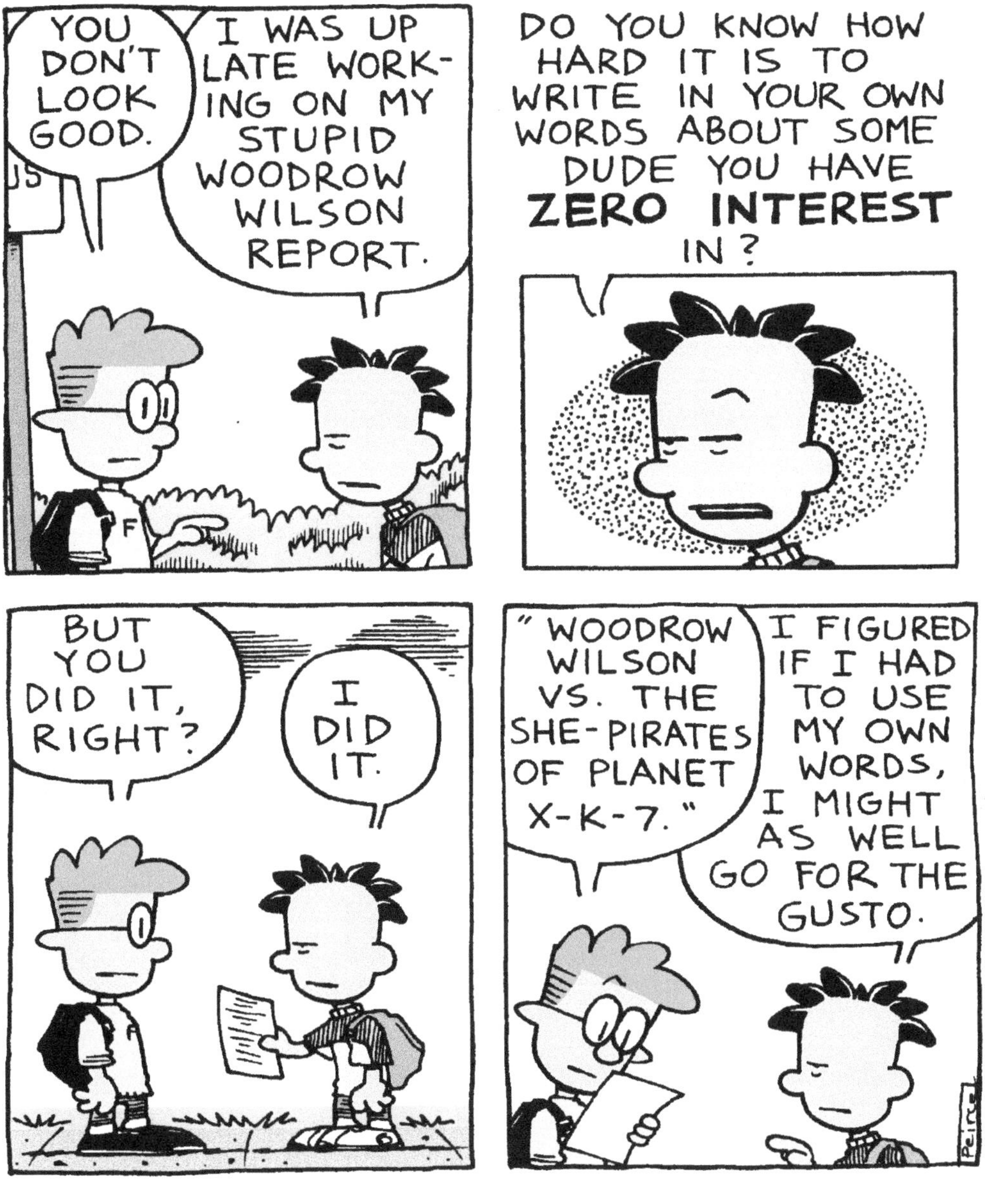
YOU DON'T LOOK GOOD.
I WAS UP LATE WORKING ON MY STUPID WOODROW WILSON REPORT.
DO YOU KNOW HOW HARD IT IS TO WRITE IN YOUR OWN WORDS ABOUT SOME DUDE YOU HAVE **ZERO INTEREST** IN?
BUT YOU DID IT, RIGHT?
I DID IT.
"WOODROW WILSON VS. THE SHE-PIRATES OF PLANET X-K-7."
I FIGURED IF I HAD TO USE MY OWN WORDS, I MIGHT AS WELL GO FOR THE GUSTO.
Peirce

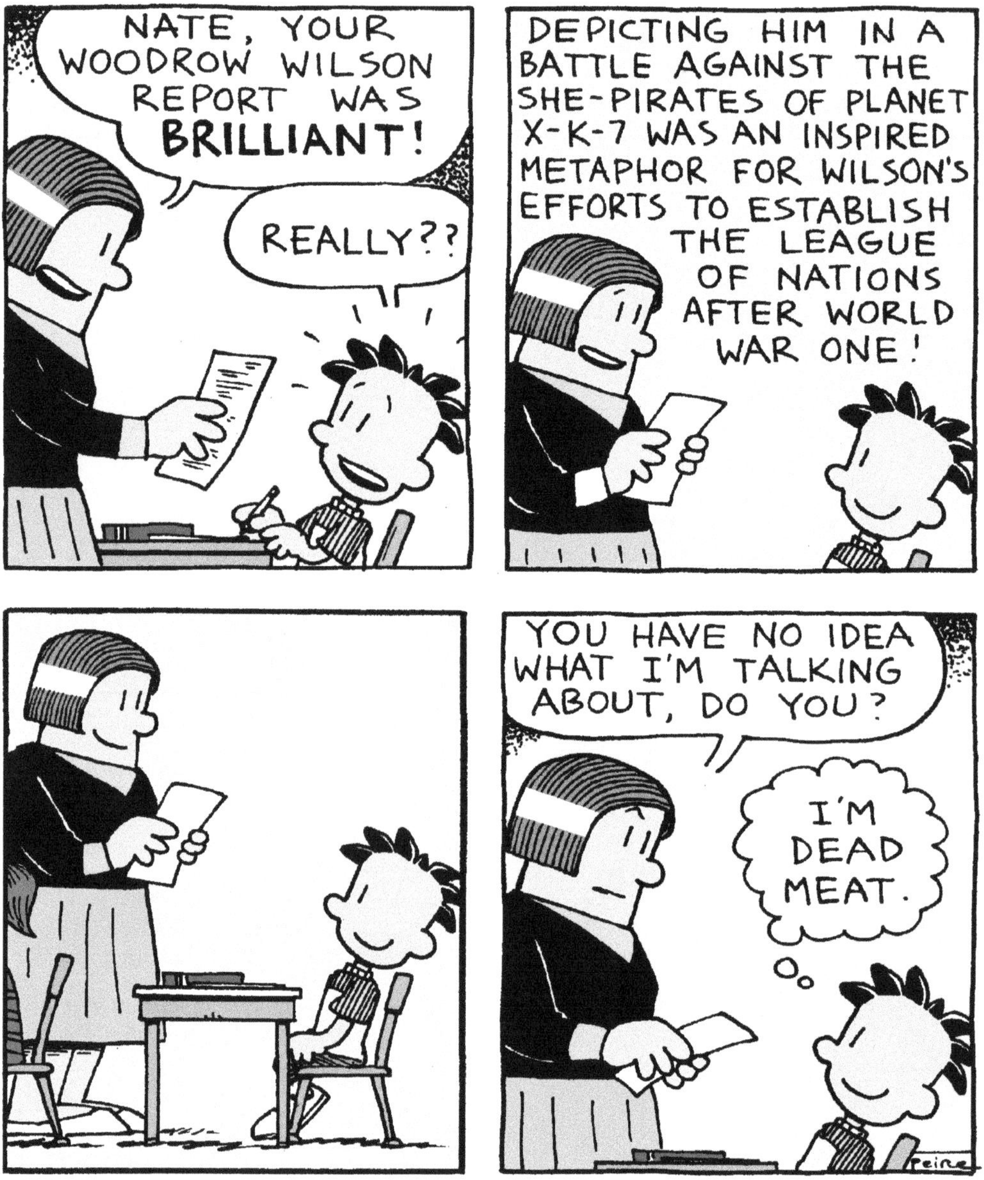
NATE, YOUR WOODROW WILSON REPORT WAS BRILLIANT!
REALLY??
DEPICTING HIM IN A BATTLE AGAINST THE SHE-PIRATES OF PLANET X-K-7 WAS AN INSPIRED METAPHOR FOR WILSON'S EFFORTS TO ESTABLISH THE LEAGUE OF NATIONS AFTER WORLD WAR ONE!
YOU HAVE NO IDEA WHAT I'M TALKING ABOUT, DO YOU?
I'M DEAD MEAT.
Peirce

Big Nate is distributed internationally by Universal Uclick.

Big Nate: Say Good-bye to Dork City copyright © 2015 by United Feature Syndicate, Inc. All rights reserved. Printed in the United States of America. No part of this book may be used or reproduced in any manner whatsoever without written permission except in the case of reprints in the context of reviews.

Andrews McMeel Publishing, LLC
an Andrews McMeel Universal company
1130 Walnut Street, Kansas City, Missouri 64106

www.andrewsmcmeel.com

ISBN: 978-1-4494-7401-0

Library of Congress Control Number: 2014952150

These strips appeared in newspapers from
October 10, 2010, through May 14, 2011.

Big Nate can be viewed on the Internet at
www.gocomics.com/big_nate

Check out these and other books at ampkids.com

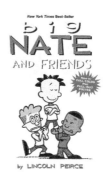

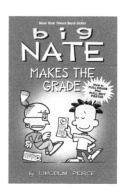

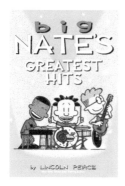

Also available:
Teaching and activity guides for each title.
AMP! Comics for Kids books make reading FUN!

CPSIA information can be obtained
at www.ICGtesting.com
Printed in the USA
LVHW071917130222
710754LV00039B/229